About the Authors

Kate Hewitt has worked a variety of different jobs, from drama teacher to editorial assistant to youth worker, but writing romance is the best one yet. She also writes women's fiction and all her stories celebrate the healing and redemptive power of love. Kate lives in a tiny village in the English Cotswolds with her husband, five children, and an overly affectionate Golden Retriever.

Besides writing, **Ann Major** enjoys her husband, kids, grandchildren, cats, hobbies, and travels. A Texan, Ann holds a B.A. from UT, and an M.A. from Texas A&M. A former teacher on both the secondary and college levels, Ann is an experienced speaker. She's written over sixty books for Mills & Boon and frequently makes bestseller lists.

Pamela Yaye has a bachelor's degree in Christian Education and her love for African American fiction prompted her to pursue a career in writing romance. When she's not working on her latest novel, this busy wife, mother and teacher is watching basketball, cooking or planning her next holiday. Pamela lives in Alberta, Canada with her gorgeous husband and adorable, but mischievous son and daughter.

Dangerous Liaisons

Dangerous Liaisons:
Passion

KATE HEWITT

ANN MAJOR

PAMELA YAYE

MILLS & BOON

First Published in Great Britain 2021
by Mills & Boon, an imprint of HarperCollins*Publishers* Ltd,
1 London Bridge Street, London, SE1 9GF

www.harpercollins.co.uk

HarperCollins*Publishers*
1st Floor, Watermarque Building,
Ringsend Road, Dublin 4, Ireland

DANGEROUS LIAISONS: PASSION © 2021 Harlequin Books S.A.

Moretti's Marriage Command © 2016 Kate Hewitt
A Scandal So Sweet © 2012 Ann Major
Seduced by the Playboy © 2014 Pamela Sadadi Yaye

ISBN: 978-0-263-29967-0

MIX
Paper from
responsible sources
FSC™ C007454

This book is produced from independently certified FSC™ paper
to ensure responsible forest management.

For more information visit: www.harpercollins.co.uk/green

Printed and bound in Spain
by CPI, Barcelona

MORETTI'S
MARRIAGE
COMMAND

KATE HEWITT

To all my readers,

Thank you for your encouragement and support.

It's always a privilege to write stories for you.

CHAPTER ONE

LUCA MORETTI NEEDED a wife. Not a real one—heaven forbid he'd ever need *that*. No, he needed a temporary wife-to-be who was efficient, biddable, and discreet. A wife for the weekend.

'Mr Moretti?' His PA, Hannah Stewart, knocked once on the door before opening it and stepping inside his penthouse office overlooking a rain-washed Lombard Street in London's City. 'I have the letters for you to sign.'

Luca watched his PA walk towards him holding the sheaf of letters, her light brown hair neatly pulled back, her face set in calm lines. She wore a black pencil skirt, low heels, and a simple blouse of white silk. He'd never really bothered to notice his PA before, except at how quickly she could type and how discreet she could be when it came to unfortunate personal calls that occasionally came through to his office. Now he eyed her plain brown hair, and lightly freckled face that was pretty without being in any way remarkable. As for her figure…?

Luca let his gaze wander down his PA's slender form. No breathtaking or bodacious curves, but it was passable.

Could he…?

She placed the letters in front of him and took a step back, but not before he caught a waft of her understated floral perfume. He reached for his fountain pen and began to scrawl his signature on each letter.

'Will that be all, Mr Moretti?' she asked when he'd finished the last one.

'Yes.' He handed her the letters and Hannah turned towards the door, her skirt whispering against her legs as she walked. Luca watched her, eyes narrowed, certainty settling in his gut. 'Wait.'

Obedient as ever, Hannah pivoted back to face him, her pale eyebrows raised expectantly. She'd been a good PA these last three years, working hard and not making a fuss about it. He sensed ambition and willpower beneath her 'aiming to please' persona, and the weekend would require both qualities, as long as she agreed to the deception. Which he would make sure she did.

'Mr Moretti?'

Luca lounged back in his chair as he drummed his fingers on his desk. He didn't like lying. He'd been honest his whole life, proud of who he was even though so many had knocked him back, tried to keep him down. But this weekend was different. This weekend was everything to him, and Hannah Stewart was no more than a cog in his plans. A very important cog.

'I have an important meeting this weekend.'

'Yes, on Santa Nicola,' Hannah replied. 'Your ticket is in your passport wallet, and the limo is set to pick you up tomorrow morning at nine, from your flat. The flight leaves from Heathrow at noon.'

'Right.' He hadn't known any of those details, but he'd expected Hannah to inform him. She really was quite marvellously efficient. 'It turns out I'm going to need some assistance,' he said.

Hannah's eyebrows went a fraction higher, but her face remained calm. 'Administrative assistance, you mean?'

Luca hesitated. He didn't have time to explain his intentions now, and he suspected that his PA would balk at what he was about to ask. 'Yes, that's right.' He could tell Hannah was surprised although she hid it well.

'What exactly do you require?'

A wife. A temporary, compliant woman. 'I require you to accompany me to Santa Nicola for the weekend.' Luca hadn't asked Hannah to accompany him on any business trips before; he preferred to travel and work alone, having been a solitary person from childhood. When you were alone you didn't have to be on your guard, waiting for someone to trip you up. There were no expectations save the ones you put on yourself.

Luca knew that Hannah's contract stipulated 'extra hours or engagements as required', and in the past she'd been willing to work long evenings, the occasional Saturday. He smiled, his eyebrows raised expectantly. 'I trust that won't be a problem?' He would inform her later just what extra duties would be required.

Hannah hesitated, but only briefly, and then gave one graceful nod of her head. 'Not at all, Mr Moretti.'

Hannah's mind raced as she tried to figure out how to handle this unexpected request from her boss. In her three years of working for Luca Moretti, she'd never gone on a business trip with him. There had been the odd, or not so odd, late night; the occasional all-nighter where she supplied him with black coffee and popped caffeine pills to keep sharp as she took notes. But she'd never *travelled* with him. Never gone somewhere as exotic as a Mediterranean island for the weekend. The possibility gave her a surprising frisson of excitement; she'd thought she'd put her would-be travelling days behind her long ago.

'Shall I book an extra ticket?' she asked, trying to sound as efficient and capable as she always was.

'Yes.'

She nodded, her mind still spinning. She needed to call her mother as soon as possible, make arrangements… 'I'll book an economy ticket—'

'Why on earth would you do that?' Luca demanded. He sounded irritated, and Hannah blinked in surprise.

'I hardly think, as your PA, I'd need to travel first class, and the expense—'

'Forget the expense.' He cut her off, waving a hand in dismissal. 'I'll need you seated with me. I'll work on the flight.'

'Very well.' She held the letters to her chest, wondering what else she'd need to do to prepare for such a trip. And wondering why Luca Moretti needed her on this trip when he hadn't needed her on any other. She studied him covertly, lounging as he was in his office chair, his midnight-dark hair rumpled, his thick, straight brows drawn into frowning lines, one hand still drumming the top of his ebony desk.

He was an incredibly handsome man, a compelling, charismatic, driven man; one business magazine had called him 'an elegant steamroller'. Hannah thought the nickname apt; Luca Moretti could turn on the charm, but it was only to get what he wanted. She'd observed him from the sidelines for three years and learned how to be the most efficient PA possible, and invisible when necessary. She liked her job; she liked Luca's force of personality, his boundless energy for his work. She'd always admired his determined work ethic, his drive for success. She might only be a PA, but she shared that drive, if not quite to the same degree.

'Very well,' she said now. 'I'll make the arrangements.' Luca nodded her dismissal and Hannah left his office, expelling her breath in a rush as she sat down at her desk. She and Luca were the only occupants of the top floor of his office building, and she appreciated the quiet to organise her thoughts.

First things first. She called the airline and booked an additional first-class ticket for herself, wincing at the expense even though Luca Moretti could well afford it. As CEO of his own real-estate development empire, he could have afforded his own jet.

That done, she quickly emailed her mother. She would have called, but Luca forbade personal calls from the office, and Hannah had always obeyed the rules. This job meant too much to her to flaunt them. She'd just hit Send when Luca emerged from his office, shrugging on his suit jacket and checking his watch.

'Mr Moretti?'

'You'll need suitable clothes for this weekend.'

Hannah blinked. 'Of course.'

'I don't mean that.' Luca gestured to her clothes, and Hannah was unable to keep from looking down at her professional yet understated outfit. She took pride in how she dressed, and she made sure to buy as high quality clothes as she could afford.

'I'm sorry…?'

'This weekend is as much a social occasion as a business one,' he explained tersely. 'You'll need appropriate clothing—evening gowns and the like.'

Evening gowns? She certainly didn't have any of those in her wardrobe, and couldn't imagine the need for them. 'As your PA—'

'As my PA you need to be dressed appropriately. This isn't going to be a board meeting.'

'What is it, exactly? Because I'm not sure—'

'Think of it more as a weekend house party with a little business thrown in.'

Which made it even more mystifying as to why he needed her along.

'I'm afraid I don't own any evening gowns—' Hannah began, and Luca shrugged her words aside.

'That's easy enough to take care of.' He slid his smartphone out of his pocket and thumbed a few buttons before speaking rapidly in Italian. Although she heard the occasional familiar word, Hannah had no idea what he'd said or who he'd called.

A few minutes later he disconnected the call and nodded towards Hannah. 'Sorted. You'll accompany me to Diavola after work.'

'Diavola...?'

'You know the boutique?'

She'd heard of it. It was an incredibly high-end fashion boutique in Mayfair. She might have walked past the elegant sashed windows once, seen a single dress hanging there in an elegant fall of shimmery silk, no price tag visible.

She swallowed hard, striving to seem calm, as if this whole, unexpected venture hadn't completely thrown her. 'That might be a bit out of my price range—'

'I will pay, of course.' His brows snapped together as he frowned at her. 'It's all part of the business expense. I'd hardly expect you to buy a gown you'll only be wearing because of your work.'

'Very well.' She tried not to squirm under his fierce gaze. She felt as if he was examining her and she was not meeting his expectations, which was disconcerting, as she always had before. She took pride in how well she performed her job. Luca Moretti had never had any cause to criticise her. 'Thank you.'

'We'll leave in an hour,' Luca said, and strode back into his office.

Hannah spent a frantic hour finishing up her work and making arrangements for the trip, ensuring that each part of the journey could accommodate an extra passenger. She knew Luca was staying with his client, hotelier Andrew Tyson, and she hesitated to contact the man directly to make sure there was an extra bedroom. It seemed a bit cheeky, asking for a room for herself in the tycoon's luxurious villa, but what else could she do?

She was just composing an email to Andrew Tyson's PA when Luca came out of his office, shrugging into his suit jacket, his face settling into a frown as he caught sight of her.

'Aren't you ready?'

'I'm sorry, I'm just emailing Mr Tyson's PA—'

His frown deepened. 'What for?'

'To arrange for an extra bedroom—'

'That won't be necessary,' Luca said swiftly, and then leaned over and closed her laptop with a snap.

Hannah stared at him, too surprised to mask the emotion. 'But if I don't email—'

'It's taken care of.'

'It is?'

'Don't question me, Hannah. And in future please leave all communications with Mr Tyson to me.'

Stung, she recoiled a bit at his tone. 'I've always—'

'This negotiation is delicate. I'll explain the particulars later. Now let's go. I have a lot of things to do tonight besides buy you some clothes.'

Her cheeks burned at his dismissive tone. Her boss was often restless and impatient, but he wasn't *rude*. Was it her fault that her wardrobe wasn't that of a socialite? Wordlessly she rose from her desk and took her laptop, about to slide it into her messenger bag.

'Leave that.'

'My laptop?' She stared at him, flummoxed. 'But I'll need it if we're to work on the plane—'

'It won't be necessary.'

A finger of unease crept along her spine. Something felt very off about this weekend, and yet she could not imagine what it was. 'Mr Moretti, I don't understand...'

'What is there to understand? You're accompanying me on a weekend that is as much a social occasion as it is a business one. I'm asking you to use some sensitivity and discretion, as the situation is delicate. Is that beyond your capabilities, Miss Stewart?'

Her face burned at being given such a dressing-down. 'No, of course not.'

'Good.' He nodded towards the lift doors. 'Now let's go.'

Stiff with affront, Hannah took her coat and followed Luca to the lift. She waited, staring straight ahead, trying to master her irritation, until the doors pinged open and Luca gestured for her to go in first. She did so, and as he followed her she was conscious in an entirely new way of how he filled the space of the lift. Surely they'd ridden in the lift together before, many times. Yet now, as Luca stabbed the button for the ground floor, she felt how big he was. How male. His shoulders strained the seams of his suit jacket, and his rangy, restless energy made the very air seem as if it were charged. She snuck a glance at his profile, the square jaw shadowed with stubble, the straight nose and angular cheekbones. Long, surprisingly lush lashes, and hard, dark eyes.

Hannah knew women flocked to Luca Moretti. They were attracted to his air of restless remoteness as much as his blatant sexuality and effortless charisma. Perhaps they fooled themselves into thinking they could tame or trap him; no one ever could. Hannah had kept more than one tearful beauty from her boss's door. He never thanked her for that little service; he acted as if the women who practically threw themselves at him didn't exist, at least not outside the bedroom. Or so Hannah assumed—she had no idea how Luca Moretti acted in the bedroom.

Just the thought sent a blush heating her cheeks now, even though she was still annoyed with his uncharacteristically terse attitude. High-handed she could take, when it was tempered with wry charm and grace. But Luca Moretti merely barking out orders was hard to stomach.

Thankfully the doors opened and they left the confined space of the lift, Luca ushering her out into the impressive marble foyer of Moretti Enterprises. A receptionist bid them good day and then they were out in the rain-washed streets, the damp air cooling her face, the twilight hiding her blush.

A limo pulled to the kerb the moment they stepped out, and Luca's driver jumped out to open the door.

'After you,' Luca said, and Hannah slid inside the luxurious interior. Luca followed, his thigh nudging hers before he shifted closer to the window.

Hannah couldn't resist stroking the buttery soft leather of the seat. 'I've never been in a limo before,' she admitted, and Luca cocked an eyebrow at her.

'Never?'

'No.' Why would she? He might travel in this sort of style all over the world, but she stayed firmly on the top floor of Moretti Enterprises. Of course, she'd seen plenty of luxury from a distance. She'd ordered champagne to celebrate his business deals, heard the pop of the cork in the meeting room down from his office. She'd booked dozens of first-class tickets and five-star hotel rooms, had instructed concierges around the world on Luca Moretti's preferences: no lilies in any flower arrangements in his suite and sheets with a five hundred thread count. She'd just never experienced any of that expense or luxury herself. 'I haven't stayed in a five-star hotel or flown first class either,' she informed him a bit tartly. Not everyone was as privileged as he was. 'I haven't even tasted champagne.'

'Well, you can enjoy some of that this weekend,' Luca said, and turned to stare out of the window, the lights from the traffic casting his face in a yellow wash. 'I'm sorry,' he said abruptly. 'I know I must seem...tense.'

Hannah eyed him warily. 'Ye—es...'

He turned to her with a small, rueful smile. 'I think that was an inward "you've been an absolute rotter".' His expression softened, his gaze sweeping over her, lashes lowering in a way that made Hannah feel the need to shift in her seat. 'I am sorry.'

'Why are you so tense?'

'As I said before, this weekend is delicate.' He turned back to the window, one long-fingered hand rubbing his jaw. 'Very delicate.'

Hannah knew better than to press. She had no idea why this business deal was so delicate; as far as she could tell, the chain of family resort hotels Luca was planning to take over was a relatively small addition to his real-estate portfolio.

The limo pulled up to Diavola, the windows lit although it was nearly seven o'clock at night. Hannah suppressed a shiver of apprehension. How was this supposed to *work*? Would she choose the dress, or would her boss? She'd done many things for Luca Moretti, but she hadn't bought herself an evening gown for him. She didn't relish the idea of parading clothes in front of him, but maybe he'd just let her choose a gown and get on with it.

Of course he would. He was already impatient, wanting to get onto the next thing; Luca Moretti wasn't going to entertain himself watching his PA try on different dresses. Comforted by this thought, Hannah slid out of the limo.

Luca followed her quickly, placing one hand on her elbow. The touch shocked her; Luca *never* touched her. Not so much as a hug or a pat on the back in three years of working for him. Hannah had always got the sense that he was a solitary man, despite the parade of women through his life, and she hadn't minded because she appreciated the focus on work. She didn't have room in her life for much else.

Now Luca kept his hand on her elbow as he guided her into the boutique, and then slid it to the small of her back as a shop assistant came forward. Hannah felt as if he were branding her back, his palm warm through the thin material of her skirt, his fingers splayed so she could feel the light yet firm pressure of each one. His pinkie finger reached the curve of her bottom, and her whole body stiffened in response as a treacherous flash of heat jolted through her.

'I would like a complete wardrobe for the weekend for my companion,' he said to the woman, who batted over-mascaraed lashes at him. 'Evening gowns, day wear, a swimming costume, nightgown, underthings.' He glanced at the gold and silver watch on one wrist. 'In under an hour.'

'Very good, Mr Moretti.'

Underthings? Hannah felt she had to object. 'Mr Moretti, I don't need all those things,' she protested in a low voice. She certainly didn't need her boss to buy her a bra. She felt the pressure on the small of her back increase, so she could feel the joints of each of his fingers.

'Humour me. And why don't you call me Luca?' Her jaw nearly dropped at this suggestion. He'd never invited such intimacy before. 'You've been working for me for what, three years?' he murmured so only she could hear, his head close enough to hers that she breathed in the cedarwood-scented aftershave he wore. When she turned her head she could see the hint of stubble on his jaw. 'Perhaps we should progress to first names... Hannah.'

For some reason her name on his lips made her want to shiver. She stepped away from his hand, her body bizarrely missing the warmth and pressure of it as soon as it had gone.

'Very well.' Yet she couldn't quite make herself call

him Luca. It seemed so odd, so intimate, after three years of starchy formality and respectable distance. Why was Luca shaking everything up now?

The sales assistant was collecting various garments from around the boutique, and another had come forward to usher them both to a U-shaped divan in cream velvet. A third was bringing flutes of champagne and caviar-topped crackers.

Luca sat down, clearly accustomed to all this luxury, and the sales assistant beckoned to Hannah.

'If the *signorina* will come this way…?'

Numbly Hannah followed the woman into a dressing room that was larger than the entire upstairs of her house.

'First this?' the woman suggested, holding up an evening gown in pale blue chiffon and satin. It was the most exquisite thing Hannah had ever seen.

'Okay,' she said, and, feeling as if she were in a surreal dream, she started to unbutton her blouse.

CHAPTER TWO

LUCA WAITED FOR Hannah to emerge from the dressing room as he sipped champagne and tried to relax. He was way too wound up about this whole endeavour, and his too-clever PA had noticed. He didn't want her guessing his game before they'd arrived on Santa Nicola. He couldn't risk the possibility of her refusal. Although Hannah Stewart had proved to be biddable enough, he suspected she had more backbone than he'd initially realised. And he didn't want her to use it against him.

Moodily Luca took a sip of champagne and stared out at the rainy streets of Mayfair. In less than twenty-four hours he'd be on Santa Nicola, facing Andrew Tyson. Would the man recognise him? It had been such a long time. Would there be so much as a flicker of awareness in those cold eyes? If there was it would completely ruin Luca's plan, and yet he couldn't keep from hoping that he would garner some reaction. Something to justify the emotion that had burned in his chest for far too long.

'Well?' he called to Hannah. She'd been in the dressing room for nearly ten minutes. 'Have you tried something on?'

'Yes, but this one's a bit...' She trailed off, and Luca snapped his gaze to the heavy velvet curtain drawn across the dressing room's doorway.

'Come out and let me see it.'

'It's fine.' She sounded a little panicked but also quite firm. 'I'll try something else on—'

'*Hannah.*' Luca tried to curb his impatience. 'I would like to see the dress, please.' What woman didn't enjoy showing off haute couture for a man? And he needed to make sure Hannah looked the part.

'I'm already changing,' she called, and in one fluid movement Luca rose from the divan and crossed to the dressing room, pulling aside the heavy curtain.

He didn't know who gasped—Hannah, in shock that he'd intruded, or himself, for the sudden dart of lust that had arrowed through his body at the sight of his PA.

She stood with her back to him, the dress pooling about her waist in gauzy blue folds as she held the front up to her chest, her face in profile, every inch the outraged maiden.

'Mr Moretti—' she muttered and he watched a blush crawl up her back and neck to her face.

'Luca,' he reminded her, and sent an iron glare of warning to the assistant, who was waiting discreetly in the corner. He did not want anyone gossiping about the oddity of the occasion.

'Luca,' Hannah acquiesced, but she sounded annoyed. Luca felt a surprising flicker of amusement. His little sparrow of a secretary sometimes pretended she was a hawk. 'Please leave. I am *changing.*'

'I wanted to see the gown. I'm paying for it, after all.' He folded his arms, feeling no more than a flash of remorse for pulling that particular trump card. Hannah, however, did not look particularly impressed. 'How much is this gown?' he asked the sales assistant.

The woman hesitated, but only for a millisecond. 'Nine thousand pounds, Signor Moretti.'

'Nine thousand—' Hannah whirled around, the dress nearly slipping from her hands. Luca caught a glimpse of pale, lightly freckled fresh, the hint of a small, perfectly round breast. Then she hauled the gown up to her chin, her face now bright red with mortification.

'Careful,' he advised. 'That material looks delicate.'

'As delicate as this weekend?' she retorted, and he smiled.

'I never knew you had a temper.'

'I never knew you could spend nine thousand pounds on a *dress*.'

He raised his eyebrows, genuinely surprised. 'Most women of my acquaintance enjoy spending my money.'

'Your acquaintance is quite limited, then,' Hannah snapped. 'Plenty of women aren't interested only in shopping and money.'

'Point taken.'

'Anyway,' Hannah muttered, 'it's wrong.' She turned around so her back was once more to him.

'Wrong? But how can you object if it's my money?'

'Do you know what could be done with nine thousand pounds?' she demanded, her back straight and quivering with tension.

'Oh, no, tell me you're not one of those bleeding hearts,' Luca drawled. 'I expected more of you, Hannah.'

'I'm not,' she said stiffly. 'I've never objected to you spending money on yourself. But when it's for me—'

'It's still my choice.' He cut her off. 'Now zip up that dress and let me see it on you.'

Taking her cue, the sales assistant stepped forward and zipped up the back, although in truth there wasn't much to zip up. The dress was almost entirely backless, with a halter top and a gauzy chiffon overlay that lent some respectability to the plunging neckline, as Luca saw when Hannah reluctantly turned around.

He schooled his face into an expression of businesslike interest, as if he were assessing the gown simply as an appropriate garment for the occasion rather than for the effect it had on his libido. Why on earth he was reacting to his PA's unexceptional body this way he had no idea. He supposed that was what you paid for with Diavola. The dresses worked.

'Very good,' he told the assistant. 'We'll take it. Now we need something casual to wear for the day, and a semiformal dress for the first night.'

'I have some of these things at home,' Hannah protested.

Luca held up a hand. 'Please cease this pointless arguing, Hannah. This is a business expense, I told you.'

She went silent, tight-lipped, her brown eyes flashing suppressed fury. Unable to resist baiting her just a little bit, or maybe just wanting to touch her, Luca reached over and pulled the tie of the halter top of her dress.

'There,' he said as she caught the folds of the dress, her eyes wide with shock. 'Now hurry up. I want to be out of here in forty-five minutes.'

Hannah's hands trembled as she stripped off the evening gown and flung it at the assistant, too unsettled and overwhelmed to care how she treated the delicate material.

What was going on? Why was Luca treating her this way? And why had she reacted to the sight of him in the dressing room, her body tightening, heat flaring deep inside when she'd turned around and seen his gaze dip to her unimpressive cleavage?

Perhaps, she thought resentfully, she'd simply never seen this side of her boss before. Outside the office, Luca Moretti might well be the kind of man who flirted and teased and stormed into women's dressing rooms and undid their gowns...

She suppressed a shiver at the memory of his fingers skimming her back as he'd tugged on the tie. Stupid, to react to the man that way. At this moment she wasn't even sure she liked him. And yet it had been a long, long time since she'd been touched like that.

Not, of course, that Luca had had any intention other than discomfiting her when he'd undone her dress. Hannah was savvy enough to realise that.

And as for the cost… Maybe it was irrational to protest when a millionaire spent what was essentially pocket change, but it was a lot of money to her. With nine thousand pounds she could have redone her kitchen or afforded a better life insurance policy…

'*Signorina?* Would you like to try on the next ensemble?'

Letting out a long, low breath, Hannah nodded. 'Yes, please.' This whole evening had entered into the realm of the utterly surreal, including her own reactions. When had she ever dared to talk back to her boss? Yet he didn't feel like her boss when she was in a dressing room, her back bare, her breasts practically on display. And yet at the same time he felt more like her boss than ever, demanding and autocratic, expecting instant compliance. It was all so incredibly bizarre.

The assistant handed her a shift dress in pale pink linen that fitted perfectly. Would Luca want to see this dress as well? And what about her swimming costume, or the lacy, frothy underthings she could see waiting on a chair? A blaze of heat went through her at the thought, leaving her more disconcerted than ever.

'It's fine,' she told the assistant, and then took it off as fast as she could. Maybe if she worked quickly enough Luca wouldn't bother striding into her dressing room, acting as if he owned the world, acting as if he owned *her*.

Forty-two minutes later all the clothes Hannah had tried on, including the most modest bikini she'd been able to find and two sets of lingerie in beige silk and cream lace, were wrapped in tissue paper and put in expensive-looking bags with satin ribbons for handles. She hadn't even seen Luca hand over a credit card, and she dreaded to think what the bill was. Why on earth was he spending a fortune on her clothes, and for such a negligible business deal? She didn't like feeling beholden to him in such a way. She worked hard and earned everything she got, and she preferred it like that.

'I think you've spent more on me tonight than you'll make taking over these resorts,' she remarked as they stepped out into the street. The rain had cleared and a pale sickle moon rose above the elegant town houses of Mayfair. 'Andrew Tyson only owns about half a dozen resorts, doesn't he?'

'The land alone makes it worth it,' Luca replied, buttoning his jacket. Seconds later the limo appeared at the kerb, and the sales assistant loaded the bags into the boot.

'I should get home,' Hannah said. She felt relieved at the thought of being away from Luca's unsettling presence, and yet reluctant to end the bizarre magic of the evening. But it was a forty-five-minute Tube ride to her small terraced house on the end of the Northern Line, and she'd be late enough as it was.

'I'll drive you,' Luca answered. 'Get in.'

'I live rather far away…'

'I know where you live.'

His calm assertion discomfited her. Of course her boss knew where she lived; it was on her employment record. And yet the thought of Luca invading her home, seeing even just a glimpse her private life, made her resist.

'I don't…'

'Hannah, get in. It's nearly eight and we're leaving at nine tomorrow morning. Why spend nearly an hour on the Tube when you don't have to?'

He had a point. As it was she'd be getting back later than she liked. 'All right, thank you.' She climbed into the limo, sitting well away from Luca. She could still remember the feel of his fingers on her back. *Stupid, stupid, stupid.* He'd probably been amused at how embarrassed she'd been. He probably undressed women in his sleep. The only reason she'd responded to him like that was because he was attractive and she hadn't been touched by a man in over five years. Her mother had told her it was more than time to jump back in the dating pool, but Hannah hadn't had time even to think about dipping a toe in.

The limo pulled into the street and Hannah sat back, suddenly overwhelmed with fatigue. The last few hours had taken an emotional toll.

'Here.' Luca pressed a glass into her hands, and her fingers closed around the fragile stem automatically. She looked in surprise at the flute of champagne. The driver must have had it ready. 'You didn't have any in the boutique,' Luca explained, 'and you said you had never tasted it before.'

'Oh.' She was touched by his thoughtfulness, and yet she felt weirdly exposed too. When had her boss ever considered what she wanted in such a way? 'Thank you.'

'Drink,' Luca said, and Hannah took a cautious sip, wrinkling her nose as the bubbles fizzed their way upward. Luca smiled at her faintly, no doubt amused by her inexperience.

'It's a bit more tickly than I thought,' she said. She felt incredibly gauche. Luca had most likely first imbibed Dom Perignon from a baby's bottle. He kept a bottle in his limo, after all. And here she was, saying how the bubbles tickled her nose.

She handed back the champagne with an awkward smile, and Luca took it, one dark eyebrow arched. 'Is it not to your liking?'

'It's just…I haven't eaten anything. And you know, alcohol on an empty stomach, never a good idea…' She was babbling, out of her element in so many ways. She, the calm, capable, unflappable PA, had been reduced to stammering and blushing by her boss, who was acting more like a man than an employer. She couldn't understand him or herself, and it was incredibly annoying.

'I'm sorry,' Luca murmured. 'I should have thought.' He pressed the intercom button and issued some directions in Italian. Hannah eyed him askance.

'What are you doing…?'

'I asked him to stop so we can eat. You don't have plans?'

Surprised alarm had her lurching upright. 'No, but really, it's not necessary—'

'Hannah, you're hungry. When you work late at the office, I provide dinner. Consider this the same thing.'

Except this didn't *feel* like the same thing. And when the limo stopped in front of an elegant bistro with red velvet curtains in the windows and curling gold script on the door, Hannah knew their meal would be a far cry from the sandwiches and coffee Luca usually had her order in when they were both working late.

She swallowed audibly, and then forced back the feelings of uncertainty and inadequacy. She'd been working as PA to one of the most powerful men in real estate for three years. She could handle dinner at a restaurant.

Straightening her spine, she got out of the car. Luca opened the door to the restaurant for her and then followed her in. The muted, understated elegance of the place fell over her like a soothing blanket.

'A table for two, Monsieur Moretti?' The French waiter asked, menus already in hand. Was her boss known *everywhere*?

Luca nodded and within seconds they were escorted to a private table in the corner, tucked away from the few other diners in the restaurant.

Hannah scanned the menu; it provided a temporary escape from Luca's penetrating gaze. *Foie gras. Roasted quail. Braised fillet of brill.* Okay, she could do this.

'Do you see something you like?' Luca asked.

'Yes.' She closed the menu and gave him a perfunctory smile. 'Thank you.'

The waiter came with the wine list, and Luca barely glanced at it before ordering a bottle. He turned to Hannah the moment the man had gone, his gaze resting on her. Again she had the sense of coming up short, of not being quite what he wanted, and she didn't understand it.

'It occurs to me that I know very little about you.'

'I didn't realise you wanted to,' Hannah answered. Luca had never asked her a single personal question in her three years of employment.

'Information is always valuable,' he answered with a negligent shrug. 'Where did you grow up?'

'A village outside Birmingham.' She eyed him warily. Where was this coming from? And why?

'Brothers? Sisters?'

'No.' Deciding this could go both ways, Hannah raised her eyebrows. 'What about you?'

Luca looked slightly taken aback, his eyes flaring, mouth compressing. In the dim lighting of the restaurant he looked darker and more alluring than usual, the candlelight from the table throwing his face into stark contrast from the snowy whiteness of his shirt, his whole being exuding restless power, barely leashed energy. 'What about me?'

'Do you have brothers or sisters?'

His mouth flattened into a hard line and he looked away briefly. 'No.'

So apparently he didn't like answering personal questions, just asking them. Hannah couldn't say she was surprised. The waiter came to take their order, and she chose a simple salad and the roasted quail, which she hoped would taste like chicken. Luca ordered steak and then the sommelier was proffering an expensive-looking bottle. Hannah watched as Luca expertly swilled a mouthful and then nodded in acceptance. The sommelier poured them both full glasses.

'I really shouldn't…' Hannah began. She didn't drink alcohol very often and she wanted to be fresh for tomorrow. And she didn't relish getting a bit of a buzz in Luca's presence. The last thing she needed was to feel even sillier in front of her boss.

'It won't be on an empty stomach,' Luca replied. 'And I think you need to relax.'

'Do you?' Hannah returned tartly. 'I must confess, this is all a bit out of the ordinary, Mr—'

'Luca.'

'Why?' she burst out. 'Why now?'

His dark gaze rested on her for a moment, and she had the sense he was weighing his words, choosing them with care. 'Why not?' he finally replied, and reached for his wine glass. Hannah deflated, frustrated but also a tiny bit relieved by his non-answer. She didn't know if she could handle some sort of weird revelation.

Fortunately Luca stopped with the personal questions after that, and they ate their meal mainly in silence, which was far more comfortable than being the subject of her boss's scrutiny, but even so she felt on edge, brittle and restless.

Which was too bad, she realised as Luca was paying the bill, because, really, she'd just had the most amazing evening—being bought a designer wardrobe and then treated to a fantastic meal by an undeniably sexy and charismatic man. Too bad it didn't feel like that. It felt…weird. Like something she could enjoy if she let herself, but she didn't think she should. Luca Moretti might have dozens of women at his beck and call, at his feet, but Hannah didn't intend to be one of them. Not if she wanted to keep her job, not to mention her sanity.

They drove in silence to her little house; by the time they'd arrived it was nearly ten o'clock. Her mother, Hannah thought with a flash of guilt, would be both tired and worried.

'I'll see you here tomorrow at nine,' Luca said, and Hannah turned to him in surprise.

'I thought I would be making my own way to the airport.'

'By Tube? And what if you're later? It's better this way. Here, let me get your bags.'

Hannah groped for her keys while Luca took the bags from the boutique to her doorstep. 'Thank you,' she muttered. 'You can go—'

But he was waiting for her to open her front door. She fumbled with the key, breathing a sigh of relief when the door finally swung open.

'Hannah?' her mother called. 'I've been wondering where you were—'

'I'm fine—' Hannah turned to Luca, practically grabbing the bags from him. 'Thank you very much. I'll see you tomorrow at nine.'

He was frowning, his gaze moving from her to the narrow hallway behind her, her mother coming around the corner. Clearly he was wondering about her living situation.

'Goodnight,' Hannah said, and closed the door.

Her mother, Diane, stopped short, her eyes widening as she saw all the expensive-looking bags by Hannah's feet. 'What on earth…?'

'It's a long story,' Hannah said. 'Sorry I'm so late. Did Jamie…?'

'Went to bed without a whimper, bless him,' Diane said. Her gaze moved to the bags. 'Goodness, that's a lot of shopping.'

'Yes, it is,' Hannah agreed rather grimly. 'Let me go see Jamie and then I'll tell you all about it.' Or at least some of it. She'd probably omit a few details, like Luca undoing her dress. The memory alone was enough to make a shiver go through her. Again.

'I'll make you a cup of tea,' Diane said. Hannah was already heading up the narrow stairway and then down the darkened hall to the small second bedroom. She tiptoed inside, her heart lifting at the familiar and beloved sight: her son. He slept on his back, arms and legs flung out like a starfish, his breathing deep and even.

Gently Hannah reached down and brushed the sandy hair from his forehead, her fingers skimming his plump, baby-soft cheek. He was five years old and the light of her life. And she wouldn't see him for a whole weekend.

Guilt niggled at her at the thought. Hannah knew her job was demanding and she wasn't able to spend as much time with Jamie as she would like. She also knew, all too well, the importance of financial independence and freedom. Working for Luca Moretti had given her both. She would never regret making that choice.

With a soft sigh Hannah leaned down and kissed her son's forehead, and then quietly left the room. She needed to get ready for her weekend with her boss.

CHAPTER THREE

LUCA DRUMMED HIS fingers against his thigh as the limo pulled up in front of Hannah's house. He'd been there less than twelve hours ago, dropping her off after their shopping and meal. He'd been strangely disquieted to have a tiny glimpse into her life—the narrow hall with its clutter of coats and boots, the sound of a woman's voice. Her mother? Why did he care?

Perhaps because since he'd met her he'd viewed Hannah Stewart as nothing more than a means to his own end. First as his PA, efficient and capable, and now as his stand-in wife-to-be. Last night he'd realised that if this ridiculous charade was going to work, he needed to know more about Hannah. And he hadn't learned much, but what he had discovered was that getting to know Hannah even a little bit made him feel guilty for using her.

Sighing impatiently at his own pointless thoughts, Luca opened the door to the limo and stepped out into the street. It wasn't as if he was making Hannah's life difficult. She was getting a luxurious weekend on a Mediterranean island, all expenses paid. And if she had to play-act a bit, what was the big deal? He'd make it worth her while.

He pressed the doorbell, and Hannah answered the door almost immediately. She wore her usual work outfit of a dark pencil skirt and a pale silk blouse, this time grey and pink. Pearls at her throat and ears and low black heels complemented the outfit. There was nothing wrong with it, but it wasn't what his fiancée would be wearing to accompany him on a weekend house party. She looked like a PA, not a woman in love on a holiday.

'What happened to the outfits I bought you yesterday?' Luca demanded.

'Hello to you too,' Hannah answered. 'I'm saving them for when I'm actually on Santa Nicola.' She arched an eyebrow. 'Being on the aeroplane isn't part of the social occasion, is it?'

'Of course not.' Luca knew he couldn't actually fault Hannah. She was acting in accordance to the brief he had given her. He'd tell her the truth soon enough…when there was no chance of anything going wrong. Nothing could risk his plan for this weekend. 'Are you packed?'

'Of course.' She reached for her suitcase but Luca took it first. 'I'll put it in the boot.'

'Hello, Mr Moretti.' An older woman with faded eyes and grey, bobbed hair emerged from behind Hannah to give him a tentative smile.

'Good morning.' Belatedly Luca realised how snappish he must have sounded when talking to Hannah. This whole experience was making him lose his cool, his control. He forced as charming a smile as he could and extended his hand to the woman who took it.

'I'm Diane Stewart, Hannah's mother—'

'Lovely to meet you.'

'I should go, Mum,' Hannah said. She slipped on a black wool coat, lifting her neat ponytail away from the collar. Luca had a sudden, unsettling glimpse of the nape of her neck, the skin pale, the tiny hairs golden and curling.

'I'll say goodbye to Jamie for you,' Diane promised and Luca looked sharply at Hannah, who flushed.

Jamie—a boyfriend? Clearly someone close to her.

Although maybe Jamie was a girl's name. A friend? A sister?

'Thanks, Mum,' she muttered, and quickly hugged her mother before walking towards the limo.

Luca handed the suitcase to his driver before getting in the back with Hannah. She was sitting close to the window, her face turned towards the glass.

'Do you live with your mother?' he asked.

'No, she just stayed the night because I was so late getting home.'

'Why was she there at all?'

She gave him a quick, quelling look. 'She's visiting.'

Hannah Stewart seemed as private as he was. Luca settled back in the seat. 'I'm sorry if I've cut your visit short.' He paused. 'You could have told me she was visiting. I would have made allowances.'

Hannah's look of disbelief was rather eloquent. Luca felt a dart of annoyance, which was unreasonable since he knew he wouldn't have made allowances. He needed Hannah's attendance this weekend too much. Still he defended himself. 'I'm not that unreasonable an employer.'

'I never said you were.'

Which was true. But he felt nettled anyway, as if he'd done something wrong. It was that damned guilt, for tricking her into this. He didn't like lying. He'd always played a straight bat, prided himself on his plain dealing. He'd lived with too many lies to act otherwise. But this was different, this was decades-deep, right down to his soul, and his revenge on Andrew Tyson was far more important than his PA's tender feelings. Feeling better for that reminder, Luca reached for his smartphone and started scrolling through messages.

Hannah sat back in her seat, glad to have that awkward goodbye scene over with. Luca had been surprisingly curious about her life, and she'd thankfully managed to deflect his questions. She'd never told her boss about her son, and she wanted to keep it that way. She knew instinctively that Luca Moretti would not take kindly to his PA having such an obligation of responsibility, no matter what he said about allowances. She was fortunate that her mother lived nearby and had always been happy to help out. Without Diane's help, Hannah never would have been able to take the job as Luca Moretti's PA. She certainly wouldn't have been able to perform it with the same level of capability.

Now she tried to banish all the thoughts and worries that had kept her up last night as she'd wondered what she was getting into, and if she was doing the right thing in leaving her son for two days. She wanted to stop wondering if she was coming across as gauche as she felt, or why her normally taciturn boss was suddenly turning his narrow-eyed attention to her.

No, today she'd told herself she was going to simply enjoy everything that came her way, whether it was champagne and caviar or a first-class plane ticket. This was an adventure, and she'd got out of the habit of enjoying or even looking for adventures. Since she'd had Jamie her life had become predictable and safe, which wasn't a bad thing but sometimes it was boring. She realised she was actually looking forward to a little bit of a shake-up.

'You're smiling,' Luca observed and, startled, Hannah refocused her gaze on her boss. He'd been watching her, she realised with a lurch of alarm. Or maybe it was simply awareness that she felt. A tingling spread through her body as his gaze remained resting on her, his mahogany-brown eyes crinkled at the corners, a faint smile tugging at his own mobile mouth. He wore a navy blue suit she'd probably seen before, with a crisp white shirt and silver-grey tie. Standard business wear, elegant and expensive, the suit cut perfectly to his broad shoulders and trim hips. Why was she noticing it today? Why was she feeling so *aware*?

'I was just thinking about flying first class,' she said.

'Ah yes. Something else you haven't done before.'

'No, and I'm looking forward to it.' She smiled wryly. 'I'm sure it's same old, same old for you.'

'It's refreshing to see someone experience something for the first time.' His mouth curved in a deeper smile, the look in his eyes disconcertingly warm. 'Tickly or not.'

She lifted her chin, fighting a flush. 'I admit, I'm not very experienced in the ways of the world.'

'Why aren't you?'

'Maybe because I'm not a millionaire?' Hannah returned dryly. 'Most people don't travel first class, you know.'

'I'm well aware. But plenty of people have tasted champagne.' He cocked his head, his warm gaze turning thoughtful. 'You seem to have missed out a bit on life, Hannah.'

Which was all too perceptive of him. And even though she knew it was true, it still stung. 'I've been working,' she replied with a shrug. 'And I have responsibilities...' She left it at that but Luca's eyes had narrowed.

'What kind of responsibilities?'

'Family,' she hedged. 'Nothing that interferes with my work,' she defended and he nodded, hands spread palm upward.

'As well I know. I do appreciate you coming for the weekend.'

'I didn't think I really had much choice,' Hannah returned, then drew an even breath. 'Why don't you tell me more about this weekend? You said it was a social occasion? How so?'

The warmth left Luca's eyes and Hannah felt tension steal into his body even though he'd barely moved.

'Andrew Tyson is a family man,' he stated. 'Wife, two children, resorts dedicated to providing people with the ultimate family experience.'

'Yes, I did some research on them when I was booking your travel,' Hannah recalled. '"A Tyson Holiday is a memory for ever,"' she quoted and Luca grimaced.

'Right.'

'You don't like the idea?'

'Not particularly.'

She shouldn't have been surprised. Luca Moretti had never struck her as the wife-and-kids type, which was why she'd kept her own son secret from him. He was never short of female company, though, and none of them lasted very long. A week at the most. 'Why are you going after these resorts if you don't really like the idea behind them?'

'I don't make business decisions based on personal preferences,' Luca answered shortly. One hand closed in a fist on his powerful thigh and he straightened it out slowly, deliberately, his palm flat on his leg, his fingers, long and tapered, stretching towards his knee. 'I make business decisions based on what is financially sound and potentially profitable.'

'But Andrew Tyson only has a handful of resorts, doesn't he? The Santa Nicola resort, one on Tenerife, one on Kos, one on—'

'Sicily, and then a couple in the Caribbean. Yes.'

'It's small potatoes to a man like you,' Hannah pointed out. Luca had orchestrated multibillion-dollar deals all around the world. A couple of family resorts, especially ones that looked as if they needed a bit of updating, hardly seemed his sort of thing.

Luca shifted in his seat. 'As I told you before, the land alone makes this a lucrative deal.'

'Okay, but you still haven't told me why this is a social occasion.'

'Because Tyson wants it to be one. He's always es-
poused family values, and so he wants each potential
owner to socialise with him and his family.'

'So chatting up little kids?' Hannah couldn't quite keep
the note of amusement from her voice. 'It sounds like your
worst nightmare.'

'His children are grown up,' Luca answered. 'The son
is only a year younger than I am.'

'Do his children have children?'

'I have no idea.' Luca sounded eminently bored. 'Probably. The son is married.'

Hannah considered the implications of everything he'd
just said. So she'd be socialising with Andrew Tyson and
his family, chatting up his children and generally being
friendly? She was starting to realise why Luca had wanted
her to come along.

'So you want me to be your front man,' she said slowly.

Luca swivelled to face her. 'Excuse me?'

'To do the talking,' Hannah explained. 'Chatting to his
wife and children while you get on with the business side
of things. Right?'

He gave one terse nod. 'Right.'

She settled back in her seat. 'All right. I can do that.'

'Good,' Luca answered, and he turned back to his
phone.

The VIP lounge at the airport fully lived up to Hannah's expectations. She enjoyed the plush seats, the com-
plimentary mimosas and breakfast buffet, and when Luca
suggested she take advantage of the adjoining spa and get
a manicure and pedicure, she decided to go for it. Why not
enjoy all the opportunities that were on offer? It wasn't as
if she had many chances to relax in a spa.

By the time they boarded the plane she was feeling
pleasantly relaxed; one of the spa attendants had given her
a head and neck massage while her feet had been soaking.

It had felt lovely, as had Luca's look of blatant male appreciation when she'd emerged from the spa—the attendant had insisted on doing her hair and make-up as well.

'You look good,' he said in approval, and, while Hannah knew she shouldn't care what Luca thought of her looks, his masculine admiration spoke to the feminine heart of her.

'I think,' she told him as they took their seats in the plane's first-class section, 'I could get used to this.'

Luca's mouth quirked up at one corner. 'I'm sure you could.' He accepted two flutes of champagne from the airline steward and handed one to Hannah. 'And now you should get used to this.'

'Why are you so determined to have me become used to champagne?' Hannah asked as she took a sip. Second time round the bubbles didn't tickle her nose quite so much.

'Why not? You should enjoy all of these new experiences.'

'True,' Hannah answered. 'And since you said this was a social occasion, I might as well.' She took another sip of champagne. '*Are* we meant to be working during the flight?'

'No.'

'So why did you put me up in first class?'

'I wanted to watch you enjoy the experience.'

Hannah felt her stomach dip at this implication of his words, the intimacy of them. She was suddenly conscious of how this all seemed: the champagne flute dangling from her fingers, the cosy enclave of their first-class seats, and Luca Moretti lounging next to her, not taking his warm gaze from hers. She swallowed hard.

'Well, I am enjoying it,' she said, striving for normality. 'Thank you.' The last thing she needed was to start crushing on her boss. He'd probably find that amusing—or maybe offensive, and fire her. She handed her half-drunk champagne to the steward and buckled her seat belt. Time to get things back to the way they'd always been.

Luca must have been thinking along the same lines because he reached for the in-flight magazine as the plane took off, and then spent the rest of the four-hour flight looking over some paperwork. Hannah asked him once if he needed her to do anything, and he snapped at her that he didn't.

In fact, with each passing hour of the flight, he seemed to get more and more tense, his muscles taut, his eyes shadowed, his face grim. Hannah wondered what was going on, but she didn't dare ask.

She tried to watch a movie but her mind was pinging all over the place, and so she ended up simply staring out of the window at the azure sky, waiting for the minutes and hours to pass.

And then they did, and they landed on Santa Nicola, the Mediterranean glittering like a bright blue promise in the distance.

'Is someone meeting us at the airport?'

'Yes, one of Tyson's staff is picking us up.' Luca rose from his seat and shrugged into his suit jacket. 'Let me do the talking.'

Okay... 'I thought you wanted me to socialise.'

'I do. But not with the staff.'

Bewildered, Hannah stared at him, but Luca's deliberately bland expression gave nothing away. He held a hand out to her to help her from her seat, and after a second's hesitation she took it.

The feel of his warm, dry palm sliding across and then enfolding hers was a jolt to her system, like missing the last step in a staircase. Instinctively she started to withdraw her hand but Luca tightened his hands over hers and pulled her forward.

'Come on,' he murmured. 'People are waiting.'

With his hand still encasing hers she followed him out of the plane, blinking in the bright sunlight as she navigated the narrow steps down to the tarmac. She was just thinking that she wished she'd packed her sunglasses in her carry-on rather than her suitcase when she heard someone call a greeting to Luca and then felt his arm snake around her waist.

Hannah went rigid in shock at the feel of his fingers splayed on one hip, her other hip pressed against his thigh.

'Signor Moretti! We are so pleased to welcome you to Santa Nicola.' A tanned, friendly-looking man in khaki shorts and a red polo shirt with the Tyson logo on the breast pocket came striding towards them. 'And this is…?' he asked, glancing at Hannah with a smile.

'Hannah Stewart,' Luca filled in smoothly, his arm still firmly about her waist. 'My fiancée.'

CHAPTER FOUR

HANNAH STOOD BLINKING stupidly at the man who had come forward. He reached for her hand and numbly she gave it to him.

'Signorina Stewart. So pleased to meet you! Signor Moretti mentioned he was bringing his fiancée, and we look forward to getting to know you. I am Stefano, one of the members of Mr Tyson's staff.'

Hannah could only stare at Stefano, trying to find the brain cells to string two words together. The only word she could think of was the one Luca had used with such confident precision. *Fiancée.*

What on earth…?

'Hannah,' Luca murmured, and she felt the pressure of his hand on her waist, the warmth of his palm seeping through her skirt.

Still reeling, she forced a smile onto her face. 'Pleased to meet you, I'm sure.'

As soon as she said the words she wished she hadn't. Now she was complicit in this…whatever *this* was. A lie, obviously. A ruthless deception—and for what purpose? Why on earth would Luca pretend she was something she wasn't?

Because he was pretending he was something he wasn't.

The answer was so blindingly obvious Hannah couldn't

believe she hadn't twigged earlier. Andrew Tyson was a family man, and this weekend was meant to be a social occasion. *Of course.* Luca Moretti, the famous womaniser, needed a woman. A fiancée to show he was the kind of family man Tyson must want him to be. What other reason could he have possibly had for introducing her that way? For *lying*?

'Come this way,' Stefano said, beckoning towards the waiting open-topped Jeep emblazoned with the Tyson logo, a dolphin jumping in front of a sun. 'Mr Tyson's villa is only a few minutes away.'

Hannah walked like an automaton towards the Jeep, Luca next to her, his arm still around her. She wanted to shrug it off but she didn't think she'd be able to; his grip was like a vice. She tried to catch his eye but he was staring blandly ahead. Damn the man. What on earth was she supposed to do now?

They got in the back of the Jeep and Stefano hopped in the front. Hannah was barely aware of the gorgeous surroundings: mountains provided a stunning, jagged backdrop to lush greenery that framed both sides of the paved single-track road. She'd read that Santa Nicola was virtually unspoilt, save for the resort, and she could see it now in the jungle of bright flowers that gave way to superbly landscaped gardens and high walls of pink sandstone.

'*Luca,*' she muttered meaningfully, although she hardly knew where to begin, how to protest. 'You can't—'

'I already have,' he murmured as the Jeep came to a stop in front of a sprawling villa, its pale stone walls climbing with ivy and bougainvillea.

'I know,' Hannah snapped. 'And you shouldn't have—' She was prevented from saying anything more by Stefano coming around to open the door on her side and help her out onto the cobbled pavement.

'Mr Tyson looks forward to welcoming you properly

this evening, during the cocktail hour. In the meantime you can both rest and refresh yourselves.'

'Thank you,' Hannah muttered, although everything in her cried out to end this absurd charade. She was so angry and shocked she could barely manage to speak civilly to Stefano, who of course had no idea what was going on. *Yet.*

And Hannah wondered how on earth she could tell him, or anyone here, the truth. Luca had made it virtually impossible, and yet still she fantasised about coming clean and watching Luca Moretti get the send-up he undoubtedly deserved. How dare he put her in this position?

Stefano led them into the gracious entryway of the villa, a soaring foyer that made the most of the house's unparalleled view of the sea. Down a long terracotta-tiled corridor, and then through double louvred doors into a spacious and elegant bedroom, a massive king-sized bed its impressive centrepiece, the French windows opened to a private terrace that led to the beach, gauzy curtains blowing in the sea breeze.

'This is marvellous, thank you,' Luca said, shaking Stefano's hand, and with a murmured farewell Stefano closed the doors behind them, finally, thankfully, leaving them alone.

Hannah whirled around to face Luca, who stood in the centre of the bedroom, hands in the pockets of his trousers, a faint frown on his face as he surveyed the room with its elegant furnishings in cream and light green.

'How could you?' she gasped out. 'How *dare* you?'

Luca moved his gaze to her. He seemed utterly unmoved, without a shred of remorse or embarrassment. 'If you are referring to the way I introduced you—'

'Of *course* I'm referring to that!'

'It was necessary.' And he strolled over to the windows as if that was actually the end of the discussion.

Hannah stared at his broad back, watching as he closed

and fastened the windows. Finally she managed to say in what she hoped was a level, reasonable voice, 'Do you actually think this can work?'

Luca turned around to face her, eyebrows arrogantly raised. 'I don't embark on ventures that are doomed to failure.'

'I think you may be in for a new experience, then,' Hannah snapped.

'Why? Why shouldn't Andrew Tyson believe you're my fiancée?'

'Because I'm *not*—'

'Are you not suitable?' Luca steamrolled over her, his voice silky and yet underlaid with iron. 'Are you not pretty or smart or sophisticated enough?'

A hot flush broke out over Hannah's body as she glared at him. 'No, I'm not,' she answered flatly. 'As you well know. I hadn't even flown first class before today—or drunk champagne—' Suddenly the memory of him pressing the flute into her hands, smiling at her with such gentle amusement, was enough to make her burst into tears. She swallowed hard before continuing furiously, realisation ripping away any illusions she'd had left. 'So everything you've done has been to maintain this…this ridiculous facade.' She glanced down at her varnished nails, her hands curling instinctively into fists. 'The manicure and pedicure?' she spat. 'The hair and make-up…' She remembered the look of approval in his eyes. *You look good.* And she'd inwardly preened at his praise. 'You just wanted me to look the part.'

'Is that so objectionable?'

'This whole farce is objectionable! You *tricked* me.'

Luca sighed, as if she were being so very tedious by objecting. 'I'm asking for very little, Hannah.'

'Very little? You're asking me to lie to strangers. To pretend to—to be in love with you!' The words rang out, making her wince. She hadn't meant it quite like *that*, and yet…that was what he was asking. Wasn't it?

'I'm not asking anything of the kind,' Luca returned evenly. 'Although surely it wouldn't be too hard?'

Hannah recoiled, horrified at the implication. Did he think he was so desirable—or simply that she was so desperate? 'Yes, it would,' she said stiffly. 'Since in actuality I barely know you. Which was the point of the little "getting to know you" spiel last night at dinner, wasn't it?' She shook her head, disgusted with both him and herself. She'd known something was off, but how on earth could she have suspected this? 'Well, at least now you know I'm an only child. That's something, I suppose. Make sure to mention it during the cocktail hour.'

'You know me well enough,' Luca answered, his tone deliberately unruffled. 'You've worked for me for three years. In fact,' he continued, strolling towards her, 'you probably know me better than anyone else does.'

'I do?' She blinked at him, surprised and a little saddened by this admission. She'd known Luca was a solitary man, but surely he had closer people in his life than his PA. 'What about your family?'

'Not around.'

'Where—?'

'You're the only person who sees me every day, Hannah. Who knows my preferences, my foibles and quirks. Yes, I think you know me very well.'

'Yes, but you don't know *me*.' And she didn't care whether she knew him or not. She wouldn't want to playact as his fiancée even if they'd been best friends. Which they were most decidedly not.

'I think I know you a little bit,' Luca said, a smile curving the sensuous mouth Hannah suddenly couldn't look away from.

'What? How?' He didn't know anything. 'You've never asked me anything about my life until last night.'

'Maybe I don't need to ask.'

'What are you saying?' He'd taken a step closer to her and her stomach writhed and leapt in response, as if she'd swallowed snakes. She pressed one hand to her middle, knowing the gesture to be revealing, and stood her ground even though she desperately wanted to take a step away from him.

Instead he took a step closer. 'Let's see,' he murmured, his voice a low hum that seemed to reverberate right through her bones. He was close enough so that she could inhale the cedarwood scent of his aftershave, see the muscles corded in his neck. Some time since entering the room he'd loosened his silver silk tie and undone the top two buttons of his shirt, so she could see the strong brown column of his throat, the dark hairs sprinkling his chest below. She jerked her gaze away from the sight.

'You don't know me,' she stated firmly. 'At all. Because if you did, you'd know I'd never agree to something like this.'

'Which is why I didn't ask you, so perhaps I do know you after all.'

'You don't,' she insisted. He was close enough to breathe in, to feel his heat. If she reached one hand out she could place a palm on his chest, feel the crisp cotton of his shirt, the steady thud of his heart, the flex of his powerful muscles…

Hannah drew her breath in sharply, horrified by the nature of her thoughts. What kind of sorcerer was Luca Moretti, to weave this spell over her so easily?

'I think I do,' Luca murmured. He stood right in front of her, his gaze roving over her, searching, finding, feeling as intimate as a caress. 'I know you drink your coffee with milk and two sugars, although you pretend you have it black.'

'What…?' Her breath came out in a rush. It was such a little thing, but he was right. She added the sugar when she was alone because she was self-conscious about taking it. Every working woman in London seemed to drink their coffee black and eat lettuce leaves for lunch.

Somehow she managed to rally. 'That's not very much,' she scoffed.

'I'm only beginning,' Luca answered. 'I know you look at travel blogs on your lunch break. I know you have an incredible work ethic but you seem embarrassed by it sometimes. I know you're determined to be cheerful but sometimes, when you think no one is looking, you seem sad.'

Hannah drew a deep breath, too shocked to respond or even to blush. How had he seen all these things? How did he *know*?

'And,' Luca finished softly as he turned away, 'I know there is someone in your life named Jamie whom you care about very much.'

She stiffened. 'Well done, Sherlock,' she managed. 'You're obviously very perceptive, but it doesn't change what I think—that this is wrong, and you never should have forced me into this position.'

Luca turned back to her, the warmth she'd just seen in his eyes evaporated, leaving only chilly darkness. 'How exactly,' he asked, his voice dangerously soft, 'did I force you?'

'It's not as if you gave me a choice,' Hannah exclaimed. 'Introducing me as your fiancée! What was I supposed to do, tell them you were a liar?'

He shrugged, the movement elegant, muscles rippling underneath his shirt. 'You could have done.' He lifted his gaze to hers, those dark, cold eyes so penetrating. 'Why didn't you?'

'Because…'

'Because?' Luca prompted softly.

'It would have been very awkward,' Hannah said. 'For both of us.'

'What's a little awkwardness?'

'You might have fired me—'

He arched an eyebrow. 'And be sued for sexual harassment?'

'I could already sue you for that,' Hannah dared to suggest. Luca's eyes narrowed.

'And then you really would lose your job, just as I would lose mine.'

She swallowed. 'You could have paid me off.'

The smile he gave her was cynical and hard. 'Is that what you're suggesting?'

'No.' Appalled, Hannah wondered how on earth they'd pursued this line of conversation. She wasn't going to sue him, even if part of her inwardly railed that she should, that Luca Moretti deserved everything he had coming to him, including a whole lot of *awkwardness*.

'I don't want money,' she informed him stiffly. 'I simply don't want to be in this position, and I resent that you put me in it. Why didn't you tell me before?'

'Because you would have refused.'

She stared at his calm expression, his hard eyes. He stood before her, arrogant and assured, utterly unrepentant. 'You don't have a shred of remorse, do you?' she asked wonderingly.

'No,' Luca agreed, 'I don't. Because if you let go of your huffy indignation for a moment, Hannah, you'll realise I'm not asking very much of you.'

'You're asking me to lie.'

'And you've never lied before?'

She bit her lip. 'Of course, everyone's lied, but this is different—'

'Andrew Tyson is putting unreasonable expectations on the real-estate developer who buys his precious resorts,' Luca cut across her flatly. 'I *know* I'm the best man for the job, and I shouldn't have to be married to be selected. The injustice is his, not mine.'

'How many other developers are bidding on it?'

'Two, and they're both married.'

Somehow she found the temerity to joke. 'You weren't tempted to say I was your wife?'

'I was tempted,' Luca admitted. 'But I figured that would be too hard to pull off.'

'How pragmatic of you,' Hannah murmured. Her mind was still spinning but some of her self-righteous fury had deflated. She didn't know whether it was simply the awesome force of Luca's personality or because she actually sympathised with him a little. Or maybe it was because she was just too tired to keep it up.

Slowly she walked to a cream divan positioned in an alcove and sank onto its soft seat. 'So how do you propose—no pun intended—to make this work? Not,' she informed him with swift asperity, 'that I'm actually thinking of going along with this idea.'

'Of course not,' Luca murmured. Hannah watched, mesmerised, as he tugged off his tie and then began to unbutton his shirt.

'What are you doing?' she squeaked.

'Changing. We're due for cocktails in less than an hour.'

'Can't you use the bathroom?' She nodded towards the door that led to what looked like a sumptuous en suite.

'Why should I?' Luca's smile was wicked. 'We're engaged to be married, after all.'

'You're impossible.' Hannah closed her eyes against the sight of Luca shrugging off his shirt. Even so she'd had a glimpse of bronzed, burnished skin, rippling muscles, and crisp, dark hair that veed down to the waistband of his trousers.

'You're not the first person to say so,' Luca answered. She could hear him undressing and even with her eyes closed she could imagine it, picture him kicking off his trousers, revealing long, muscular legs, wearing nothing but a pair of boxer shorts, perhaps in navy satin…

Good grief, but she needed to get a grip. Hannah took a deep breath. 'So you still haven't told me how this is going to work.'

'We're going to act like we're engaged. Simple.'

'Simple?' She opened her eyes to glare at Luca; he stood across the room, buckling the belt on a pair of grey trousers. His chest was still gloriously bare. 'It's not simple, Luca. We're not engaged. We barely know each other. If someone asks either one of us anything about our relationship or how we met, we'll have no idea what to say.'

'It's best to keep as close to the truth as possible,' Luca advised as he reached for a light blue shirt and shrugged into it. 'You're still my PA.'

'And we just happen to be engaged. Convenient.'

He shot her a quick, hard smile. 'It is, isn't it? Now you should get ready. We're due to meet Tyson for cocktails shortly.'

CHAPTER FIVE

LUCA STARED OUT at the setting sun turning the placid sea to gold and waited for Hannah to emerge from the bathroom. He tried to ignore the guilt that flickered through him, an unpleasant ripple of sensation. All right, so he'd tricked her. He shouldn't have. But he hadn't had any choice. Not that Hannah would be able to understand that, and he had no intention of explaining it to her. She didn't seem to be quite so angry now, although she had shut the door rather firmly after flouncing in there to get changed.

Sighing restlessly, Luca turned away from the spectacular view. Every nerve ending tingled with anticipation at coming face to face with Andrew Tyson. In the three months since Tyson had announced he was selling his chain of family resorts, Luca hadn't actually spoken to the man, not even on the telephone. Everything had been done through intermediaries, until this weekend. Until now, when he would finally look upon the man he'd hated for so long. He *had* to close this deal. And he'd do whatever it took to accomplish that.

'Are you ready?' he called to Hannah. They were due on the terrace for drinks in five minutes.

'Yes.' She unlocked and opened the door, emerging from the bathroom with her head held high even as uncertainty flickered in her eyes. Luca felt the breath rush from his lungs as he took in her appearance.

She wore a cocktail dress in plum-coloured silk; the pure, clean line of the material across her collarbone drew his attention to the elegance of her shoulders and neck as well as the slight, enticing curve of her breasts. The dress fitted perfectly to her tiny waist and then flared out around her thighs, ending at her knees. Her long, shapely legs were encased in sheer stockings and she'd worn her hair not in its usual neat ponytail, but in loose waves about her face. She looked clean and fresh and utterly alluring.

Luca finally found his voice. 'You look...good.'

'I meet with your approval?' Hannah surmised tartly. 'Well, I need to look the part, don't I?' She went over to her suitcase and riffled through her belongings. 'I don't feel at all guilty for letting you buy me a fortune in clothes, by the way.'

'And so you shouldn't.' The rays of the setting sun caught the golden glints in her hair. Luca watched as she moved her hair over to one shoulder in order to put on her earrings. He found something almost unbearably erotic about watching her do this, her neck exposed, her slender hands fitting the earring into her ear. Her feet, he saw, were bare.

'I suppose I'll have to give them back when this charade is over?' she asked as she reached for a pearl necklace.

'No, not at all. You may keep them. They're yours.'

She fiddled with the necklace, unable to do the clasp, and Luca walked towards her. 'Here, let me.' His fingers brushed her nape as he did the clasp and he felt a shudder go through her. Felt it go through himself. He couldn't resist brushing his fingers against that tender, silky skin one more time before he stepped away.

'Thank you,' she murmured, not looking at him. He could see a rosy flush spreading across the creamy skin of her throat and face.

'I should have bought you some appropriate jewellery.'

'I think that would be going above and beyond,' she answered lightly. 'Pearls surely suffice.'

'Yes…but I'd like to see you with diamonds. And sapphires. They'd look lovely against your pale skin.'

She dipped her head, hiding her expression. 'Thank you.'

Luca watched her, wishing he had a reason to touch her again. 'You don't seem as angry as you were before.'

She glanced quickly at him before lowering her lashes. 'I suppose I'm not. The truth is, I actually do like you, Mr—'

'Surely now is the time to call me Luca.'

'Luca. Sorry, old habits die hard, I suppose.' She sighed and then straightened before moving away from him. 'I'd better not slip up with that one, huh? Anyway.' She reached for a wrap in matching plum-coloured lace; it looked as fragile and delicate as cobwebs. 'I like working for you, even if I resent having to participate in this farce of an engagement. I don't want you to lose face or your job, and I certainly don't want to lose mine. So.' She turned to him, a determined smile on her face. 'Here we are.'

'Here we are.' He gazed at her and she gazed back, and the moment stretched and spun out while the sun continued to set and the room became dark with shadows.

Eventually, Luca didn't know how long it took, he roused himself and reached for her hand. 'We should go.'

'All right.'

And with her fingers loosely threaded through his, he led her out of the room.

The terrace was bathed with the last rays of the setting sun as Luca led her through the open French windows and out onto the smooth paving stones. Torches flickered in the deepening twilight and couples milled around along with several staff members proffering trays of champagne and frothy-looking cocktails.

Smiling wryly to herself, Hannah took a flute of champagne with murmured thanks. She took a sip, enjoying the crisp bubbles bursting on her tongue, and gazed around at the assortment of people. There were two other couples, an urbane, blond man with a tall, bony-looking woman who Hannah vaguely recognised, and a middle-aged man with greying hair and a smiling wife who had squeezed herself into a dress of green satin. Their host, as far as she could tell, was nowhere to be seen.

Next to her Luca looked relaxed and faintly amused, but Hannah could feel the tension emanating from him. The fingers that clasped his flute of champagne were white-knuckled. She wondered again why he cared so much, and knew he would never tell her. And she would probably never work up the courage to ask.

'Greetings!' A jovial-looking man in his seventies appeared in the French windows, rubbing his hands and smiling in expectation. Hannah recognised Andrew Tyson from the photograph she'd seen on the Tyson Resorts website. Genial, running slightly to fat, with sandy silvery hair and deep-set brown eyes. In his youth he must have been quite handsome. He still possessed a vigorous charisma now.

'I'm so pleased to have you here at last,' he said as he strolled onto the terrace. 'Luca, James, and Simon. You all know each other?'

The men exchanged quick glances and terse nods. 'Excellent, excellent. And you all have drinks?' His gaze moved over the crowd to rest on Luca.

'Luca Moretti,' he said as if accessing a mental Rolodex. 'We've never actually met, but I have, of course, heard of your many accomplishments in the world of real estate.'

Hannah glanced at Luca and saw his expression was bland. 'Thank you,' he murmured.

'And you are recently engaged?' Andrew's gaze sharpened, his smile turning almost sly. 'For I've heard of your accomplishments elsewhere.'

Luca drew Hannah forward, as if displaying a trophy. She tried to smile even though she didn't like being pushed forward as if for inspection. 'Indeed. Please meet my wife-to-be, Hannah Stewart.'

'Hannah.' Tyson glanced at her appraisingly, and for one horrible second Hannah wondered if he would see through this whole ridiculous charade. And she realised she didn't want to be exposed in such a way, and she didn't want Luca to be exposed. He might have lied and tricked her terribly, but now that she was embroiled in this ploy she wanted it to succeed.

'I'm very pleased to meet you,' she told Tyson, and stuck out her hand for him to shake. He kissed it instead, his lips a little damp, and next to her Luca shifted restlessly.

'Likewise, of course,' Tyson said. 'Now how did the two of you meet?'

'Hannah is my PA,' Luca intervened swiftly. 'We met at work. I'm not one to advocate mixing business with pleasure, but in this instance it was impossible not to.' He sent Hannah a lingering, loving glance that didn't quite meet his eyes. Still she felt herself tingle. Her body was reacting to Luca's, or maybe it was her mind reacting to his words. She knew them to be lies but they affected her anyway. It had been a long time since she'd been complimented by a man in any shape or form.

'I can see why,' Andrew said with a charmingly flirtatious smile for her. 'How did he propose, Hannah? If you don't mind me asking?'

Uh-oh. Her mind blanked for one awful second before she thought *screw it* and gave a light, teasing laugh. 'Oh, it was so romantic, wasn't it, Luca?' she practically purred, sliding an arm around her intended's waist. His body tensed under her hand and she enjoyed the feel of bunched muscle and taut abs before she continued with her story. 'He surprised me with a trip to Paris for the weekend—on a private jet.' She slid Luca what she hoped was an adoring look from under her lashes, enjoying the way his wary expression changed to one of cautious interest. He wanted to know where she was going with this. 'And then one magical evening he took me to the top of the Eiffel Tower—he'd rented the whole thing out so it was completely private.'

'I didn't think you could rent the Eiffel Tower,' Andrew said and Hannah continued without missing a beat.

'Oh, you can, if you know the right people.' She dared to wink. 'Isn't that right, Luca?'

He smiled blandly. 'It is.'

'And then what happened?' The woman in green satin had asked. Everyone was listening to her story now, clearly intrigued by the over-the-top romanticism. Hannah knew she shouldn't lay it on too thick; this was Luca Moretti, after all, and his reputation had clearly preceded him. And yet…if Luca was going to do a thing, she knew he'd do it properly, proposing marriage included.

'And then he told me how madly in love he was with me,' she finished blithely, 'and he proposed. Down on one knee.' She ended this utter fabrication with a happy sigh.

Andrew Tyson smiled faintly as he nodded towards her hand. 'But you don't have a ring, my dear.'

'Oh, but I do,' Hannah assured him. 'Luca presented me with the most magnificent ring—a family heirloom, actually, hundreds of years old, although he changed the design for me. Sapphires and diamonds,' she added, remembering what Luca had said earlier. 'Gorgeous.' She paused for a moment, picturing the fictitious ring, while everyone remained silent and spellbound.

'What happened to it, then?' asked the lanky woman rather sulkily.

'Oh, it was too big. Silly Luca.' She patted him playfully on the cheek and ignored the glimmer of warning in his mahogany eyes. 'It's at the jeweller's being resized.' She turned a twinkling smile onto Andrew Tyson. 'But I assure you, the next time I see you, you'll be suitably blinded.' Now *why* had she said that? She didn't want to see Andrew Tyson again. She certainly didn't want to keep up this pretence. She'd just got carried away.

'I'm sure,' Andrew murmured. 'Charmed, my dear, charmed.' He turned to another guest and Hannah only just kept from sagging with relief, now that the adrenaline was leaving her in a cold rush. She could feel the watchful gazes of the other businessmen and their wives, no doubt wondering what a man like Luca Moretti saw in her.

'You're a natural,' Luca murmured in her ear. 'You should be on the stage.'

'Shh,' Hannah chided. They eased away from the group as they both gazed out at the sea, now swathed in darkness. The moon was just rising, sending a sheen of silver over the water. 'Actually, I quite enjoyed myself.'

'I could tell.' He shot her an amused look, although Hannah could still feel how tense he was. 'You almost had me believing I gave you an heirloom ring.'

'Well, that's the point, isn't it?' Hannah replied. Actually, she had enjoyed believing in the fantasy for a few moments. Wearing the dress, drinking the champagne, acting as if a gorgeous, powerful man adored her. It could get addictive, enjoying all this attention and luxury, and she needed to remember none of this was real.

'If I'd known how much you'd get into the spirit of the thing,' Luca remarked, 'I would have let you in on the secret earlier.'

'I think it's more of a case of needs must,' Hannah returned. She glanced back at the assembled group. 'We should mingle, I suppose.'

'I suppose.'

'Tyson's wife isn't here? Or his children?'

The traces of amusement on Luca's face disappeared. 'They're joining him tomorrow. Tomorrow's dinner will be the big black-tie event.'

'When will he announce who has won the bid?'

Luca shrugged. 'Who knows? I think he's toying with all of us.'

Hannah glanced at Andrew, who was working his way through the crowd, talking to everyone individually. 'He seems a nice man.'

'Appearances can be deceiving.'

She turned back to Luca, surprised by the hardness in his voice. 'You don't like him.'

'I don't know the man,' Luca answered as he tossed back the rest of his drink. 'But I don't like being forced into play-acting. His demands are unreasonable and irrelevant.'

'And yet you still chose to go after his resorts.'

'I told you twice now, the land is valuable. Now let's go.' He took her arm and moved back to the crowd, and Hannah had no choice but to follow his lead. The Luca Moretti she knew wouldn't kowtow to anyone's demands, especially if he thought they were unreasonable. So why was he in this case?

She had no time to ponder the question as they were plunged back into the complicated social dynamics of three men who clearly respected if not liked each other, and were all bidding for the same job, while Andrew Tyson presided over them all.

At dinner Hannah sat next to Daniela, the sulky, beautiful woman who was partner to James, the CEO of a slick development company in the City. 'So how long have you been working for Luca?' she asked Hannah as the first course was served.

Luca, was it? Hannah covertly studied Daniela's tall,

lithe build, the long blond hair she kept tossing over her shoulder in an artful, deliberate way. 'Three years.'

'And you have been engaged for how long?'

A couple of hours. 'A few weeks.' Hannah took a sip of the cold cucumber soup to keep from having to say anything else.

'I never thought a man like Luca would marry,' Daniela said with a burning stare for the man in question, who was chatting with Simon, the third developer, across the table. 'He always seemed like the type to love and leave.'

'Until he found someone he wanted to stay with,' Hannah returned.

Daniela arched an eyebrow, the scepticism evident on her face. 'You're quite different from the women Luca is usually seen with. Not quite as...polished.'

Stung by this unsubtle put-down, Hannah lifted her chin. 'I didn't realise you knew him.'

'Oh, I know him,' Daniela said darkly and Hannah inwardly seethed. Luca could have warned her that a former paramour would be here, unsheathing her claws and trying to draw blood. And what if she gave something away to this elegant harpy? Daniela might know more about Luca than she did. Judging by her smouldering looks, it seemed almost a certainty. The idea made her feel unsettled in a way she didn't like. She wasn't *jealous*, just annoyed and angry all over again at Luca putting her in this position.

By the time the dessert plates had been cleared and coffee served, Hannah was having trouble keeping up her sparkly pretence. The excitement of pretending to be someone she wasn't had worn thin, and she longed only to return to their room and go to sleep. Actually, what she really wanted to do was go back to London and snuggle with her son. When she'd been in the bathroom changing she'd managed to speak to Jamie on the phone for a few minutes, listening to him chatter about his day, but it wasn't enough. It was never enough.

Luca must have seen the slump of her shoulders or the fatigue on her face for in one graceful movement he rose from the table. 'It's been a lovely evening, but I fear I've tired my fiancée out. Do you mind if we excuse ourselves?'

'Not at all, not at all,' Andrew replied as he also rose. 'We'll see you both in the morning.'

Luca and Hannah made their farewells to the rest of the group and then they walked in silence to their bedroom; with each step Hannah was remembering that big bed and how small it now actually seemed. They surely wouldn't share it. Luca would be a gentleman and make up a bed on the divan. Or so she hoped.

And yet even the thought of sharing the same room with Luca made her head go light and her palms turn damp. He was so *male*, so potently virile and sexual. She'd been immune—mostly—in their usual office environment, but she felt it keenly here, when they were sharing a bedroom and the moonlight and the gentle whooshing of the sea conspired to make everything seem romantic.

Luca opened the door to their bedroom, stepping aside so Hannah could go in first. He shrugged off his jacket while Hannah kicked off her heels with a groan. 'Wretched things.'

'You're not a fan of high heels?'

'I like taking them off.' The room was bathed in moonlight, the windows open to the sea breeze, the light from the lamps on the bedside tables giving out a cosy glow. Hannah glanced at the bed, which had been turned down, the cream duvet folded back to reveal the silky sheet beneath. A heart-shaped chocolate in gold foil nestled on each pillow. 'How is that going to work?' she asked, deciding to tackle the problem head-on.

Luca barely glanced at the bed. 'How is what going

to work?' His fingers had already gone to the buttons of his shirt, and, heaven help her, he was going to take it off again. And this time she might let herself watch.

'Sleeping arrangements,' Hannah said, dragging her gaze away from the tantalising glimpse of Luca's chest. 'We can't both sleep in the bed.'

'Oh?' He sounded amused. 'Why can't we?'

'Because!' Startled, she turned back to him and watched as he shrugged out of his shirt and then went for his belt buckle. '*Luca.* Can't you change in the bathroom?'

'What are you, a nun? If it makes you feel better, I won't sleep in the nude as I usually do.'

'What a prince,' Hannah gritted through her teeth. 'Seriously, Luca—'

'Seriously,' he said as he reached for a pair of drawstring pyjama pants that were going to leave very little to the imagination. 'It's a bed. It's huge. We can both sleep in it. I need my sleep, and I don't want anyone suspecting that we're not sleeping together. And, in case you're worried, I'm perfectly capable of sharing a bed without ravishing the other occupant.'

Hannah swung away as Luca dropped his trousers to change into his pyjamas. 'I'm not afraid of that,' she said, staring hard at the curtains drawn against the French windows. She could hear the whisper of fabric over Luca's legs, imagined his powerful thighs, muscles flexing…

Stop. Hannah pressed one hand to her flaming cheek. She really had to get a grip on her imagination. *And* her hormones.

'I'm dressed,' he said mildly. 'You can turn around.'

Taking a deep breath, Hannah did so. And dropped her gaze to his bare chest, his perfectly sculpted pectoral muscles lightly dusted with dark hair. The pyjama bottoms were slung low on his hips, so she could see the taut muscles of his abdomen, tapering down to... Quickly she jerked her gaze back up.

'If you're not worried that I'm going to ravish you, what are you afraid of?' Luca asked.

Why did he have to sound so reasonable? And make her feel so ridiculous? 'It just doesn't seem appropriate,' Hannah muttered.

'Hannah, we passed "appropriate" a while ago.' He took a step towards her, his hands outstretched. 'Look, you were magnificent back there. The whole thing about the Eiffel tower and the ring? I was practically believing it myself. And you seemed like you were having fun.' Hannah looked away, biting her lip. 'Well?' Luca pressed. 'Were you?'

'Sort of,' she admitted. What woman wouldn't like to step into a fairy tale for an evening, even if it was fake?

'So maybe you should let go of what's appropriate in this situation,' Luca suggested, his voice dropping to a beguiling murmur, standing only a step away from her.

She had the insane urge to reach out and *stroke* his chest.

'Let yourself enter into the spirit of the thing,' Luca continued, his voice all honeyed persuasion. 'Like you did tonight.'

'And share your bed.'

'In the literal sense only.'

'Oh, you know I didn't mean *that*,' Hannah protested, her face flaming once more. She shook her head. 'Honestly, you're incorrigible.'

'You've only just realised that?' He turned to the huge bed and plucked the chocolate from the pillow. 'So what are you waiting for?' he asked as he unwrapped the chocolate and popped it into his mouth. 'Come to bed.'

CHAPTER SIX

LUCA LAY IN BED, his arms braced behind his head, as he waited for Hannah to emerge from the bathroom. She'd been in there for quite a while, no doubt summoning her nerve to come out.

He didn't feel bad about sharing the bed with her. He'd even suggested, before she'd huffed into the bathroom clutching her pyjamas, that she was free to construct a barrier of pillows between them if she really did fear for her virtue.

She'd rolled her eyes. 'I can handle it,' she'd retorted, which amused him because she'd been the one to get all worked up about the issue in the first place.

She'd been incredible tonight, though. Sparkling and funny and charming, and he'd seen how Andrew Tyson had come under her spell. *He* almost had. Luca had found his gaze continually moving towards her, ensnared by her tinkling laugh, her teasing smile, the way the light caught the honeyed highlights in her hair.

Several times he'd leaned forward to try to catch what she was saying, needing to know and not because of the pretence. Because he really wanted to hear.

Then he'd reminded himself that she was playing a part and so was he, and Andrew Tyson was falling for it. That was all that mattered. He had no sympathy for the man, no pity whatsoever. Watching Tyson, Luca had barely been able to sit across from him and keep a smile on his face. Hannah had at least provided a distraction from the rage that simmered beneath the surface, threatening to bubble over.

The door to the bathroom opened and Hannah stepped out. Her hair was loose about her face and she wore…

'What the hell is that?'

Hannah glanced down at her roomy, faded T-shirt and shapeless boxer shorts. 'My pyjamas.'

'Didn't you get pyjamas at the boutique?'

'If you mean the scrap of lace that barely passes for a negligee, then yes. But I am not wearing that.' She glowered at him, a flush firing her face. 'There are limits, Luca.'

'You can't wear those. The staff come in to serve us breakfast in bed in the morning.'

Hannah didn't look at him as she crossed the room and climbed into bed, dragging the duvet up to her chin. 'So?'

'So,' Luca answered, 'I want them thinking that we spent the night ravishing each other as any newly engaged couple on holiday would.'

The minute he said the words images emblazoned themselves on his brain. Heat flared inside him. And he felt Hannah stiffen next to him.

'And they won't think of that if I'm dressed like this?' Hannah said after a moment. Her voice sounded suffocated. 'Too bad.'

She turned away from him, her body radiating tension. Luca sighed and snapped off the lights. He'd pushed it far enough, he supposed, although in truth he wanted to see Hannah in a sexy nightgown for his own sake, never mind the staff who would come in the next morning.

'You could have warned me about your friend,' Hannah said after a tense silence when Luca had been willing the desire coursing through his body to fade.

'My friend?' he asked, nonplussed.

'Daniela. She obviously knows you.'

'We've met.'

'You mean you've slept with her.'

Luca was silent, considering the assumption. He hadn't slept with Daniela, although the Russian model had made it clear she'd wanted to. And considering what he was asking Hannah to do, he supposed she deserved to know the truth. 'We went on a date,' he said. 'About a year ago. But nothing happened.'

'I suppose she wished something did.' Her voice was slightly muffled.

'Maybe,' Luca allowed.

'Judging by the burning looks she was giving you over dinner, I'd say definitely. And she wasn't impressed with me either. Not like that's too surprising, though.'

Hannah's words ended on a sigh and surprise flickered through him. 'Why do you say that?' he asked quietly.

Hannah didn't answer for a moment. In the darkness he couldn't see her features, only the taut shape of her body under the duvet. He heard the soft draw of her breath and it felt weirdly intimate. He realised he'd never actually slept in the same bed with a woman before. His assignations—he couldn't even call them relationships—had always ended with a definitive post-coital farewell.

'Well,' Hannah said at last, 'it's obvious, isn't it? A Plain Jane PA is hardly your type.'

'You're not a Plain Jane, Hannah.'

She laughed, a snort of genuine amusement that made him smile. 'Come on, Luca. Your normal type is supermodels and socialites, right? I'm neither.'

'That doesn't mean you're plain.'

'I'm not glamorous or gorgeous,' she returned. 'I don't

mind.' She shifted where she lay, so he felt the mattress dip beneath them. 'Why do you date socialites and supermodels? I mean, why not a normal woman?'

'Well.' Luca cleared his throat, caught between amusement and a surprising embarrassment. 'I'm not really interested in their personalities.'

Hannah was silent for a moment. 'Well, that's blunt,' she said at last.

'I try to be honest.'

'Except when you're duping a houseful of people into believing you're about to be married.' She rolled over so she was turned towards him, although Luca couldn't actually see her face in the darkness. He had the alarming impulse to reach out to her, curve a hand around her neck and draw her closer. Kiss those lush lips he'd found himself sneaking looks at all evening. 'Why do you go for shallow?' she asked. 'Why is it just sex for you? Because that's what you're saying, isn't it?'

Luca was silent for a long moment, struggling to form an answer that was honest without being too revealing. 'Because it isn't worth it,' he finally said. 'To have more.'

He waited for Hannah's response, his body tensing against the possible onslaught of questions. Her voice came out in a soft, sorrowful sigh.

'Maybe it isn't,' she agreed quietly.

Luca waited for her to say more but she didn't. He closed his eyes, telling himself it was better that way, because he didn't want to explain his answer even if part of him wanted to know why Hannah agreed with him.

With his eyes closed, his other senses were heightened, so he could breathe in her light floral scent, feel the warmth of her body so close to his, hear the gentle draw and sigh of her breathing.

Desire flared through him again and more intensely this time, and ruefully Luca acknowledged that he might be the one in need of a pillow barrier. He rolled onto his other side, away from Hannah, and tried to will himself to sleep.

If this were a romcom, Hannah thought wryly, she and Luca would fall asleep and then somehow, in the night, they would wake tangled up in each other's arms. They'd gaze into each other's eyes, still caught in the throes of sleep, and then Luca would brush a kiss across her lips, slide his hand down her body, everything fogged with sleep...

Hannah realised her rueful imagination was fast turning into fantasy, and heat flooded her belly at just the thought of Luca looking at her that way. Touching her that way.

She squeezed her eyes shut, trying to banish the images. Maybe her mother was right, and she needed to start dating again. Diane was always worried that Hannah worked too much, that she didn't have a social life of her own. Hannah replied that she didn't have the time for a social life, but the truth was relationships were too much risk. Maybe that was something she and Luca had in common.

She sighed, the sound loud in the stillness of the room.

'Problem?' Luca asked, his voice sounding strained.

'This is a bit awkward,' Hannah said into the darkness.

'Just go to sleep, Hannah.' Luca sounded annoyed now, and, chastised, Hannah rolled away from him. She could do this. She was exhausted, for heaven's sake. She needed her sleep. Yet all she could think about, all she could focus on, was Luca's body a few feet from hers. Maybe only a foot. And his chest was bare. She imagined resting her cheek against it, her arms around his waist, their legs tangled together.

She stifled a groan. It was going to be a very long night.

Hannah woke to a light knock on the door and she blinked blearily as she raised her head from the pillow.

'Just a moment,' Luca called, and then his arm snaked out, hooking around her waist, and drawing her towards the hard wall of the chest. The feel of his body coming into full, intimate contact with hers stole the breath from her lungs and she froze in shock. Then she felt his obvious arousal nudging her thighs and she gasped aloud.

'It's morning,' Luca muttered. 'That's all it is.'

All right, fine. She was a grown-up; she understood basic biological functions. But *honestly*. This was way, way past the call of duty. And yet it felt so very nice.

As the door opened, Hannah adjusted to the feel of Luca's body against her own. This was what she had fantasised about last night, and the reality felt even better than she had imagined. His chest was warm and solid and the smell of him was intoxicating, overwhelming. The press of his hand on her lower back made her rock helplessly into his hips, his erection settling between her thighs, making heat flare sharply inside her. Luca's breath hissed between his teeth as his body instinctively pushed back before he stilled.

'Hannah.'

Mortified, she tried to move away, but Luca's arms were like steel bands around her. 'Stay still,' he commanded in a low voice that was as hard as iron.

Two staff members wheeled in a cart laden with two breakfast trays, and Luca eased up in bed, taking Hannah with him so they were both reclining against the pillows, the duvet pulled demurely across their laps. Hannah wished, bizarrely perhaps, that she were wearing the gorgeous lace negligee, revealing as it was. She felt ridiculous in her oversized T-shirt that had faded to an unappealing grey colour from too many washes. And her hair... She lifted her hands to the tangle around her face and Luca smiled at her, tucking a stray strand behind her ear.

'Nothing like a little bedhead in the morning,' he said

with a teasing smile, and Hannah blinked, discomfited, until she realised he was putting on a show for the staff.

'I'm glad you love me no matter what I look like,' she replied sweetly. 'Or what I wear.'

The staff handed them their trays and with murmured thanks Hannah sat up straighter, taking in the freshly squeezed orange juice, the carafe of coffee, toast and fresh fruit and the most delicious-looking omelette. She could definitely get used to this.

The members of staff left quietly and Hannah reached for a piece of toast. She was not going to look at Luca, and remember how it had felt to have his arms around her, to arch into him… *What* had possessed her to do that?

'So what's the plan for today?' she asked, deciding that ignoring that whole brief interlude was the best way to go. Luca, it seemed, did not agree.

'Just to be clear,' he said flatly, 'we're going to keep this as play-acting, and nothing more.'

Hannah eyed him resentfully, trying to keep the hot tide of embarrassment at bay. 'You're the one who insisted we share a bed.'

'You're the one who rocked against me like a wanton,' Luca snapped.

'A wanton?' Hannah pushed aside the breakfast tray, her appetite having vanished, and scrambled out of the bed. 'What century do you live in?'

'I mean it, Hannah—'

'Trust me, I take the warning. And just like you, Luca Moretti, I am perfectly able to sleep in the same bed as someone without ravishing them!' Caught between fury, mortification, and tears, she grabbed her clothes and slammed into the bathroom.

Luca sighed and closed his eyes as the slam of the bathroom door echoed through the room. He'd handled that about as badly as possible. Calling Hannah Stewart a wanton was like calling Andrew Tyson a saint. Absurd. Laughable, except there was nothing remotely funny about either situation.

He opened his eyes and raked a hand through his hair, wondering how best to do damage control. Honesty? The truth was, he'd been far more aroused and tempted by Hannah's slender body than he'd any right to be. When she'd rocked into him he'd felt his precious control starting to disintegrate, and it had taken its last shreds to keep from shouting at the staff to leave them alone so he could bury himself deep in her willing body. *He* was the wanton, not Hannah.

He had no idea why his pretty enough PA affected him this way; perhaps it was simply the strangeness of the situation, or that his senses and emotions felt raw from facing Tyson again after so many years. He couldn't deny it, though; he'd been fighting an unreasonable and most inconvenient attraction to her since this whole charade had begun.

He drank his coffee, musing on the unwelcome distraction of his surprisingly delectable PA. He needed to focus on the real reason he'd come to Santa Nicola. He couldn't let anything distract him from his purpose. Having Hannah upset or embarrassed was just as difficult and distracting as having them both fighting—and flirting with—a sexual attraction he didn't think either of them had expected. It was time to nip this in the bud.

Fifteen minutes later Hannah emerged from the bathroom, her hair damp, her face composed. She wore a pretty pink linen sundress that skimmed her breasts and hugged her slim waist. She didn't so much as look at Luca.

'I'm sorry,' Luca said as he pushed his breakfast tray away. 'I shouldn't have said that.'

'You do have a tendency towards bluntness,' Hannah

replied as she struggled to put on her pearl necklace. This time Luca didn't offer to help.

'I wasn't being blunt,' he said. 'I was dissembling.'

She glanced at him and then quickly away again. 'How so?'

'I'm attracted to you,' he stated flatly. 'To my own surprise.'

'I thought it was just the morning,' she returned tartly, but he could see her cheeks pinken.

'It was more than the morning,' Luca admitted gruffly. 'I was angry at myself, and my body's reaction, rather than at you.'

'It must be terribly irritating to be attracted to someone like me,' Hannah agreed. Luca realised that underneath her embarrassment, she was blisteringly angry. 'Someone with feelings and a normal bra size.'

'Hannah,' he warned through gritted teeth. The last thing he needed this morning was a big, messy row with the woman who was supposed to be his compliant, biddable faux fiancée.

'Luca,' Hannah returned mockingly. She whirled around, her colour high, her golden-brown eyes blazing. 'How about you listen to me for a change? I didn't ask to come to this island. I didn't ask to pretend to be your fiancée. I didn't ask to share your bed! In fact, at every step, I've asked for the opposite. I've wanted more space, not less. And then you have the audacity, the wretched nerve, to call me a wanton!'

'I told you why—'

'And you think that makes it better? You said it like you couldn't even understand why you were attracted to someone like me. *To my surprise.* Well, thanks for that, Luca. Thanks very much.' She turned away again, her hands shaking as she reached for her pearl earrings.

All right, he could see how what he'd said might have sounded insulting, but… 'I didn't mean it that way.'

'Actually, I think you did. But never mind. I don't really care.' She put her earrings in, shaking her hair over her shoulders. 'Let's just get this day over with, shall we?'

Luca hesitated, wanting to defuse her anger, but sensing that she wasn't in the mood to be placated. Wordlessly he headed into the bathroom to shower.

As soon as the door closed Hannah released a shaky breath and slumped onto the divan. She couldn't take much more of this ping-ponging from one emotion to the next, from overwhelming desire to incredible rage. *What was happening to her?*

She knew the answer to that one. Luca Moretti was. She took a steadying breath, and then, taking advantage of Luca being in the shower, reached for her phone.

Diane answered on the first ring. 'Hey, Mum,' Hannah said, her voice sounding weary and just a little bit wobbly. 'It's me.'

'Hannah. Are you all right?'

'Why— Do I sound that bad?' She tried for a laugh, pressing a hand to her forehead. It didn't help her seesawing emotions that she'd got very little sleep last night.

'You sound tired,' Diane admitted cautiously. 'Is everything okay?'

'Fine. Just an intense work weekend.' Work being the word she could drop from that sentence. 'Is Jamie awake yet?'

'Yes, he's just having his breakfast. I'll put him on for you.'

Hannah closed her eyes, listening to the familiar sound of her mother's murmur, her son's excited answer. The squeak of a chair, and then the sound of him scrabbling for the phone.

'Mummy?'

A tidal wave of homesickness crashed over her, threatening to pull her under. 'Hello, sweetheart. I miss you.'

'I miss you, too. Nana says you're on an island.'

'Yes, it's very pretty. I'll try to bring you back a present. Maybe some shells or rocks for your collection?'

'Ooh, yes,' Jamie crowed. 'Can you bring back a big one? A conch?'

'I don't know about that,' Hannah said with a little laugh. 'I think they might be protected. But I'll bring you back something, Jamie, I promise. Be good for Nana now.'

'I will.'

'He always is,' Diane assured her when Hannah had said goodbye to her son. 'Don't work too hard.'

'I always work hard,' Hannah answered, and heard how grim she sounded. Maybe she did work too hard. Maybe the sacrifices weren't worth it, no matter what she believed about being financially independent and free. 'I love you, Mum,' she said.

'Hannah, are you sure you're all right…?'

'I'm fine,' Hannah said, and then, hearing the bathroom door open, she quickly said goodbye and disconnected the call.

She was just putting the phone away when Luca emerged from the bathroom, freshly shaven, his hair damp, a towel slung low on his hips. 'Were you on the phone?'

Hannah turned away from the alluring sight of his nearly naked body. 'Is that a crime?'

Luca sighed. 'No, of course not. I just wondered.'

'Then the answer is yes, I was.'

'Hannah, look, I said I was sorry.'

'In about the worst way possible.'

'Can we please call a truce?'

Hannah took a deep breath, knowing she was being childish and emotional. She was a professional, for heaven's sake, and Luca was her boss. She could handle this. 'I'm sorry,' she said evenly. 'Let's forget it. Clean slate today, all right?' She turned to him with a bright, determined smile just as Luca dropped his towel.

CHAPTER SEVEN

HANNAH WHIRLED AWAY from the sight of Luca's naked body, one hand clapped to her eyes.

She let out a trembling laugh. 'You are so not making this easier.'

'I'm sorry. I don't like dressing in the bathroom.'

'That message has been received, trust me.'

'I'm dressed now,' Luca told her dryly, and Hannah lowered her hand.

'Wearing a pair of boxer briefs does not, in my opinion, constitute dressed.'

'The important bits are covered,' he answered and reached for a shirt.

'I don't understand you,' Hannah said slowly. 'You flirt and drop your clothes and act like it's ridiculous for me to be outraged, and then you get angry with me and basically accuse me of being a slut for responding when you're practically naked next to me.' She tried for a wry smile but felt too confused and weary to manage it. 'I thought it was women who usually sent mixed messages.'

Luca stilled, his hands on the buttons of his shirt, his gaze lowered. 'This is a new situation for me,' he admitted gruffly. 'And a tense one. I know I'm acting out of character.'

'Considering you're acting as my fiancé, you certainly

are.' She sighed and reached for the strappy sandals that went with her sundress. 'So what is the schedule for today, anyway?'

'You spend the day with the other wives, touring the island, and I give my presentation.'

'Wow, that's not sexist or anything.'

Luca arched an eyebrow and resumed buttoning his shirt. 'You're not here as my PA.'

'Well I know. So you spend your day in the boardroom while I fend off Daniela's digs?'

'She's harmless. I barely know her.'

'She might disagree.' Hannah hesitated, noticing the lines of strain from Luca's nose to mouth, the fatigue she could see in his eyes and the weary set of his shoulders. She felt a surprising dart of sympathy and even compassion for him. For whatever reason, this weekend was difficult for him. 'So what is your presentation about?'

He stilled for a second and then reached for a pair of charcoal-grey trousers. 'How I'm going to rehabilitate the Tyson brand.'

'The resorts did look a bit shabby on the website.'

'They're tired,' Luca affirmed with a terse nod. 'They haven't been updated in over twenty years.'

'Why is Tyson selling them, anyway? Don't his children want to take over his business?'

A grim smile curved Luca's mouth. 'No, they're not interested.'

'That's sad, considering what a family man he is.'

'Heartbreaking,' Luca agreed dryly. He selected a cobalt-blue tie and began to knot it. There was, Hannah reflected, something quite sexy about a man putting on a tie, long, lean fingers manipulating the bright silk. Especially a man who looked like Luca.

'So what are your plans for the resorts?' she asked as she forced her gaze away from the mesmerising sight of

Luca getting dressed. 'How are you going to rehabilitate them? I never printed any documents out about it.'

'No, I did it myself.' He slid her a quick smile. 'I am capable of working a printer, despite how often I ask you to do it.'

'May I see them?' Hannah asked, and surprise flashed across Luca's face. 'I'm curious.'

His fingers slowed as he finished knotting his tie, his forehead furrowed. 'All right,' he said at last, and he went to his briefcase and took out a manila folder of documents.

Hannah joined him on the divan, their thighs nudging, while Luca opened the folder and took out the presentation he'd put together. The colourful image on the front page was an architect's visualisation of what the resort could look like, with villas in different pastel colours, cascading pools with water slides and whirlpools, and lots of colourful flowers and shrubbery. It looked inviting and fresh and friendly.

Hannah reached over to turn a page, scanning the paragraphs that described Luca's plans in detail. She knew Luca's real-estate projects always focused on sustainable energy and recyclable materials, and this was no different. But this proposal went a step further, and sought to incorporate the local culture and economy of each of the islands where there was a Tyson resort, instead of making it an exclusive enclave behind high stone walls, separate from the local residents.

She saw how family-friendly it was too, with hotel rooms and changing areas to accommodate both children and adults. Jamie would love the cascading pools and water slides outlined in one of the resorts' plans. She glanced up at Luca, who was frowning down at the images.

'For someone who doesn't have children, this is very astute.'

He shrugged one powerful shoulder. 'I did the research.'

'I like it,' she said and handed the folder back to him. 'I really like it.' Luca might have done the research, but there had been a passion and commitment to his ideas that spoke of more than just having a finger on the marketing pulse. It surprised and touched her, and it felt as if his plans for the resort had revealed something about him, something he didn't even seem to realise. He *cared*.

The last of her reservation about performing in this fake engagement fell away. She was here, and she'd agreed to help Luca. She was going to do the job properly, and maybe she'd even have fun while she was at it.

'Okay,' she said as she stood up with a bright smile. 'It's time to face the fearsome Daniela.'

A smile tugged at Luca's mouth. 'She's not that bad.'

'Why didn't it work out between you two, anyway?' Hannah asked lightly, ignoring the sting of jealousy her question caused.

'She was too clingy.'

'What, she wanted to stay the night?' Hannah quipped.

'I told you. It never got that far. Anyway, last night you agreed with me that relationships weren't worth it,' Luca reminded her.

Hannah stilled. How had they got onto this? 'I said "maybe",' she corrected him. 'The verdict is still out.'

'But you're not in a relationship?' Luca pressed, his gaze narrowed.

Hannah cocked her head. 'Is that really any of your business?'

Luca's gaze flicked to the bed, reminding him all too well of what had just happened there. 'Considering the nature of this weekend,' he answered, 'yes.'

'Fine. No, I'm not.' And hadn't been in anything close to one for over five years. 'Work keeps me busy,' she added before turning away.

They left the bedroom to join the other guests for coffee and pastries in the spacious front hall. A marble table held a huge centrepiece of lilies, and Hannah saw Luca's mouth compress as he turned away from the ostentatious display. She knew he disliked lilies, but now she wondered at the nature of that particular quirk. She was curious about Luca in a lot of new and unsettling ways, thanks to the nature of this weekend.

After about half an hour of chit-chat, Andrew Tyson called the men away to his private office for a day of presentations. Meanwhile one of his staff ushered the three women towards a waiting car, where they would be given a tour of Santa Nicola.

Hannah was looking forward to seeing some of the island, but she didn't relish Daniela's hostile company. Fortunately the third woman of their trio, Rose, plopped herself next to Hannah and chatted to her about her three young children for the drive into the island's one town, Petra. Daniela sat in the back, sulking and staring out of the window.

Hannah spent a surprisingly enjoyable morning, strolling through Petra's cobbled streets, admiring the whitewashed buildings with their colourfully painted shutters and terracotta roof tiles.

At an open-air market she bought a wooden toy boat with a sail made of shells for Jamie, smiling to think of him receiving the present. It was even better than a conch shell.

'And who is that for?' Daniela asked, coming up next to her at the stall of toys in the market square. Hannah accepted the paper-wrapped boat from the vendor with a smile of thanks. She'd managed to avoid Daniela for most of the day, but she supposed a confrontation was inevitable. Daniela dripped with the venom of a woman scorned.

'It's a boat,' she said pleasantly. 'For my nephew.' She didn't like lying about her son, but Daniela was the last person she'd trust with any confidence, and her having a child Luca didn't know about would shatter any illusions that their engagement was real.

Daniela raised perfectly plucked eyebrows. 'Have you met Luca's parents yet?' she asked, and Hannah tensed.

The question might seem innocent enough, but she knew Daniela well enough to know it was loaded. She tucked the present for Jamie in the straw bag she'd brought, stalling for time. Luca had told her to stick as close to the truth as she could, so she supposed that was what she'd have to do.

'No, I haven't,' she said as she looked into Daniela's pinched face, trying for a pleasant tone and smile. 'Not yet.'

'Not yet?' Daniela repeated, a sneer entering her voice and twisting her pretty features. 'Then you don't know he's an orphan? His parents died when he was young.' She smirked in triumph and Hannah tried to school her features into an acceptably bland expression although inwardly she cursed herself. She knew Daniela had been setting her up somehow. She'd seemed to suspect her from the start. *Because you're not the kind of woman Luca Moretti is normally seen with. Certainly not the kind of woman he'd fall in love with.*

'We had a whirlwind courtship,' she dismissed as best she could. 'We're still learning all sorts of things about each other.'

'We went on one date and he told me,' Daniela returned.

'One date?' Hannah couldn't keep from matching the woman's cattiness. 'Then perhaps it's time you got over him.'

The conversation dogged her for the rest of the day, and she breathed a sigh of relief when they headed back to the resort. Luca wasn't in the bedroom when she arrived, and she put her purchases away before running a deep bubble bath. Before dropping them off, the member of staff had informed the three women of the evening's itinerary: cocktails on the terrace with Tyson and his family, followed by a formal dinner and dancing.

Hours and hours of pretending, a prospect that made Hannah feel both tense and exhausted, even as she tingled with anticipation at spending an evening with Luca. Would he dance with her? The thought of swaying silently with him, breathing in his heat and scent, his arms strong about her, was enough to make her stomach flip-flop.

Which was *fine*, Hannah assured herself. So she was attracted to Luca. What woman wouldn't be? Why shouldn't she enjoy dancing with him? It wasn't as if it were going anywhere. She wasn't looking for a relationship or even a one-night stand. Both were too risky. All she wanted was a few moments of enjoyment and pleasure.

Except Luca had admitted he was attracted to her. Reluctantly, yes, and to his surprise, but *still*. Over the course of the day she'd got over the sting of his obvious bemusement at being attracted to her, and accepted the compliment that it was.

The door to the bedroom opened just as Hannah was stepping out of the bathroom, swathed in an enormous terrycloth bathrobe.

'How did it go?' she asked and then watched in dismay as Luca jerked his tie from his collar and strode over to the minibar, pouring himself two fingers' worth of whisky and downing it in one hard gulp.

'Fine.'

Hannah knotted the sash on her robe and pulled her damp hair out from under its thick collar. 'You're not acting like it's fine,' she observed cautiously.

'I said it was fine, it's fine,' Luca snapped, and poured another drink.

Hannah watched him, wondering what demon was riding his back. Because that was what Luca looked like: a man who was haunted. Tormented. And she didn't understand why.

'Daniela asked me about your parents,' she said, knowing she needed to tell him what had happened that afternoon. Luca stiffened, his glass halfway raised to his lips.

'Why would she do that?'

'Because she was trying to trip me up. I think she suspects something.'

'Daniela?' He shook his head, the movement curtly dismissive. 'I barely know the woman. I haven't seen her in over a year. She's been married to James Garrison for nearly six months.'

'Well, I think she still holds a candle for you. And she asked me about your parents and I told her I hadn't met them. Yet.' She waited, but Luca's face was blank.

'And?' he said after a pause.

'And she informed you were an orphan. I didn't know that, Luca, and clearly I should have. *She* knew it.'

Hannah couldn't tell anything from his expression; his eyes looked pitilessly blank. 'I'm sorry,' she said inadequately. 'For your loss.'

'It was a long time ago.'

'Still, it's a big thing.' She knew that all too well. 'And now Daniela knows I didn't know it.'

Luca pressed his lips together and tossed his empty glass on top of the bar, where it clattered and then rolled onto its side. 'There's nothing we can do about it now.'

'All right.' Hannah didn't know how to handle him in this mood; his usual energy had been transformed into a disturbing restlessness, a latent anger. 'I just thought you should know.'

'Fine. I know.'

Stung, Hannah did not reply. The tentative enjoyment she'd been nurturing for this evening was draining away like her cold bathwater. If Luca stayed in this foul mood, the night was going to be interminable.

'I'll go get ready," she said stiffly, and went to gather her clothes. She was definitely changing in the bathroom.

Luca stared at the closed bathroom door and swore under his breath. The afternoon with Tyson had been nearly unbearable, the latent fury he'd felt for so long bubbling far too close to the surface, threatening to spill over. Maintaining a professional manner had been the acting job of the century; all he'd wanted to do was haul Tyson out of his chair by his lapels and slap the smug smile off his face.

He hadn't expected to be this angry, this raw. He'd thought he'd mastered his emotions far better than that, and it only exacerbated his fury to know that he hadn't. But he shouldn't have taken it out on Hannah.

As for Daniela's suspicions… Raking a hand through his hair, Luca swore again. If his fake engagement was exposed, the humiliation he'd face in front of the man who had flayed him once already would be unendurable. He could not even contemplate it.

Luca's mouth twisted grimly as he considered the options. If Daniela or anyone suspected something, then he and Hannah would have to make doubly sure that they were convincing. Striding towards the wardrobe, he reached for his tux.

He was just straightening his bow tie when Hannah emerged from the bathroom, her chin held high, her eyes veiled. Luca's gaze dropped to her dress and his throat went dry. It was the one she'd modelled at the boutique, ice-blue with a plunging neckline only partially obscured by the gauzy overlay. She'd styled her hair in an elegant chignon, exposing the delicate, swanlike curve of her neck.

'It's all right, isn't it?' Hannah asked, nervousness making her voice wobble a bit.

'Yes…' Luca's voice came out gruff and hoarse.

Hannah tugged at the material self-consciously. 'It's just you're looking at me strangely.'

'It's only…' He cleared his throat. 'You look beautiful, Hannah.'

Colour flared in her face. 'So why are you glaring, then?' She turned away, fidgeting with her earrings, her necklace, clearly uncomfortable in the sexy, diaphanous gown.

'Hannah.' Luca crossed the room to put a hand on her shoulder, her skin cool and soft beneath his palm. 'I'm sorry I've been in such a foul mood. It's not fair to you.' He paused and then admitted with more honesty than he'd been planning to give, 'Nothing about this weekend has been fair to you.'

Hannah bowed her head, a tendril of soft brown hair falling against her cheek, making Luca want to tuck it behind her ear, trail his fingers along her skin. 'I was actually looking forward to this evening, you know,' she admitted. 'Until…'

'Until I returned to our room?' Luca finished with a wry wince, and then sighed. 'I am sorry. You don't deserve to bear the brunt of my bad mood.'

'So many apologies.' She turned around, a teasing smile curving her lips. 'I should record this conversation, otherwise I might never believe it actually happened.'

'I'll deny it, of course,' he teased back. He'd dropped his hand from her shoulder when she'd turned around but he itched to touch her again. Her waist looked so tiny he thought he could span it with his hands. The gauzy overlay of the dress made him want to peel it away and touch the pale, creamy flesh beneath. He remembered untying the halter top of the dress back when she'd first tried it on and he wanted to do it again. He wanted her…and he could tell she wanted him.

He saw it in the way she swallowed convulsively, her eyes huge and dark in her pale face. She bit her lip and Luca nearly groaned aloud. The attraction he felt for his PA was both overwhelming and inconvenient, but in that moment he couldn't even think about the consequences, the difficulties, the dangers. He just wanted to touch her.

And so he did.

He reached out with one finger and stroked her cheek; her skin was just as soft as he'd imagined, silky and cool. She shuddered under his touch, her whole body quivering in response, and that made Luca ache all the more.

'Hannah…' he began, although he didn't even know what he would say. How much he would admit.

Hannah didn't let him finish. She took a halting step away, nearly tripping on the trailing hem of her gown. 'It's—it's getting late,' she stammered. 'We should go.'

And Luca told himself he felt relieved and not crushingly disappointed that he'd had such a narrow escape.

CHAPTER EIGHT

HANNAH SIPPED THE frothy cocktail Andrew Tyson had insisted she try, an island speciality involving fruit and strong liquor, and tried to soothe the ferment inside her. Now more than ever she felt confused and disturbed, and, more alarmingly, *tempted* by Luca Moretti.

She couldn't understand how one moment he could be so aggravating and arrogant and the next so sweet and sincere. She'd gone from wanting to slug him to wanting to purr under that single, seductive stroke of his finger. The tiniest touch had created a blaze of want inside her that was still making her hot and bothered. She imagined what he could do with his whole hand, his whole body, and felt another sizzling dart of heat arrow through her.

She could not start thinking about Luca Moretti that way. All right, yes, his sex appeal had started affecting her ever since they'd left their normal employer–employee relationship behind at the office, but she hadn't taken it *seriously*. She hadn't actually entertained the possibility of something happening between them.

Now her mind skirted around that intriguing thought, flirted with the possibility of—what? A fling? A one-night stand? Hannah was sensible enough to know Luca Moretti wasn't interested in anything more, and she wasn't interested in any relationship, much less one with a man who had sworn off marriage and children, and was a notorious womaniser. But she wasn't the type to have casual sex; she never had before. And to contemplate it with her *boss*...

And yet desire was a powerful thing. The sight of him in his tuxedo was enough to make her head spin and her mouth dry. The crisp white shirt emphasised his bronzed skin, and the tuxedo jacket fit his broad shoulders and narrow hips perfectly. He was incredible, darkly magnificent, so next to him James Garrison looked like a weedy fop, Simon Tucker a corpulent would-be Santa Claus. Luca was literally head and shoulders above the other men, a gorgeous, arrogant Colossus who looked as if he could straddle the world. The only man who nearly matched his height was Andrew Tyson, and his shoulders were stooped with age, his face lined and eyes faded.

Luca had spent the first part of the evening by her side, charming and solicitous to everyone, clearly working the room. When Tyson had entered the opulent sitting room, Luca had slid an arm around Hannah's waist, practically gluing her to his side. The bump of his hip against hers was enough to make sensation sizzle through her. She could feel the heat of his thigh through the thin material of her dress, and her insides tightened to an exquisite, aching point of desire.

She'd never responded so physically, so overwhelmingly, to a man before. Not, Hannah acknowledged, that she had a lot of experience. Ben, Jamie's father, had been her only lover, and while she'd enjoyed being with him she hadn't felt this desperate, craving physical touch like water in a parched desert.

Sliding sideways glances at Luca, she felt an overwhelming urge to touch him, to feel the rough stubble on his jaw, to discover if his lips felt soft or hard against hers. To feel his body against hers as she had that morning, and rock against him again, and then deeper still.

Heat flashed through her at the thought and Luca must have felt it, must have sensed her response, because he gave her a single, burning look before turning back to address Simon Tucker.

He knew how he affected her, maybe even how much. The thought would have been mortifying except that she knew she affected him too. He'd told her he'd been attracted to her that morning, and surely she couldn't feel this kind of chemistry if it were merely one-sided.

So the question was, could she do anything about it? Did she dare? She wasn't looking for a relationship, wouldn't put herself or Jamie at risk of being hurt. She knew what happened when you loved people. You risked losing them. She'd lost too many times already to try again.

'Hannah?' Luca prompted, and she realised she had no idea what anyone had been saying for the last few minutes.

'Sorry?' She tried for a conciliatory yet loving smile. 'I'm afraid I was a million miles away.'

'No doubt planning your wedding,' Simon joked good-naturedly. 'Have you set a date?'

'As soon as possible, as far as I'm concerned,' Luca answered swiftly, with a squeeze of Hannah's waist. 'But Hannah wants more of a do.'

Hannah lifted her shoulders in a helpless shrug. 'You only get married once.'

'Hopefully,' James joked, an edge to his voice that made a frozen silence descend on the little group for a few seconds.

'What's your secret to a happy marriage, then, James?' Simon asked, trying for jocular.

'A limit-free credit card and no questions asked,' James replied with a pointed look at his wife. Daniela pressed her lips together and said nothing.

Hardly a response of a family man, Hannah thought.

James Garrison was a slick study, and looked to share Luca's view on relationships.

'I'll take that on board,' Luca answered in a tone that suggested he would do no such thing.

'Falling for your PA isn't like you, is it, Luca?' James said, malice entering his ice-blue eyes. 'I thought you made sure never to mix business and pleasure.'

'As I said last night, this time it was impossible to resist.' He glanced down at Hannah, who tilted her head up to look at him so their mouths were only a few inches apart. She felt her insides shudder even though she knew Luca was only play-acting. That simmering heat in his eyes might not have been real, but the response Hannah's body gave certainly was. Her lips parted in helpless expectation, her whole being trained on Luca's sleepy, hooded gaze.

'Irresistible,' he murmured, and then closed those scant inches separating them.

The feel of his mouth on hers was a complete surprise and yet also a sigh of relief and wonder. *At last.* Her mouth opened underneath his and Hannah clutched at his lapels, barely aware of what she was doing. Luca's tongue swept into her mouth with sure possession, turning her insides weak and liquid. Her fingers tightened on his jacket.

'No doubt that you two are heading for the altar,' Simon joked, and Luca finally broke the kiss. Hannah sagged against him, her heart thudding, her mind spinning, her whole body feeling as if she'd been lit up inside like a firework.

'Like I said,' Luca said with a wry smile. 'Irresistible. I didn't stand a chance.'

And neither did she.

Her lips were still buzzing from his kiss when they headed out to the terrace where tables had been set up for dinner, laden with crystal and silver that glinted under the moonlight. Torches flickered, casting warm shadows across the terrace, and the sea was no more than a gleam of blackness in the distance, the tide a gentle shooshing sound as the waves lapped the shore.

They were just about to take their seats when Andrew Tyson turned expectantly to the open French windows. 'Ah,' he said, his voice filled with pleasure. 'My family has finally arrived from New York. Please let me introduce you all to my wife and children.'

Luca froze before slowly turning to face the French windows, where Andrew Tyson's wife, Mirabella, and their two children stood, framed by the gauzy white curtains.

He'd been waiting for this moment, both expecting and bracing himself for it, and yet now that it was finally here he found every thought had emptied from his head, the smile wiped from his face. Even the electric, intoxicating buzz of Hannah's kiss was forgotten in that horrendous, endless moment.

Distantly, as if he were down a long tunnel, he heard people exchanging pleasantries. Words were said, but it was as if everyone had started speaking another language. Tyson's two children, Stephen and Laura, came forward, smiling and shaking hands. Stephen had the dark hair of his mother and Tyson's brown eyes. Laura was the opposite, with her father's sandy hair and her mother's blue eyes. They were both relaxed, friendly, completely in their element, and in a few seconds he was going to have to shake their hands. Say hello. Act normal.

He acknowledged this even as he didn't move. Had no idea what the expression on his face was. Felt nothing but the relentless, painful thud of his heart. He'd been waiting for this moment for years, decades, and yet he hadn't been prepared for it, not remotely.

Then he felt a soft, slender hand slide into his, fingers squeezing tightly, imbuing warmth and strength. He glanced down at Hannah's face, the worry and concern in her eyes, the compassion in her smile, and he felt as if he'd fallen out of that tunnel with a thud, as if he'd rejoined reality, and was strong enough to deal with it—thanks to the woman next to him.

'Stephen. Laura.' His voice came out on a croak that he quickly covered, extending his hand for them both to shake. 'Luca Moretti and my fiancée, Hannah Stewart.'

Hannah stepped forward to greet them both and Luca forced himself to breathe normally, to school the expression on his face into one of friendly interest. To will his heart rate to slow.

He felt the delayed reaction of shock kick in, an icy wave that swept over him and left his knees weak, his whole body near to trembling. He had to get out of there.

'If you'll excuse me,' he murmured, and went in search of the bathroom.

Once inside, safely away from all the prying eyes, he splashed his face with cold water and then stared hard into the mirror, willing himself to get a grip. He'd climbed his way out of appalling poverty, negotiated dozens of million-and billion-dollar deals, was a man of power and authority and wealth. He'd conquered all these old fears and insecurities. He didn't need to feel this way now. He *wouldn't*.

Except he did.

He released a shuddering breath and rubbed a hand over his face. He needed to get back to the dinner. James Garrison was chomping at the bit to take this deal out from under him, simply out of spite. Garrison had always been jealous of Luca's success, of the huge deals he brokered that James hadn't a chance in hell of managing. Luca knew he couldn't afford to throw himself a damned pity party in the bathroom.

Taking a deep breath, he straightened his tux and then

opened the door to the hall, stopping short when he saw Hannah there waiting for him.

'What are you—?'

'I was worried about you.' She put a hand on his sleeve, and he glanced down at her fingers, long and slender, the nails buffed and glistening with clear varnish. Every part of her was simple and yet so elegant. 'Luca, what's going on? Can't you tell me?'

'It's nothing.'

'That's not true.' Concern threaded her voice. 'Please, Luca. Do you know how hard it is to act the part when I have no idea what you're going through?'

'You're doing fine, Hannah.' He shrugged off her hand. 'You certainly acted the part when I kissed you.'

Colour surged into her face but her gaze was steady, her voice calm. 'Don't take out your frustrations on me, Luca. All I'm asking for is the truth.'

He raked a hand through his hair, knowing she had a right to understand at least a little of what was going on. 'Tyson and I have a history,' he said in a low voice. 'Not a pleasant one. I didn't expect it, but seeing him again brings it all back.'

'And his family?' Hannah asked. Luca tensed.

'What about his family?'

'You obviously didn't like their arrival. You went white—'

'I did not,' he denied shortly, even though it was point-less. Hannah was gazing at him in a cringing mixture of pity and disbelief.

'Luca—'

'We need to get back in there.' He cut her off, and then reached for her hand. Tonight he'd show Andrew Tyson and his damned family just how much he had, how happy he was.

By the time they arrived back on the terrace, everyone

was seated and the first course had been served. Luca and Hannah took their places with murmured apologies. Luca saw he was seated next to Stephen Tyson, and he braced himself to talk to the man.

Stephen, he knew, had chosen not to take on the family's business but was a doctor in New York instead. Now he gave Luca a friendly smile.

'I'm sorry, but have we met before?'

A hollow laugh echoed through the emptiness inside him and he swallowed it down. 'No, I'm quite sure we haven't.'

Luca could feel Hannah's concern, the tension tautening her slender body. It was strange how attuned they'd become to each other and their moods, but perhaps that was simply an effect of the parts they had to play.

'Really?' Stephen shrugged, still smiling. 'Strange, but you look familiar.'

'Perhaps you've seen his photograph in one of the industry magazines?' Hannah suggested with a smile of her own. 'Luca is quite famous in his own right.' She placed a hand over his, squeezing his fingers, and Luca felt his heart twist inside him. He'd never had someone fight his corner before, even in the smallest way. He'd always been alone, had gone through childhood with his fists up and his nose bloody. Seeing Tyson made him feel like that battered boy again, and yet having Hannah hold his hand reminded him that he wasn't.

'Of course you are,' Stephen acknowledged. 'I know you developed the cancer centre in Ohio. It was really a masterwork of art and functionality. Utterly brilliant.'

'Thank you,' Luca said gruffly. He hadn't expected Stephen Tyson to be so friendly and sincere. It made it hard to hate him.

Somehow he managed to get through three courses, making small talk, smiling when necessary. He'd brought

Hannah's hand underneath the table after the first course to rest on his thigh and he wrapped his fingers around hers, clinging to her, craving her warmth. She didn't let go.

As the coffee and petits fours were being served, Andrew Tyson rose to make a toast.

'It's such a pleasure to have three dedicated family men here,' he began with a genial smile for all of them. 'As someone who has always determined to put family first, it is of course important to me that the man who takes on Tyson Resorts share my values.' He paused, his smiling gaze moving to his wife and then to his children. 'While I am saddened that my own children have not chosen this task, I understand completely why they've decided to pursue their own dreams—as I of course wish them to. My children are my pride and my joy, the touchstone of my life, along with my wife. The happiness I've experienced with my family is what I wish for each of you, and for every family who visits a Tyson resort.'

Luca couldn't bear to hear any more. He shifted in his seat, and Hannah squeezed his hand in warning. He couldn't leave now, but he could at least tune out Tyson's words.

Finally Tyson raised his glass and everyone else did as well, murmuring 'Hear, hear…' dutifully. Luca drained his glass of wine and then pulled away from Hannah.

'Luca,' she began, but he just shook his head.

'Later,' he managed, and then strode down the terrace steps, out into the darkness.

Hannah dabbed her mouth with her napkin, trying to cover the worry that she was sure was visible on her face. What kind of terrible history could Luca possibly have with Andrew Tyson? She glanced at the man who was now chatting with Simon and Rose Tucker, and decided she would make her excuses as well. If Luca left without her, it might look as if they were having a lovers' tiff. If they both left, people might assume it was a romantic tryst instead.

She made her farewells to the Tysons, telling them that Luca had wanted to steal her away for a moonlit walk on the beach.

'Ah, young love,' Andrew answered with a genial smile. 'There's nothing like it.'

No indeed, Hannah thought grimly as she held handfuls of her dress to keep from tripping down the stone steps that led directly to the beach.

Away from the candlelit terrace, the beach was awash in darkness, the white sand lit only by a pale sickle of moon. Hannah couldn't see Luca anywhere. Impatiently she kicked off the silver stiletto heels that made walking in sand impossible, and gathered a big handful of gauzy dress around her knees so she could walk unimpeded. Then she set off in search of her erstwhile fiancé.

CHAPTER NINE

HANNAH FOUND LUCA about half a mile down the beach, away from the villa, with nothing but a few palm trees for company. He sat with his elbows resting on his knees, his head cradled in his hands. Hannah had never seen such an abject pose; every powerful line of Luca's body seemed to radiate despair.

She hesitated, not wanting to intrude on his moment of sorrowful solitude, but not wanting to leave him alone either. He looked too lonely.

'I'm not going to bite your head off,' Luca said, his voice low and so very weary. 'Although you have good reason to think I would.'

She came closer, her dress trailing on the sand that was cool and silky under her bare feet.

'I wasn't thinking that,' she said quietly, and came to sit beside him, drawing her knees up as his were. He didn't lift his head. She thought about asking him yet again what pain and secrets he was hiding, but she didn't think there was much point. Luca didn't want to tell her and, truthfully, she didn't blame him. She had pain and secrets of her own she didn't want spilling out. Still, she felt she had to say something.

'The petits fours weren't actually that good,' she ventured after a moment. 'So you really didn't miss much.'

Luca let out a soft huff of laughter, and somehow that sounded sad too.

'I know what it's like to grieve, Luca,' Hannah said quietly.

'Is that what you think I'm doing?'

'I don't know, and I won't ask because I know you don't want to tell me. But…' she let out her breath slowly '…I know what it's like to feel angry and cheated and in despair.'

'Do you?' Luca lifted his head to gaze at her speculatively; she could only just make out the strong lines and angles of his face in the moonlit darkness. 'Who do you grieve, Hannah?'

It was such a personal question, and one whose answer she didn't talk about much. Yet she was the one who had started this conversation, and if Luca wasn't able to talk about his pain, perhaps she should talk about hers.

'My father, for one,' Hannah answered. 'He died when I was fifteen.'

'I'm sorry.' Luca stared straight ahead, his arms braced against his knees. 'How did it happen?'

'A heart attack out of the blue. He went to work and dropped dead at his desk. It was a complete shock to everyone.'

'Which must have made it even harder.'

'Yes, in a way. My mother wasn't prepared emotionally, obviously, or financially.'

Luca glanced at her. 'Your father didn't leave her provided for?'

'No, not really. He'd always meant to take out a life insurance policy, but he never got around to it. He was only forty-two years old. And savings were slim… He wasn't irresponsible,' she hastened to add. 'Just not planning for the disaster that happened.' And she'd decided long ago not to be bitter about that. She'd simply chosen to make different choices.

'So what did your mother do?'

'Got a job. She'd been a housewife for sixteen years, since before I was born, and she'd been a part-time pre-school teacher before that. It was tough to find work that earned more than a pittance.'

'And what about you?'

'I worked too, after school. We sold our house and rented a small flat. That helped with expenses.' But it had been hard, so hard, to go from the simple, smiling suburban life she'd had as a child to working all hours and living in a small, shabby flat.

'I'm sorry,' Luca said again. 'I never knew.'

'I never told you.' She paused, waiting for him to volunteer something of his own situation, but he didn't. 'What about you?' she asked at last. 'What happened to your parents?'

Luca was silent for a long moment. 'My mother died when I was fourteen.'

'I'm sorry.'

His cynical smile gleamed in the darkness. 'We're both so sorry, aren't we? But it doesn't change anything.'

'No, but sometimes it can make you feel less alone.'

'How do you know I feel alone?'

She took a deep breath. 'Because I do, sometimes.' Another breath. 'Do you?'

Luca didn't answer for a long moment. 'Yes,' he said finally. 'Yes, all the time.' He let out a hollow laugh. 'And no more so than when I was looking at Andrew Tyson and his damn kids.' His voice broke on the words and he averted his head from her, hiding his face, shielding his emotion.

'Oh, Luca.' Hannah's voice broke too, for her heart ached to see this proud, powerful man brought to such sadness.

'Don't.' His voice was muffled, his head still turned away from her. 'Don't pity me, Hannah. I couldn't bear it.'

'I don't—'

'I'd rather someone attacked me than pitied me. It's the worst kind of violence, cloaked as something kind or virtuous.' He spoke scathingly, the words spat out, making her wonder.

'Who pitied you, Luca?' she asked quietly. 'Because you seem the least likely person for anyone ever to feel sorry for.'

'I wasn't always.'

'When you were a child? When you lost your mother?'

He nodded tersely. 'Yes. Then.'

But she felt he wasn't telling her the whole truth. 'What happened to you after your mother's death? Did you live with your father?'

'No, he wasn't around.' Luca expelled a low breath. 'I went into foster care, and managed to secure a scholarship to a boarding school in Rome. It saved me, lifted me up from the gutter, but not everyone liked that fact. I stayed on my own.'

It sounded like a terribly lonely childhood. Even though she'd lost her father, Hannah was grateful for the fifteen years of happy memories that he'd given her. 'How did your mother die?' she asked.

He let out a long, weary sigh and tilted his head towards the sky. 'She killed herself.'

Startled, Hannah stared at him in horror. 'Oh, but that's terrible—'

'Yes, but I could understand why she did it. Life had become unendurable.'

'But you were only fourteen—'

'I think,' Luca said slowly, still staring at the starlit sky, 'when you feel that trapped and desperate and sad, you stop thinking about anything else. You can't reason your way out of it. You can only try to end the sadness.'

Tears stung Hannah's eyes at the thought. 'You have great compassion and understanding, to be able to think that.'

'I've never been angry with her,' Luca answered flatly. He lowered his head to gaze out at the sea, washed in darkness. 'She was a victim.'

'And were you a victim?' Hannah asked. She felt as if she were feeling her way through the dark, groping with her words, trying to shape an understanding out of his reluctant half-answers.

'No, I've never wanted to think of myself as victim. That ends only in defeat.'

'I suppose I felt the same,' Hannah offered cautiously. 'My father's death left my mother in a difficult situation, and I wanted to make sure I never ended up that way as an adult.'

He gave her a swift, searching glance. 'Is that why you agreed with me that relationships aren't worth it?'

'I only said maybe,' Hannah reminded him. 'But yes, that has something to do with it.' She thought of Jamie's father and felt a lump form in her throat. She'd moved on from her grief years ago, but opening those old wounds still hurt, still made her wonder and regret. If she'd done something differently…if she'd handled their last argument better… 'When you lose someone,' she said, 'you don't feel like taking the chance again.'

'But he was your father, not a boyfriend or husband.'

'I lost one of those too,' Hannah admitted. 'A boyfriend, not a husband.' They'd never got that far. They'd never had the chance. And she had to believe that they would have, if Ben hadn't died. That he would have changed his mind, she would have had a second chance.

'When?'

'Almost six years ago.'

Luca turned to her, the moonlight washing half his face in lambent silver. 'You bear your sorrows so well. You don't look like someone haunted by grief.'

'I'm not,' Hannah answered staunchly. 'I choose not to be.' Even if it was hard, a choice she had to make every day not to wallow in grief and regret.

'That's a strong choice to make.'

'It hasn't always been easy,' Hannah allowed. 'And I can't say I haven't had my moments of self-pity or evenings alone with a tub of mint-chocolate-chip ice cream,' she added. 'But I try not to wallow.'

His mouth twisted wryly. 'Is that what you think I'm doing? Wallowing?'

Horrified, Hannah clapped a hand to her mouth. 'Luca, no—'

'No, it is.' He cut her off. 'And I despise myself for it. I thought I could come here and stare Andrew Tyson in the face. I thought I could smile and shake the man's hand and feel nothing, because I'd schooled myself to feel nothing for so long. But I can't. I *can't*.' His voice broke on a ragged gasp and he dropped his head in his hands. 'I don't want to feel this,' he muttered. 'I don't want to be enslaved by something that happened so long ago. I wanted this to be a clean slate, a second chance—' He drew in a ragged breath, his head in his hands, and Hannah did the only thing she could, the only thing she felt she could do in that moment. She hugged him.

She wrapped her arms around him, pressing her cheek into his back, trying to imbue him with her comfort. 'Oh, Luca,' she whispered. *'Luca.'*

He went rigid underneath her touch but she hung on anyway. Luca could be as strong and stoic as he liked, but he still needed comfort, and in that moment she was determined to give it to him.

He reached up to grip her wrists that were locked across his chest as if he'd force her away from him, but he didn't.

'Why are you so kind?' he demanded in a raw mutter.

'Why are you so afraid of kindness?' Hannah returned softly.

He turned, his hands still on her wrists, and for a second she thought he would reject her offer of comfort and push her away, but then his features twisted and with a muttered curse he reached for her instead.

Their mouths met and clashed and the fierce desire to comfort him turned into something far more primal and urgent. His hands were everywhere, clenching in her hair, stroking her back, cupping her breasts, and all the while his mouth didn't leave hers.

They fell back on the sand in a tangle of limbs, and when Luca's thumb brushed over the taut peak of her nipple Hannah arched into his hand, craving an even deeper caress.

She tore at his shirt, studs popping, desperate to feel his bare, glorious skin. She let out a gasp of pleasure and satisfaction when she finally parted the shirt and ran her palms along his hair-roughened chest, revelling in the feel of sculpted muscle and hot skin.

Luca's breath came out in a hiss and then he was pulling at her dress, the gauzy folds tearing under his urgent touch, and Hannah didn't even care.

'Luca,' she gasped, and it was both a demand and a plea. She needed to feel his hands on her body. She felt as if she'd explode if she didn't. He pulled the tattered dress down to her waist, leaving her completely bare on top as she hadn't worn a bra with the halter-style dress.

Then he bent his head to her breasts, his tongue now touching where his hands had been, and Hannah clutched his head to her, nearly sobbing in pleasure at the feel of him tasting her.

But even that wasn't enough. She needed more from him, of him, and when his hand slipped under her bunched dress, his fingers deftly finding and stroking her centre, she thought she almost had it. The pleasure was so acute it was akin to pain, a sharp ache that left her gasping. She skimmed the length of his erection, sucking her breath in at the way his body throbbed in insistent response to her touch. She pulled at his trousers, fumbling with the ties of his cummerbund, and with a muttered oath Luca ripped it away from him and tossed it on the sand. Hannah let out a gurgle of laughter that he swallowed with his mouth as he kissed her again and she gave herself to him, offering everything as her hands clutched at his shoulders and her hips rocked against his.

'Hannah,' Luca muttered against her mouth. 'Hannah, I need…'

'Yes,' she answered almost frantically. 'Yes, *please*, Luca, now.'

She parted her legs as he fumbled with the zip on his trousers. She didn't have a second to consider if this was a good idea, if she'd regret this afterwards. She couldn't think past the haze of overwhelming need that consumed her.

Then Luca was inside her, an invasion so sudden, so sweet, so *much*, that Hannah felt tears sting her eyes. It had been so long since she'd given her body to a man. So long since she'd felt completed, conquered. She wrapped her legs around him, enfolding herself around him as she accepted him into her body.

He stilled inside her as they both adjusted to the intense sensation. Luca's eyes were closed, his arms braced by her shoulders. Then Hannah flexed around him and with a groan of surrender he started to move.

It had been a while, and it took her a few exquisite thrusts before she managed to find the rhythm and match it, and then with each thrust she felt her body respond, opening up like a flower, everything in her spiralling upward, straining towards that glittering summit that was just out of her reach—

Until she found it, her body convulsing around Luca's as she cried out his name and the climax rushed over them both, their bodies shuddering in tandem, tears slipping down her face as she gave herself to the tidal wave of pleasure.

In the aftermath Hannah lay there, Luca's body on top of hers, the thud of his heart matching her own. She felt dazed and dizzy and yet utterly sated. She couldn't regret what had happened, not even for a second.

Then Luca rolled off her with a curse, lying on the sand on his back, one arm thrown over his eyes. Okay, maybe she could.

Hannah felt a whole bunch of things at once: the cold sand underneath her, the stickiness on her thighs, the grit in her hair, the torn dress about her waist. The pleasure that had overwhelmed her only moments before now felt like mere vapour, a ghost of a memory.

She pulled her torn dress down over herself, wincing at the shredded gauze. To think Luca had spent nine thousand pounds on this one gown. Not that she would have had a chance to wear it again, even if it hadn't been ruined.

Luca lifted his arm from his face and turned his head to rake her with one quick glance. Even in the moonlit darkness Hannah could see how indifferent he looked, and inwardly she quelled.

This had been a mistake. A wonderful, terrible mistake, and one she would most certainly regret no matter the pleasure she'd experienced. How could she work with Luca from now on? What if he fired her? But even worse than the fears for her job was the piercing loneliness of the thought that he might shut her out of his life. He already was, and she'd barely been in it to begin with.

She took a deep, calming breath and told herself not to jump to conclusions.

'Your dress,' Luca stated flatly.

Hannah glanced down at it. 'I'm afraid it's past repair.'

'I'm thinking of getting back to the room,' he clarified impatiently. 'I don't care about the dress.'

'Oh. Okay.' She bit her lip, trying not to feel hurt. This was a far cry from pillow talk, but then they hadn't even had a bed. They'd had a few moments of frenzied, mindless passion that Luca undoubtedly regretted, just as she was starting to.

Luca sat up, readjusting his trousers and then searching for the studs on his shirt. He found enough to keep the shirt mostly fastened, and he stuffed his tie and cummerbund in his pocket. Then he shrugged off his tuxedo jacket and draped it over her shoulders.

'There. You're mostly decent. Hopefully we can sneak into the room without anyone seeing us.'

'And if they do?' Hannah asked, thankful her voice didn't wobble. 'Wouldn't they just think we'd done exactly what they'd expect us to do, and made love under the stars?'

Luca's mouth compressed and he stood up, brushing the sand from his legs before he reached a hand down to her. She took it only because she knew she'd struggle getting up on her own. She was torn between an irrational anger—how had she expected Luca to act?—and a deep and disturbing hurt. She shouldn't care this much. She hadn't had *feelings* for Luca, not really.

Except somehow, in the last twenty-four hours, she had begun to develop them. She'd seen intriguing glimpses into a man whom she'd already respected and admired— glimpses of strength and emotion. She'd seen him determined and arrogant but also humble, concerned for her even while he was in the throes of his own emotional agony. Luca Moretti had depths she'd discovered this weekend that he hadn't even hinted at before.

And he was hiding them all from her now. He dropped her hand the moment she was upright and started walking back towards the villa, its lights glimmering in the distance. Hannah followed him, clutching his jacket around her shoulders, wincing at the sand she could feel in her hair and clothes.

They skirted around the terrace that was now empty to the other side of the house, where the bedrooms' French windows overlooked the beach.

'You'd better pick the right room,' Hannah muttered darkly. Hurt and anger were giving way to a weary resignation as she scrambled to think of a way to navigate this awful aftermath.

Luca didn't even reply, just stalked ahead and then flung open a pair of windows and ushered her into their bedroom. Hannah stepped inside, her glance taking in the turned-down bed, the chocolate hearts on the pillows. Had it been only twenty-four hours ago that she'd been in this same room, this same position, except now everything felt drastically different?

'Why don't you get cleaned up?' Luca said, nodding towards the bathroom without looking at her. 'And then we'll talk.'

CHAPTER TEN

LUCA SHRUGGED OFF his torn shirt as Hannah disappeared into the bathroom. What had he been *thinking*, slaking his lust with his PA? The trouble was, he hadn't been thinking. He'd been utterly in the grip of his own awful emotions, and Hannah's tentative comfort had been the balm he'd so desperately craved. It was only afterwards, after the most sexually and emotionally explosive encounter he'd ever experienced, that the regrets came rushing in. Regret to have slept with his PA at all, and, worse, shame that he'd allowed her to see him in such a vulnerable state. What must Hannah think of him? It had practically been a pity lay.

Except she had been just as gripped by the raw, urgent need that he'd felt consume him. She'd been just as desperate to have him inside her as he'd been to be there.

The knowledge didn't make him feel any better. The whole thing was an appalling mistake, made about a thousand times worse by the fact that they hadn't used any protection.

Hannah emerged from the bathroom, dressed in the same awful pyjamas she'd worn last night, but at least tonight Luca was grateful for the way they hid her body. The last thing he needed was to feel tempted again.

She didn't look at him as she came into the room, going

directly to the bed. Her body was stiff with affront and Luca watched in bemused disbelief as she reached for her book by the bedside table and then buried her nose in it.

He took a deep breath. 'Hannah.' She didn't so much as look up from her book. 'We need to talk.'

'Oh, *now* we need to talk?' Finally she looked up, and Luca saw anger firing her brown eyes, turning them to gold. Her hair was tousled about her shoulders, her face flushed, and, pyjamas aside, she looked utterly lovely.

But he had to stop thinking that way.

'Yes, now we need to talk.'

'Not right after?' Hannah filled in. 'No, you couldn't bother to say boo to me then.'

Luca's insides tightened with both irritation and remorse. He hadn't treated her very well, back on the beach, but she'd blindsided him, in so many ways. 'Clearly what happened took us both by surprise.' She took a deep breath and nodded, her hands folded across her abandoned book. 'So much so that I didn't think to use any protection.'

Hannah's lips parted on a soundless gasp as her eyes widened in shocked realisation. 'I didn't even think of that.' She nibbled her lip. 'But it's not…I mean, based on the time of the month, I don't think it's risky.'

'You'd let me know? I mean, if…?'

Her gaze locked with his and her breath came out in a rush. Luca felt the import of the moment, the enormous impact of what they'd shared together. More than he'd ever shared with any other woman, pregnancy or not. 'Yes, of course,' she answered. '*If.* But I really don't think there's going to be an if. So that's one less thing to worry about.' She tried for a smile but it wobbled and slid off her face, and she looked away, blinking rapidly.

'Hannah…' He expelled a shaky breath. He was finding this all a lot harder than he would have wished. He didn't like the realisation that he'd hurt her.

Hannah glanced down at her laced fingers. 'You don't need to worry about me, Luca,' she said quietly. 'I wasn't looking for some kind of fairy tale, and I certainly don't have any expectations because of...well, you know.'

And that proclamation, which should have only brought blessed relief, caused him the most absurd flicker of disappointment. His emotions were clearly all over the place. 'Good,' Luca said shortly. 'Then we can forget this ever happened and move on.'

With effort Hannah kept her face blank. *Forget this ever happened.* As if she could ever do that. Those passionate moments with Luca were emblazoned on her brain, his touch branded on her body. She swallowed and nodded.

'Yes,' she agreed, because what else could she say? Luca wasn't looking for a relationship, and neither was she—and certainly not with a man like him. If she ever dared to risk her heart—and her son's—it would be with someone who valued family, who wanted a child. *Her* child.

And yet Luca had put so much care into his plans for the family resort, and just a moment ago he'd almost looked disappointed that she was most likely not pregnant.

But she couldn't go chasing after rainbows where none existed. He'd made his intentions more than clear.

Luca nodded, seemingly satisfied with her agreement. 'You'll tell me if the situation changes?'

'If I'm pregnant?' she clarified wryly. 'Yes, Luca, I'll tell you. It's not as if it's something I could hide, working for you.'

'But you wouldn't try to hide it?'

'No, of course not.' She frowned at him. 'But let's cross that bridge when we come to it, shall we?'

A terse nod was all the response she got and he disappeared into the bathroom while she tossed her book on the bedside table, too unsettled to read.

Even though she'd just told Luca they didn't need to think about how to handle a pregnancy yet, she found herself doing just that—and her scattered thoughts soon morphed into the most absurd fantasy of Luca as a doting dad. This child could have what Jamie had missed out on. She pictured Luca cradling their newborn, his big, strong hands so tender with that tiny scrap of humanity. She thought of all the things that Jamie would experience without a dad—a lost tooth, riding a bike, Christmas and birthdays. This child wouldn't miss out at all.

Then Luca came out of the bathroom and got into bed, his movements brisk and businesslike, and Hannah forced her wayward thoughts to a screeching halt. What on earth was she thinking, casting Luca Moretti of all people, into the role of a devoted father? He was anything but—not to the imaginary child they most likely hadn't conceived, and certainly not to her son by another man. If she was pregnant, he'd probably pay her off and remain completely uninvolved. The antithesis of a happily-ever-after.

No, she had to clamp down on that kind of dangerous and foolish thinking right now. Luca wasn't interested in relationships, and neither was she. As he'd told her, it simply wasn't worth it.

The next morning Hannah woke to an empty bed; she'd been so exhausted from everything that had happened, she'd fallen asleep without any restless wondering of what Luca was thinking or feeling next to her.

Now, in the bright light of a Mediterranean morning, the events of last night took on a sordid and reproachable cast. What had seemed irresistible and exciting in the sultry darkness now felt shameful. She was glad Luca wasn't in the room because she didn't think she could look him in the eye. Just the memory of how she'd begged him to touch her made Hannah's face flame.

Half an hour later, after eating breakfast delivered by staff and dressed in another one of her ensembles from Diavola, her hair and make-up done, Hannah felt more in control of the situation, or at least as if a mask of calm respectability had been put in place.

Luca hadn't returned to the room and so she decided to go in search of him. She saw several suitcases in the foyer and realised Andrew Tyson's guests were starting to depart. She'd known she and Luca would be leaving some time today, and the thought of returning home to Jamie, to her mother, to normal life, brought a rush of relief. She couldn't handle any more of her seesawing emotions.

She wandered through a few more rooms before she found some of Tyson's guests along with his family in a breakfast room, enjoying coffee and pastries. Laura Tyson gave her a friendly smile as she came into the room.

'You're Luca Moretti's fiancée, isn't that right?'

'Yes…'

'I saw the two of you sneak out at the end of the dinner last night,' Laura said confidentially, her eyes sparkling. 'I don't blame you. Luca is certainly a handsome man, and he obviously adores you.'

That sincerely delivered statement nearly made Hannah choke. 'Thank you,' she murmured. She couldn't manage any more. This awful pretence was straining at its seams. Another lie and it would explode. *She* would.

Laura leaned closer to Hannah and lowered her voice. 'To tell you the truth, I think my father favours your fiancé to take over the resorts. He mentioned how impressed he was with his plans.'

'Oh…well, that's encouraging to hear.' Hannah smiled, genuinely glad for Luca even amidst the turmoil of all her feelings. Based on the proposal she'd seen, he deserved to win the commission.

'He'll make the announcement shortly, I'm sure.'

'Today…?'

Laura wrinkled her nose. 'Probably not for a week or two. This is a big decision for him.' Her smile fell as she admitted, 'I think he's still hoping one of us will show an interest, but Stephen and I had different dreams.'

'He's a doctor…'

'And I work in pharmaceutical research. Our little sister died of leukaemia when she was only four years old,' Laura explained quietly. 'It had a big impact on all of us… and I think we've chosen to honour her memory in different ways.'

'I'm sorry for your loss,' Hannah said, knowing the words were inadequate yet meaning them utterly. She knew what it was like to lose someone at a young age.

'I'm glad that someone is interested in taking the resorts on,' Laura said. 'I know they're a bit worn. Dad hasn't had as much energy as he used to, and he's never been good at delegating. But I hope with your Luca on board things will change for the better.'

Her Luca. As if. 'I hope so too,' Hannah said and Laura gave her one more smile before turning away.

Luca came in the room a short while later, his face and body both tense. Even grim-faced as he was he looked devastatingly attractive in a grey pinstriped suit matched with a crisp white shirt and dark blue tie. The elegantly cut suit showed off his muscular body to perfection, and he strode into the room as if he owned it, his gaze searching out Hannah.

As his deep brown eyes locked with hers Hannah felt a fiery heat start a blaze in her belly, much to her irritation. She'd worked for the man for three years and he'd never caused that reaction in her in all that time. Yet right now she couldn't deny the magnetic pull of attraction that had her unable to break away from his penetrating stare. She could only pretend it didn't exist.

'Hannah.' He nodded towards the door. 'Are you ready to leave?'

No lovey-dovey play-acting this morning, she noted. He must have known that he'd sealed the deal.

'I didn't realise we were leaving so soon,' Hannah answered. 'I'll pack right away.'

Luca followed her down the hall and into their bedroom. The huge, airy room felt claustrophobic as she got out her suitcase and started neatly folding her clothes into it. Her hands trembled and she hid them in the folds of a dress.

'I spoke to Laura just now,' she said, her voice an octave higher than normal. She cleared her throat and tried again. 'She seems quite sure that you've secured the bid.'

'Tyson is keeping us on leading strings,' Luca answered. He prowled around the room, his hands shoved into his pockets, every stride predatory and restless.

'Laura said it was a big decision for him to make.'

'I think he just likes toying with us,' Luca answered dismissively. 'That's the kind of man he is.'

'If there really is bad blood between you,' Hannah said slowly, amazed that she hadn't thought of this earlier, 'why would he sell the resorts to you?'

Luca stilled, his back to her as he gazed out at the sparkling sea. 'Because he doesn't know it was me.'

'What do you mean?'

'It's complicated,' he answered on a shrug, his voice gruff. 'Suffice it to say, Tyson doesn't realise there is any history between us. Only I do.'

Hannah frowned, Luca's admission making her uneasy. How was what he'd said even possible? And yet Luca clearly meant it. He also very clearly wasn't going to tell her anything else, and she didn't want to ask. She'd got in too deep with Luca Moretti already.

'I just need to get my wash bag from the bathroom,' she said. 'And then I'll be ready to go.'

Fifteen minutes later they'd made their farewells and were bumping down the road to the airport in the same Jeep they'd arrived in only forty-eight hours ago, which seemed unbelievable. Hannah felt as if she'd lived an entire lifetime in the space of a few short and incredible days. And that lifetime, she reminded herself, was over.

An hour later they were settled in first class in the aeroplane to London. Luca waved away the offers of champagne and Hannah looked out of the window, stupidly stung. A few days ago he'd said he'd enjoyed watching her taste champagne. But she'd had quite a bit of champagne since then, and she had a feeling it would taste flat now anyway. So much for tickly.

As soon as they'd taken off Luca got some papers out of his briefcase and spent the entire flight immersed in work. Hannah told herself she was grateful not to have to make awkward small talk, but silence gave her the unwelcome space to remember every second of last night's encounter.

Just thinking about the way Luca had kissed her, with such overwhelming intensity and passion and *desperation*, made her inner muscles clench and she shifted restlessly in her seat. She *had* to get over this. Her job and her sanity were both at stake. She couldn't work with Luca every day and remember how he'd felt. How he'd tasted.

And she'd forget in time, Hannah assured herself. Of course she was still thinking about his kiss. It hadn't even been twenty-four hours. But the memory would fade in time, and who knew? Maybe in a week or month or ten years, she and Luca would laugh about the one bizarre interlude they'd had on a Mediterranean island.

Hannah settled back into her seat and started to flick through the films available on her entertainment console. Yes. That was exactly how it was going to be.

CHAPTER ELEVEN

THE NEXT MORNING Hannah dressed for work in her smartest pencil skirt and silk blouse, slipped on her highest, sharpest stiletto heels. She needed armour.

On the Tube on the way into the Moretti Enterprises office, she worried if she was making too much effort. Maybe Luca would think she was trying to impress him. But she'd nip that prospect right in the bud the second she arrived. She'd make it quite clear to Luca that she was as interested and invested as he was in getting their relationship back on a firm, professional footing.

She needed to get her life back to normal, both for Jamie's sake as well as her own. She'd had a happy reunion with her son last night, reading stories and cuddling before bed.

Once Jamie had been tucked in bed, Diane had regaled Hannah with stories of their weekend together: a trip to the zoo, baking fairy cakes on a rainy afternoon. Then her mother had cocked her head and swept her with a knowing yet inquisitive gaze.

'I didn't realise Luca Moretti was so handsome.'

'Haven't you seen his picture in the tabloids?' Hannah had answered a touch too sharply. 'He's often photographed with some socialite or other.'

'You know I don't read the tabloids.' Her mother had

sat back, arms folded. 'But going on a business trip with him was a departure from the way things usually are, wasn't it?'

That, Hannah had reflected sourly, was a complete understatement. 'Yes, it was,' she'd answered.

'Do you think you'll go on another trip with him?'

'No,' Hannah had answered firmly, and thankfully her mother hadn't asked her any more questions.

That morning as dawn light had filtered through the curtains Jamie had crept into her bedroom, teddy bear dangling from one chubby fist, and climbed into bed with her. Hannah had snuggled his warm little body against her, savouring the precious moment. It had reminded her of her priorities, and put the events of the weekend firmly into their place—a moment out of reality, nothing more.

Luca had not yet arrived when she reached the penthouse office, and Hannah breathed a sigh of relief that she had a few moments to compose herself and begin work without worrying about her boss.

She was well into her in-tray when he arrived, striding through the lift doors, looking devastatingly sexy in a navy blue suit, his close-cropped dark hair bristly and damp from the rain.

Hannah looked up as he entered, and the breath bottled in her lungs, every thought emptying from her head as her gaze locked on his body and her mind played a reel of X-rated memories. With effort she yanked her gaze away, staring down at the spreadsheet she'd been working on, the numbers blurring before her distracted gaze.

'Good morning.' Luca's voice was brisk and business-like, giving nothing away. 'I'll be in my office if you need anything.' And he strode past her desk, closing the door behind him with a decisive click.

Hannah ignored the pinpricks of hurt and disappointment she felt at his obvious dismissal and refocused on her work.

Luca didn't emerge from his office all morning, and Hannah managed to plough through paperwork until just before lunch, when she needed Luca's signature on some letters.

She approached his door with trepidation, bracing herself for his hostility.

'Come in,' Luca barked after she knocked on the door, and she pushed it open, the letters in her hand.

'I just need you to sign these,' she murmured, and Luca beckoned her forward. It was no more than he would have done a week ago, but now the command seemed autocratic and unfeeling. Her problem, she told herself. She had to get over her unreasonable reaction to this man.

She placed the letters on the desk, taking a careful step away as he signed them so she wouldn't breathe in his cedarwood scent or feel the heat emanating from his powerful body.

'Here.' Luca handed her the letters, and his hand brushed hers as she took them. Hannah felt as if she'd been scorched. A tremor went through her body, followed by a wave of helpless longing that she knew she couldn't disguise. Everything in her yearned to have him touch her again, and this time with intent.

Luca cursed under his breath and heat surged into Hannah's face. 'I'm… I'm sorry,' she muttered, embarrassed beyond belief that her reaction was so cringingly obvious to him. 'I thought I'd go to lunch if you don't need me.' *Wrong* choice of words. 'I mean, if there's nothing you need me to do…in the office…' Could she make this any worse?

'I know what you meant,' Luca answered tersely. 'Yes, you can go.'

With relief Hannah fled from the room.

* * *

Luca watched Hannah leave his office as if she had the fires of hell on her heels, and let out a weary groan. This was all much more difficult than he'd thought it would be. Much more tempting. The merest brush of Hannah's hand against his own had made his body pulse with desire, hardly the distraction he needed during the working day.

They'd both settle down, he told himself. Their attraction, without anything to nurture it, would surely fade. Perhaps he'd take a business trip to the US, check on some of his properties in development there. Give them both a chance to cool off. An opportunity to forget.

Except Luca didn't think he'd ever forget the feel of Hannah's slender body yielding to his, or, more worryingly, the way she'd held him when he'd been so angry and defeated, the sweet, heartfelt way she'd comforted him. That was something he definitely needed to forget.

Abruptly Luca rose from his desk to stare out at the bustling city streets. He wasn't used to craving another person's company or comfort. He'd lived his life alone, ever since his mother had died, battling his way through boarding school and foster care, and even before then, when she'd been too busy or despairing to care for him.

He'd chosen to lift his chin and ignore the taunts and scorn that had been heaped upon him as a bastard growing up fatherless in a remote Sicilian village. He'd pretended the snubs and jibes of the entitled boys at school had bounced off him. He'd always acted as if he didn't care and he'd almost convinced himself he didn't…until he'd come face to face with Andrew Tyson, the man who had rejected him once already. His father.

Letting out a shuddering breath, Luca turned from the window. In a week or so Tyson would seal the property deal, and he'd be the owner of the resorts his father's legitimate children had refused to take on. He'd have control of the inheritance that would have been his, as firstborn son, if Tyson, the alleged family man, had deigned to marry the woman he'd impregnated.

Then he would finally have his revenge.

In the meantime, he needed to get hold of his rampaging libido and shut Hannah Stewart firmly back in the box where she belonged: as his PA, an employee like any other.

Hannah took an unaccustomed full hour for lunch, walking the streets of the City, trying to talk herself out of this ridiculous reaction to Luca Moretti. She reminded herself of how she used to be with the man, calm and cool and professional. That was how she needed to be again.

She felt more herself when she'd returned to the office, and thankfully Luca was closeted behind a closed door, taking a conference call. Hannah got on with her day and had just about convinced herself that she had this thing under control.

Then Luca opened the door to his office and heat and memory and longing all surged through her body, an unstoppable force.

'I'm going home for the day, to pack,' Luca announced. Hannah kept her gaze glued to her computer screen and willed her hands not to tremble.

'Pack…?'

'I'm going to America for a week, to check on some of my properties there.'

'Would you like me to make travel arrangements?' Hannah asked.

'No, I've taken care of it myself.' He paused, and Hannah forced herself to meet his iron gaze. 'This thing between us, Hannah. It will fade.'

Hannah didn't know whether to be gratified or embarrassed that he was acknowledging it. Was he actually saying that he felt it too, as much as she did? 'Of course,' she managed. 'I'm sorry, I don't mean things to be awkward.'

Luca shrugged. 'It never should have happened. I'm sorry it did.'

Ouch. 'Of course,' Hannah said stiffly, trying to keep the hurt from her voice. She shouldn't care. She really shouldn't.

'But,' he continued, his voice and expression both inflexible, 'you will tell me if there is a result?'

A result? It took Hannah a second to realise he meant a pregnancy. 'I told you I would. But I don't think—'

'Good.' For a second she thought she saw regret in his eyes, longing in his face. But no, she was imagining it; he looked as hard and unyielding as ever as he nodded once in farewell and then walked out of the office.

Hannah spent the week trying to get on with her life. She spring-cleaned her house and bought several new outfits and had her hair and nails done, not for Luca Moretti's sake, but her own. She took Jamie to the cinema and the park on the weekend, and told herself she was blessed in so many ways, and she didn't need anything more in her life. Certainly not a man who would only break her heart—again.

At least, she discovered a few days after Luca had left, she wasn't pregnant. The realisation brought relief that was tinged by a little impractical disappointment. Honestly, what on earth would she have done with another baby? It was hard enough being a single mum to one child.

The day Luca arrived back at work she'd dressed carefully in one of her new outfits, a slim-fitting dress in silvery grey silk with a tailored black blazer. She had her hair in a more glamorous chignon rather than her usual practical ponytail, and she felt polished and confident and strong.

Then Luca walked through the lift doors. Hannah's

heart seemed to stop as her gaze swept over him and she noticed the weariness in his eyes, the lines of strain from nose to mouth. She had a nearly irresistible urge to go to him, offer him comfort as she had once before.

And look where that had ended.

'Hello,' she said stiffly, turning back to her computer. 'Welcome back.'

'Thank you.' Luca paused by her desk, and Hannah breathed in the spicy male scent of him. 'Has anything of note happened while I've been away?'

'No, not particularly.' She'd kept him abreast by email, and even that had felt like too much contact. 'The post is on your desk.'

'Thank you.' Still he didn't move away, and Hannah tore her gaze away from her computer to look up at him. His gaze locked on and burned into hers, and she felt as if she could lose herself in the deep brown of his eyes.

'Luca,' she whispered, her voice breathy and soft. Luca's expression hardened.

'I'll be in my office.'

A week away hadn't changed anything. Luca swivelled in his chair, restless and angry with himself for still responding to Hannah in such a basic and yet overwhelming way. The mere sight of her looking so poised and elegant had made him yearn to sweep her into his arms, pluck the pins from her hair and lose himself in the glories of her mouth.

While in New York he'd tried to distance himself from the memory of her touch by going out with a model he'd once been friendly with, but the elegant, gorgeous woman had left him completely cold. He hadn't been able to summon the interest even to kiss her, and she'd been quite put out as a result.

Maybe, he mused, he was going about this the wrong way. Maybe instead of forgetting Hannah he needed to get her out of his system. He'd been able to tell, simply from that one small exchange, that she still reacted to him just as powerfully as he did to her. Why not have a fling? They'd work out this inconvenient attraction and then resume their professional relationship. He didn't want to lose his PA, and he knew Hannah didn't want to lose her job. Surely they could be sensible about this. Businesslike, even. They'd both agreed that neither of them wanted the risk of a real relationship, so Hannah should surely be amenable to the kind of arrangement he was thinking about. All he had to do was offer.

CHAPTER TWELVE

HANNAH HAD JUST put Jamie to bed and changed into comfy yoga pants and a fleece hoodie when the doorbell rang. She was exhausted, emotionally spent from having been on high alert with Luca in the office, and she wanted to do nothing more than kick back with a glass of wine and maybe some ice cream and watch several hours of soothingly mindless reality TV.

Suspecting her elderly neighbour needed help opening a jar or reaching something on a high shelf—Hannah was called on for these kinds of services several times a week—she opened her front door with a sunny smile pasted onto her face and felt it slide right off when her stunned gaze took in the sight of the powerful form filling her doorway.

'Luca…what are you doing here?'

'I want to talk.' He bent his head so as not to hit the low stone lintel. 'May I come in?'

Hannah had a kneejerk reaction to refuse. She didn't want him in her house, overwhelming her life with his presence, his power. She glanced behind her, as if looking for assistance but none was forthcoming. 'All right.'

She led Luca to the small sitting room, which, after a quick post-tea tidy-up, was free of any evidence of her son. 'Is something wrong?'

'Not exactly.' Luca's perceptive gaze took in the little

room with its worn sofa and coffee table, the small TV in the corner. With framed prints on the walls and bookcases overflowing with paperbacks, it was homey and cosy but a far cry from the luxury Hannah knew he was accustomed to.

'I'm not pregnant,' she blurted. 'If that's why you came. It's certain.'

'Oh.' Luca looked surprised, and then discomfited. 'No, that's not why I'm here.'

'Oh. Okay.' Flummoxed, she gestured to a chair. 'Would you like to sit down?' It felt surreal to have Luca in her little house, taking up all the space and air. She sat on the sofa and he sat in a chair opposite, his hands resting on his muscular thighs.

'This isn't working, Hannah.'

Her stomach lurched unpleasantly. She couldn't pretend not to understand what he was talking about. 'I'll get over it,' she said a bit desperately. 'It *can* work—'

'It's not just you,' he interjected. 'I feel it too.'

Her heart somersaulted at that admission but she still felt wary. She *couldn't* lose her job. 'So what are you suggesting? I need my job—'

Luca grimaced in distaste. 'Do you actually think I'd fire you over this?'

'You might think of a convenient reason to let me go or at least shift me to another position in the company.' The latter wouldn't necessarily be a bad thing, even if she'd miss the status and salary, not to mention the challenge, of being the CEO's executive assistant. And, she admitted painfully, she'd miss Luca.

'That's not the kind of man I am,' he answered stonily, and Hannah thought she detected hurt underneath his hard manner.

'I'm sorry, I'm just paranoid, I suppose.' She spread her hands. 'You hold all the cards, Luca.'

'Then let me play one now. I want you, Hannah. I want you in my bed. Properly, and not just for a few mindless minutes.'

Hannah stared at him in shock, the blood draining from her head, making her dizzy. She could not think to string two words together.

'I don't see any reason why we shouldn't have an affair,' Luca stated. 'We're obviously attracted to one another, and those feelings are not going away. I think it would be far better to explore this mutual attraction to our satisfaction, and then part on good terms.' His eyes glittered as he pinned her with his stare. 'I'm a very considerate and generous lover, Hannah.'

'I know you are,' she answered numbly. The shock was dissipating, replaced by anger, and, far worse, hurt. 'I've arranged the courier from Tiffany & Co. enough times to realise,' she added tartly.

Luca didn't look remotely abashed at this statement. 'Then you agree?'

'To what, exactly? Being your mistress?' Her voice rang out, making him blink in surprise. Hannah held on to her rage. Better to be angry than to break down into tears, bitterly disappointed that *this* was what he was offering her. No-strings sex. How could she even be surprised?

'"Mistress" is an outdated term,' Luca observed. 'And not one I'm entirely comfortable with.'

'But isn't that what you have? Mistresses?'

'Lovers,' he corrected swiftly. 'And one at a time. You're an independent woman, Hannah. I'm not suggesting I take that away from you.'

'But what are you suggesting? Because I've seen you with other women enough to know what you want.'

Ire flashed briefly in his eyes. 'I had no idea you were so knowledgeable of my desires,' he remarked. 'What is it that you think I want?'

'Availability,' Hannah answered. 'You like your women to drop everything when you crook your little finger. Yet at the same time you like them not to fuss when you don't reciprocate.'

'I'm a busy man.'

'And I'm a busy woman,' Hannah snapped.

Luca raised his eyebrows in eloquent disbelief. 'Is that your only reservation? Because I feel quite confident that we can work something out.'

'I bet you do.'

'Why are you so offended?'

'Because I don't want to be your bit on the side,' Hannah cried, rising from the sofa and pacing the confines of the room in her agitation. 'I don't want to be *anyone's* bit on the side.'

'You wouldn't be. To say that is to suggest I'd be entertaining other women at the same time, and I assure you I am always faithful to my current partner.'

'Oh, well, then.' Hannah rolled her eyes. '*That's* a relief.'

Luca pressed his lips together. 'What, exactly, is your objection?'

Hannah stared at him, knowing she was being emotional and unreasonable. This offer was *exactly* the sort of thing she should have expected from Luca. It was what she'd been contemplating herself over that fateful weekend. So why was she acting all outraged now?

With a sigh Hannah ceased her pacing and sat back down on the sofa. 'I'm sorry, Luca, but I find everything about your offer objectionable. It's tempting, of course it is, because you're right. I am attracted to you, very much so, and it's hard to ignore that.'

Luca's eyes glittered starkly in his set expression. 'Then don't.'

'But I don't want an affair,' Hannah explained, even

though at the moment she was questioning her own sanity at turning down the most desirable and compelling man she'd ever known. 'At least, I don't want *just* an affair.'

'Ah.' Comprehension dawned on Luca's features and his lips gave a cynical twist. 'So that really was a "maybe".'

Hannah laughed sadly. 'I suppose it was.' She took a deep breath, needing to explain herself further. 'I know what it's like when a man wants you to simply slot into his life, and that's not what a relationship is about.'

'The boyfriend of six years ago?'

'Yes.'

'But you miss him.'

'Yes, although it isn't as simple as that. But a relationship, for me, is give and take. Wanting to be with a person no matter what comes your way, not only in a set of circumstances arranged to your liking. And frankly, Luca, I don't want to be dropped when you've burned through this thing between us.'

Luca's mouth quirked upwards even as his eyes remained hard. 'Maybe I'd be the one to be dropped.'

'Considering how quickly you've worked through women, I think that's unlikely,' Hannah answered. 'You're only the second man I've ever been with. Perhaps I'm responding more emotionally because of that. But the answer has to be no, Luca.' Her heart twisted in protest but Hannah remained firm. 'I want more from a relationship, if I ever choose to have one. I'm not even sure I would. It *is* risky. We both know that. You clearly don't want to take the risk and I'm not sure I do, either.'

'So you want more than I'm offering, except you're not even sure you'd be willing to risk it?' Luca surmised tersely. 'You can't have it both ways, Hannah.'

'I'm not having it any way,' Hannah answered with wry sorrow. 'But I'm definitely not interested in the kind of arrangement you're suggesting.' She took a deep breath and squared her shoulders. 'It's not for me.' Even though it hurt, more than she'd ever admit, to turn him, and her only offer of happiness and companionship, down.

It wouldn't end well, she knew that. She'd start to care too much and Luca would get bored with her. He'd treat her like any of his other women and that would shatter her confidence and break her heart. It was better this way, to end it before it began, even if it felt as if she were being torn in two.

Luca stared at her for a long moment. 'If you're sure,' he said quietly.

'I'm not sure,' Hannah admitted on a despondent laugh. She couldn't keep the yearning from her voice or the desire from pooling inside her. 'All you'd have to do is touch me, Luca,' she admitted, and she knew she wasn't warning him; she was asking him.

Knew Luca realised it as well as heat flared in his eyes, turning them nearly black, as he eased off his chair, coming to kneel before her. She could see the light glinting on the blue-black strands of his hair and wonderingly she reached out and touched the rough-smooth stubble on his jaw. She shouldn't do this. She really shouldn't do this, and yet she *had* to.

'Hannah, do you *know* what you do to me?' he breathed.

'Tell me,' Hannah answered. She felt transfixed, almost drugged, by the desire that stole through her veins at the mere thought of Luca touching her. Wanting her.

'You drive me crazy,' Luca muttered as his hands slid under her hair, cradling her face and tilting her towards him so their lips were a whisper apart. 'You make me lose my mind. All I've been thinking about for the last week is this.' And then he kissed hers, his lips slanting across hers in blatant, primal possession.

Hannah opened herself up to his kiss, yielding everything under the delicious onslaught of his mouth and hands, her body arching towards his as her hands tangled in his hair.

'How can you say no to this?' Luca demanded as he slid his hands under her hoodie, his bare palms cupping her breasts, the friction of skin on skin making her shudder with longing.

'I'm not saying no, am I?' she muttered thickly as Luca tugged the zipper down her hoodie.

'Don't ever say no,' Luca commanded as he pulled her hoodie off. 'I can't bear it. Don't ever say no to me, Hannah.'

Hannah knew she was powerless to say anything at that moment. Her hands roved greedily over his chest, tugging his shirt out of his trousers, for she longed to feel his skin against hers. With a groan Luca tore at his shirt and Hannah was about to tug her own shirt over her head when some distant, desire-fogged part of her brain registered the creak on the stair.

Her hands stilled and Luca glanced at her, his breathing ragged, a question in his eyes.

No, Hannah thought. *No, please...*

The door creaked open. 'Mummy...?'

CHAPTER THIRTEEN

LUCA FROZE AT the same moment that Hannah frantically pushed her T-shirt down and scrambled up from the sofa. He turned, his whole being numb with shock, as she went to the sleepy little boy standing in the doorway. *Her son.*

'Hello, sweetheart.' Hannah scooped up the boy in her arm, nuzzling her cheek against his hair even as she shot Luca a nervous look. 'You're meant to be asleep.'

'I had a bad dream.'

'Let me tuck you back up in bed, Jamie.'

Jamie. So this was the man in her life. He realised he'd stopped wondering who Jamie was, mainly because he'd been so consumed by his desire for Hannah. Now the realisation slammed into him with the force of a sledgehammer, leaving him winded and reeling.

Jamie's eyes rounded as he looked directly at Luca. 'Who's that, Mummy?'

'The man I work for, Jamie. He…he was just here for a meeting.' She shot Luca another look, almost as if she were angry with him. And shouldn't he be the one to be angry? He was the one who had been duped, deceived…

A *son.* Why had Hannah never told him she had a child?

With Jamie cuddled in her arms, Hannah turned towards Luca. 'You can see yourself out…?'

Luca gazed at her for a tense moment. 'I'll wait here,' he answered coolly.

He was questioning that decision when Hannah disappeared upstairs to settle her son, and he was left alone with the ferment of his own thoughts. Hannah had a child. In light of this new information his suggestion of an affair seemed sordid and distasteful.

A *mother* wasn't going to drop everything to parade about in sexy lingerie in the penthouse suite of the next up-and-coming five-star hotel. He might not have outlined his proposal in such vivid detail, but Hannah knew him well enough to understand what he'd had in mind. Sex, uncomplicated and available, without questions, demands, or prevarications. That was how he'd conducted all his affairs. It was what he'd been aiming for with Hannah.

No wonder she'd rejected him.

With a groan of frustration Luca sank onto the sofa. His mind was spinning with this new information. He had no idea what to do with it, but he knew he was angry that Hannah had kept it from him.

He heard the creak of the stairs and then the door opened. He looked up and saw Hannah looking calm and determined, her face pale.

'Why didn't you tell me?' he demanded in a low voice.

'You have no right to know anything about my personal life.'

He jerked back, stung by this biting assessment. 'Didn't this last weekend give me some right?'

Her chin lifted a fraction and she remained by the door, her arms folded, her look haughty. 'Honestly? No.'

Luca suppressed the angry retort he wanted to make. If he calmed down for a second, he could acknowledge that she had a point. He'd dismissed their encounter out of hand last weekend. The fact that she wasn't falling in with his plans now was a source of frustration and disappointment, but it didn't mean she'd been duplicitous or unreasonable. Betrayal couldn't be involved when there had been no relationship to begin with.

He just *felt* betrayed.

'Tell me about him,' he said.

Hannah's eyebrows rose. 'Why, Luca? There's nothing between us. I think it's better if we try to—'

'Humour me.' He cut her off, his teeth gritted.

She stared at him for a long moment, and then finally, thankfully, she unbent. She dropped her haughty stance and came to sit across from him. 'What do you want to know?'

'How old is he?'

'Five.'

'His father?'

'The man I told you about.'

'Your boyfriend? You weren't married?' He heard the prudish censure in his voice and inwardly winced.

'No, we weren't married,' Hannah answered evenly, 'although I think we would have got married if he hadn't died.'

'How did he die?'

'A motorcycle accident.' She pressed her lips together. 'Why do you want to know all this now?'

'I don't know,' he admitted. 'This blindsided me, Hannah. Everything about you has blindsided me, since we first landed on Santa Nicola.'

'Are you regretting ever introducing me as your fiancée?' Hannah asked with a weary laugh. She looked sad, and that made him feel sad. His earlier determination to make her his mistress—and, yes, he would use that word—felt as if it had happened to a different man. Been intended for a different woman.

In truth, though, he didn't regret anything about the

weekend on Santa Nicola. He didn't regret getting to know Hannah, or experiencing the wonder of her body. He just wanted more.

But not that much more.

'So why didn't you ever mention you had a child?' he asked after a moment. 'It's kind of a big thing. Most employers know such details about their employees.'

'You're not most employers, Luca. You never asked.'

'I assumed you were single.'

'I *am* single.'

'And childless,' he clarified. 'If you'd had a child, I would have expected you to mention it.'

She folded her arms, her stance turning defensive again. 'Well, I didn't. I like to keep my personal life private. And frankly, I suspected you wouldn't be thrilled to know I had such a demand on my time. Executive assistants are expected to drop everything for work.'

'And you did drop everything, on many occasions,' Luca observed. 'Who had Jamie?' It felt strange to say the boy's name.

Hannah's mouth tightened. 'My mother.'

'So she lives nearby?'

'Yes.'

Which was why she'd been here the night he'd dropped her off after their shopping and dinner. He sat back, still absorbing all the implications of what he'd discovered.

'Are you asking all these questions as my employer,' Hannah asked slowly, 'or something else?'

Surprised, Luca jerked his gaze to Hannah's. And realised he didn't know the answer to that question. 'I'm just surprised,' he said gruffly, knowing that was no answer at all.

'Well, now you know the truth. And I can assure you, it won't affect my work. It never has.'

Luca thought of the all-nighters and weekends they'd

worked together, suppressing a stab of angry guilt at the realisation. She should have told him she had a child at home who needed her care. He would have made provisions.

Maybe. Or maybe he would have informed her that she really wasn't suited to the demands of the role.

'I should go,' he said, rising from his chair. Hannah watched him, a look of sadness on her face that he didn't understand. *She* was the one who had rejected him. Not that he'd have made that offer if he'd *known*...

'I'll see you tomorrow,' he said and with a brusque nod of farewell he stalked out of the room.

Hannah spent a sleepless night wondering if she should have done things differently. Maybe if she'd been upfront about Jamie from the beginning, or at least from last weekend, Luca wouldn't have made his offer of an arrangement. Maybe he would have tried for something more.

Or maybe he would have run a million miles in the opposite direction. She'd known all along that Luca wasn't dad material. She'd known full well he wasn't interested in a relationship. Her stupid, stubborn heart had insisted on feeling differently, but it didn't change facts.

Rejecting Luca's proposal of an affair made her realise just how much more she wanted—if she dared. Not just with anyone, but with him. With Luca, a man whose heart was clearly off limits.

At least, Hannah reflected, the knowledge of her son would probably put Luca right off her. And, God willing, her attraction to him would fade when it wasn't reciprocated. That was a relief, even if it didn't feel like one.

Her heart couldn't be that broken, considering how quickly things had progressed between them. A little dented maybe, but she'd survived much worse before, and she would again. It really was better this way.

She was still giving herself this pep talk when she dropped Jamie off at school, mentally kicking herself when she saw that his class was having a bake sale and she was the only mother who hadn't brought in a home-made tray bake.

'Didn't you read the letter we sent home?' the teacher asked, her concerned tone still managing to hold a note of reproach.

'I must have forgotten,' Hannah said. She turned to Jamie, who was watching the parade of parents with their offerings of baked goods with a stoic expression that strangely reminded her of Luca. 'Sorry, sweetheart.'

Her little man squared his shoulders. 'It's okay.'

But it wasn't. She tried not to drop the ball like this, but occasionally it happened. Hannah supposed she could excuse herself considering all the distractions she'd had, but she still felt guilty for not putting Jamie first even in such a small matter.

She rang her mother on the way to work, hating to call in yet another favour but also wanting to please her son, asking if Diane could run something in that morning.

'Oh, Hannah, I'm sorry,' her mother said. 'I'm volunteering at the day centre today. I would otherwise...'

'Of course.' Her mother volunteered several times a week with a centre for elderly people and Hannah knew she enjoyed the work. It wasn't fair of her to call her mother away from her own life. 'Don't worry, it's not a big deal,' she said as brightly as she could. And then spent half an hour on the Tube battling a crushing sense of guilt.

She supposed she could blame Luca for this, for questioning her choices, but Hannah was honest enough to admit, at least to herself, that she'd always struggled with working mother's remorse. It might not have been fair or reasonable, but she felt it all the same.

Luca was shut away in his office when Hannah arrived,

and so she got right down to work, trying to push away all the distracting thoughts and worries that circled her mind.

Luca came to discuss some travel arrangements about an hour later, and she instinctively tensed as he approached her desk. She felt both weary and wired, but at least it kept her from shaming herself with an obvious physical response to his presence.

'What's wrong?' he asked after she'd taken down some dates for a trip he was planning to Asia next month.

'What do you mean?' she asked, startled. 'Nothing's wrong.'

'You look worried.' His whisky-brown gaze swept over her as he cocked his head. 'Is it Jamie?'

Hannah stared at him, dumbfounded. 'You've never asked me that before.'

'I never knew you had a child before.'

'Yes, but…' She shook her head, more confused than ever. 'If you had known, you would have been annoyed that I seemed worried and distracted while at work. Not…'

'Not what?' Luca prompted, his gaze locked on hers.

'Not concerned.'

'Perhaps you don't know me as well as you thought you did.'

'Perhaps I don't.' She had thought she knew what kind of man he was. But that had been a week ago, and everything had changed since then.

'So is it your son?' Luca asked. 'That's worrying you?'

Still surprised by his perception as well as his interest, Hannah relented. 'Yes, but it's only a small thing.'

'What?'

'I forgot his class had a bake sale today. Everyone brought in biscuits and cakes, lovely home-made ones, except for me.' She shook her head, almost wanting to laugh at the bemused look on Luca's face. This was so outside his zones of both familiarity and comfort. 'I told you it was a small thing.'

Luca didn't answer for a moment. Hannah sighed and turned back to the notes she'd been making. Clearly she hadn't advanced the cause of working mothers through this exchange.

'So,' Luca said slowly, 'Jamie is the only child in the class without cakes or biscuits?'

'Yes, but it doesn't really matter—'

'It does matter,' Luca stated definitively. 'Let me make a few calls.'

Hannah stared at him in stunned disbelief as he went back into his office. Not knowing what else to do, she got on with making his travel arrangements. Fifteen minutes later, Luca reappeared.

'Come on,' he said. 'My limo is waiting downstairs.'

'Your limo—where are we going?'

'To your son's school.'

'What—?'

'He can't be the only one without cakes,' Luca stated, and stabbed the button for the lift.

Hannah had no choice but to grab her handbag and coat and follow him into the lift. 'Luca, what are you doing? He can manage—'

'But why should he, when I can do something about it?'

'I could have done something,' Hannah muttered. 'Couriered a cake to the school—' Now she felt even more guilt.

'We'll do better than that,' Luca announced. 'We'll deliver them in person.'

The cakes turned out to be forty-eight of the most glorious creations from a nearby exclusive patisserie. Hannah peeked into the white cake box and her jaw dropped at the berries glistening like jewels in folds of perfectly whipped cream.

'These are amazing,' she told Luca. 'And they must have cost—'

'It was no trouble.'

Hannah closed the cake box. 'I'll pay.'

'You will not,' Luca returned swiftly. 'This is my gift. Do not presume to take it from me, Hannah.'

She shook her head slowly, overwhelmed but also befuddled by his generosity. 'I really don't understand you. Last night you seemed angry…'

'I was surprised,' he corrected. 'And I don't deal well with surprises.'

'And now?'

'Now I want to help.'

'But you don't even like children,' Hannah burst out.

Luca glanced at her, affronted. 'Why would you think that?'

'Maybe because you had to make me masquerade as your fiancée to impress a self-proclaimed family man?' Hannah returned dryly. 'Just a thought.'

'Just because I don't want children myself it doesn't mean I don't like them.'

'But why don't you want them, if you like them? Most people do.'

Luca was silent for a long moment, his gaze hooded, his jaw bunched tight. Hannah held her breath as she waited; she realised she really wanted to know the answer.

'I told you it wasn't worth it,' he finally said.

'But what does that even mean—?'

'Since you partially agreed with me, what do you think it meant?' he shot back, his eyes glittering.

Hannah considered the question for a moment. 'It means that you're scared of getting hurt,' she said quietly. 'Afraid of someone leaving you, or stopping to love you. Of loving someone causing you pain rather than joy.'

She held Luca's gaze, willing him to answer, to admit

the truth. 'Well, then,' he said, breaking their locked gazes as he looked out of the window. 'Then you know why.'

Hannah was silent, struggling with her own emotions as well as Luca's. 'It sounds very lonely,' she said finally.

Luca shrugged, his gaze still averted. 'I'm used to being alone.'

She remembered what he'd said on the beach, how he'd felt alone all the time. 'You don't even want to try?' she asked, her voice squeezed from her throat. She didn't know when the conversation had gone from the abstract to the personal, but she knew she was asking him more—and revealing more herself—than just what he thought about relationships in general. She was asking him what he thought about her.

'I don't know if I can,' Luca said in a voice so low Hannah had to strain to hear it.

'You'll never find out if you don't,' Hannah answered and he turned to look at her, his eyes like burning black holes in his tense face.

'That's a very pat answer, and the reality is more complex when there are people involved,' he said. 'Children involved.'

Hannah's breath hitched. She wasn't the only one who had made this conversation intensely personal. 'Luca…'

'If you want to know why I want to help Jamie, it's because I know how he feels,' Luca continued, and her world, which had tilted on its axis for one glorious moment, righted itself with a thud. 'As a child. My mother wasn't often capable of being there for me. Not,' he cut across any protest she'd been going to make, 'that I'm equating you to her. I'm not. I'm quite sure you're a very good mother to your son.'

'Thank you,' Hannah said uncertainly.

'But it doesn't feel good, being the only kid in your class who doesn't have the right kit for PE, or who can't pay for the school dinner. Not that those things happened to Jamie—'

'They happened to you,' Hannah said softly.

'Yes.' Luca's gaze shuttered. 'After my mother died, I had a scholarship to an exclusive boarding school, but it didn't cover everything. I might as well have had "charity orphan" tattooed on my forehead.' He sighed, rolling his shoulders to excise the tension. 'I can relate to feeling left out.'

And the fact that he was doing something about it, trying to make it better for her son, made Hannah's heart feel as if it could burst. Luca was making it very difficult to stop caring about him. One more little act of kindness and she'd be halfway to falling in love with him. More than halfway; she was almost there.

She gave the driver directions to Jamie's school, and the limo pulled up outside the gates while the children were at playtime. They all ran up to the fence, eyes rounded at the sight of the stretch limo. When she and Luca got out, Hannah could hear the whispers running through the huddle of children.

'Isn't that Jamie's mummy—?'

'What is she doing in that fancy car—?'

'That man is so *big*.'

'He's got cakes!'

The whispers turned into excited jabbers as Luca proffered the huge white cake box. 'These are for Jamie Stewart,' he announced in a voice that managed to be both commanding and friendly. 'I heard he needed some cakes for the school bake sale.'

And as the children clambered excitedly around him, Hannah realised that Luca had needed to do this for his sake as much as Jamie's. The knowledge was enough to bring tears to her eyes. After a childhood that had been far too sad and neglected, and an adolescence that hadn't been much better, Luca was finally able to be the boy who had the cakes. Who could make things better.

Jamie beamed at both of them as Luca handed the box into Reception. 'Thank you, Mummy,' he whispered, and threw his arms around her waist, squeezing tight.

Hannah ruffled his baby-soft hair. 'Thank Mr Moretti,' she answered with a smile. 'He was the one who insisted we bring the cakes.'

Jamie turned the full wattage of his smile onto Luca. 'Thank you, Mr Moretti!'

Luca looked startled, and then moved. He nodded once. 'It was my pleasure,' he said gruffly.

They didn't speak as they got back into the limo. Luca looked lost in thought, and Hannah felt as if she might burst into tears. Finally she managed, 'You're a good man, Luca Moretti.'

He turned his startled gaze on her, his expression ironing out to a familiar and heart-sinking blandness. 'You might not think that in a moment.'

'Why not?' Hannah asked, her heart now nearing her toes.

'Because Andrew Tyson emailed me this morning. He wants to have dinner with us tomorrow night.'

CHAPTER FOURTEEN

HANNAH GAZED AT herself in the mirror, frowning at her pale cheeks and sparkling eyes. She felt both terrified and elated at the thought of the evening ahead, posing once again as Luca's loving fiancée, and it showed in her face. She had no idea what to expect of this evening, of Luca. Her hopes careened wildly, and it was impossible to keep a leash on them.

Her mother's eyebrows rose as Hannah appeared in the sitting room. 'This is a business dinner?' she asked sceptically, because the emerald-green satin dress hugged her slender curves lovingly and was a far cry from her usual pencil skirt and silk blouse ensemble. She'd bought it on her lunch break, spending far more on a single garment than she ever had before, and she couldn't make herself regret it.

'It's more of a social occasion,' Hannah hedged.

Her mother's eyebrows rose higher. 'A date?'

'Maybe,' Hannah admitted, and then added hastily, before her mother got completely carried away, 'But probably not.'

Almost certainly not, she reminded herself sternly. No matter how much her stubborn heart couldn't help hoping since she'd seen a softer side of Luca yesterday, Hannah knew tonight was about donning the pretence once more. If

Luca acted lovingly towards her, it was because he needed to convince Andrew Tyson, not because he actually felt something for her. And if he did feel something for her... was she even willing to try? To risk her heart again, to lose someone she loved again?

Because Luca Moretti was a dangerous proposition.

The burden of pretending felt heavier that night than it had over the weekend in Santa Nicola. How was she supposed to pretend to love a man she was afraid she already had those feelings for? She didn't know what part of herself to hide, and what part to reveal. And she didn't like the thought of deceiving Andrew Tyson again, no matter what kind of history existed between him and Luca. The man was kind, with a genuine desire to see a family man take over his resorts. No matter that Luca had a good plan for the resort, lying was still lying.

Despite these concerns, Hannah's insides lit up with excitement when Luca's limo pulled up in front of her house. Jamie was still awake, his face pressed to the glass as he inspected the limo.

'That is a *cool* car.'

'Yes, well.' Hannah kissed her son's cheek. 'Be good for Nana.'

'I will.' His gaze was glued on the limo, and Luca's powerful form as he exited the vehicle and started towards their front door. Hannah's heart flipped over at the sight of him in a grey business suit with a crimson tie. *Why* did she react this way to him, when she'd seen him in such a suit dozens, hundreds of times? Her body didn't care. Everything had changed.

Luca knocked on the door and Jamie raced to open it.

'Jamie—' Hannah began half-heartedly, because she hated to dampen her son's excitement.

'Did you bring me any cakes?' Jamie demanded of Luca, and Hannah put a restraining hand on her son's shoulder.

'Jamie, don't be rude.'

'But of course I did,' Luca answered with an easy smile, and took a perfectly wrapped mini chocolate cake from behind his back. Jamie crowed in delight. 'Share with your grandmother,' Luca advised while Hannah simply stared, dumbfounded.

'What?' he asked as he caught her stunned look. 'Why are you so surprised?'

'I'm just...' Hannah shrugged helplessly. 'I didn't expect you to be so thoughtful.' Towards her son. He was turning all her preconceived notions on their head, and that was dangerous. Her head was counselling her heart to hold back, stop hoping. Meanwhile her heart was doing cartwheels.

'That's quite a backhanded compliment,' Luca remarked. 'But I'll take it.' His heated gaze scorched her for one breathtaking second. 'You look amazing.'

'Thank you.' Hannah's breath dried in her throat. He looked amazing too, his eyes burning almost gold in his bronzed face, his lithe, muscular body encased in a superbly cut suit, every atom of him radiating both beauty and power.

'Enjoy yourself,' Diane said, a knowing twinkle in her eye, and Hannah decided it was time to get themselves out of there, before her mother said—or she did—something revealing.

'Thank you,' she said belatedly, once they were settled in the car. 'For giving Jamie the cake. You're practically spoiling him.'

'I don't mind.' He sat back against the sumptuous leather seat, and Hannah eased away from him a little bit, because the temptation was to snuggle closer.

'So why does Andrew Tyson want to meet us again?' she asked, determined to keep focused on why they were there together.

'I don't know. He simply said he wanted to have dinner with us, to discuss the plans and get to know us better.'

'Get to know us better?' Hannah repeated as alarm bells started clanging. 'But what if he suspects something? We could get tripped up easily enough.'

'Could we?' Luca asked softly. His eyes glittered in the darkness of the car. 'I think we know each other rather well by now.'

Hannah was glad the darkness hid her blush. 'That may be so, but there are still questions he could ask us, about how you proposed—'

'On top of the Eiffel Tower.'

'*Luca.*' Hannah's breath came out in a rush. 'You know what I mean.'

'Yes, I know you're tired of the pretence, just as I am. But tonight will be the last, Hannah. I'm hoping Tyson will announce his intentions for the resorts tonight.' He glanced out of the window. 'I need him to,' he said in a low voice.

Hannah gazed at his tense profile for a few seconds before asking quietly, 'What is the source of the bad blood between you and Tyson, Luca? What happened, that he doesn't even know about it?'

'It was a long time ago.'

'That's not an answer.'

'It's all the answer I'm going to give.' Luca hesitated. 'I'm sorry, Hannah. That part of my life is not up for discussion.'

Luca saw Hannah's expression close up and knew she was hurt that he'd put her off. But how could he admit the truth? He'd already revealed enough about his childhood. He didn't want to invite more pity—or condemnation, for his plans for Tyson. That part of his life wasn't up for discussion, and neither was it negotiable.

And while his plans for revenge remained crystalline

clear, his feelings for Hannah were more confused than ever. He'd surprised himself by going to Jamie's school yesterday, and then buying the boy a cake tonight. Even more unsettling was the excitement he'd felt at seeing Hannah; she looked amazing in the emerald-green dress that clung to her like a second skin and brought out the golden glints in her hair and eyes. His palms itched to smooth over her curves, to tug down the zip and watch the bright, satiny material fall away.

Nothing had dampened his desire for her, not the discovery that she had a son, not the flat refusal of his offer. In fact, both things made him want her more, which was contrary and frustrating. He'd enjoyed seeing her cuddle her son, and witnessing her obvious love for her child made a powerful ache reside inside him, for what he'd missed as a child himself, but also for what he hadn't attempted to have as a man. The fact that she'd refused his sex-only offer made him respect her—more than he respected himself. She wanted more from a relationship. She wasn't afraid to try for it.

But he was.

It was fear, pure and simple, that was keeping him from asking Hannah to have a real relationship. The knowledge was shaming. When had fear ever held him back? He'd brokered huge deals, taking massive business risks. He'd started virtually empty-handed, a twenty-two-year-old fresh out of university with nothing to recommend him but a degree. How could he be afraid now? And not just now, but all along?

He'd thought staying solitary was being strong, but since coming to know Hannah, since witnessing her own particular brand of courage, he wondered if it was actually weakness.

And that thought was the most terrifying of all. Because if he did try just as Hannah had asked him to, if he risked

himself, heart and soul, what then? What happened if—
when—Hannah walked away from him?

The limo pulled up in front of the upscale restaurant
Tyson had suggested for their meeting. Luca glanced at
Hannah, the lights from the streets washing over her pale,
strained features. She wasn't looking forward to pretending again, and, God knew, he wasn't either.

'Hannah.' He rested a hand over hers, savouring the
warmth of her skin, the comfort of the contact. 'I promise this is the last time. We won't have to pretend again,
ever, no matter what.'

She turned to face him, her eyes huge in her face. 'Do
you really mean that?'

'Yes.'

'What if Tyson asks for another meeting? What if he
wants us to come to the opening of the resorts?'

'He won't,' Luca stated flatly and Hannah shook her
head, her expression turning wild.

'But don't you see, Luca? The pretence never ends. He
might be expecting an invitation to our wedding—'

'He won't. And in a few weeks or months, we can quietly announce our broken engagement.'

'Oh.' She sat back against the seat as if she'd been
winded. 'I see. So I'm thrown over for the next supermodel?'

'I never suggested such a thing,' Luca returned sharply.
'We can make it a mutual decision, or you can be the one to
throw me over. I deserve it, after all I've put you through.'
And yet the thought made everything inside him clench in
denial. They were talking about a fake engagement and yet
he still felt rejected. Because he didn't want to end things
with Hannah. Not yet. Not until…when?

He knew he was being ridiculous. It was better to be
safe than sorry. Better to be alone and strong than brokenhearted and weak. He'd *lived* by that. He'd built his life on
that knowledge. He couldn't change now.

Could he?

'We should go in,' Hannah said tiredly as she reached for the door handle. She turned her face from him, and Luca felt the loss.

The excitement Hannah had felt at spending the evening with Luca had fizzled out. She felt tired and sad and strangely empty, and the prospect of pretending for several hours filled her with despair. She didn't want this. She wanted Luca to love her for real. She wanted to be honest about her feelings, not play this wretched game—and for what? A business deal that was practically pocket change to a man like Luca?

He hadn't wanted to tell her about his history with Tyson, and his flat, final tone had made her afraid to push. Luca had made it clear she had no rights in his life, even if she wanted them.

The restaurant was quiet and elegant, with each table afforded maximum privacy. Waiters moved discreetly around the room with its frescoed walls and plush carpeting, and the only sound was the tinkle of expensive crystal and silver, the low murmur of conversation.

The understated ambiance reminded Hannah poignantly of that first dinner she'd had with Luca, when he'd bought her clothes and she'd felt gauche and unsure and yet also excited. Before everything had begun. It hadn't even been two weeks ago, and yet it felt like a lifetime. She felt like a different person, one who had lived and loved and lost.

Hannah told herself she was being melodramatic. Two weeks. You couldn't fall in love with someone in two weeks, especially when you hadn't even been looking for love in the first place.

But you've known him for three years.

'Luca, Hannah.' Andrew Tyson's melodious voice floated out to them as he stood up at the private table he'd reserved for them in a corner of the restaurant. 'So nice to see you again.'

Luca's arm snaked around her waist and he drew her close enough so their hips nudged. Heat stroked along Hannah's veins at the contact. The attraction she felt for Luca was as potent as ever.

Tyson stuck out his hand for Luca to shake and after the tiniest pause Luca shook it. 'Andrew.' His voice was even, businesslike without being friendly.

Tyson kissed Hannah's cheek and then they all sat down while he had the waiter bring them a bottle of the restaurant's best champagne.

'To celebrate your engagement,' he said with a smile. 'Among other things. Have you set a date?'

Hannah snuck a glance at Luca, waiting for his cue, and watched as he smiled easily. 'In the summer. You always hear talk of June weddings.'

June? That was only two months away. Hannah schooled her face into a smile as Tyson turned to her. 'Will that give you enough time to plan, Hannah?'

'Oh, I think so.' Her smile felt as if it were stretching like a rubber band across her face, ready to snap. 'With Luca's contacts, things can happen quite quickly.'

'Oh, I'm sure.' Andrew gazed at them both speculatively, and Hannah tensed, wondering if he suspected. What if Daniela had whispered something into his ear? Then his face relaxed and the waiter popped the cork on the champagne, and then Andrew raised his glass of bubbly in a toast.

'To marriage,' he said. 'And family. And true love, of course.'

'To all three,' Hannah said as gamely as she could, and they clinked glasses.

'Are you planning on having a family?' Andrew asked. 'I know that's a personal question, but—'

'We both want children,' Luca cut in swiftly. 'Two or three, at least. I prefer an even number.'

'Why not four, then?' Hannah suggested a bit tartly. This from the man who had told her less than an hour ago that he didn't want children at all.

Luca slid her a burning glance. 'Four it is, then.'

And just like that she imagined a dark-haired baby in her arms, a toddler on Luca's shoulders, which was idiotic. This was *pretend*.

'Good thing they come one at a time,' Andrew said with a laugh. 'Generally speaking.'

They ordered their food then, and Hannah tried to relax. Tried not to take every smiling glance or casual caress that Luca gave her like a dagger to the heart, but they hurt all the same. Because he was only acting for Andrew Tyson's sake, and yet no amount of reminders could keep her body from responding, her heart from yearning.

When he held her hand throughout the first course, and gave her a bite of his dessert as he smiled into her eyes, and referenced an in-joke she hadn't even known they'd had…all of it made her feel a potent, impossible mixture of hope and despair. This wasn't real, she knew that, and yet it *felt* real. She wanted it to be real.

By the end of the evening her nerves were well and truly frayed. Andrew had remained jovial, Luca loving. Hannah had been the only one who had seemed to feel the strain.

As they were settling the bill she excused herself to go to the ladies'. She needed a break from the play-acting. In the bathroom mirror her face looked pale, her eyes too dark. She touched up her make-up and tried to find a smile. Not much longer now, a thought that brought both relief and disappointment. As soon as they left the restaurant, would Luca revert to his normal, businesslike self?

Luca and Tyson were shaking hands as she came out of the bathroom. 'I'll be in touch soon,' Tyson promised.

'Has he not told you for certain yet?' Hannah asked as they left the restaurant for the waiting limo. Luca opened the door for her before sliding in beside her.

'Not yet, but I think it's almost certain.'

'Why did he want to see us?'

'To make sure he's making the right decision, I suppose.'

The limo pulled away from the kerb and in the wash of streetlights Hannah saw the lines of tension bracketing Luca's mouth and eyes.

'At least it's over,' she said quietly.

He glanced at her, a frown pulling his eyebrows together. 'You didn't enjoy it.'

It was a statement, and one Hannah couldn't contradict, at least not completely. 'I'm tired of pretending,' she said. 'You know that.' But that wasn't the whole truth, and the events of the evening, as well as the past couple of weeks, compelled her to continue. 'But it's not just that. I don't like pretending, Luca. With you.' She took a deep breath and turned away so he couldn't see the tears sparkling on her lashes. 'It hurts.'

Luca was silent for so long Hannah was afraid she'd appalled him with her honesty, and yet she felt too sad to be embarrassed. This hurt past mere humiliation.

'Hannah.' He cupped her cheek in his palm, turning her face so she was looking at him. He caught the tear trembling on her lash with his thumb. 'Don't cry. I can't stand it if you cry.' His other hand came up to cup her face, and his voice came out on a groan. 'I can't stand the thought of hurting you,' he said, and then he kissed her.

CHAPTER FIFTEEN

Luca's lips crashed down on Hannah's and it felt like coming home. Her mouth opened under his and her hands clutched his lapels. He heard her soft moan and it incited him further. He wanted her. He *needed* her.

'Luca…' she muttered and he pulled her to him, his hands sliding over the slippery satin, anchoring on her hips, wanting to keep her as close as possible.

She pressed against him, the softest part of her arching against him so he could barely restrain himself from peeling her dress away from her body and burying himself inside her warmth.

The limo began to slow to a stop and with a gasp Hannah pulled back, her face flushed, her lips swollen.

'I'm home…'

'This is home,' Luca growled, and pulled her towards him. She came willingly, melting into him, her lips finding his as she rubbed against him.

'I can't, Luca,' she mumbled but then let out a breathy sigh as his hand cupped her breast.

'You really can.'

She laughed shakily. 'Is this really a good idea?' She pulled back again, and even in the darkness of the limo he saw the unhappy confusion in her eyes.

Luca took a deep breath, willing the fire in his body to fade. 'It seems like a very good idea to me.'

'I still don't want a fling, Luca.'

He glanced away, feeling cornered and yet knowing it was unfair. Just because Hannah didn't want what he did...

And hell if he actually knew what he wanted.

'Couldn't we just take one day at a time?' he asked. 'And see what happens?'

Hannah stilled and he turned to face her. She looked delectable, half-sprawled on his lap, her hair falling down from its chignon, her eyes bright and luminous, rosy lips parted.

'What exactly are you saying?'

'That I don't want to lose you. But I don't know how much I have to give.'

She let out a trembling laugh. 'That's honest, I suppose.'

'Most people don't start a relationship promising for ever,' Luca said gruffly.

Hannah's gaze sharpened. 'Is that what you're suggesting? A relationship, rather than a fling?'

'Yes.' The word came reluctantly, and Hannah could tell. She laughed again, the sound one of both sorrow and hope.

'Well?' Luca asked. 'What about it?'

'One day at a time?' she said slowly, and Luca nodded, holding his breath, amazed at how much this meant to him. How much he needed her to say yes.

A slow, shy smile bloomed across her lovely face. 'Sounds pretty good to me.'

The next morning, as she headed into work, Hannah was fizzing with both anticipation and anxiety. She couldn't wait to see Luca, but she was afraid he might have changed his mind. Afraid that one day at a time might mean one day, full stop. Last night, in the darkness of the limo, after the intensity of their charade for Tyson and then that passionate, overwhelming kiss, maybe Luca had said things he regretted in the cold light of morning.

Her doubts were swept away when Luca strode into the office and, going right to her desk, pulled her towards him for a thorough kiss.

'Good thing no one else is on this floor,' Hannah exclaimed, her lips buzzing, when he'd finally released her. 'What if someone saw?'

'No one did,' he returned before heading into his office. Hannah sat down at her desk, her lips buzzing, her heart singing with joy.

She told herself to slow down, to take one day at a time just as Luca had said, because neither of them had any idea what tomorrow could bring. But her mind and heart both went leaping ahead anyway. Seemed as soon as she'd got over the anxiety of actually starting a relationship she went tumbling in, head-and-heart-first.

Luca asked her to spend Saturday with him—the day with Jamie and the night the two of them alone. Both prospects filled Hannah with both excitement and nervousness. Introducing her son properly to Luca was a big step—and as for the night...

She just felt excitement about that.

Luca had asked her what kinds of things Jamie liked to do, and she'd told him the usual five-year-old-boy pursuits: the park, the zoo, football. 'And he's mad about planes,' she'd confided. 'We always go outside to look at them heading for Heathrow.'

Luca had typed it all into his smartphone, looking as serious as he did when conducting a million-pound business deal. Hannah's heart had ached with love.

Yes, she was falling in love with this man, and it was happening so hard and fast it scared her. Luca might not be keeping up. In fact, she was quite sure he wasn't. Every interaction that didn't have his hands on her body and his mouth on hers was difficult for him, the words stilted but sincere. He was trying, but it was hard. And maybe one day, even one day soon, it would become too hard.

But in the meantime…

She would do as Luca said and enjoy each day as it came. She knew she couldn't stop herself from falling in love with Luca, even when her mother worried about her, even when she stared at her son's sleeping face and wondered if she was setting everyone up for a catastrophic fall. She knew what it was like to love and lose. She didn't want that to happen again, no matter what she'd told Luca about wanting to try.

Saturday dawned sunny and warm, a perfect spring day that felt like a promise. Luca picked them up not in his usual limo, but in a flashy sports convertible that Hannah had never seen before. Jamie leapt up and down with excitement at the prospect of travelling in such a vehicle; Luca had even gone to the trouble of installing an appropriate car seat.

'It's perfectly safe,' he told Hannah, even though she hadn't said anything. 'I can see the worry in your eyes. But this car has been crash-tested in all sorts of situations.'

'Is it yours?'

'Yes, although I don't drive it as often as I could. I usually prefer to be driven, and use the time to work.'

'You do have an admirable work ethic,' Hannah said with a smile. She buckled Jamie into his seat. 'So where are we going?'

Luca waggled his eyebrows. 'You'll see.'

She smiled, enjoying seeing this lighter side to the man she loved. 'It's a surprise?'

'Yep.'

The surprise turned out to be a visit to a private airfield, with Jamie being allowed to scramble in and out of planes, from private jets to a retired fighter plane, culminating in a helicopter ride over London. Jamie's eyes were huge as he pressed his face to the window and Luca pointed out the London Eye, Big Ben. Hannah's heart felt so full she couldn't keep from grinning. From squeezing Luca's hand the whole ride, simply because she needed to show him how much he meant to her.

They had a luxurious picnic lunch that Luca had arranged on a field overlooking the planes, and as Jamie cavorted around, running off his excess energy, Hannah turned to Luca and put her hand over his.

'Thank you. This day has been amazing. Jamie will remember it for ever.' She squeezed his hand. 'But, you know, the park or the zoo would have been fine, too.'

'I know not every day can be like this,' Luca admitted wryly. 'But I suppose I wanted to make a good first impression.'

'Trust me, you'd already done that with the cakes.' She paused, her hand still over his, longing to know more about this man her heart had already yielded to. 'How is it you grew up with so little and yet now you have so much?'

Luca shrugged. 'Hard work, a lot of determination, and a good dose of luck.'

'Where did you grow up?' Hannah asked. 'I'm ashamed to admit I don't even know.'

'A small village in Sicily.' Luca's expression closed, and Hannah knew this had to be hard for him. 'My mother was unwed when she had me, and in that kind of remote, traditional community we both suffered badly, albeit in different ways.'

'Oh, Luca, I'm sorry.' Now she understood why he'd asked if she'd been married when she'd had Jamie.

'It made me determined to escape.'

'And foster care? Was that hard?'

He shrugged, the negligent movement belying the deep emotion she saw fermenting in his eyes. 'It was what it was. A home for orphan boys in rural Sicily—what do you expect? But I had a good teacher and he encouraged me to apply for a scholarship. From there I went to university, and when I was twenty-two I bought my first property, a falling-down building in one of the worst districts in Naples.'

'And what did you do with it?' she asked, intrigued.

'I developed it into a halfway house for homeless teens and sold it to the government.'

'You've never forgotten your roots,' Hannah said slowly. She'd known that Luca had been committed to certain principles in all of his property deals. She just hadn't understood what had motivated him.

'I never have,' Luca agreed, his voice going a bit flat. 'And I never will.' His tone had turned ruthless, almost menacing, and it made Hannah afraid to ask any more questions. In any case, Luca asked one instead. 'Tell me about Jamie's father.'

Hannah tensed even though she knew he had a right to ask the question. 'What about him?'

'Did you love him?'

'Yes, but it feels a long time ago now.'

'You told me you knew what it felt like for someone to expect you to slot in his life.'

Hannah sighed. 'Yes, that was what Ben expected, and I didn't realise it until I stopped.'

'What do you mean?'

She hesitated, not wanting to access all these old memories yet accepting that Luca had a right to the truth. 'I met Ben while in college. He had dreams of travelling afterwards, seeing the world. When we'd started dating we planned this carefree life, traipsing around Europe and Asia, taking jobs as we could, living totally free.'

Luca studied her, his gaze both serious and intent. 'And then what happened?'

'And then I fell pregnant. Accidentally. And I realised

that I wanted to keep the baby, that Ben's dreams of travelling the world weren't really my dreams, even though I'd convinced myself they were. I'd never been anywhere, as you know, and I liked the idea of an adventure. I just liked the idea of a bigger adventure, of being a mother, better. I couldn't turn away from that.'

'And how did... Ben react?'

'He wasn't pleased, to say the least. He was furious with me, and he demanded I have an abortion.' She tucked her knees up to her chest, resting her chin on top as she recalled that last, awful confrontation, felt the ensuing, needling guilt. 'I could sympathise with him a little, because I'd done a complete about-face, and now wanted something we'd both agreed to *not* wanting, at least not for a long while.' She paused, her gaze unfocused as she recalled Ben's parting words. *I'll damn well go alone, then.*

'Hannah?' Luca's voice was gentle, breaking into her unhappy thoughts. He squeezed her fingers. 'What happened?'

'We had a huge row. He said he was going to travel anyway, and leave me behind. And then he stormed out and jumped onto his motorcycle, and twenty minutes later crashed into a lorry. He died instantly.' She raised her eyes, giving Luca a sorrowful smile. 'I've chosen to believe that he might have come round. He was shocked, and understandably so, and he always did have a temper. And I felt terribly guilty, still do really, for yelling right back at him. But he would have come round. He wouldn't have left me or our child, not if he had a choice.' Luca didn't answer and Hannah let out a wobbly laugh. 'You probably don't believe that. And maybe he wouldn't have, but I don't want Jamie to know that about his father. You're actually the only person I've told.'

'Not even your mother...?'

'I didn't want her to think badly of Jamie's father...and I

felt guilty for my part in the whole mess.' She sighed. 'But it did make me realise what I wanted a relationship to be, and it's not simply wanting to be with someone when they go along with your plans. It's wanting to be with someone *whatever* the plans. Because plans fall apart. People change. I've learned that lesson more than once.'

Luca turned her hand over, stroking her palm with his thumb. 'So have I.'

'I don't want to rush you,' Hannah blurted. 'I know this is new…for both of us. But with Jamie involved…'

'I understand.'

'It can't all be fancy cakes and helicopter rides.'

'I know.' Luca's expression turned distant. 'But I can't help but want to give Jamie some of the things I never had.' He gave her a quick, reassuring smile. 'I won't spoil him, I promise.'

'I know you won't. I can't believe we're even talking about this. You've exceeded my expectations in so many ways,' she admitted with a laugh. 'I should have told you I had a child ages ago.'

'I would have reacted differently,' Luca said sombrely. 'You've changed me, Hannah.'

Her heart lifted and she lifted his hand to her mouth to press a kiss to his palm. 'Not too much, though. Because I like you the way you are.'

'Just enough,' Luca assured her, and then leaned across to kiss her tenderly.

Jamie fell asleep on the way back home, and Luca carried him inside to a waiting Diane.

'Have fun,' Diane said, kissing her daughter on the cheek, and then Hannah was back in the sports car with Luca driving to his flat in Mayfair.

She'd never been to his home before, had no idea what to expect. She'd been touched that Luca had wanted to bring her there, and not to some anonymous luxury hotel. He was inviting her into his life in so many ways.

As excited as she was to be alone with Luca, she was also incredibly nervous. The last and only time they'd made love it had been hurried and desperate, a moment of passion neither of them had been expecting. Tonight would be completely different…a deliberate coming together and giving of themselves. Hannah didn't want to disappoint him.

'I feel a little nervous,' she admitted after Luca had parked the car in the underground garage and they were riding up the lift to his penthouse flat.

'Nervous? Why?'

'Because this is different. What if…what if I'm not good enough?'

Luca's eyebrows rose nearly to his hairline. 'Trust me, Hannah, you're more than good enough. I feel like I've been waiting for this night for most of my life.'

She smiled tremulously, pleased by his words but not quite sure if she could believe them. Luca had had dozens, hundreds of women, and was the most powerful, compelling, and attractive man she'd ever met.

And what was she? A single mum with stretchmarks and a B-cup bra size.

The doors of the lift opened directly onto his flat, a single open space with a soaring ceiling and panoramic views of the city. Hannah stepped out onto the marble parquet floor, her heart making its way up to her mouth.

Luca stepped behind her and rested his hands on her shoulders. 'Hannah. Trust me. I want to be with you more than I've wanted to be with anyone in my life.' Gently he brushed her hair aside to kiss the curve of her shoulder, his lips lingering on her skin so a shudder ran through her body.

'I feel the same way,' she whispered, because how could

she not? Luca was amazing. He'd blown her world clean apart.

'Good,' Luca said gruffly, and slid his arms around her waist, drawing her back to rest against the hard wall of his chest. She could already feel his arousal, felt an answering desire race through her veins, pool between her thighs.

'I brought lingerie,' she told him on a shaky breath. 'But I don't know if I want to wait long enough to put it on, just so you can take it off again.'

'I don't,' Luca answered in a growl. 'Save it for another night.' He spun her around, his hands delving into her hair as his mouth found purchase. Hannah returned the kiss, revelling in it, in him, in the freedom and luxury of the whole evening ahead of them.

Still kissing her, Luca backed her towards his bedroom, separated from the living area by linen-covered screens. The bedroom contained nothing but a massive bed, the navy silk duvet stretched invitingly across. With a little smile Luca pushed her back onto it, and then covered her body with his own.

They kissed and kissed, legs and limbs tangling, hands smoothing over every body part they could find. Laughing, both of them, breathless with anticipation and joy.

After a few frenzied moments Luca rolled away, his breath ragged. 'We don't need to rush.'

'I rather feel like rushing,' Hannah admitted. Every part of her ached with the need for Luca to touch her, and, more than that, to feel that glorious sense of completion and unity she'd felt before.

'Well,' Luca answered as he rolled back to rest lightly on top of her. 'You can't always have everything you want.' He popped the button on her jeans and ran his hand lightly over her belly. 'Sometimes you have to be patient.'

'Are you going to teach me, then?' Hannah asked, her

breath coming out in a shudder as Luca tugged down her zip.

'If I can,' he admitted and pressed a kiss to her belly. 'If I can be patient myself. I want you so very much, Hannah.'

His heartfelt words made her heart sing even as his hands made her body burn. He stripped off her clothes and then it was her turn to unbutton his shirt, tug down his jeans. She ran her hands over the sculpted muscles she'd only glimpsed in the dark.

'You really are the most beautiful man. It's most unfair,' she complained laughingly.

'Unfair? Do you really want to look like me?'

She curled a hand around his impressive biceps as his mouth dipped to her breasts. 'No,' she confessed breathlessly, 'but sometimes I feel like an ugly duckling to your swan.'

Luca lifted his head, his gaze locking on hers. 'Hannah, you're beautiful.'

'To you, maybe, but from a purely objective—'

'To me, yes. Completely to me.' He brushed the hair away from her face and pressed a gentle kiss to her lips before saying, 'I can't be objective when it comes to you. All I see is a woman who makes me burn. Who cares what anyone else thinks?'

'When you put it like that…' Hannah said, her laugh turning to a gasp as Luca's mouth moved lower.

She writhed underneath his sure and knowing touch as he used his mouth and hands on her most sensitive places. Arched her hips, inviting him to a deeper caress and then sighing with both satisfaction and need as he took her up on her blatant offer.

And she touched him, revelling in the hard planes of his chest, the sharp curve of his hip, and the pulsing strength of his arousal.

Luca groaned as she wrapped her hand around him. 'You're going to kill me.'

'But you'll die happy,' Hannah teased.

Then, finally, he was moving inside her, her body stretching to accommodate him, her eyes widening as she felt him in her deepest part. She wrapped her legs around his waist, her hands clutching his shoulders as he began to move and she matched his rhythm.

'Luca…'

She closed her eyes as she surrendered herself to the wave of pleasure they were both riding to the crest, until Luca touched her cheek and whispered raggedly, 'Look at me, Hannah. I want to see you as I make love to you. I want you to see me.'

Hannah opened her eyes to see Luca gazing at her with burning need, and that blazing look was what had her tumbling over the edge of that wave, until they were both lost in pleasure.

Afterwards they lay in a tangle of limbs and covers, their heart rates slowing as their breathing settled. Hannah stretched and then snuggled into Luca, his arm coming around her shoulders. She felt sated and happy, her body nearly boneless.

She smoothed her hand down Luca's chest, enjoying the liberty of touching him. Her hand drifted lower and he caught it in his.

'Give me a few minutes, at least,' he murmured, and she laughed softly. 'Vixen,' he teased, and pressed a kiss to her hair.

'I like taking one day at a time,' Hannah told him lazily. 'And one night at a time.'

'Glad to hear it.'

'It's funny to think that if you hadn't needed a fake fiancée we wouldn't be here like this.' She'd meant to tease but she felt Luca tense next to her. She rolled onto her side, her hair brushing his chest as she looked at him. His expression was bland, and she'd learned how he used that to hide his true, deeper feelings. 'Luca? What is the history between you and Tyson?'

'I told you before, it happened a long time ago.'

'But it matters,' Hannah said quietly. 'It certainly mattered to you during that weekend. And yet he doesn't even know...how can that be?'

'Leave it, Hannah.'

She recoiled at the taut note of warning in his voice. She'd thought they'd moved past that kind of thing. She'd thought they'd been opening up to each other. She'd certainly told Luca more about herself than she had anyone else.

'Why can't you tell me about it?' she asked, and Luca rolled off the bed so he was sitting on the edge, his back to her.

'Because it's not important.'

Hannah knew she shouldn't push. She might be risking everything they'd only just started to build, and yet...what *had* they built, if they couldn't talk about this?

She took a deep breath. 'It is important, but you obviously don't want to tell me.' She waited for something from Luca, but he didn't reply.

CHAPTER SIXTEEN

'ANDREW TYSON FOR you on line one.'

Hannah's deliberately neutral voice made Luca grimace. They'd managed to get beyond that awkward moment on Saturday night, when she'd asked about Tyson and he hadn't given her any answers, but only just.

Part of him had wanted to admit to her what Tyson was to him, but he'd held back out of instinct, not willing to part with that painful information yet. Not wanting to be so exposed. Now he wondered if he should have, because once the deal was signed Hannah would know his plans for the resorts. And what would she think then?

It didn't matter. This had nothing to do with Hannah. What they had together was sacred, and what had happened with Tyson had no part in that.

Realising he was keeping Tyson waiting, Luca picked up the phone.

'Moretti here.'

'Luca.' Tyson's voice oozed genial warmth, making Luca flinch. Tyson had turned away from him once before, utterly and without any remorse. The fact that he was friendly now, not knowing who Luca really was, made his kindness grate.

'Hello, Andrew.' He managed to keep his tone neutral. When he'd decided to go after Tyson's resorts, he hadn't considered the impact of dealing with the man himself. He'd told himself he didn't care, that he felt nothing for the man who'd fathered him, the man he'd seen only once. Even if the scent of lilies still made him retch. Every interaction with the man showed those assertions for the lies they were.

'I have good news for you, Luca,' Andrew said. 'And I'm sure you know what it is.'

'I believe I do.' Luca listened as Andrew outlined the deal he'd been waiting for: a takeover of the Tyson resorts.

'Because,' Andrew finished, 'if I can't have one of my own children running the place, I'd like to have you.' A sentiment that nearly made Luca choke.

They finished the conversation with plans to finalise the paperwork next week, when Tyson was in London. Luca put down the phone and stared vacantly out of the window at the busy streets far below, the sky cloudless and blue above.

Distantly he registered a tap at the door, and then the sound of it opening. 'Luca?' Hannah asked, her expression wary. 'That was Andrew Tyson, wasn't it? Did he give you an answer?'

'Yes.' Luca forced himself to face Hannah and smile. 'He's accepted my bid.'

Hannah's answering smile morphed into an uncertain frown. 'But...aren't you happy?'

Was he happy? He'd been happy this last week with Hannah. As for Tyson... He didn't feel the satisfaction, the triumph and the sense of retribution that he'd thought he'd feel upon owning his father's business. When it came to Tyson, he felt...empty.

'Luca?' Hannah asked softly. She walked towards him, laying a hand on his arm. 'I wish you'd tell me what was wrong.'

This was the time to tell her about Tyson. To tell her the truth. Luca gazed up into Hannah's voice, saw the concern and care shining in her eyes, and his throat closed.

'Nothing's wrong,' he said gruffly, the words squeezed out of his too-tight throat. The smile on his face felt plastic and he reached for her so she couldn't see how fake it was. 'Nothing's wrong at all.'

He didn't think he'd fooled her because she just frowned before kissing him gently on the lips, making Luca feel as if something inside him were breaking.

'I've got a good idea,' he said afterwards, his arms still around her. 'I have a boring black-tie dinner tonight that I was thinking of skipping. Why don't we go to it together instead?'

Hannah pulled away from him so she could study his face. 'You mean…as a couple?'

'Yes, that's exactly what I mean. I've become part of your world, but you haven't yet become part of mine.'

Tremulous hope lit her eyes even as she frowned uncertainly. 'I don't have anything to wear.'

'Hmm, your last evening gown didn't survive the trip, did it?' Luca teased. 'I think it's time for another visit to Diavola.' Hannah didn't light up at this prospect as he'd expected her to. 'What? You don't want to buy a new dress?'

'You'd be buying the dress,' Hannah replied. 'And I don't want to be treated like your mistress.'

Luca suppressed a sigh. 'So am I never allowed to buy you things? It's as much, if not more, of a pleasure for me, Hannah.'

She chewed her lip, clearly torn. 'I don't know,' she admitted. 'But I don't want to be treated like one of your women.'

'You aren't.' Luca's lips twisted in wry self-deprecation. 'I never even spent the entire night with a woman before you, Hannah. Not that I want to admit that, but you're different. I'm different when I'm with you.'

She studied him for a moment, a faint frown creasing her forehead, and Luca could practically read the thoughts going through her mind. *How different are you, really? Why won't you tell me about Tyson?*

She didn't say any of it though, just smiled and kissed him. 'I suppose you can buy me a dress.'

Eight hours later Hannah stood next to Luca, sheathed in an elegant Grecian-style gown of ivory silk. She'd had her hair and make-up done at the boutique, and felt every inch the regal princess as Luca introduced her to various acquaintances.

'Ah, so this is your fiancée,' a paunchy man remarked with a sweeping, appreciative gaze for Hannah. She stiffened, as did Luca. Clearly the rumour of their forthcoming nuptials had got around. Had they really thought it wouldn't?

'When is the date, by the way?' the man asked.

'Soon,' Luca answered in a tone that brooked no more questions. The man moved on.

'You must really be starting to regret the whole fake-fiancée thing,' Hannah murmured.

Luca shot her a swift, searching look. 'I don't regret anything, because it brought us together. But I'll be glad to put it behind us.'

But would it ever be behind them? This was the danger of taking one day at a time, Hannah acknowledged bleakly. You never knew what was lurking just ahead.

She still felt worried that Luca might tire of her or of the whole 'happy families' routine he'd entered into with such surprising enthusiasm. Maybe she—and Jamie—were nothing more than a novelty.

And maybe she needed to choose to believe what Luca said, that he was different, that he did care. Maybe she needed to believe in him. She'd made that choice with Ben after he'd died, when it had been too late. She'd decided to believe the best would have happened, even if they'd never got the chance to see it become a reality.

Now she needed to believe the best *could* happen, that Luca could be the man he wanted to be. That she could help him be that man. They just needed time.

They didn't leave the reception until after midnight, and Hannah's feet ached in the silver stilettos Luca had bought her to go with the dress.

'You were magnificent,' he said as he opened the door to the limo waiting at the kerb.

'I liked being by your side even if it all felt a bit grand for me,' Hannah admitted.

Once inside the limo Luca reached for her hand. 'Stay the night?'

Guilt and temptation warred within her. 'I can't,' she said regretfully. 'I've been away too much as it is.'

Luca didn't answer, just played with her fingers, his head lowered. Hannah resisted the impulse to apologise. Luca knew what he was taking on. Her responsibility for Jamie was part of the package, and she wouldn't say sorry for that.

'I don't want to be apart from you,' Luca said finally.

Hannah's heart lifted at this admission. 'You could stay with me,' she suggested tentatively.

Luca lifted his head. 'What about Jamie?'

'What about him?' She smiled teasingly. 'He has his own bedroom, you know.'

'You don't mind me being there? When he wakes up, I mean?'

'I don't think Jamie's old enough to realise exactly what it means,' Hannah returned. 'But even a five-year-old will get the message that you're an important part of our lives.' She hesitated, feeling as if she had one foot poised over a precipice. 'And you are, Luca.' He didn't respond and she couldn't keep herself from rushing in with caveats. 'I mean, I know it's happened so quickly and we're taking one day at a time...'

'Hannah.' Luca took her face in his hands and kissed her lips. 'You don't need to say things like that. You're an important part of my life.' He paused. 'The most important part.'

Relief rushed through her even as doubts niggled at her mind. If she was the most important part, why wasn't he being more open? Why didn't she feel as if she could totally trust him?

Time, she reminded herself. It would come with time.

'Let's go home,' Luca said, and leaned forward to tell his driver where to go.

Back at her house, Hannah tiptoed upstairs, Luca behind her. Her mother had left with a smile on her face, glad to see Hannah finally finding some happiness.

Her bedroom felt small and shabby compared to Luca's glorious open-plan penthouse, but he assured her he didn't mind as he framed her face with his hands.

'All I want is you. One day you will believe that.'

'Why don't you keep trying to convince me?' Hannah murmured, and Luca did just that.

They'd made love many times since that first unexpected encounter on the beach, and yet Hannah never tired of the feel of Luca's body against hers, inside her. Now, as he slid inside her and filled her up, he looked in her eyes, his body shuddering with the effort of holding back.

'I love you,' he said, his voice ragged with emotion, and Hannah blinked back tears.

'I love you too,' she whispered, wrapping her arms around him, and Luca began to move.

Afterwards they lay together, silent and happy, needing no words.

'You sign the contract for the Tyson resorts next week,'

Hannah said as she ran a hand down his chest, loving the play of his muscles under her palm.

Luca wrapped his hand around her own. 'Yes.'

'Maybe we could go there one day, the three of us,' Hannah said. 'I'd love to see how you implement all your ideas.'

Luca didn't answer and Hannah wondered if she'd presumed too much. Talking about anything to do with the resorts felt fraught. Then he rolled over and drew her tightly into his arms, his head buried in her shoulder as a shudder went through his body. Surprised and unsettled, she returned the embrace. Luca didn't say anything, and Hannah could only wonder what emotion gripped him. She decided not to ask; it was enough he was sharing this with her, and she knew some things went too deep for words.

A week later Luca shook hands with Tyson for the last time as the contracts were signed and witnessed. Tyson's resorts were officially his.

'I look forward to seeing you implement your plans,' Tyson told him as he closed his briefcase. 'I was deeply impressed by your ethos.'

Luca smiled tightly and said nothing. He told himself that he wouldn't feel so flat and empty once he'd put his plans in motion. Once he'd taken from Tyson what the older man had refused him all along, he'd finally sense that satisfaction that had eluded him. The justice that he had deserved for his whole life.

'Stephen mentioned that you looked familiar,' Tyson remarked as he shrugged on his coat. 'But we hadn't met before Santa Nicola, had we?'

Words bubbled in Luca's throat, thick with rage and remembrance. He remembered staring into Tyson's face, those faded brown eyes flat and hard. *You will leave here. Now.*

A push at the small of the back, the overpowering stench

of lilies from the vase in the foyer. Then a door closed in his face.

'No,' he said coolly. 'We haven't.'

After Tyson had left, Luca looked down at the contract with the signatures boldly scrawled. For a moment he imagined what Hannah had suggested last week: the Tyson resorts as he'd proposed them to be, a holiday with her and Jamie. The family life he'd never had, the *happiness* he'd never had. He had a diamond ring in his jacket pocket he was intending to give to Hannah that evening. A whole life about to unfold, a life he now realised he wanted desperately.

Then Luca's jaw hardened and his fist clenched. It couldn't be that simple, that easy for Tyson. He wouldn't let it be. He'd been waiting for this, working for this, his whole life. Justice would be had. How could he hold up his head otherwise? How could he let go of the one thing that had driven his ambition, his whole life?

Grimly focused, Luca reached for his phone. It was time to make a few calls.

Hannah was humming as she stepped onto the Tube. She'd been humming or smiling or practically prancing down the street for over two weeks now, ever since she and Luca had started a real relationship. Ever since it had felt as if her life had finally begun.

Already her mind was jumping ahead to scenarios she wouldn't have dreamt of a month ago. Images of frothy wedding dresses and newborn babies, a house in the country, a whole life unfolding that she knew she wanted desperately—with Luca.

Her mother had cautioned her to slow down, and Hannah had tried, but it was hard when she was so happy, and Luca seemed so happy as well. He was a changed man just as he'd told her, and she needed to believe in that. Trust in his love for her and not let the small things worry her. If Luca still harboured secrets, he would tell her in his own time. She simply needed to be patient.

Her unfocused gaze skimmed across the train car of commuters on smartphones or reading newspapers. Some distant part of her brain clanged in alarm and she tensed, her gaze moving back to a headline she'd only dimly registered in the newspaper across from her. It was the business section, and in big black letters it blared *Tyson Resorts to Close*.

She leaned forward, sure it must be misinformation, and made out the first words of the news story.

In a shock move by real-estate tycoon and property developer Luca Moretti, the newly acquired Tyson Resorts, a chain of six family-orientated vacation spots, are set to close—effective immediately. When contacted, Moretti gave no comment.

Hannah sat back, her mind a welter of confusion. It couldn't be right. The newspaper must have got it wrong, or was attempting to stir up trouble. Luca wasn't going to close the resorts. He was going to turn them into something wonderful. She'd seen the plans herself.

Despite these reassurances a sense of foreboding dogged Hannah as she made her way into the Moretti Enterprises building and up to the penthouse. She'd known Luca was hiding something, something that tormented him. Had seen how affected he'd been on Santa Nicola, having to leave the table after Tyson's toast. She'd tried to find out what was going on but she'd been afraid to press too hard. But maybe she should have. Maybe she should have seen this coming.

The reception area was empty as the lift doors opened onto the penthouse floor, but Hannah could see the lights in Luca's office were on. She dropped her bag and coat on her desk and went straight to his door.

'Come in,' he called at her knock.

Hannah opened the door, her heart starting to thud. Luca sat at his desk, his gaze on his computer screen. He glanced up at Hannah as she came in, a smile transforming his features even as the expression in his eyes remained guarded.

'Good morning.' His voice was low and honeyed and it made both heat and hope unfurl inside her. Here was the man she knew, the man she loved. He would explain everything to her now. He *had* to.

'I read the most ridiculous thing in the newspaper this morning,' she said, and Luca stilled.

'Oh?'

'Yes, in the business section. It said that you were going to close the Tyson resorts, effective immediately.' She waited for his disbelieving laugh. Willed him to rise from his desk and take her in his arms. She needed to believe this wasn't true, that Luca was the man she'd thought he was. He didn't move. 'Luca?' she asked, her voice starting to wobble. 'It's not true, is it? I mean…it can't be true.' Silence stretched and spun out, started to snap. *'Luca.'*

'It is true,' he said finally, his voice flat. 'I'm closing the resorts.'

'Why?' she cried. 'After all your plans…' She snagged at a fragile thread of hope and pulled. 'Is something wrong with them? Did you discover something—the buildings need to be condemned, or—?'

'No.' Luca snipped off that thread with a single word. 'Nothing's wrong with them besides being a bit shabby.' He took a deep breath and laid his hands flat on his desk, his gaze direct and cold and yet somehow also vulnerable. 'The truth is, Hannah, it was always my intention to close them.'

CHAPTER SEVENTEEN

LUCA STARED AT Hannah's shocked and lovely face and wondered at the wisdom in telling her this much truth. But how could he have avoided it? She would have found out about his plans at some point. He'd accepted that he needed to come clean, but he'd been delaying the revelation because he'd known instinctively that Hannah wouldn't like it.

'This decision has nothing to do with us,' he stated.

She shook her head slowly, her face pale, her eyes wide and dark. 'What does it have to do with, then?'

'With Tyson and me. That's it. Old history.'

'So this is revenge,' she said, realisation dawning in her face. Slowly she made her way to the chair in front of his desk and sat down with a thud. 'It was always about revenge.'

'Justice,' Luca corrected. His hands clenched into fists on top of his desk and he forced himself to flatten them out. 'This is about justice, Hannah. It always was.'

'Justice for whom? For what? What did Andrew Tyson ever do to you, Luca, that he doesn't even know about?'

Luca stared at her for a long moment, his jaw clenched so hard it ached. 'He fathered me,' he stated flatly.

Hannah jerked back with surprise. *'Fathered...'* She shook her head slowly. 'I don't understand.'

'My mother was a chambermaid at his resort in Sicily.

He seduced her and then, when she fell pregnant, he promised to marry her. She went back to her home village with her head held high, certain that he'd come for her like he said he would.'

Hannah's face looked pale and waxy with shock. 'And he never did…?'

'No. My mother waited for him for six years. Six *years.* All the while insisting he would come. At first she told me there were letters. Promises. And then nothing.' His throat worked and he swallowed down the lump that had formed there. 'Do you know what it's like to grow up in a place like that as a bastard? My mother was branded a whore, and I was no better. Everyone made our lives a misery, and we couldn't escape. My mother had no money and she was still waiting for Andrew Tyson to ride in like a white knight on his charger.' Bitterness surged through him, bile rising in his throat, and he rose from the desk and paced the room, unable to keep still.

'What happened after six years?' Hannah asked quietly.

Memories jangled and clanged in Luca's mind, an unholy cacophony of unhappiness. 'My mother decided to find him. She discovered when he was going to be back in Sicily, and she went to his house in Palermo. Took me with her.' He closed his eyes against the tidal rush of pain.

'So you saw him? You met him?'

'"Met" may be stretching things,' Luca returned, his voice sharp and hard, cutting. 'We stood in his doorway while he told us to get out. He didn't even let my mother tell him my name. He never looked me in the eye. Just pushed me right out the door and told us never to come back.'

'No…'

Luca's eyes snapped open. 'You think I'm lying?'

'No, of course not,' Hannah whispered. 'It's just so terrible to think a man like him would do that.'

'A man like him? Do you even know who he is? That

kindly-old-man shtick he's got going? It's a *lie*. I know who he is, Hannah. I've always known who he is.'

Hannah was silent for a moment, struggling with her own emotions just as Luca was struggling with his. He felt so angry, so raw and wounded, and he hated it. He wanted to lash out to cover his pain, and he only just kept himself from it.

'So all this time you've been waiting to get back at him? To take his resorts, his life's work, and ruin it all?'

Luca stared at her in disbelief, even as realisation crystal lised inside him. She was taking Tyson's side. Of course she was. His whole life he'd been the interloper, the un-wanted. Nothing had ever changed that.

'Yes, that's exactly what I've been doing,' he said, his voice hard. 'That's exactly what I've wanted to do since I was five years old. There were lilies in his foyer, when my mother took me there.' He didn't know why he told her that; maybe he wanted her to understand how much that encounter had affected him. 'Even now the smell makes me retch.'

Her face started to crumple. 'Oh, Luca.'

Luca took a step away. 'Don't. Don't pity me. I just want you to understand.' He took a deep, jagged breath. 'This doesn't have to change anything between us, Hannah. I still love you.' He reached into his pocket, his hand closing over the little black velvet box, its presence reassuring him.

But Hannah was shaking her head, her eyes swimming with tears. Luca felt the bottom of his stomach drop out; it felt as if his empty insides had been suddenly filled with ice water. Hannah was looking at him as if she didn't love him, as if she didn't even know him.

'Hannah…'

'Do you know,' she asked quietly, a jagged edge to her voice, 'why Andrew Tyson built so much into these family resorts? Why his son is a doctor and his daughter a pharmaceutical researcher?'

Luca stared at her, his eyes narrowed. 'No, and I don't care.'

'Because his youngest child died of leukaemia when she was only four years old. And they all responded to her death in different ways.' Hannah gazed at him, her face full of pain, a tear splashing onto her cheek. 'Your half-sister, Luca.'

'Don't.'

'I made a choice a long time ago, when my father died,' she continued as she sniffed back her tears. 'I wasn't going to be angry with him for leaving my mother and me virtually destitute. I accepted that he had no idea he was going to have a heart attack at only forty-two, that he would have provided for us if he could have.'

'And you think Tyson is the same?' Luca surmised incredulously. 'You think he would have provided for my mother and me, if he could have? Because what I saw then was a choice, very clearly made, to get us the hell out of his life.'

'And when Ben didn't want our baby,' Hannah continued over him, 'when he screamed at me to get rid of it and walked out of my life, I made a choice to believe he would have come back when he'd cooled down. He would have married me.' Luca shook his head. He could see where she was going with this, and he didn't buy it. Not for Tyson. Not for him.

'Maybe you think I'm naïve,' Hannah stated with quiet dignity. 'Stupidly optimistic. And maybe my father wouldn't have provided for us. Maybe Ben really would have chucked me over for the carefree life he wanted. But I didn't believe otherwise for their sakes, Luca. I believed it for mine.' He stared at her, uncomprehending, a muscle ticcing in his jaw. 'I didn't want to be consumed by bitterness and anger. I wanted to live my life free and forgiving. I wanted to make different choices, *right* choices, and not be bound and ensnared by the past. And I want the same for you.'

'It's different.' He could barely squeeze the words out from his constricted throat.

'It feels different,' Hannah allowed. 'It always does. But think about what you're doing, Luca. Those resorts employ hundreds and maybe even thousands of innocent people. They could revitalise the economy of so many deprived places—you know what it's like from your childhood, don't you, to live near luxury but never be a part of it? You wanted to change that. Those plans for the resort came from your heart, your soul. They showed me the man I fell in love with.'

Luca let out a hard, disbelieving laugh. 'You fell in love with me because of some real-estate plans?'

'Partly. I fell in love with a man who had vision and hope.' She took a deep breath. 'Not a man bent on revenge.'

Luca stared at her, feeling sick. 'So you're giving me an ultimatum.'

'I'm asking you not to do this,' Hannah cried, her hands stretched out to him. 'Not for Tyson's sake or all the employees' sake, but for your own. Don't let the past define you, Luca. Don't let revenge guide you.'

Luca was silent for a long moment, struggling with all the emotions he felt. Anger, that it had come to this, and fear, that he was losing her, and underneath all that a deep-seated certainty that Hannah would have left him at some point anyway. 'So what are you saying, Hannah? That if I go through this you'll leave me?' He took the velvet jewellery box out of his pocket and tossed it on the desk. 'I was planning to give you that tonight. I want to marry you, Hannah.'

Pain flashed across her features. As far as a proposal

went, Luca knew it was terrible, but he felt too cornered to care. Too hurt.

Hannah's expression smoothed out and she picked up the box, snapped it open. She stared at the ring nestled inside, a diamond with sapphires on either side, for a long moment. 'It's beautiful,' she said, and then she closed the box and put it back on the desk. Luca watched, saying nothing, not trusting himself to speak.

'I love you, Luca,' Hannah said. 'But I can't marry you. Not if you're going to be consumed by revenge and hatred and bitterness. I feel for you,' she continued, tears trickling down her face, making him ache to comfort her, even now. 'I grieve for you and the hard childhood you had. Part of me wants to punch Andrew Tyson in the face.' She gave him a wobbly, heartbreaking smile. 'But this level of revenge? This depth of hatred? I can't have that in my life. I can't have that in my son's life. And I don't want it in your life.' She took a deep breath, not bothering to swipe at the tears that trickled down her cheeks unchecked. 'You're a better man than this, Luca. You're a good man. A great one, and I love you so much it hurts. But I can't...' Her voice choked, the last of her composure slipping away. 'I can't,' she managed on a half sob, and turned quickly and ran from the room.

Hannah wiped the tears from her face as she grabbed her bag and coat. She couldn't stay here. She couldn't bear to be so close to Luca and yet feel so agonisingly far away from him.

How could she not have known?

She'd known something was off with the whole deal. She should have asked him more about the history between him and Tyson; she should have tried to make it better. If only she could have done something before they'd reached this awful point, with Luca bent on revenge and her heart breaking.

Even through her agony she knew she'd made the right decision. She couldn't be with someone who was so bent on revenge. It would twist their entire relationship, their whole future, out of shape. And yet right now the shape she was in was broken, shattered into a million desolate pieces.

Hannah stumbled into the lift and then out of the office building, at a loss as to where to go or what to do. Her whole life was in tatters. Her job, her love, all her hopes…

For a second she wondered if she'd been unfair to Luca. God knew she understood how hurting he had to be. And yet he'd been so angry and cold, so determined not to give up on his plan for revenge. How could she cope with that? How could she compete with it?

Tears starting afresh, Hannah walked numbly down the street, going nowhere.

Luca stood completely still for a good five minutes, the silence of the office and the emptiness of his own heart reverberating around him. Then the pain rushed in and he bent over, breathing hard, as if he'd just been punched in the gut. He felt as if he had. He felt as if he'd had a dagger directly to his heart.

Hannah had left him. Hadn't he been waiting for this, secretly? Hadn't he feared that she wouldn't stick around, because nobody ever had? He'd told her relationships weren't worth the risk. He'd told her he wanted to try. And he *had* tried, and he'd failed.

Fury bubbled through him, adding to the pain and grief. Hannah had no right to judge him, no call whatsoever to make demands. She had no idea what he'd been through, what it felt like to be pushed out of Tyson's house, cut out of his life. He wasn't motivated by revenge so much as by justice. Why couldn't Hannah have seen that? Why had she ruined everything, simply because of a business deal?

Frustrated, furious, Luca spun away from his desk, paced his office like the cage it had become. His office phone buzzed and he waited for Hannah to answer it before he remembered that she was gone. He thought about ignoring the call but then decided he shouldn't. He wasn't going to change one iota of his life, damn it, not for anyone or anything.

Grabbing the phone, he bit out a terse greeting.

The building's receptionist answered imperviously. 'Andrew Tyson is in the foyer, requesting to see you.'

'Tyson?' Luca demanded in disbelief. Had his father come to beg for his precious resorts? Now he could send him away, just as Tyson had once done to him. 'Send him…' he began, and then stopped. Why not see Tyson, acknowledge the defeat in the older man's eyes? Maybe this was the reckoning he needed. Maybe now he would finally find the satisfaction he craved. 'Send him up,' he ordered, and slammed the receiver back in its cradle.

When the lift doors opened and Andrew Tyson emerged, Luca recoiled at how much older the man looked, as if he'd aged ten or even twenty years. He walked slowly, almost shuffling, his shoulders stooped, his head bowed in defeat. And Luca felt no satisfaction.

Andrew lifted his head to gaze straight into Luca's eyes. 'I know who you are,' he said, and he sounded sad.

Luca didn't flinch or look away. 'Do you?' he asked, as if it were a matter of little interest.

'Yes.' Andrew drew a deep breath. 'You're my son.'

Something broke inside Luca at that simple admission, and he resisted it, the feeling that the shell he'd constructed about himself was starting to crack. 'No,' he said. 'I've never been that.'

'You're right.' Andrew moved slowly past him to Luca's private office. After a pause Luca followed him. He found Andrew standing by the floor-to-ceiling window, gazing out at the city streets. 'You've done well for yourself. But I already knew that.'

'No thanks to you.' As soon as he spoke the bitter, childish words he regretted them. 'Why are you here?' he asked. 'And how did you know?'

'I think some part of me suspected all along,' Andrew answered as he turned to face him. 'Some ashamed part of my subconscious.'

Luca's gaze narrowed, his lips compressed. 'Ashamed?'

'I've always been ashamed of the way I treated you, Luca,' Andrew said quietly.

Rage spiked so hard and fast Luca struggled to frame a response. 'You say that now? Thirty years later? You've been *ashamed*?' His voice rang out, angry and, worse, agonised. Andrew bowed his head, a supplicant.

'I know it doesn't do much good now.'

'It doesn't do *any* good.'

Andrew lifted his head, and with a cold ripple of shock Luca saw that his father's eyes were damp. 'I know. And I'm sorry, which I also know doesn't do any good.' Andrew drew a ragged breath. 'I'm the worst sort of hypocrite, Luca. You were right to close the resorts.'

Luca's jaw dropped. His father thought he was *right*? Where was the savage satisfaction of vengeance now? 'You can't mean that.'

'No?' Andrew lifted shaggy eyebrows, his mouth twisting in a sad parody of a smile. 'You don't think I regret treating you the way I did?'

'No,' Luca gritted. 'I don't. Considering you never once found me in thirty years, never sought out my mother... She killed herself,' he told him, the words raw with pain. 'Did you know? When I was fourteen.'

Andrew's face slackened, his colour turning grey. 'I didn't know that,' he said hoarsely.

'If you regretted turning us away,' Luca asked, 'why did you never come find us?'

'Because I was afraid to,' Andrew admitted starkly. 'When I told Angelina to wait for me, I meant it. I was going to come to her. But then my father was pressuring me to take over the resorts and marry a suitable woman—'

'And my mother wasn't.'

'No,' Andrew said. 'A Sicilian chambermaid? My father would have disowned me.'

'So you disowned us instead.'

'Yes.' Andrew lifted his chin, meeting Luca's gaze squarely. 'I was a coward, Luca. A dishonourable coward.'

'And it never occurred to you that going on to present yourself as a wonderful family man was just a little bit hypocritical?' Luca demanded.

'Yes, of course it did.' Andrew seemed to visibly diminish. 'It occurred to me all the time.'

'Not enough to do anything about it, though.'

'No.' Andrew was silent for a moment. 'I never even knew your name.'

'You never gave my mother the chance to tell you.' Luca could feel his throat thickening with emotion, a telltale sting at the backs of his eyes. 'It helped me, in the end,' he forced out. 'I knew you wouldn't recognise my name.'

Andrew smiled sadly. 'And you didn't think I'd remember you from back then? When you were…five?'

'No, I didn't. Considering you never even looked directly at me.'

'I was a coward, Luca. I admit it fully and freely. I'm sorry.' He paused. 'I know I don't deserve your forgiveness, but I will ask for it.'

The softly spoken words filled Luca with a fresh rage that possessed an intensity akin to sorrow or grief. Perhaps he felt all three. 'My forgiveness?' he repeated hoarsely. 'How do you even dare?'

'You're right,' Andrew said quietly. 'I don't have the right to dare. I shouldn't presume. But in the thirty years since I rejected you, Luca, I've realised how wrong I was. I've loved and lost…even my own child. Another child,' he clarified quickly. 'In addition to you.'

Luca remembered what Hannah had told him, about the daughter who had died of leukaemia. He could not quite frame the words of condolence that bubbled in his throat. Suddenly he felt confused, mired in sadness, the rage trickling away. He didn't understand himself.

'I'll go,' Andrew said, rising from the chair where he'd sat slumped. 'I only came to ask for your forgiveness, and to say I understand why you did what you did. I don't begrudge you anything, Luca.' And with one last tired smile, Andrew left.

Luca stood there for a moment, his mouth agape, his heart thudding and yet also strangely empty. After so many years planning his revenge, so long craving for a blazing moment of justice and vengeance, he got this? Sorrow and forgiveness and no satisfaction whatsoever?

Luca swore aloud. The sting at the backs of his eyes intensified and he closed them, willing it back. Willing it all back. And then he thought of Hannah.

'Where's Luca?'

Jamie's plaintive question was enough to make Hannah swallow back a sob.

'He's not coming tonight, sweetheart.'

In just a few short weeks Luca had become an important, integral part of her son's life. *And hers.* How was she supposed to go on without him?

All day, since leaving Luca's office in a state of numb grief, Hannah had wondered if she'd made a mistake.

Been too harsh. Why hadn't she tried to understand Luca's perspective more? Why hadn't she practised what she'd preached to him and been more forgiving of *him*? She'd told him she'd chosen not to be bitter, but that morning she'd acted bitterly towards him. She'd turned away from him when he might have needed her understanding most.

But he hadn't acted as if he needed her. He'd been iron-hard, refusing to change or even acknowledge that his decision might have been wrong. And to close all the resorts...

Laura Tyson had somehow managed to find Hannah's home number and had called her in tears, begging her to ask Luca to reconsider.

'Why would he do something like that?' she'd said, more sad than angry. 'I don't understand.'

Hannah did, but she couldn't explain it to Laura. That was Luca's prerogative.

'Mummy...?' Jamie took her face in his hands, his gaze serious. 'Are you sad?'

'No,' Hannah assured him, but her voice wobbled. She put her arms around her son and hugged him tightly. At least she had him. She'd always have him, and she'd always put him first. It was small comfort when her heart felt as if it were in pieces on the floor, but she clung to it all the same.

A little while later she put Jamie to bed and then drifted around the downstairs of her house, unable to do anything but wonder and mourn. After an hour of simply staring into space she broke down and called Luca. She'd do what Laura had asked and beg him to reconsider. She'd apologise for her own harshness, even as she recognised that Luca wasn't the kind of man to back down or unbend. But he'd changed... She'd changed him.

Except, to make the decision he had, had he really changed that much, or even at all?

In any case his mobile switched over to voicemail and Hannah disconnected the call without leaving a message, feeling lonelier and more desolate than ever.

A few minutes later a knock sounded on the door, a determined tap-tap that had her heart turning over. It couldn't be Luca, she told herself. She was thinking it might be simply because he was dominating her thoughts. Because she wanted it to be him so badly.

It was most likely her elderly neighbour, Veronica, asking her to open a pickle jar. Sighing, Hannah rose from the sofa. And opened the door to see Luca standing there, just as she'd been hoping he would.

It took her a few seconds for her mind to catch up to her sight. Her mouth gaped as she struggled to find words. Luca found them first.

'May I come in?'

'Yes—' She stepped aside even though she longed to throw herself into his arms. She reminded herself she didn't actually know why he was here.

Luca walked into the sitting room where they had already spent so many enjoyable evenings. It felt like a lifetime ago that he'd first walked into this room, that he'd asked her to be his mistress.

He turned around slowly. Hannah's heart quelled because he didn't look like a man who had made the right decision, who was buoyed by hope. He looked tired and defeated.

'Andrew Tyson came to see me,' he said.

Hannah pressed one hand against her chest, as if she could will her heart to slow. 'And?'

'And he asked for my forgiveness.' Luca let out a harsh laugh and Hannah recoiled. Maybe he hadn't changed, after all.

'And?' she asked softly.

'And I don't know what to do with that.' Luca shook his

head. 'I don't know what to do or how to feel.' His voice broke as he looked at her in genuine confusion and hurt. 'If I let go of my anger, what am I? If I stop seeking justice, what do I do?'

'Oh, Luca.' In that moment Hannah realised this was her second chance as much as it was Luca's. She could offer him the comfort now that she hadn't that morning. She could give him the encouragement to make the right choice instead of judging him for making the wrong one. 'I'm so sorry.'

'Why?' Luca asked, his handsome face filled with a new and unhappy bewilderment. 'What are you sorry for, Hannah? That I didn't get what I wanted? But you didn't want me to get that.'

'I'm sorry because you're hurting,' Hannah answered. 'And I love you and I don't want you to hurt.'

His face twisted. 'Even now, you love me?'

'Yes.' She spoke with such certainty that Luca took a step towards her, his hands outstretched.

'Do you mean that, Hannah? Even though I tried to destroy a man's life? Even though I put hundreds of people out of a job?'

'Even though,' Hannah said quietly. 'I should have been more understanding this morning, Luca, but I still mean what I said. Revenge is a road to self-destruction—'

'I know.' His mouth twisted wryly. 'I think I self-destructed this afternoon. Having Tyson admit everything… He knew I was his son, and he was sorry. He said I was justified in closing the resorts.' He let out a weary laugh. 'Talk about stealing your thunder.'

'And what's left?' Hannah asked softly. 'Without your thunder?'

'Regret. Sorrow.' He stared at her, his eyes burning. 'And love. Regret and sorrow will fade and heal with time, but the love never will. If you can still love me, Hannah…'

Hannah went to him then, arms outstretched, voice cracking. 'You know I do.'

His arms closed around, his face buried in her hair. 'I love you. So much. You gave me something else to live for. Something good.'

'You gave that too, Luca.' She let out a shaky laugh, her voice ragged with tears. 'The last twelve hours have been the longest of my life.' Luca didn't answer, just held her more tightly. And Hannah rested there, content to live in that moment. She wasn't going to press Luca for promises he couldn't give. She wasn't going to ask—

'I'm not going to close the resorts,' Luca said quietly. Hannah eased back to look at his face.

'Is that what you want?'

'It is now. What you said…the way Tyson was…I realised you were right. I would only be hurting—even destroying—myself. And us. And that's the last thing I want, Hannah. I love you too much to throw away both our futures.'

'And I love you,' Hannah answered fiercely.

Luca tipped her head up so his lips could meet hers. 'Then that's all I need,' he said softly.

EPILOGUE

HANNAH OPENED THE French window of the villa and stepped out onto the silky sand. The waves were shooshing gently onto the beach; the sky was a brilliant blue above. Behind her she could hear Jamie scampering around, exclaiming over everything, and Luca's answering chuckle.

They'd arrived at the newly renovated Tyson resort on Tenerife that morning, and Jamie hadn't stopped for a second. Fortunately Luca had the energy to keep up with his newly adopted son.

This was their honeymoon, taken with Jamie after a wedding in London and a weekend just the two of them in Paris. It had been the wedding she'd always wanted, with family and friends and a gorgeous white dress from Diavola. Jamie had been the ring bearer and Andrew Tyson and his family had been among the guests. It had been another step onto the road to both healing and happiness.

The weekend in Paris had been glorious, too. Luca had surprised her by renting out the Eiffel Tower just as she'd dreamed up on Santa Nicola, and they'd danced alone on the terrace with the stars spangled above them, their hearts full to overflowing…just as they were now.

Hannah let out a sigh, the sound replete with both contentment and thankfulness.

'Now, that was quite a sigh, Signora Moretti.' Luca

stepped out onto the sand, standing behind her as he rested his hands on her shoulders.

Hannah leaned her head against the solid wall of his chest. 'It was a happy sound,' she assured him.

'I'm glad to hear it.' Luca slid his arms around her waist. 'Because I'm happy. Happier than I ever thought I had a right to be.'

The last year had been full of blessings and challenges as Luca had reopened the Tyson resorts and made steps to building a relationship with his father as well as being a father to Jamie. They'd become a family, a proper one, strong and loving, and Hannah had hopes that they would add a fourth person to their little tribe before too long.

She'd continued to work for Moretti Enterprises, and to enjoy the challenges of her job, although she'd reduced her hours to spend more time with Jamie. It hadn't always been easy, learning and loving and changing, but it had been wonderful.

Luca tilted her head up to brush her lips in a kiss. 'To think that just over a year ago we were on a beach like this one, but only pretending. Although perhaps not as much as I thought I was.'

Hannah laughed softly. 'Are you rewriting history?'

'No. I think I was taken with you from the moment I saw you try on that dress. It was as if a switch flipped inside me. I started seeing you differently. I started feeling different myself.'

'I did too,' Hannah admitted. 'I was quite annoyed by it, actually.'

Luca laughed at that. 'As long as you're not annoyed now.'

'Annoyed?' Hannah smiled and shook her head. 'No, I'm overwhelmingly happy and thankful that you love me as much as I love you.'

'More,' Luca assured her, and pulled her to him. 'I love you more.'

'I don't think that's possible,' Hannah murmured, her head tilting back as Luca kissed her.

'Then we'll call it even,' Luca murmured, and deepened the kiss.

* * * * *

A SCANDAL
SO SWEET

ANN MAJOR

A special thank you to Stacy Boyd, my editor,
for her patience and brilliance.

A special thank you to Nicole, a fan,
who sent me an e-mail encouraging me
while writing this book.

And a thank you to Ted.

Prologue

A man's life could change in a heartbeat.

Seven days ago Zach Torr had been in the Bahamas, elated to be closing the biggest deal of his career. Then he'd received an emergency call about his uncle.

The one person who'd held Zach's back these past fifteen years was gone.

Now, still dressed in the suit he'd worn to give his uncle's eulogy, Zach stood on the same narrow girder from which his uncle had fallen. He stared fearlessly down at his contractors, bulldozers, generators, cranes and men, big tough men, who appeared smaller than ants in their yellow hard hats sixty-five stories below.

Zach was a tall man with thick black hair and wide shoulders; a man his competitors swore was as ruthless as the fiercest jungle predator. The women he'd left behind agreed, saying he'd walked out on them without ever looking back.

Normally, his eyes were colder than black ice. Today they felt moist and stung. How had Uncle Zachery felt when he'd stood here for the last time?

A shudder went through Zach. Men who walked iron were no less afraid of heights than other men.

The chill breeze buffeting him whipped his tie against his face, almost causing him to step backward. He froze, caught his balance…hissed in a breath. A sneeze or a slip— was that how it had happened? Up here the smallest mistake could be fatal.

Had Uncle Zachery jumped? Been startled by a bird? Been pushed? Suffered a heart attack? Or simply fallen as the fore-man had said? Zach would never know for sure.

As Uncle Zachery's sole heir, Zach had endured several tough interviews with the police.

The newspaper coverage had been more critical of him than usual because he'd stayed in the Bahamas to close the deal before coming home.

He hated the invasion of the limelight, hated being writ-ten about by idiots who went for the jugular with or without the facts.

Because the fact was, for Zach, the world had gone dark after that phone call.

When he'd been nineteen and in trouble with the law for something he hadn't done, Uncle Zachery had come back to Louisiana from the Middle East, where he'd been building a city for a sheik. Uncle Zachery had saved him. If not for his uncle, Zach would still be serving hard time.

Houston-bred, Zach had been cast out of town by his beau-tiful stepmother after his father's death. Her reason—she'd wanted everything. His father had naively assumed she'd be generous with his sixteen-year-old son and had left her his entire fortune.

If it hadn't been for Nick Landry, a rough Louisiana shrimper who'd found Zach in a gutter after he'd been beaten by his stepmother's goons, Zach might not have survived. Nick had taken Zach to his shack in Bonne Terre, Louisiana, where Zach had spent three years.

It was in Bonne Terre where he'd met the girl he'd given his heart and soul to. It was in Bonne Terre where he'd been charged with statutory rape. And it was in Bonne Terre where the girl he'd loved had stood silently by while he was tried and condemned.

Fortunately, that's when Uncle Zachery had returned. He'd discovered his sister-in-law's perfidy, tracked Zach to Louisiana, gone up against the town of Bonne Terre and won. He'd brought Zach back to Houston, educated him and put him to work. With his powerful uncle behind him, Zach had become one of the richest men in America.

His cell phone vibrated. He strode off the girder and to the lift, taking the call as he descended.

To his surprise it was Nick Landry.

"Zach, I feel bad about your uncle, yes. I be calling you to offer my condolences. I read about you in the papers. I be as proud as a papa of your accomplishments, yes."

So many people had called this past week, but this call meant everything. For years, Zach had avoided Nick and anything to do with Bonne Terre, Louisiana, but the warmth in Nick's rough voice cheered him.

"It's good to hear from you."

"I've missed you, yes. And maybe you miss me a little, too? I don't go out in the boat so often now. I tell people it be because the fishin' ain't so good like it used to be, but maybe it's just me and my boat, we're gettin' old."

Zach's eyes burned as he remembered the dark brown waters of the bayou and how he'd loved to watch the herons skim low late in the evening as the mist came up from the swamp.

"I've missed you, too, yes," he said softly. "I didn't know how much—until I heard your voice. It takes me back."

Not all his memories of Bonne Terre were bad.

"So why don't you come to Bonne Terre and see this old man before he falls off his shrimp boat and the crabs eat him?"

"I will."

"We'll go shrimpin' just like old times."

After some quick goodbyes, Zach hung up, feeling better than he had in a week.

Maybe it was time to go back to Bonne Terre.

Then he thought about the Louisiana girl he'd once loved— blonde, blue-eyed, beautiful Summer, with the sweet, innocent face and the big dreams. The girl who'd torn out his heart.

She lived in New York now, a Broadway actress. Unlike him, she was the press's darling. Her pictures were everywhere.

Did she ever come home…to Bonne Terre?

Maybe it was time he found out.

One

Eight Months Later
Bonne Terre, Louisiana

Zach Torr was back in town, stirring up trouble for her, and because he was, a tumult of dark emotions consumed her.

Summer Wallace parked her rental car in front of Gram's rambling, two-story home. Sighing because she dreaded the thought of tangling with her grandmother and her brother over Zach, she took her time gathering her bag, her purse and her briefcase. Then she saw the loose pages of her script on the floorboard and the slim white Bible she kept with her always. Picking them up, she jammed them into her briefcase.

When she finally slammed the door and headed toward the house she saw Silas, Gram's black-and-white cat, napping in the warm shade beneath the crape myrtle.

"You lazy old thing."

A gentle wind swayed in the dogwood and jasmine, carrying with it the steamy, aromatic scent of the pine forest that fringed her grandmother's property. Not that Summer was in the mood to enjoy the lush, verdant, late-August beauty of her childhood home. No, she was walking through the sweltering heat toward a sure argument with Gram. About Zach, of all people.

Fifteen years ago, when she'd run away after her mother's death, she'd felt sure he was out of her life forever.

Then Gram had called a week ago.

It had been late, and Summer had been dead on her feet from workshopping an important new play.

"You'll never guess who's making a big splash here in Bonne Terre, buying up property to develop into a casino," Gram had said in a sly tone.

Gram had a habit of calling late and dropping her little bombs in a seemingly innocent way, so, wary, Summer had sunk into her favorite chair and curled up to await the explosion.

"And who do you think bought the old Thibodeaux place and hired your brother Tuck as his pool boy and all-around gopher?" her grandmother had asked.

Tuck had a job? This should have been good news. Gram had been worried about him after his latest run-in with Sheriff Arcenaux. But somehow Summer had known the news wouldn't be good.

"Okay! *Who?*"

"*Zach* Torr."

Summer had frozen. Her brother, who had poor judgment in nearly every area of his life, could not work for Zach, who couldn't possibly have her family's best interests at heart. Not after what had happened. Not when their names would be forever linked in the eyes of the media and, therefore, the world.

She'd become too famous and he too rich, and their tragic youthful love affair was too juicy. And every time the story was rehashed, it always surprised her how much it still hurt, even though she was seen as the innocent victim and he the villain.

From time to time, she'd read about how hard and cold he was now. She'd never forget the story about how ruthlessly he'd taken revenge on his stepmother.

Any new connection between Zach and her family was a disaster in the making.

"You're not the only former resident of Bonne Terre who's famous, you know."

Summer's breath had caught in her throat as she'd struggled to take the news in.

"Zach's a billionaire now."

Summer had already known that, of course. Everybody knew that.

"Even so, he's not too busy to stop by to play Hearts with an old lady when he's in town...or to tell me how Tuck's doing on the job."

Zach had been taking the time to play cards with Gram? To personally report on Tuck, his pool boy? *This was bad.*

"Gram, he's just trying to get to me."

"Maybe this isn't about you. You two were finished fifteen years ago."

Yes, it had been fifteen years. But it *was* about her. She was sure of it.

Summer had tried to make Gram understand why Tuck had to quit his job, but Gram, who'd been exasperated by all the stunts Tuck had pulled ever since high school, had refused to hear anything against Zach, whom she now saw as her knight in shining armor. Then she'd punched Summer's guilt button.

"You never come home, and Zach's visits are fun. He's awful good with Tuck. Why, the other night he and Nick took Tuck shrimping."

"A billionaire in a shrimp boat?"

"Yes, well he did buy Nick a brand-new boat, and his men are remodeling Nick's shack. And you should see Zach. He's lean and fit and more handsome than ever."

Lean and fit. Rich and handsome. She'd seen his photos in the press and knew just how handsome he was. Oh, why couldn't he be the no-good homeless person her stepfather had predicted he'd be?

"Rich as he is—an old lady like me with a beautiful, unmarried granddaughter can't help wondering why a catch like him is still single."

"Gram! We have a history. An unsavory, scandalous history that I'm sure he wants to forget as much as I do! Not that that's possible when there are always reporters around who love nothing better than to rehash the dirt in celebrities' lives. Don't you see, I can't afford to have anything to do with him."

"No, your stations in life have changed. You're both enormously successful. Your career would threaten most men, but it wouldn't threaten Zach. Whatever happened to letting bygones be bygones?"

"Not possible! He hates me!" *And with good reason.*

"Well, he's never said a word about that scandal or against you. You wouldn't be so dead set against him, either—if you saw him. The townspeople have changed their narrow minds about him. Well, everybody except Thurman."

Thurman was Summer's impossible stepfather.

There was no arguing with Gram. So here Summer was—home in Bonne Terre—to remove Tuck from his job and, by doing so, remove Zach from their lives. She didn't want to confront Zach, and maybe, if she could get through to Tuck and Gram, she wouldn't have to. All it had ever taken for Summer to remember the secrets and heartbreak of her past, and the man who'd caused them, was to visit Gram.

Nothing ever changed in Bonne Terre.

Here, under the ancient cypress trees that edged the bayou,

as she listened to a chorus of late-summer cicadas and endured the stifling heat, the wounds to her soul felt as fresh and raw as they had fifteen years ago.

Unlike Tuck, Summer had been an ambitious teen, one who'd decided that if she couldn't have Zach Torr, she had to forget him and follow her dreams. That's what had been best for everybody.

She'd worked hard in her acting career to get where she was, to prove herself. She was independent. Famous, even. And she was happy. Very happy. So happy she'd braved coming back to Bonne Terre for the first time in two years.

Summer pushed the screen door open and let it bang behind her.

"I'm home!"

Upstairs she heard a stampede of footsteps. "Gram, she's here!"

Yanking earbuds from his ears, Tuck slid down the banister with the exuberance of an overgrown kid. She was about to cry out in fear that he'd slam into the newel post and kill himself, but he hopped off in the nick of time, landing on his feet as deftly as a cat.

"Come here and give me a hug, stranger," she whispered.

Looking sheepish, with his long hair falling over his eyes and his baseball cap on backward, Tuck shyly obliged. But then he pulled away quickly.

"If I didn't know better, I'd say you were even taller," she said."

"No, you're shorter."

"Am not!" she cried.

"God, this place is quiet without you here to fight with."

"I do have a career."

"It must be nice," he muttered. "My famous sister."

"I'm doing what I love, and it's great," she said much too

enthusiastically. "Just great. I'm here to try to teach you about ambition."

"I got a job. Didn't Gram tell you?"

Gram walked into the room and took Summer into her arms before Summer could reply.

"I was wondering what it would take to get my Babygirl home."

"Don't you dare call me that!" Summer smiled, fondly remembering how she used to be embarrassed by the nickname when she was a teenager.

"Set your bag down and then go sit out on the screened porch. Tuck, you join her. I'll bring you something you can't get in that big city of yours, Babygirl—a glass of my delicious, mint-flavored tea."

Summer sighed. "Gram, I don't want you wearing yourself out waiting on us. Tuck, we're going to help her, you hear?"

Tuck, who was lazy by nature, frowned, but since he adored his big sister, he didn't argue. He trailed behind them into the kitchen where he leaned against a wall and watched them do everything.

"At least you're going to carry the tray," Summer ordered as she placed the last tea cup on it.

Tuck grabbed a chocolate-chip cookie instead.

Then the phone rang and he shrugged helplessly before disappearing to answer it.

As Summer took the tray out to the porch and set it on the table, she sank into her favorite rocker, finally taking the time to appreciate the deep solitude of the trees that wrapped around Gram's big old house. In New York or L.A., Summer's phones rang constantly with calls from her agent, producers and directors…and, especially of late, reporters.

She was A-list now, sought after by directors on both coasts. She'd worked hard and was living her dream.

She had it all.

Or so she'd believed. Then her costar and sometimes lover, Edward, had walked out on her. The night their hit play closed, he'd declared to the entire cast that he was through with her. That had been a month ago. Ever since, nosy reporters had been hounding her for the full story, which she still didn't want to share. That night, back in her apartment after the wrap party, she'd tried to tell herself that Edward's departure hadn't made her painfully aware of how empty her personal life had become.

No well-known Broadway actress was ever alone, especially when she was under contract for a major Hollywood film. Even when she was between shows and movies, she couldn't walk out of her apartment without some stranger trying to take her picture or get her autograph. She was always multitasking—juggling workshops, PR events, rehearsals and script readings. Who had time for a personal life?

She was thirty-one. Forty, that age that was the death knell to actresses, didn't seem quite so far away anymore. And Gram, being old-fashioned and Southern, constantly reminded Summer about her biological clock. Lately, Gram had started emailing pictures of all Summer's childhood girlfriends' children and gushing about how cute they were.

"Where would I be without you and Tuck? Mark my words, you'll be sorry if you end up old and alone."

Gram's longings were part of the reason Summer had let Hugh Jones, the hottest young actor on the west coast, rush her into a new relationship not two weeks after Edward had jilted her so publicly. Had she actually felt a little desperate at realizing how alone she was?

Not wanting to think about her personal life a moment longer, Summer picked up her glass and drank some of her iced tea.

Where was Gram? And what was taking Tuck so long on the phone?

Was he talking to Zach?

She took another sip of tea.

Reporters constantly asked her if she was in love with Hugh. But unfortunately for her, it wasn't Hugh who came to mind at the mention of the word *love*. No, for her, love and Zach would always be tangled together like an impossible knot. Her chest tightened. She'd only felt that exquisitely painful rush of excitement once.

She never wanted to feel it again.

She'd been sixteen, and he nineteen, when their romance had ended in unbearable heartbreak. For a brief moment she allowed herself to remember New Orleans and the terrible, secret loss she'd suffered there, a loss that had shattered her youthful illusions forever, a loss that had taught her some mistakes could never be made right.

Zach was the reason why she almost never came home. Bonne Terre was a small, gossipy Cajun town. If she hadn't forgotten her past, the town wouldn't have forgotten it, either. Even if the town's citizens didn't ask her about him, she always *felt* him everywhere when she was home. She had too many painful memories and…secrets.

Here on this very porch *he* had kissed her that first time.

Just as she was remembering how her mouth had felt scorched after he'd brushed his lips against hers, her grandmother's low, gravelly whisper interrupted her thoughts.

"You're not the only person who loves to sit in that chair."

The sly, mischievous note in her grandmother's tone sent a frisson of alarm through Summer.

"Oh." She didn't turn and smile because her cheeks were still burning.

"Zach always sits there."

Summer stiffened.

"I can't believe you allow him to come over, much less allow him to sit in *my* chair. What if someone tips off the press about his visits to see my grandmother and this causes another nasty story to be published about us? And why is he developing in Bonne Terre anyway? In all these years he's never once come back, until now."

"When his uncle died back in the fall he came to visit Nick. When he saw the land prices, he started talking to people. He already has a casino in Vegas. One thing led to another. The city fathers decided to court him...."

When Summer noticed the ice cubes in her glass tinkling, she set the glass down with a harsh *clink*.

"Careful, dear, that's your mama's best crystal." They paused, as they both reflected on the sweetness of Anna, Summer's dear, departed mother, whom they would miss forever. "Zach's bought up all that land across from our place."

"I still can't believe that with his history, with so many in this town set against him, Zach would come back here."

"He says it's time to set the record straight. He's certainly winning the town over."

How exactly did he intend to set the record straight? Summer thought of the one secret she'd kept from him and trembled. "He's made a fortune in Houston. Isn't that vindication enough? Why would he care what the people here think of him?"

"They nearly sent him to prison."

Because of me, Summer thought with genuine regret.

"Old wounds run deep sometimes...and need healin'. He's got everybody around here excited. His casino's going to be a fancy riverboat."

"Gambling? It's a vicious, addictive sport."

"Gaming will bring jobs.... And jobs will buy a lot of forgiveness. Bonne Terre's fallen on really hard times of late."

"Gram, you sound brainwashed. It makes me wonder how often Zach comes by."

"Well, he dropped by the first time because he wanted to see if I'd sell this place to him."

Summer would watch the swamp freeze over before she let that happen.

"Zach's been by about once a week ever since. We have coffee and cookies. Chocolate chip are his favorite."

Summer took great pains to center her glass in its condensation ring on the coaster. "I hope you didn't tell Zach you might sell or that I was coming to see you about all this."

Her grandmother hesitated. "I'm afraid I might have told him he could make me an offer. And… You know how I can never resist bragging about you. I've shown him my scrapbooks."

Summer frowned. "I can't imagine I'm his favorite subject."

"Well, like I said, he's always ever-so polite. He's been especially interested in your romance with Hugh." Gram smiled. "Asked me whom I thought was more fun—Hugh or himself?

I said Hugh was a rich movie star, who probably wouldn't waste his time on an old lady. I told Zach he had nothing to worry about."

Summer squeezed her eyes shut and counted to ten.

Kneading the knot between her eyes, she said, "Did you or didn't you tell him I was coming home because I'm upset about Tuck's job?"

"It's hard for me to remember exactly what I do or say these days, but if I did tell him, what can it matter? You said that what happened between you two was over a long time ago."

Summer frowned. Yes, of course, it was over. So, why was she obsessing about him?

"I think Thurman had Zach all wrong. I told your stepfather he was too hard on the boy at the time, that you were just youngsters in love. But Thurman doesn't ever listen to anybody."

He hadn't listened when Summer and her mother had begged him to drop the charges against Zach, and the stress of that time had ended her mother's remission. Her mother's death was just one of the reasons Summer was estranged from him. The other had to do with a tiny grave in New Orleans.

But Summer didn't want to think about that. "Okay, back to selling this place to Zach. That can't happen."

"I can't help it if I'm not averse to moving into a modern condo, if Zach comes up with some favorable financin'."

"But I love this house," Summer protested. "I can't believe you've actually gone this far with a deal without once mentioning it to me. What's his next move?"

"He said he'd put an offer together, but so far he's been too busy."

"Maybe we'll get lucky and he'll stay busy," Summer muttered, squeezing her eyes shut.

Somehow she didn't really think Zach, who could be relentless, would leave her grandmother alone until he got exactly what he wanted. Had he hired Tuck to win over Gram? So she'd sell him her home, which had been in the family for more than a hundred years?

"Word has it he closed on that tract across from us just yesterday. That's where he'll build the dock," Gram said. "So he'd like to control this property. He definitely doesn't want me selling to anybody else."

Inspiration struck.

"Gram, I'll buy the house from you. Then you can live here or in a condo. Your choice."

"Oh?"

"I want you to call Zach and tell him you won't sell. Hopefully, when he learns I'm here checking up on you, he'll back off."

Her grandmother watched her intently for a long moment. "You never looked at Edward the way you used to look at Zach. Fifteen years is a long time for you to still be bothered by a man," said her grandmother wisely. "Have you ever asked yourself why?"

"No." Summer yanked her scrunchy out of her hair and pulled her ponytail even tighter. "Because I'm perfectly happy with my life as it is. Can we quit talking about him and not start on your dissatisfaction with my single state?"

"Oh, all right, dear. I won't bring him up again—or the fact that you're an old maid—not unless you do."

"Old maid? Gram, there's no such thing anymore."

"Maybe that's so in Manhattan, but that's definitely not so in Bonne Terre. Ask anybody."

Gram's set expression stung way more than it should have.

Tuck stuck his head out the door. "Zach called and needs me to come in, so I've got to get to work."

"Hey, Tuck, your job is one of the reasons I came home. Can we talk?" Summer said.

"Later. He needs me to run an errand."

Summer ground her teeth as she watched her brother lope out the door.

Tuck refused to quit his job. Summer and he had quarreled about it briefly, but Zach had just promoted Tuck to full-time status and he now spent his whole day running errands for Zach's contractor.

As for Gram, she was as good as her word. Two whole days had passed without her ever once mentioning Zach.

She was the only one silent on the subject, however. The whole town was buzzing because Summer and Zach were both in town. Whenever Summer went shopping, the curious sneaked sidelong glances at her. The audacious stopped her on the street and demanded to know how she felt about Zach now.

"Do you regret what you and Thurman did—now that Zach's so rich and nice and set on saving this town from economic disaster?" Sally Carson, the postmistress, had demanded.

"Your grandmother told me he's been real sweet to her, too," Margaret York, one of Gram's oldest friends, said with a look of envy.

"Well, his return to this town has nothing to do with me," Summer replied.

"Doesn't it?" Margaret's face was sly and eager. "Men don't forget...."

"Well, I have."

"I wonder how you'll feel when you see him again. *We all wonder.*"

One of the worst things about fame was that it made everyone think they had a right to know about her private life. Some things were too personal and painful to share with anyone, even well-meaning neighbors.

So Summer stopped going into town. Instead, she stayed at the house to work on her script and formulate a new way to approach Tuck.

On this particular afternoon she'd set a plate of cookies and a glass of tea garnished with a sprig of mint beside a chaise longue on the screened veranda. She paced in frustration, gesturing passionately as she fought to discover her character, a young mother. The role eluded Summer because, for her, young motherhood was a painful theme.

But today she did something she'd never let herself do before—remember how she'd felt in New Orleans when she'd been expecting her own child. Suddenly, she broke through the protective walls inside her, and grief washed over her in waves.

Her eyes grew wet, and she began to tremble, but she didn't relent. So deeply was she immersed in painful memories, she didn't hear the hard, purposeful crunch of gravel beneath a man's boots until he was nearly upon her.

A low vicious oath startled her. Expecting Tuck, Summer whirled, dabbing at her damp eyes with the back of her hand.

And there *he* was.

At the sight of Zach's hard, chiseled features swimming through her tears, the pages she'd been holding fell to the wooden floor.

"Well, hello there," he said.

"Zach." She hated the way his low, velvet voice made her heart accelerate, made the air feel even hotter. Frantically, she dabbed at her eyes so he wouldn't see her tears. "Gram said you'd been visiting a lot." Her voice sounded choked and unnatural.

"Did she?" Black eyes narrowed as he pushed the screen door open. "She told me you were coming home." Zach scowled. "You're pale, and your eyes are red. Have you been crying?"

"No! It's nothing," she whispered. "I was just acting out a part."

His lips thinned. "You always were damn talented at that."

Good, he bought it.

Tall and dark in a long-sleeved white shirt and jeans, and as lethally handsome as ever, Zach's tight expression told her he wasn't happy to see her.

As she bent over to retrieve her script, his insolent dark eyes raked her body in a way that made her aware of how skimpily clad she was in her snug blue shorts and thin, clingy blouse.

Feeling strangely warm and too vulnerable suddenly, she bristled and sprang to her feet. "I told Gram to tell you. If she decides to sell, she'll sell to me. So, why are you here now?"

"I haven't spoken to her. My secretary arranged my appointment with your grandmother," he said, striding closer. "When I saw you in those shorts, I imagined she told you I was coming and you were lying in wait...."

"As if I'd do—and, hey, it's August. I...I have a perfect right to wear shorts," she sputtered.

"Yes." His gaze drifted over her appreciatively. "You look good in them. Too good—which I'm sure you know."

"Gram didn't tell me you were coming."

"And she didn't tell me to cancel my visit. I wonder why. Maybe she likes my company. Or maybe she'd prefer to sell to me. This old place and that brother of yours are way too much for her."

"None of that is any of your business."

"Your Tuck was running pretty wild, got himself fired from a bar because money went missing...."

"As if you know anything about Tuck. He doesn't steal!"

Zach's black brows arched. "Still thinking the worst of me while you defend everybody else. Your stepfather's been giving me hell, too."

The comparison to her stepfather cut her...deeply. Zach hadn't been there for her when she'd needed him either, had he? He hadn't cared....

Maybe because he hadn't known.

"As a matter of fact, I like your grandmother. That's why I hired Tuck. When I happened on him late one night, he'd had a flat tire. He didn't have a spare or money or a credit card, and his phone was dead. So he accepted my offer to haul him to a service station and buy him a new tire on the condition that he become my pool and errand boy and work it off."

"I see through your Good Samaritan act."

"I was sort of suspicious about it myself."

"You're just using Tuck to get at me in some way. So go,"

she whispered. "You are the last person I want involved with my family, especially with Tuck, who's extremely vulnerable."

"Well, sorry if my return to Bonne Terre upsets you, or if Tuck's being my employee bothers you," he said, not sounding the least apologetic. "But since I've got business in this town for some time to come, and Tuck works for me, I suppose you and I were bound to meet again…sooner or later."

"Gambling? Is that your business?"

"Yes. What of it? You're an actress, someone skilled at weaving seductive illusions. You sure seduced me with your little act. And I let you off easy. You should feel lucky. I'm not known for lenience with people who betray me."

Easy? Lucky? New Orleans lay like a weight on her heart.

"All you see is your side."

"I was the one who damn near got strung up because of your lies," he said. "I'm the one who's still found guilty every time some reporter decides to write another story about us."

"Well, maybe you don't know everything!" She stopped. She would never make the mistake of trying to confide in him. But despite her best intentions, she said, "You…you can't believe I ever wanted to accuse you, not when I begged you to run off with me, and when it was my idea to…"

"To seduce me?" he finished.

His silky whisper and the intense fire in his black eyes rubbed her nerves raw.

"It wasn't like that and you know it. I…I couldn't help it if Thurman hated you for what I did."

"Let's not kid ourselves. You did what you did. I don't give a damn anymore about why you did it."

Shame and some darker emotion she didn't want him to sense scorched her cheeks as she turned away from the coldness in his face. "If I could have undone what I did or said, or what I caused people to believe about you, I would have."

"Hollow words…since you could have stepped up and

cleared my name at any point. You didn't. Like a fool, I waited for you to do just that. I was young. I believed in you back then." His mouth tightened into a hard, forbidding line. "But, no, you ran off to New Orleans where you probably seduced somebody else."

"There was never anyone but you...." She swallowed tightly. "I—I tried to apologize...and explain. You refused to take my calls. I even went to Houston looking for you after your uncle took you away, but you wouldn't see me."

"By then I knew what a talented manipulator you were."

At his dark, unforgiving scowl, she sucked in a tortured breath. "If you hate me so much, why won't you just go?"

"I don't hate you. Frankly, I don't consider you worth the waste of any more emotion. What I'm doing here isn't about you. I've made a name for myself in other places. When Nick called me a few months ago, I realized I'd never let go of what happened here and neither have the people of this town or the media. Maybe I've decided it's time I changed a few people's minds.

"Your stepfather used to be the biggest man in these parts. Not anymore. I intend to be bigger than he ever was. I intend to make him pay for what he did—to kill him with kindness, bestowed upon his town."

"I want you to leave Gram and Tuck alone. I'm buying this property from her because I won't have you cheating her to get back at me."

"You'd better not make accusations like that in public."

"And you'd better stop trying to make me look bad to my grandmother, who's started nagging me about not coming home often enough!"

"Haven't you been neglecting her?"

"Well, if I don't come home, it's because of you. I—I can't forget...when I'm home," she finished raggedly.

Dark hurt flashed in his eyes but was gone so fast she was sure she'd only imagined it.

When he stomped toward the front door, she blocked his way. At her nearness, his hard body tensed. When their gazes locked, a muscle in his jawline jerked savagely. His breathing had roughened.

He wasn't nearly as indifferent as he'd said.

Nor was she.

"Move aside," he muttered.

Hurt, she lashed out. "No—this is my grandmother's house. I won't allow you to use her to get at me. So—leave."

"Like hell!"

When she stood her ground, his hands closed over her forearms. But as he tried to edge her aside, she stomped down on his foot with her heel.

Cursing, he tightened his grip and crushed her against his muscular length.

Despite the unwanted shiver of excitement his touch caused, her tone was mild. "Would you please let me go?"

A dozen warring emotions played across his dark face as she struggled to free herself.

"I don't think I will."

Locking her slim, wriggling body to his made their embrace even more alarmingly intimate.

"You're trembling," he said. "Why? Are you acting now? Or do you feel what I…." He broke off with a look of self-contempt.

"Damn you for this," he muttered. "You're not the only one who can't forget."

Even if she hadn't felt his powerful arousal against her pelvis, his blazing eyes betrayed his potent male need. Then his gaze hardened with determination, and she watched breathlessly as he lowered his mouth to hers.

"I shouldn't do this," he whispered fiercely, bending her

backward, molding her even more tightly to the hard contours of his body. "God help me, I know what you are, what you did."

"You did things, too...." He'd hurt her terribly. Yet she wanted him, ached for him.

"I can't stop myself," he muttered. "But then I never could where you were concerned."

No sooner did his warm mouth close over hers than she turned to flame. If he'd flung her onto the chaise longue and followed her down, she would have forgotten the hurt that had turned her heart to stone for fifteen years. She would have ripped his jeans apart at the waist, sliding her hands inside.

She wanted to touch him, kiss him everywhere, wind her legs and arms around him and surrender completely—even though she knew his need was based on the desire to punish while hers was due to temporary insanity.

On a sigh, her arms circled his tanned neck, and she clung, welding herself to his lean frame in a way that told him all that she felt. She was a woman now, a woman whose needs had been too long denied. When he shuddered violently, she gasped his name.

"Zach... I'm sorry," she murmured as warm tears leaked from her eyes and trickled down her cheek. She feathered gentle fingertips through his thick, inky hair. "I wronged you, and I'm so sorry. For years I've wanted to make it up to you." She hesitated. "But... You hurt me, too."

For fifteen years, she'd been dead in the arms of every other man who'd held her.

She hadn't felt this alive since she'd last been in Zach's embrace.

His hand closed over her breast, stroking a nipple until it hardened. The other hand had moved down to cup her hip.

Next he undid the buttons of her blouse so that it parted for his exploration. For one glorious moment she was her younger self and wildly in love with him again. Back then she had trusted him completely. She'd given him everything of herself. With a sigh, she leaned into him as he stroked her, and her response sent him over some edge.

He rasped in a breath. Then, in the next shuddering instant, he ended their kiss, tearing his lips free, leaving her desolate, abandoned.

Loosening his grip, he let her go and staggered free of her as if he'd been burned. He raked a large, shaking hand through his hair and swore violently, staring anywhere but at her.

"Damn you," he muttered, inhaling deeply. "I see why you do so well on Broadway. You're like a tigress in heat. Is that why Hugh Jones took up with you so fast?"

Summer was about to confess she felt nothing when Hugh kissed her—nothing—but Zach spoke first.

"Brilliant performance," he said. "You deserve an Oscar."

"So do you," she whispered in breathless agony as she dried her cheeks with the back of her hand. She couldn't let him know that for a few magical seconds she'd actually cared.

"I'd better go before I do something incredibly stupid," he said.

"Like what?" she murmured, feeling dazed from his mesmerizing kiss and savage embrace.

"Like take you back to my house to do whatever the hell I want to do with you…for as long as I want."

"Oh?"

"Don't look at me like that! I know what you are. Damn you for making me want the impossible," he muttered.

She clenched her fists, not any happier than he was to realize that she wanted the impossible, too.

He didn't like her. With good reason. Their past was too painful to revisit. What burned inside her, and in him, was lust—visceral and destructive.

Gram opened the front door. Her violet, silver-lashed eyes wide, she peered out at them with excessive interest, causing Summer, whose blouse was still unbuttoned, to blush with shame even as she quickly pulled the edges back together. The last thing she wanted to do was get Gram's hopes up about a romantic reunion with Zach.

"Oh, my go-o-o-d-ness." Gram worked hard to hide her pleasure at the sight of Zach's blazing eyes and her granddaughter's scarlet face and state of dishabille. "I'm so sorry." In a softer voice directed toward Summer, she said, "And I thought you told me you wanted nothing more to do with him." There was that sly note of satisfaction in her tone again.

"I don't," Summer cried, but the door had already closed behind her triumphant grandmother. "Why didn't you tell me he was coming over?" she called after Gram. Then Summer turned and said to Zach, "Why did I even ask, when I specifically ordered her not to mention you?"

Zach's eyes went flat and cold. "As far as I'm concerned, this never happened. But—if you see me again—you'd better run. You and I have more unfinished business than I realized. Don't give me any more reasons to come after you and finish what you started."

Suspecting he must want revenge, she swallowed. "Don't threaten me."

"It's not a threat. It's a promise, a warning. If you're smart, you'll stay away from me."

As if to emphasize his words, he strode over to her. Reaching up his hand, he ran a calloused fingertip along her damp cheek, causing her to shiver involuntarily.

"I want you in my bed. I want you to pay for what you did. In every way that I demand."

Startled, because the image he painted—of lying under him on a soft bed—aroused her to such a shocking degree, she jumped back. Out of his sensually lethal reach, her voice was firm. "I won't be seeing you again."

"Good. Tell your grandmother I'll call her after you leave town."

His gorgeous mouth curled. Looking every bit as furious and ashamed as Summer was beginning to feel, Zach turned on his heel and strode down the gravel drive, leaving her to wonder how she could have stood there like a besotted idiot and let him touch her again after sharing such an embarrassing kiss.

"None of this happened," Summer whispered consolingly to herself when she finally heard the roar of his car. Too aware of gravel spinning viciously, she sank down onto the steps and hugged her knees tightly.

She felt cold and hot at the same time.

It was all a horrible mistake. Zach didn't like that it had happened any more than she did.

She was glad he felt that way.

She was glad!

Somehow she had to make Gram and Tuck understand that Zach was dangerous, that he'd threatened her.

Tuck, who'd gotten in trouble too many times to count, could not continue to work for Zach, who would use whatever her brother did to his own advantage.

Squaring her shoulders, Summer got to her feet and picked up the remaining pages of her script. Then she ran into the house and up the stairs where she took a long, cold shower and brushed her teeth.

Not that she could wash away his taste or the memory of his touch or the answering excitement in her system.

That night, when she awoke, breathing hard from a vivid dream about Zach kissing her even more boldly, it was impossible to ignore the hunger that was both ancient and familiar lighting every nerve ending in her being.

Wild for him, she sat up in the darkness and pushed her damp hair back from her hot face. "It was just a stupid kiss. It doesn't matter! Zach can't stand me any more than I can stand him."

So, why are you dreaming about him, aching for him, even when you know he despises you?

Two

One month later

Once back in New York, Zach's kiss lingered on the edges of Summer's consciousness almost all the time, despite the fact that she'd willed herself to forget him. Despite the fact that she'd decided it was best not to obsess over things she couldn't control, like Tuck's refusal to quit his job and Gram's support of his decision.

And because the memory of Zach's kiss lingered, she drove herself to work harder than ever.

Summer read every script her agent gave her. She auditioned tirelessly for any part that was halfway right for her. When she was home alone she compulsively cleaned and dusted every item in her already immaculate apartment in a vain attempt to shove Zach Torr and his stupid kiss and his ridiculous threats back into the past where they belonged.

Not that she could stop herself from calling certain gossips in Bonne Terre to get a picture of what he was up to back home or stop herself from reading her hometown's newspaper online to get the latest news about his riverboat gambling project. Everything she read was annoyingly favorable. People were more impressed by him every day. He was the town's favorite son. Rumors abounded about the lavishness of the riverboat he was building and the luxurious amenities and hotels he was constructing onshore.

On impulse, maybe to prove to those blockheads back home how little she cared for Zach, she let Hugh Jones join one of her interviews.

Naturally, the young, bright-eyed journalist went gaga over beautiful, golden Hugh, whose immense ego was hugely gratified at being fawned over.

At first, the young woman's eager questions had been standard fare. Summer tossed off her ritual answers.

Her favorite role was the one she was creating. She was always nervous opening nights. And, yes, the play she was workshopping today was ever-so exciting.

Naturally, when the journalist wasn't entirely focused on Hugh, he grew bored.

Hugh shuffled from one foot to the other and yawned, and the reporter laughed and leaned into him so her breast brushed his elbow.

"Okay, let's talk about this hot new man in your life. Every woman in America is dying to be you, Summer." The woman was staring into Hugh's baby-blues as if she'd been hypnotized.

Idiotically, the phrase *hot new man* put Summer back on Gram's screened porch, in the arms of that certain individual she would give anything to forget.

Again she tasted the sweet, blistering warmth of Zach's mouth and felt his muscular length pressing her close. At the memory of his big hands closing over her breast and butt, the dark, musty corner she shared with Hugh and the reporter felt airless.

"So, what's the latest with you and Hugh?" the reporter asked. "If you don't mind my saying so, you two are *the* most exciting couple these days."

"I'm a pretty lucky guy." Hugh squeezed Summer closer before launching into a monologue about himself.

Summer was wondering if she and Hugh had ever once had a real conversation about anything else.

"I don't think Summer's got any complaints," the reporter said when Hugh finally ended the everybody-loves-me monologue.

Hugh laughed, pulled Summer closer and planted his mouth on hers just as a flash blinded her.

Infuriated at his brashness, Summer thumped her fists on his chest. Luckily, her cell phone vibrated and blasted rap music from her pocket.

"Excuse me," she whispered, desperate for an excuse to be done with the reporter and Hugh.

Sliding her phone open, she read the name, *Viola Guidry.* "Sorry, guys, it's my grandmother. I have to take this."

"So—that kiss makes me wonder how serious you and Hugh are?" the reporter asked.

"We're just good friends," Summer snapped in a flat, cool tone.

"That's all you're going to give me—"

Nodding, Summer smiled brightly as she shook the woman's hand. "Thanks so much." Cupping the phone to her ear, Summer walked away.

"Hey, girls, much as I loved doing this interview, I've got a meeting before I catch my plane to L.A.," Hugh said carelessly, blowing Summer an air kiss. "See you, angel."

Summer waved absently and fought to concentrate on her grandmother's frantic words.

"You have to come home! Tuck's in the hospital. He's going to be okay, but Sheriff Arcenaux says he may have to arrest him!"

"For what?"

"Tuck invited some friends over to Zach's and they got into his liquor. When Zach came home, Tuck was so drunk he'd passed out. Two of Zach's cars were missing, and Tuck's friends were busily looting the place."

"Oh, my God! Did I warn you or not?"

"Zach's threatening to press charges. So—you've got to come home."

Fear was a cold fist squeezing Summer's heart so tightly she could barely breathe. Practically speaking, she didn't have time for this. Her calendar was jam-packed with work commitments. Emotionally, she knew her family needed her.

"Zach wants to meet with you. He gave me his attorney's number and told me to have you call him. He said maybe he'd be willing to work something out with you, instead of pressing charges, if you meet with him. But he'll only meet with you."

Summer felt so frustrated and panic-stricken it was all she could do not to throw the phone.

Zach had her right where he wanted her—cornered.

In a soft voice, she said, "I'm on my way, Gram."

She was late.

Zach hated wasting time, and that was exactly what he was doing as he waited for Summer, a woman he'd spent years trying to forget. His empire should be his focus, not some woman from his past.

Hell, he'd wasted too much time worrying about her ever since he'd seen her on Viola's porch. She'd looked so sad and fragile before they'd spoken. He was almost sure she'd been crying. The pain in her eyes had been so profound he still wanted to know what she'd been thinking.

Then, like a fool, he'd kissed her.

Her mouth had been hot and yielding, almost desperate with pent-up passion. But tender, too. Ever since that kiss, it was as if her lips and her taste and her softness and her sweet vulnerability had relit the passion he'd once felt for her. It seemed nothing, not all the ugliness or news coverage or even reason, had been able to destroy his desire for her.

The woman's kiss had made him remember the girl he'd loved and trusted.

She didn't matter; she couldn't ever matter again.

Summer had been a virgin when she'd given herself to him. His one and only. Never would he forget how lush, lovely and shyly innocent she'd been, nor how her shy blue eyes had shone. He'd been deeply touched that such a beautiful girl with such a radiant soul had chosen him.

For the first two years they'd known each other, his focus had been their friendship and protecting her from her controlling stepfather. Then they'd fallen in love during her senior year, so he'd stayed in Bonne Terre to wait for her to graduate. He hadn't pushed for sex, but somehow, after they'd run away together, she'd gotten through his defenses.

One night when they'd been alone in that remote cabin, she'd cried, asking him what she should do about her stepfather. What would happen if they didn't go back, if she didn't finish school? Would he come to New York with her?

He'd realized then that Summer saw him as part of her future; saw her stepfather and Bonne Terre as something she was finished with forever.

Intending to comfort her, to reassure her that he wanted her in his future as well, he'd gone to the bed, taken her in his arms and held her close. Her hair had smelled of jasmine, so he'd nuzzled it. Then she'd kissed him, her soft mouth open, her body pressing against his eagerly. She probably hadn't understood how she'd tempted him.

He'd stroked her hair, caressing her, and she'd moaned. Her tears had stopped, but she'd clung anyway. Then they'd come together as if it were the most natural thing in the world. Their union had been both sexual and spiritual. He'd believed they'd marry after she graduated, that they would be together forever.

Never again had he felt like that about a woman.

Forget it.

Zach forced his mind to the present. He couldn't afford to reminisce. Time was more precious than money. His uncle's death had taught him that.

Zach had his briefcase stuffed with foreclosure cases he'd intended to review as he sat in his attorney's sumptuous conference room. Waiting for *her*. Plate-glass windows afforded him an excellent view of the bayou four stories below. Not that he was enjoying the scene of cypress and dogwood trees. No, he couldn't stop thinking about her.

Why was she late? Was she remembering their last encounter and his promise to make her pay?

When he heard the desperate click of her high heels in the hall, he glanced up, tense with expectation. Even as he steeled himself to feel nothing, his heart began to race.

The door opened, framing her slim, elegant body before she entered. Her delicate, classical features and radiant complexion were too lovely for words.

He wanted her so much he couldn't breathe.

They looked at each other and then away while the silent tension between them crackled. On some deep level, she drew him. Her incredible blond beauty alone made her unforgettable. Then there was her fame. Hell, how could he forget her when her face was plastered on the covers of gossip magazines and cheap, weekly newspapers?

She was everywhere.

Only a few days ago he hadn't been able to resist reading

the latest about her budding romance with Hugh Jones in one of those sensational newspapers he despised. He'd grabbed it off a wire shelf in a drugstore and jammed it into his brief-case. He'd carried it up to his office and pored over the story that went with the front-page photo of the famous couple sharing a kiss. Summer had claimed they were just friends, but Jones had expounded about how crazy they were about each other. Which one of them was lying?

Probably her.

Zach had wadded the newspaper and thrown it in the trash. In his penthouse suite, staring out at the city of Houston, which was littered with the skyscrapers he'd built and owned, he'd never felt more isolated.

She had a life—perhaps she even loved that famous, ego-tistical movie star—while he had only his fierce ambition and immense wealth. He'd gone through his contact list on his smart phone, called a beautiful blonde who resembled Sum-mer and asked her out. But that night, after dinner, when she'd invited him up to her loft, he'd said he had to work. Driving home, feeling empty and more alone than ever, he'd burned for Summer.

So, he'd seized his opportunity. He'd used her brother to get her here.

"Coffee?" His attorney's pretty secretary offered from the doorway.

"No," Zach thundered without even bothering to ask Sum-mer, for whom he felt irrational fury because she wouldn't stop consuming his thoughts.

He wasn't in the mood for niceties. When the secretary left and Summer's long-lashed, legendary violet-blue eyes flicked in alarm, he felt as if she'd sucker punched him in the gut. Damn her, for having this much power over him.

His heart hardened against her knockout beauty even as other parts of his body hardened because of it. He wished he could forget the softness of her breast and the firmness of her butt and the sweet taste of her lips. He wished he didn't ache to hold her and touch her again. He wanted to kiss her and force her to forget all about Jones.

How many others had there been in her bed since Zach? Legions, he imagined with a rush of bitterness. A Broadway star with a face and figure like hers, not to mention a budding movie career, could have anybody—directors, producers, actors, fans.

Hell, she had Hugh Jones, didn't she? But was she as responsive when Jones touched her? Had Zach only imagined she'd been pushing against Jones, trying to free herself, when that picture had been taken?

None of it mattered. Zach wanted her in his bed with an all-consuming hunger. And he was determined to have her.

As if she read his thoughts, she flushed and glanced down, staring at her white, ice-pick heels rather than at him. Still, her sultry voice made him burn when she whispered, almost shyly, "Sorry I'm late. Traffic. I had to go by Gram's first... to check on Tuck."

"How's he doing?" Zach asked, standing up and placing his hand on the back of the chair he intended to offer her.

He'd found Tuck drunk and unconscious on the living-room floor of Zach's new house. The garage doors had been open, and Zach's Lamborghini and second Mercedes had been missing.

Fortunately, Zach had come home unexpectedly and had caught two of Tuck's friends, also drunk, ransacking his house, or he might have suffered worse losses. Since then, the automobiles had been found abandoned in New Orleans.

Zach blamed himself, in part, for not having hired an appropriate staff for the house.

"Tuck's doing okay." Summer answered his question as she stepped farther into the room, her legs as light and graceful as a dancer's, her silky white dress flowing against her hips. He remembered how sexy she'd looked when she'd bent over in her short shorts on her grandmother's porch.

And why shouldn't she be graceful and sexy? She was a performer, a highly paid one. Everything she did was part of a deliberate, well-rehearsed act. Maybe the kiss they'd shared when she'd seemed to quiver so breathlessly had been a performance, as well.

She sat down in the chair he'd indicated and crossed her legs prettily. He stayed on his feet because staring down at her gave him the advantage.

Even though he knew what she was, and what she was capable of, the years slid away. Again he was sixteen, the bad new homeless kid in school with the sullen, bruised face. Everybody had been scared of him. Summer had been the popular, pampered high-school freshman, a princess who'd had every reason to feel superior to him.

People talked in a town the size of Bonne Terre. Everybody knew everybody. Nobody approved of Nick dragging such a rough kid home and foisting him upon the school. Thurman Wallace had even demanded Zach be thrown out.

Only Summer, who'd been a precocious thirteen and two years ahead of her age in school, hadn't looked down on Zach. Not even when all the other kids and her step-daddy thought she should. No, even on that first day, when Roger Nelson, a football star, had demanded to know what Zach had done to make a guy hate him so much he'd beaten him nearly to death, she'd butted in and defended him.

"Maybe that's not what happened," she'd said. "Maybe Zach was in the right, defending himself, and the other guy was in the wrong. We don't know."

"So what happened, Torr?" Nelson had demanded.

"Why should I tell you?"

"See, he's trash, Pollyanna," Nelson had jeered. "Anybody can see that!"

"Well, then maybe I'm blind, because I can't," she'd insisted. "I see a person who needs a friend."

Not long after that Summer had become his secret best friend.

The memories slipped away, and Zach was heatedly aware of the woman seated before him.

As if she couldn't resist using her power on him, Summer tipped her head his way, sending that thick curtain of blond hair over her shoulders as her blue eyes burned into the center of his soul.

"Zach, thanks for getting Tuck medical attention so fast. They said you had specialists flown in from Houston." Her face was soft, beguilingly grateful.

Clenching a fist, he jammed it in a pocket. He wasn't buying into her gratitude. Not when he knew she'd do anything to keep her brother from being arrested.

"The doctors are personal friends of mine in Houston. It was either fly them here or airlift him to New Orleans. He was out cold. He had a bump the size of a hen's egg on his head and a gash that needed stitches, so I wanted to make sure he was just drunk and that there was no serious head injury involved."

"Thank you," she said.

"I don't see any need for us to make a big deal about something anyone would have done."

"You paid for everything, too. We have insurance. If you'll invoice me, I'll—"

"You'll pay me. Fine," he growled.

He was blown away by his feelings. He wanted her so badly he could think of nothing else, and she was coldly talking money.

"You said you wanted to see me. I've talked to Tuck, and

he feels terrible about everything that happened. He had no idea those boys were going to steal anything or tear up your house. The last thing he remembers is hearing a noise in the garage and stumbling across the living room to check it out. Then he must have tripped."

"Oh, really? What about the money that went missing when he was fired from his last job? Your brother's been running pretty wild all summer. He's nineteen. Old enough to know what the guys he runs around with are capable of."

"He was just showing off. They said they'd never seen a billionaire's place. He wanted to impress them."

"He shouldn't have invited them over or given them my whiskey."

"I agree, and so does he…now. He just didn't think."

"Your Tuck's had too many run-ins with the law for me to buy into his innocence. He's been indulged in Bonne Terre. Maybe because he's a Wallace."

"That's what this is about, isn't it—his last name? You were hoping something like this would happen. You deliberately hired my trouble-prone brother, set him up, so you could get back at me."

He tensed at her accusation. "Since you're so quick to blame others for his actions, I'm beginning to see why he's so irresponsible."

Heat flared in her eyes. He noted that she was breathing irregularly, that her breasts were trembling.

"You have no right to use him this way. He's practically an orphan. I was twelve when he was born. He was two when our father ran off, four when Mother married Thurman and he adopted us. If my stepfather was hard on me by pushing me in school, demanding I excel and graduate two years ahead of my class, he constantly browbeat Tuck, calling him a wimp and a sissy who'd never amount to anything. I was the favorite. Tuck could never measure up.

"After our mother died, he was raised by a stepfather who disliked him and then by aunts who cared more for their own children, and later by his grandmother, who's become too old and lenient. And I admit, I don't come home often enough."

Zach had figured all that out for himself. The kid had no direction. She and Viola were protective of Tuck, but didn't demand enough responsibility from the boy.

"And what do you do—you put him in temptation's way so you can get at me," she repeated in a shaky tone. "Since he's been in trouble before, if you press charges and he's tried and convicted, he could be locked up for a long time. You knew that when you hired him. If this gets out to the media, there will be a frenzy."

Zach paced to the window. "If you believe I deliberately used Tuck to hurt you, you wouldn't believe anything I told you to defend myself. So, I won't bother."

"Oh, please. You threatened me the last time I saw you. I think you've ordered me here because you intend to make good on that threat!"

Yes, he wanted to yell.

I want to sleep with you so badly I'd do almost anything to accomplish that!

But then the intensity of her pleading look made him jerk his gaze from hers.

She was afraid of him.

He didn't want her fear. He wanted her warm and passionate and wild, as she'd been the first time.

He strode back to the table and picked up the legal documents in which he'd accused her younger brother of a felony.

When he saw his grip on the papers made his tendons stand out, Zach knew he was dangerously close to losing control. What was her hold over him?

By all rights he should have the upper hand in this situation. Her brother had brought thugs to his home to rip him off. He had every right to demand justice. But Tuck, who'd trusted him, needed help. He needed direction. Zach remembered how he himself had been derailed as a kid due to vengeful adult agendas.

Feeling torn between his ruthless desire and his personal code of ethics, Zach threw the documents onto the table. Then he glared at Summer fiercely, willing revulsion into his gaze.

But she was wide-eyed, vulnerable. Her perfect face was tight-lipped and pale; her shoulders slumped. She'd said she never wanted to see him again, but she'd come today. With a career like hers, she'd probably been busy as hell, but she'd come because she was genuinely worried about her brother and wanted to help him.

When she'd thanked Zach for getting the right doctors, he'd seen real gratitude in her eyes. And he'd liked pleasing her. Too much. In that white dress, which clung in all the right places, she looked young and innocent—not to mention breathtakingly sexy.

He wanted her in his bed. He wanted revenge for all that she'd done to him.

Do what she's accused you of. Use Tuck. Make your demands.

Yet something held him back.

For years, he'd told himself he hated her, had willed himself to hate her. But when he'd held her and kissed her at her grandmother's house, his hate had been tempered by softer, more dangerous emotions.

He'd once believed that if he had enough money and power, he would never be vulnerable to the pull of love again.

But now here she was, with her golden hair smelling of perfume and shimmering with coppery highlights so bright they dazzled him, with her lips full and moist, with her long-lashed eyes smoldering with repressed need.

Was she lonely, too? He wanted to hold her against his body and find out.

But more than that, fool that he was, he wanted to protect her. And her idiot brother.

He had to get out of here, go somewhere where he could think this through.

To her, he snarled, "This meeting's canceled." Then he punched the intercom and spoke to his lawyer's secretary. "Tell Davis to take over."

"I don't understand," Summer whispered. "What about Tuck?"

"I'll deal with you two later."

She let out a frightened sigh that cut him to the quick. "Zach, please…"

He wanted to turn to make sure she was all right.

Instead, he shrugged his broad shoulders and sucked in a breath.

To hell with her.

Without a backward glance, he strode out of the room.

Three

He was impossible! Arrogant! Rude!

If he'd slapped her, Zach couldn't have hurt Summer more than he had when he'd turned his back on her and walked out.

Fisting her hands, she got up and ran after him. But with his long legs, the elevator doors were closing before she caught up to him.

"Zach, you've got to listen—"

His glare was indifferent and cold as the doors slammed together.

"Well, you've sure got him on the run. You must have scared the hell out of him," Davis said, chuckling behind her. "That's not so easy to do. Usually he shreds his adversaries."

Zach's attorney looked slim and handsome in his tailored Italian suit and prematurely gray hair. He had been a year or two older than she in high school, but she and he had never been close. Davis worked for Zach now, not her.

Her heart swelled with uncertainty. She was afraid to say

anything to Davis because whatever she said would be repeated to Zach. She couldn't risk damaging Tuck's chances.

"Where do you think he went?" she asked.

"We've got a lot of legal work to wrap up, so he's in town for a few days. He spent his morning at the construction site, and he didn't mention having any other meetings this afternoon, so maybe he went home. I'd leave him alone for now, let him settle down. Don't push him into making a rash decision about Tuck. Believe me, he'll call you when he's ready."

But wouldn't it be better to deal with him now, when he wasn't ready? Wouldn't that give her an advantage?

Besides she was under contract to perform in New York, and her calendar was full. She didn't have a second to waste. No way could she stay here indefinitely without major consequences to her career. Directors, producers and other actors were depending on her.

Acting on a mixture of intuition and desperation, she went out to her rental car and followed the winding bayou road to the old Thibodeaux place.

His pale, beige antebellum-style home had a wide front veranda and ten stately columns. Weeds grew in the flower beds, and the grass was overgrown. Wild passion flowers had taken over the edges of the yard. She rang the bell and nobody answered, making her wonder why he didn't have adequate staff.

When she began to pace the veranda, she saw it had a few rotten boards and was in need of a thorough sweeping. She peered through the smudged pane of a front window. Inside, she saw stacks of boxes on the dusty, scarred floors of the palatial rooms.

Apparently, his people hadn't finished moving him in. Was he even here?

When she rang the bell again with no answer, she decided to walk around back by way of a redbrick path that lay in the shade of vast oak trees that needed a good trimming. All the forest-green shutters were peeling, as well.

The mansion had been built a decade before the Civil War and had served as a Yankee headquarters.

Now, the house and yard needed love and lots of money, but with enough of both, it could be a beautiful home for some lucky family. Had Zach bought it because he was thinking of settling down? Marrying and having children? Little dark-haired boys or girls? She imagined them playing out in the yard and hated the way the vision tugged at her heart.

A gleaming silver Mercedes was parked in front of Zach's three-car garage. His car? How many did the man own?

Seeing the low, white-picket fence, also in need of fresh paint, encircling the pool, she opened the gate and stepped gingerly through the high weeds to let herself inside.

Intending to knock on one of the back doors, she headed toward them only to stop when she saw a half-empty bottle of expensive scotch on a nearby table. At the sound of someone bouncing with a vengeance on the diving board, she turned just as a pair of long, tanned, muscular legs disappeared into the water.

"Zach?"

He didn't answer, of course, because he was underwater and speeding like a dark torpedo toward the shallow end. When she heard more splashing, she walked to the edge where the water lapped against the stairs. Centering her white heels precisely on one of the large navy tiles that bordered the pool, she waited for him to come up for air.

He was fast. Obviously, he'd stayed in shape since he'd been on the swim team in high school.

Oh, my God. He was naked!

Suppressing a cry at that realization, she saw his clothes discarded untidily on the far side of the pool. Still, instead of turning and fleeing, she stopped and stood her ground.

Her nervous state was such that she felt it took him forever to surface.

Thankfully, since he was in the water, when he did stand up, she couldn't see much of his lower body, but his perfect, muscular, wetly gleaming, tanned torso stimulated her overactive imagination anyway.

He shook his wet black head, flinging droplets of water all over her.

"Hey!" she cried, stepping even farther back.

He scowled up at her in shock even as his black eyes greedily raked her with male interest. Grinning, he made no effort to sink lower in the water or cover himself. "Why am I even surprised?"

"I knocked," she said defensively as hot color rose in her cheeks. "On your front door."

"Did you really?"

A warm breeze caressed her cheek. She looked anywhere except at his wide, dark chest and muscular arms. Even so, she was aware of his height, of his taut stomach and of that dark strip of hair running down his middle and disappearing into the water.

"You didn't answer," she said.

"A lot of women...women who weren't looking for trouble...would have just left."

"I...I'm not looking for trouble."

"Well, you damn sure found it."

"I have to know what you're going to do about Tuck."

"Since you're obviously determined we're going to have a chat on that subject, maybe you'd be so kind as to get me a towel out of the bathhouse. Since I thought I was alone, I didn't think I'd need one. Or... Do I—need one?"

"Yes!" she cried. "You most certainly do!"

He laughed.

Thankful for something to do other than trying to avoid

looking at his amused and much-too-sexy face, she all but flew to the bathhouse. Returning quickly, she set the fluffy, folded rectangle on the edge of the pool. Patting it primly, she turned her back on him.

Water splashed as his bare feet thudded across concrete. She felt her body warm as she listened to him towel off, visualizing his tall bronzed body behind her without a stitch on.

He was certainly taking his time. Was he trying to tempt her into turning around? She *wanted* to turn. Thankfully, she resisted. Surely he'd had time to secure the towel, but another intolerable minute passed.

Finally, as if sensing her impatience and interest in his physique, he chuckled and said, "It's safe for you to turn around now."

But it wasn't. Not when his fierce black eyes devoured her, obviously reading her wicked desires. Not when he wore only that towel and they both knew he was naked and gorgeous and completely male underneath it.

She wished she didn't feel so keenly alive every time she was anywhere near him. She wished she wasn't drawn by his tanned arms and bare chest, that she didn't remember lying with him as a girl after they'd made love and nuzzling that dark strip that vanished beneath the thick folds of his towel.

Oh, how she'd loved him that night after he'd made love to her. Like a foolish child, she'd thought he belonged to her, that he would always be hers.

Maybe he would have—if she'd fought Thurman and the town. Maybe then she wouldn't feel as she did right now, as if she was starving for love.

"You've got guts to come out here all alone. Aren't you scared of what I might do to you?"

Her heartbeat accelerated. She didn't fully understand her motives. She'd just known that she couldn't let him bully her, and that she couldn't stand by and let Tuck be hurt because of her past sins.

Moving closer to him to prove her bravery, she said, "You ran away. Maybe you're the one who's scared of me."

He flushed darkly. "And then again, sweetheart...maybe not."

Sweetheart. The word ripped her heart. In the past, he'd always said the endearment so tenderly it took her breath away. Today, his voice was harsh with irony.

Before she knew what was happening, his hand snaked toward her, and he yanked her against his body, which was wet and warm and as hard as steel.

Her heart leaped into her throat as she caught the faint scent of scotch on his breath. Too late, she wondered how much he'd drunk.

"I wasn't scared of you, you little fool. I was scared of me. Of what I might be tempted to do if I didn't get away from you. Then you come here...and deliberately invade my privacy. You tempt me...into this, into holding you again. Sweetheart, you're playing with fire."

Again too late, she realized he hadn't had time to swim off any of the liquor he'd drunk.

"Well," she hedged, "I...I see you were right.... And I was wrong. Maybe it would be smarter to set up another meeting tomorrow morning, as you suggested."

Echoing her thoughts, he said, "It's too late for such a sensible decision. You came here because you want something from me, and you want it very badly. You saw I was naked. You knew you were alone with me and you stayed. Since I told you I still wanted you, maybe you thought if you excited me again, I'd be easier to deal with."

"No!"

"Hey, don't back down. You were right. It's good for your

cause that you're here. As it turns out, I know exactly what I want from you. I was just fighting the temptation earlier."

Oh, God.

"I didn't stay because you weren't dressed…and I thought I could manipulate you…or whatever horrible thing you think I was up to."

His swift grin was savage. "You've always been good at pretending. Like back in high school—when your stepfather bullied you into graduating early, you pretended you wanted what he wanted. He wanted you to be a teacher because he thought that was a respectable career for a woman. Did you ever once tell him how important theater was to you before you starred in *Grease* and made him so angry at the end of your senior year? You dated me behind his back, too, because you knew he wouldn't approve. And when he hung me out to dry, you lied to everybody in this town about me. Your whole life was a lie. So, you'd damn sure lie now."

"No…"

"I think you've gone on lying to yourself for years. You know how I know? Because I've been doing the same thing. In my arrogance, I thought you'd taught me such a bitter lesson I was immune to women like you…and to you specifically. Until I kissed you…."

She swallowed, suddenly not liking the way he was holding her, or the way he was looking at her with that big-bad-wolf grin.

"I'd better go."

"You're so damned beautiful." He was staring at her as if she were a puzzle. "How can you look so innocent? I have enough money to buy practically anything, anybody, I want and I usually do. I want you. Why should I deny myself?"

Drawing her closer, he reached up and gently brushed away the lock of blond hair that feathered against her skin.

Her tummy flipped. Tenderness from him was the last

thing she'd expected, and it caused hot, unwanted excitement to course through her.

He smelled of chlorine and sunlight, scotch and of his own clean male scent, which somehow she'd never forgotten. All of it together intoxicated her.

Her reaction frightened her. When she tried to back away, his grip on her wrist tightened.

"I want you to move in with me for a while. I want to figure out this thing that's still between us."

"Impossible!" He wanted sex. He just wasn't going to say it. "There's nothing between us."

Again, she tried to jerk free, but his hand and body were granite hard.

"You're such a liar. Before we kissed, I would have agreed. I wanted to believe that," he said. "But unlike you, I'm uncomfortable lying to myself."

"I'm under contract in New York. I've got an opening night in eight weeks. We're going to be rehearsing, and I have several scenes to shoot for a movie in L.A. My calendar is full. Crammed."

"So reschedule."

"I have commitments, a life.… Other people are involved. Producers, my director, the rest of the cast."

"Odd—you failed to mention your movie-star boyfriend… Hugh, I believe?" His eyes darkened.

"Yes! Of course—*Hugh*. We're in the same film."

Zach's grim smile held no satisfaction. "And you think I don't have someone special or plenty on my plate?"

Someone special.

The thought of him having a girlfriend he truly cared about tugged painfully at her heart—which was ridiculous!

"Even I, who know next to nothing about the theater world, have heard the term *understudy*," he continued. "Reschedule."

"I hate you."

"Good. We're on the same page." His voice was harsh. "You'll live here, with me, weekends only—until your opening night. I don't care how you live the rest of the week. Or with whom. I'll be commuting here from Houston."

"I have to know exactly what you want from me," she whispered.

"I'm a man. You're a woman. Use your imagination."

"This is crazy."

"You forget, I'm a gambler. Ever since you pulled your little stunt and nearly destroyed me, I've gotten to where I am by operating on my gut. If I feel like it's right to go ahead with a deal, I do…whether or not I have all the facts to support my decision. Even if the facts tell me it might be the wrong thing to do—as in your case—I do it. It's worked for me so far."

"This isn't business. I won't have you gambling with my future, with Tuck's future."

"It's the way I operate. Take it or leave it. Since I hold the winning cards where your brother and his band of merry thieves are concerned, I don't think you have a better option."

"Is it sex? Do you want me to sleep with you? If that's it—just say so."

"Sex?" His black gaze raked her. "I won't say that offer doesn't tempt me. Did you mean tonight?"

When she didn't deny it, when she bit her lip and said nothing, he cupped her chin. Again, his hold was gentle, only this time it was more intimate as he studied her, his black eyes lingering on her lips before traveling lower. His hand stroked her throat. When his fingers slid briefly beneath the neckline of her dress, causing her skin to burn and her pulse to race even faster, she gasped in anticipation.

"I want you in bed, but it's not that simple," he finally murmured, removing his hand.

Only after he stopped touching her could she breathe again.

"I want you in bed, but I want you to be willing. So, this isn't just about sex. Not by a long shot."

No, it was about submission, about complete domination and control. She'd read plenty about how ruthless he was. He wanted to humiliate her as thoroughly as he'd humiliated his stepmother.

She shut her eyes because his gaze was too powerful and her own desire was beginning to feel too palpable.

"I loved you," he whispered. "I trusted you, but you betrayed me."

"I…I…loved…you, too."

"Shut up, Summer! You and your stepfather and his cronies nearly sent me to prison. For statutory rape. I was nineteen. Now, any time a reporter shows up here or in Houston to do a new story on me, they dredge up the past. That's not something I'll easily forget. Or forgive—ever."

"But…"

"Even though my uncle got me out of that mess, even though I've made a success of myself, a cloud has hung over my name. For years. No matter how much money I made. Because of you. Do you understand? At the least opportune times, when delicate deals hang in the balance, a belligerent press will hound me about those trumped-up charges, especially because you're so famous now. No matter how high I climb, somebody's always there, wanting to throw me back in the gutter where you put me. So, I came back to this town— to set things straight once and for all. I want to bury the past and silence my accusers. If you move in with me, everybody around here will think you approve of me and always have.

So, yes, this is about more than sex or revenge or whatever the hell else you think."

"You seem to have done okay in Houston."

"No thanks to you! If you'd had your way, I'd be a registered sex offender today. My uncle was at least able to get that part of my record expunged." The rough bitterness that edged his low tone made her shiver.

"Despite what you say, your plan sounds like revenge."

"You owe me," he muttered. "You don't want me to press charges and sic the crazy justice system on your brother, the way you stuck it to me. Because we both know how destructive and long-reaching the consequences for that would be.

If you do what I ask, Tuck gets a free ride. My plane and pilot will be at LaGuardia Airport every Friday at 3:00 p.m. to pick you up and fly you here for as long as your companionship amuses me. Be there, or by damn, I'll forget how beautiful and vulnerable and innocent-looking you are and do as I please with your brother."

"You wouldn't—"

"Are you willing to risk Tuck's future on that assumption? My anger over the way you railroaded me fueled my ambition to achieve all I've achieved. I doubt Tuck will be so lucky if you throw him to the wolves."

She was shuddering violently when he let her go. Still, his burning eyes didn't release her for another long moment.

"And I have one more condition—you're not to tell a soul about our little bargain."

"Don't do this," she pleaded softly.

"If it gives you any pleasure, I feel as trapped as you do," he muttered.

"Then why are you punishing us both?"

"This meeting's adjourned!" he said in a harder tone. "I intend to finish swimming laps. Naked. You can watch me or join me or leave. Your choice."

Grinning darkly with cynical, angry amusement that stung her to the quick, his hands moved to his waist to shed his towel. Even though he took his time, and she had plenty of time to turn away, she stood where she was, daring him.

Like a raptor, his black eyes gleamed diamond hard as he

ripped the white terry cloth loose. With a shocked gasp she watched, mesmerized, as it fell down his long legs and pooled in an untidy heap beside his bare feet.

His tall legs were planted firmly apart as his hard eyes locked on hers. His full, sensuous mouth smiled wickedly in invitation.

Although she willed herself to turn away, he was so uncompromisingly male, so fully aroused, she was too compelled by him not to look.

"Why don't you stay and swim, too? We could start your weekends a week early," he murmured in a low, seductive tone.

Hot color crept into her cheeks. How could just looking at him be so electrifying? If only she could have hidden her admiration. "I…I don't think that would be wise."

"We're way past wisdom," he murmured drily. "You want to. I want you to. We're both adults. You start serving your time, maybe I'll get my fill of you sooner rather than later. I could let you off early…for good behavior."

Tempted, she trembled as she fought the fierce need to move toward him, to touch him. Her hands clenched. Looking at him took her back to the most glorious, sensual night of her life. He was so virile and handsome she couldn't think.

She wasn't that foolish, naive girl any longer. She'd been fiercely independent for years.

But the foolish hopes and dreams of that girl still lurked in her heart, tormenting her. If Summer didn't turn and walk away, or run—yes, run!—she would do something incredibly stupid, something she would regret for the rest of her life.

Just as she regretted their past love.

Only, she didn't feel as if she regretted it anymore.

Why not? What was happening to her?

Did some crazy part of her want to try again? Did she

really want to risk everything she'd achieved for a second chance with him?

He got you pregnant. When you tried to tell him, he wouldn't even talk to you.

But how could she blame him for what he hadn't known?

"I see you're unsure," he murmured with a faint, derisive smile.

"I—I'm not unsure," she said even as the burning desire in his eyes made her feel as if she was melting. "I think you're a monster, so I—I'm leaving. R-right now. Really."

He laughed. "Then check with Davis for my phone numbers. Call me if you decide to take my offer so I can tell my pilot and my caretaker. Since I'm a gambling man, I'll wager that you'll be here next Friday. We can swim together then. Or do whatever else we feel like. We'll have the whole weekend to enjoy each other."

He spoke casually, as if her decision meant little to him. Then he turned and walked away.

Her stomach in knots, she watched him much too hungrily until he vanished behind a wall of shrubbery.

Four

Manhattan

Summer loved Central Park, especially on a sparkling September day when the leaves had begun to turn and a cool front had put a chill in the air.

"Hugh, I'm so sorry I can't fly out to L.A. this weekend."

Hunched over her smartphone on a bench near the fountain at Bethesda Terrace during a rare break, Summer chose her words carefully.

Guiltily, she pushed a blond strand of hair out of her eyes. "My brother's in trouble, so I have to go back to Bonne Terre."

"But…"

"Truly, there's nothing I'd rather do next weekend than be with you at the premiere of *Kill-Hard*."

"My agent swears it's my breakout role."

"I'm so sorry. Truly. I'll be there Sunday…late."

After Zach.

When Hugh hung up, seething, she was a little surprised that her guilt was overwhelmed by relief.

At least Hugh's premiere was one thing she could scratch off her to-do list.

Summer began to flip through her calendar, deleting or canceling other engagements. For the next few weekends she would be doing her own script work, so she could juggle the commute to Louisiana. Later, when rehearsals began in earnest, getting away from New York would be trickier, maybe downright impossible.

She would worry about that later. Zach would probably be tired of her by then anyway.

Daily, hourly, all through the week, she'd resented Zach for causing such immense upheaval in her life. His demand was outrageous, medieval, and she told herself she was furious with him and with herself for going along with him.

And yet, if that were true, why did her breath catch every time she remembered the avid desire in his eyes? Why did she dream of him holding her close every night? Or awaken hot and sweaty from the image of writhing in his arms like a wanton? She would toss her sheets aside, go to the window and stare out at the stars, imagining spending two days and nights with Zach.

Being a man, no matter what he'd said, all he wanted from her was sex.

But what did she want?

She didn't know. And she didn't know what she could tell Gram. Summer didn't want her grandmother to get her hopes up for no reason. Since she couldn't figure that one out and didn't want to lie, she wouldn't call Gram or take her calls until Summer saw her again in Bonne Terre. Until then, Summer would concentrate on her career goals, on developing and playing her roles. It wasn't healthy to obsess over a man whose sole goal was to punish her.

On Friday, at three o'clock sharp, she met Zach's pilot. Once aboard the jet, she pulled out her script, intending to figure out her character for the scenes with Hugh scheduled to be shot in L.A. next week.

Normally, Summer chose roles because she felt affection for the character, but in this case, her reasons had been more pragmatic. When she'd complained that she didn't think she could do a dark, unlikeable sex addict, her agent had pointed out that the money was simply too good to pass up.

So, Summer needed to study her lines and determine how her edgy sex scenes fit into the emotional context of the movie.

But her mind drifted to Zach, making it impossible for her to concentrate on the femme fatale she was to play in Hugh's film.

Staring out the windows of his Houston office as he held his phone, Zach frowned as his pilot brought him up to date.

"Yeah. She was right on time. Weather looks good until we hit Louisiana. Looks like you're going to have a nasty drive." He gave Zach the plane's arrival time, and the two men ended the call.

Outside, dark purple clouds hung over the city to the northeast. It was only three, but the freeways were already jammed with cars. Impatient, because he'd wanted to leave the city well before rush hour, especially if there was bad weather, Zach thrust his hands into his pockets and prowled his office like a caged cat.

Leroy McEver, the newly hired contractor on Zach's biggest project downtown, was late as usual. Although Zach was sorely tempted to leave, no way was Zach driving to Bonne Terre without making Leroy understand once and for all that the reason he'd fired Anderson and hired him was that he expected Leroy to stop the constant cost overruns.

But even with pressing business to deal with, Zach was anxious to be on his way to Bonne Terre. To her. As always, his inexplicable need to bed her, even after what she'd put him through, annoyed the hell out of him.

After their love affair had been exposed and made to look ugly in the newspapers, he'd zealously guarded his personal life. He kept his private life private. She was a movie star, who probably courted media attention.

There were multiple reasons not to go through with the bargain he'd made with her. But he wouldn't put a stop to it. He couldn't.

Thus, his impatience to see her again infuriated him. He hated himself for stooping to blackmail.

But he wanted her, and she owed him—big-time.

One minute the road was darkly veiled in mist. In the next the brightly lit Thibodeaux house loomed out of the shadowy cypress and oak grove. Summer got out, grabbed her bag and thanked Zach's pilot, Bob, for the lift.

"I've got orders to wait until I'm sure you're safely inside."

Summer's footsteps sounded hollow as she marched up the path, crossed the porch and rang the doorbell.

Setting her bag and briefcase down, she turned the key Bob had given her in the lock, jiggling it until the door opened.

"Zach?"

Again, as her shy, uncertain voice echoed through the empty rooms, she marveled that a man like him, with a house like this, had no staff. As she felt blindly for the light switches on the wall, she heard a man's heavier tread approaching. When she saw a tall, angular shadow splash across the floor between the stacked boxes, her heart began to pound as unwanted, craven excitement coursed through her. All week, she'd waited for this and had been too ashamed to admit it.

"Zach?"

"It's just me, Summer," Tuck said as he ambled through the door at the far end of the room. He had earbuds in his ears and was bouncing to some soundless beat. His hands were jammed into jeans that rode so low on his skinny hips she marveled that he didn't worry about them falling off.

She couldn't see much of his skinny face for the thick golden hair hanging over his eyes.

"You doing okay…since the hospital?" she asked.

"Ever since Zach told me he's not going to press charges, or even fire me, I've been fine. Can you believe he gave me a second chance?"

"Big of him."

"Course, he locked his liquor up and set some pretty strict ground rules," he muttered more resentfully. "Oh, he said I'm supposed to tell you that you can have the bedroom down the hall on the first floor. He made me stock the fridge and get the room ready for you. And he told me to carry your suitcase inside for you."

Tuck came to an abrupt stop in front of her. When she reached for him, he allowed a quick hug.

"I'm glad you're okay," she whispered, ruffling his hair. "Next time, think."

He leaned down and grabbed her suitcase. "Zach told me to tell you about the security system." He told her the code and asked her if she wanted him to write it down or show her how to set it.

She shook her head.

When he showed her the room, she was pleasantly surprised to find antique furniture, curtains and rugs that went together. A silver mirror and comb and brush set lay on a low, polished bureau.

"It's pretty," she said.

"Because Zach sent a dumb decorator and lots of other people over to boss me around and make sure it was."

"Where is Zach?"

"On the road. His meetings ran a lot later than he expected."

"Oh."

"So, why are you here tonight if you hate him so much?"

"I—I don't hate him. It's…it's complicated."

"You're not here because of what I did, are you?"

"Oh, no. It has nothing to do with you." She felt her cheeks heat. "We just…er…reconnected. That's what happens sometimes…with old flames."

He stared at her as if he didn't quite buy it. "So…okay… everything's cool, then. Can I go? I was gonna play some pool tonight before I found out about you and Zach."

She gritted her teeth, not liking that he'd accepted them as a couple so easily. He'd talk, and everybody would believe him.

He stared at her through the greasy strings of his blond hair. "You sure you're okay about this?"

"I'm great! Never better!" She gave him a bright smile.

"You've sure got the whole town talking."

She winced. "You know how people in Bonne Terre talk."

"Yeah. When I shopped for stuff, people kept asking me questions about you."

"So, who are you playing pool with?" she asked, anxious to change the subject.

"Some guys. *Good* guys."

"Hope so. Hey, did Zach say when he'll get here?"

"Maybe. I don't remember. So—can I go now?"

"Give me another minute."

She had work. Lots of it. Since she was a trained stage actress, movie roles did not come naturally to her. Scenes would be shot out of order, and she wouldn't be able to fall back on the rhythm of the play to carry her character into her scene.

Since she needed to study the *before* moments that preceded every scene, she should be happy Zach was running late, but, for some reason, the thought of being alone here in his house with her script depressed her.

Making her way into the kitchen, she opened the fridge and found it full of her favorite cheeses, eggs, fresh vegetables and sparkling water. Zach must have talked to Gram to find out things she liked before sending Tuck to get them.

Closing the fridge door, she realized she wasn't going to work tonight when she felt so empty and strange being in Zach's house without him.

"Can I go now?" her brother repeated.

"If you'll give me a ride to Gram's first."

"If I were you I wouldn't go over there. The local gossips really have her and her friends all stirred up about you. She's been hounding me for details. Says you won't return her calls."

She knew Tuck was right, but she'd rather be at Gram's facing hard questions than stay in this house alone, waiting for Zach. On the drive to Gram's, she switched the conversation back to Tuck. "So, how come you agreed to work for Zach again after you got in trouble? Is it the job you like? Or him?"

"The work's boring, but he's okay. Funny, he's almost like a friend."

Her stomach tightened with alarm. Zach was far from a friend. Tuck should have better sense than to trust that man. But there was no way she could tell Tuck that without giving herself away.

"I wish you'd go back to school and find something that interests you. Then you wouldn't have to do boring work. Or work for Zach."

"School's even more boring. And like I said, I sort of like working for Zach."

"Maybe if you tried to be interested, you'd become interested."

"That's what Zach said the other day when he drove me over to the junior college."

"He what?"

"Drove me to the tech campus. In his Lamborghini. Boy, was everybody impressed."

"I can't believe he took the time.... He's a very busy man." She couldn't hold back now. "You know, Tuck, he's not really your friend."

"Hey, where do you get off criticizing him? You're never here. He is." His tone was low as his sad eyes whipped around to regard her. "You're this big famous actress. Until Zach came back to Bonne Terre, Gram and me didn't interest you much. With your glam job, how could you understand what it's like for someone like me, somebody who's ordinary and stuck here? I can't help if it's hard for me to get excited about my life. It's not much to get excited about."

"Then you've got to do something with your life, Tuck."

"I've heard it before."

"If you don't do something, nobody else is going to do it for you. Life is what you make it."

"Easy for a big shot like you to say. Why don't you stay out of my business, and I'll stay out of yours? Deal?"

"No, it's not a deal!"

Damn. Because of Zach, she was losing precious ground with her brother.

Refusing to come in, Tuck dropped her off at Gram's. As Summer got out of the car, he sped away in an angry whirl of dust and gravel.

Dreading being grilled by Gram, especially after not taking her calls all week, Summer squared her shoulders before marching up to the house.

Summer was barely inside before Gram switched off the television and plopped Silas down on the floor.

"Why didn't you return any of my phone calls?"

Because I was too ashamed of what I was doing.

"That was…unforgiveable of me," Summer whispered. "I did listen to every single message though…if that counts."

"So, when were you going to tell me you've started seeing Zach Torr?" Gram asked excitedly.

"It's not what you think," Summer hedged, feeling acutely uncomfortable that her grandmother was hoping for a true romance.

"What is it, then?"

"Look, it was a long flight. I'm thirsty. Do you have some tea?"

"Why didn't you tell me? Why did I have to hear this from all the gossips?" Gram asked rather gloomily as she and Silas followed Summer into the kitchen.

Summer didn't say anything as Gram splashed tea from a pitcher in the fridge into a tall glass.

"Well, if you won't talk, I'll say my peace. I think it's great that you're reconnecting with Zach."

"We're not…."

"It's high time you two sorted out the past."

"Gram—"

"It will do you both a world of good…to talk it out."

"There's nothing to talk out."

"Oh, no?" After stirring in lemon and mint Gram handed Summer the tall glass of iced tea. "You could talk about New Orleans. And the baby."

Summer's chest felt hollow and tight.

"You looked like death when you came home from New Orleans. I used to wonder if you'd ever get over it. Maybe if you told Zach, let him share that grief with you, maybe then both of you could move on. He's just as stuck in the past as you are."

Summer shook her head. "That was fifteen years ago. It's way too late for us."

Losing his baby after he'd rejected her had hurt so much, Summer had locked her sorrow inside. She'd never wanted to suffer because of it again.

Tears burned behind the back of her eyelids. "I can't talk about it, not even like this, to you, Gram."

Gram's arms slid slowly around her, and Summer, fighting tears, stayed in them for quite a while.

"Spending time with him is the brave thing to do. I think it's a start in finding yourself. I, for one, am going to pray for a miracle."

"You do that," Summer whispered, not wanting to repeat that, for her and Zach, it was hopeless.

"In the meantime, we could play Hearts," Gram said more cheerfully .

"Gram…I…"

"I just love it when Zach stops by to play Hearts…. A man with as much as he has to do taking time for a little old lady… And he's not even my grandson."

Zach again…besting her. Was there no competing with him? No escaping him?

Feeling cornered, Summer sat down with Gram to play Hearts.

Except for the lights she'd left on, the Thibodeaux mansion was still dark several hours later when Summer drove up in Gram's borrowed Ford sedan, after having lost too many games of Hearts. She hadn't bothered to set the security system, so she simply unlocked the door and let herself in.

Feeling restless because Zach still wasn't there, she showered and dressed for bed in a thin T-shirt and a pair of comfortable long cotton pants. Intending to mull over her scenes for a little while, she pulled back her covers and slid into bed with her script.

But just reading through the sex scene made her squirm, so when she saw the remote, she flicked on the television, surfing until she found the weather channel.

There was a big storm over east Texas that Zach would have to drive through. Video of downed trees, traffic signs and power lines made her more apprehensive, so she turned the television off.

Was he okay? If he'd been in an accident, would anyone even think to call her?

He's fine. Just fine. And why should you care if he isn't?

Even more restless now, she got up and padded into the kitchen where she poured herself a glass of sparkling water. She was pacing when her cell phone rang. Hoping it might be Zach, she sprinted back down the hall to answer it.

"What the hell do you think you're doing?" Thurman demanded without bothering to greet her. "How can you move in with that bastard? You should be ashamed of yourself."

She *was* ashamed, and furious at Thurman for punching that hot button.

Headlights flashed across the front of the house as her stepfather lambasted her. Stiffening her spine, she stood up straighter. She wasn't some teenage girl her stepfather could blackmail or control.

"How did you get this number?" Summer said. "I've told you never to call me."

"What are you doing over there? I demand to know."

"It's none of your business. And it hasn't been for a very long time. Mother's dead. I'm an adult. Goodbye."

"You're dragging the family down into the dirt all over again!" He swore viciously.

She turned her phone off just as Zach's key turned in the lock.

Thinking she should give him a piece of her mind for putting her through all this, she stomped toward the front door. Then he stepped wearily across the threshold. She registered the slump of his broad shoulders, which looked soaked in the gray light.

"Hi," she said, feeling an unwanted mixture of relief and sympathy for him.

"Sorry." He seemed as tense and wary as she was. "I hope I didn't wake you up."

"You didn't." No way would she admit she'd been worrying about him. "Thirsty." She waved her glass of water. "Thanks for getting all my favorite stuff. For the fridge, I mean."

"All I did was have Rhonda make a phone call to your grandmother. Rhonda's my secretary." When he smiled crookedly, he was incredibly handsome despite the dark circles of fatigue shadowing his eyes.

"Long day?" she whispered, feeling slightly breathless, already having fallen under the spell of his lean, sculpted beauty.

He nodded. "Even before the drive. Long week, too. When it rains…it pours. Literally."

"Oh, and the storm. Was it bad?"

"It slowed me down."

From the late hour and his tight features, she was almost sure that was an understatement.

"Do you have any more bags? Could I help you carry something inside?"

"You're being awfully nice. Too nice," he accused, his dark eyes flashing dangerously. "Why?"

"Yes—and I don't know why. I don't trust myself, either."

When he smiled and seemed to relax, she felt her own tension ease a little. But just a little. After all, their shared weekend loomed in her imagination. She wasn't sure what he expected of her tonight.

"No," he said. "I don't need help. This is all I brought." He paused. "If you hadn't spent your night here waiting on me, what glamorous place would you have been?"

"In L.A., at Hugh's premiere."

At the mention of Hugh, Zach's eyes darkened.

"I was going out there this weekend because we start shooting together next week."

"Are you two doing a love scene?" His voice was hard now. *More than one.*

Annoyed because he'd nailed her and because, like most people, he so obviously attached undue significance to anything of a sexual nature on film, she ignored his question.

"I don't want to talk about Hugh with you."

"Good. Because neither the hell do I."

She hesitated, wondering why he sounded jealous and not knowing where to go from here. "Are you hungry?"

"Look, there's no need for you to worry about me. It's late…. And I've screwed up your schedule enough today as it is."

Of course he was right, but he looked so bone weary, as if it had taken everything out of him to get here while she'd rested on his plane and had been pampered at Gram's.

"I'll just put some cheese and ham out," she said. "You bought it, after all."

"Not so that you would stay up and wait on me. I can take care of myself."

"It won't take a minute," she insisted, stubbornly refusing to let him boss her around.

"Okay. I'll be back down after I freshen up." He left her and carried his bag and briefcase upstairs.

By the time he strode into the kitchen, she'd opened a bottle of wine and set a single place for him at the kitchen table.

When he sat down, she noted that his black hair was still gleaming wet.

"You're not eating?" he said, sipping wine, when she hovered but didn't sit.

"I ate at Gram's earlier."

"Not those chocolate-chip cookies she baked just for me, I hope?" he teased.

"She bakes them for me, too—even though I tell her not to." Summer grinned back at him. As she pulled out a chair, she couldn't stop staring into his utterly gorgeous eyes. Was there a man alive with longer lashes? A tiny pulse had begun to throb much too fast at the base of her throat, causing her breath to catch.

What was going on? How could she actually be so thrilled he was here, safe and sound, when he'd forced her to come to him, when he intended to deliberately humiliate her? When Thurman and the rest of the town were judging and accusing her? When Hugh was sulking in L.A. and her agent and director were apoplectic? When she'd disappointed poor, darling Gram, who was hoping for a happy ending to this farce?

"I had a few cookies after a chicken sandwich," she replied, striving to sound nonchalant. "Dessert is allowed sometimes, you know."

"Even for an actress who has to keep her perfect figure... so she'll look mouth-wateringly sexy in those love scenes... with Hugh?"

His angry black gaze flicked over her breasts in her thin T-shirt. His male assessment accused her even as it made her blood heat.

"Love scenes in movies aren't the least bit sexy. They're all about creating an illusion for the viewer."

"Is that so? You always were good at creating illusions."

He glanced away abruptly, trying to hide his obvious interest in her body and his fury at the thought of her with Hugh, but it was too late. Suddenly the walls of his kitchen felt as if they were closing in on her, and she couldn't breathe. How could he charge the air between them with a mere question and a hot, proprietary glance?

"You have no right to attack me or to look at me like that. No right at all."

"Then maybe you shouldn't dress the way you do," he muttered in a tone so savage she knew he was as provoked as she.

"I'm wearing an ordinary T-shirt."

His hard eyes burned her breasts again. "Right. I guess it's the fact the material's so thin and you're braless underneath that's getting to me."

"Sorry!"

When she felt her nipples tighten and poke at the cotton fabric, she clenched her hands. He was impossible. Since he'd come back to Bonne Terre, he'd been turning everything into some sort of sex game.

"Why you're determined to put us both through a weekend like this, I can't imagine."

He stared at her for a long time. "You know why. Just as you know you have it coming." He stabbed a piece of cheese.

"I think I'd better go back to bed," she said abruptly, not trusting herself, or him, or the intimacy of their cozy little situation. "We're obviously not a couple who can cohabitate easily and naturally."

At her rejection, his dark face was suddenly blank and cold. "Good idea. Go ahead. I'll clean up—alone."

"You're supposed to be a billionaire. Why don't you have staff to do all that?"

"Because they're people, and I'd have to deal with them and their problems. Because I want to live informally here and not be bothered by too many prying eyes. Because I couldn't be here…like this…with you, if I had a staff. Not that I don't have a cleaning lady. And my secretary just hired a gardener. So, do you have more questions about how I live my life before you leave me in peace?"

He wanted *her* gone! She was getting on *his* nerves! His attitude infuriated her. He'd blackmailed her into coming here, hadn't he? He'd launched the blatant sexual attack.

What had she expected—wine and roses?

Her heart pounding, she turned stiffly. Marching to her bedroom, she locked herself in and threw herself on the bed where she lay wide-awake, tossing and turning and staring up at the ceiling for what felt like an endless time.

Her mood was ridiculous. She should be thrilled he didn't want her tonight.

She heard the savage clink of dishes and silver in the kitchen, of a garbage lid being slammed, of the disposal grinding violently. His heavy tread resounded in the hall outside her door and on the stairs. Then he stomped about in the room above hers. Something crashed to his floor so hard she sprang to a sitting position. Fisting her sheets, she stared at the ceiling listening, but after that bit of violence, he quieted.

When he turned on the water, the sound of it hummed in her blood. She imagined him naked in his shower with hot suds washing over his warm, sleek muscles. And despite what he'd said to anger her, she wanted to go up and join him.

Slowly, she got out of bed and went to her bathroom. Stripping, she turned on her own shower. When the water was warm, she stepped into the steam, threw her head back and let the pulsing flow drench her. She cupped her breasts and imagined him seizing her, thrusting inside her. She imagined her hands circling his hard waist. She imagined pressing herself against him even tighter as she begged for more.

The water ran down her limbs and circled in the drain. Sighing in frustration, she fell back against the tile wall while the spray streamed over her. A strange sensation of loss and a fierce longing to move beyond their past and their present darkness possessed her.

She clenched her fists, beat the tiles, but it did no good.

He disliked her, yet he would force her to stay with him.

Did he intend to hook her on his lovemaking and then laugh at her and leave her? Would he flaunt their relationship to everybody in Bonne Terre and beyond to prove she and her stepfather had wronged him?

She closed her eyes and pushed her wet hair out of her face. Because of her own shameless desire, she was on emotionally unsafe ground.

How would she make it through the weekend without falling more deeply under his spell?

Five

When Summer awoke the next day, she sat up slowly, her heart racing, as she thought about Zach upstairs in his own bed. Except for the birds, the house seemed too quiet and dark. But that was only because she was used to pedestrians on the sidewalks and tenants on the stairs, to sirens and traffic, to garbage trucks making their early rounds as the Upper West Side woke up.

Fearing Zach might not have slept any better than she had, she crept noiselessly from her bed to the bathroom where she brushed her teeth, washed her face and combed her hair.

Rummaging through her suitcase, she put on a T-shirt and a pair of tight-fitting jeans. Okay, so he'd probably comment on how tight they were, but she didn't own any other kind.

Grabbing her script, she headed for the kitchen where she found a bag of coffee. She closed all the doors before she ground the coffee and started a pot. Listening to the birds, she decided it might be more fun to work on the porch.

She went to the door and was taking great pains to open it without making the slightest sound, when the security alarm began to blare.

With a little scream, she clamped her hands over her ears and fought without success to remember the code.

"Blast it!" she muttered as Zach slammed down the stairs.

Wearing nothing but a pair of jeans, and dragging a golf club, he hurled himself into the kitchen.

"My fault. I forgot about the alarm," she said, staring at his chest and finding him heart-throbbingly magnificent. "I was trying so hard not to wake you."

He punched in the code and set the golf club down. "It's okay. Usually I get up way before now. Coffee smells good." He raked his hands through his hair.

"It does, doesn't it?" She broke off, tongue-tied as usual around him, maybe because his gaze left her breathless.

"Did you sleep okay?" he asked in a rough tone.

"I guess."

"I had a tough night, too," he murmured, grinning sheepishly.

His super-hot gaze made her tummy flip. Suddenly, sharing the kitchen with him when he was sexily shirtless, when he kept his eyes welded to hers, seemed too intimate. She felt as awkward as she would have on a first date when she knew something might happen but didn't know what. Quickly, she turned away and poured herself a coffee. Then she scurried outside. Behind her she heard his knowing chuckle.

Not that she could work out here, she mused, not when he was bustling about in the kitchen.

Concentrate on something else! Anything else but him!

The morning air was fresh and cool, and the sky a vivid pink. As her frantic gaze wandered to the fringe of trees that edged the far corner of his property, three doe and a tiny fawn picked their way out of the woods in a swirl of ground fog to nibble a clump of damp grass.

Summer tiptoed back to the kitchen door and pushed it open. Holding a fingertip against her lips, she waved to Zach to come out.

When he joined her, he smiled, as charmed by the scene as she.

"I'll bet you never see anything like that in Manhattan."

"There are all sorts of amazing sights in Manhattan," she murmured in a futile attempt to discount the awe that sharing the dawn with him inspired.

"I'll bet somebody as famous as you could never live anywhere as boring as Louisiana or Texas again. Or be serious about anybody who wasn't a movie star like Jones."

"I didn't say that!"

His hard eyes darkened as they clashed with hers.

An awkward minute passed as she tried to imagine herself living with Zach, here, in Houston, anywhere. Impossible—she was an actress, who lived in Manhattan.

"To change the subject—what do you want to do today?" he asked casually.

"I need to study those scenes I have to shoot next week."

"That's fine. I did make tentative plans for us to meet Tuck and Gram at the new Cajun café on the bayou. Over lunch I thought we could encourage Tuck to enroll in one of the tech programs at the junior college."

"Tuck's not interested in school."

"Really? When I informed him I might press charges if he didn't take some responsible action about his future, he told me he'd like to take some courses that could lead to a career as a utility lineman."

"I can't believe this! You're threatening Tuck, too, now."

"It's way past time he stepped up to the plate. I took him over to the junior college Wednesday and introduced him to Travis Cooper, who's the young, enthusiastic head of that particular program. He was a late bloomer, like your Tuck, which may be why the two of them hit it off immediately."

"Okay—I can do lunch," she replied. "I like your results, even if I don't approve of your tactics. Then I'll need to study my scenes this afternoon...since I procrastinated last night."

"Okay. While you do that, I'll inspect one of my building projects."

He took a long breath, his black eyes assessing her with such frank male boldness her tummy went hollow. "But, I'll want to spend the evening with you. Alone. Here."

"Of course," she whispered, her skin heating even as she fought to look indifferent.

Without warning, he stepped closer and grinned down at her. "I'm glad you agreed so easily. I want you to be eager."

He bent his handsome black head toward hers, and she was so sure he would kiss her, she actually pursed her lips and stood on her tiptoes as if in feverish anticipation.

But he only laughed, as if he was pleased he had her wanting him. "Save it for tonight, sweetheart."

A very colorful curse word popped into her mind, but she bit her lips and made do with a frown.

Lunch with Tuck and Gram was amazing. First, the succulent fried shrimp, which were crunchy and light, were so addictive Summer had to sit on fisted hands to keep from stealing the one Zach left on his plate just to tempt her. As she was staring at that shrimp, Tuck finished his gumbo and astonished her by informing Zach that, yes, he'd decided he was fine with giving Cooper and his dumb program a chance. She was further amazed when she listened to him converse easily and intelligently with Zach, as Tuck rarely did with her. She could tell that Zach really had been devoting a great deal of time to Tuck, and that Tuck was lapping up the attention.

Despite all that was enjoyable about lunch, she didn't like the attention from surrounding diners, who stared and snapped pictures with their phones.

"Did you have an ulterior motive for lunching with all of us so publicly?" Summer asked after they dropped off Tuck and Gram and were driving home.

Zach's mouth was tight as he stared grimly at the road. "Being railroaded on felony charges and then being tried in the court of public opinion wasn't any picnic, either."

"That still doesn't make it right for you to use Tuck and Gram to get even with me."

"Maybe I just want people to see that I have a normal relationship with all of you," Zach said.

"But you don't. You're blackmailing me."

"Right." His dark eyes glittering, he turned toward her. The sudden intimacy between them stunned her. "Well, I want people to know that you're not afraid of me. That you never were. That you liked me, loved me even. That I was not someone who'd take a young, unwilling girl off to the woods to molest her. Is that so wrong?"

His face blurred as she forced herself to focus on the trees streaming past his window instead of him. The realization of how profoundly she'd hurt him hit her anew.

Yes, he'd hurt her, too, and yes, he'd gone on to achieve phenomenal success. But he'd never gotten over the deep injury her betrayal had inflicted—any more than she'd gotten over losing him and the baby.

Because of her, Zach had been accused of kidnapping and worse. All he'd ever tried to do was help her.

When a talent scout had been wowed by her high-school performance in *Grease,* her stepfather had forbidden her to go back to her theater-arts class. He'd sworn he wouldn't pay for her to study theater arts in college, either.

So she'd run away to Zach, who'd forced her to go back

and try to reason *with Thurman.* Only after her stepfather struck her and threatened her with more physical violence if she didn't bend to his will had Zach driven her to Nick's fishing cabin on the bayou in Texas. There they'd hidden out and made love. There they'd been found in each other's arms by Thurman and his men.

She did owe Zach. More than a few weekends. And not just because of Tuck. If Zach wanted to be seen with her and gossiped about—so be it.

"You don't have to drive me home before you go to your site," she said softly. "I'll go with you."

"I thought you needed to work on your love scenes with Hugh."

His voice hardened when he said the other man's name, and she felt vaguely guilty. Which was ridiculous, since she wasn't in a relationship with either man.

"I do, but I'll study on the plane, or later, when I get to L.A."

"Well, if you're coming with me, I've got to take you home anyway. Those sandals won't work at the construction site and neither will that tight, sexy skirt."

"Oh."

"You'll need to wear a long-sleeved shirt, jeans and boots. I'll supply you with a plastic hard hat and a safety vest with reflective tape."

"Sounds like a dangerous place."

Even though it was Saturday, cranes, bulldozers and jack-hammers were operating full force as battalions of work-ers carried out all sorts of tasks, none of which made sense to Summer as she adjusted the inner straps of her hard hat. Zach seemed as happy as a kid showing off as he led her around the site, pointing at blueprints, sketches and plans with a pocket roll-up ruler, introducing her to all of his foremen and contractors. Local men, all of them, who eyed her with open speculation.

Zach was developing hundreds of acres along the bayou, creating a dock for his riverboat casino, as well as restaurants, a hotel, a small amusement park, shops, a theater, a golf course and no telling what else.

"I've never built anything," she said, "so I'm impressed. Look, you don't have to entertain me. I'll explore on my own."

"You be careful and don't go too far."

At first she stayed close to him because the ground was rough and muddy. Then she began walking toward the dock on two-by-fours that men had laid across deep holes as makeshift bridges.

She was standing on such a bridge when Nick drove up in his battered pickup, looking for Zach. The elderly shrimper wore faded jeans, a T-shirt and scuffed boots. Even though he dipped his cowboy hat ever so slightly when he saw Summer, his cold, unsmiling face told her he hadn't forgiven her. Until Zach's uncle had shown up, Nick had been Zach's sole advocate.

"Didn't expect to see the likes of you here, *cher*," he said when he walked up to her. "Dangerous place for a woman."

Nick was thinner than the last time she'd seen him, his tanned skin crisscrossed with lines, his wispy hair steel-gray. But the penetrating blue eyes that pierced her hadn't changed much.

"And you're a dangerous woman for any man, even Zach. I warned the boy to stay away from you, but he won't listen," Nick said, eyeing Zach, who stood a hundred yards to their right, deep in conversation with a contractor. "He never did have a lick of sense where you were concerned. I don't like you settin' your hooks in him again. By coming out here with him you'll have the whole town talkin' and thinkin' you're a couple again."

"Tell him. He invited me for the weekend."

Nick spat in disbelief. "Well, you tell him I stopped by and that I'll catch up with him later. Or, if he'd prefer, he can drop by…after he gets rid of you."

She nodded.

He turned and left.

Her mood dark and remorseful, she headed toward the dock. Because of the deep holes in the ground, she was forced to cross on the makeshift bridge again. She'd nearly reached the dock when Zach called out to her.

Maybe she turned too fast—one of the boards slipped, and she tumbled several feet into the muddy hole filled with rocks and debris. When she tried to stand, her left ankle buckled under her weight.

She looked up in alarm and saw Zach running toward her, his dark eyes grave. Leaping over the boards, he was soon towering over her. "Are you okay?"

"Yes—except for my left ankle."

"I should never have brought you here."

"Nonsense. I fell. It all was my fault."

"Hang on to me, then," he commanded, jumping down into the hole.

Half carrying her, he led her out of the pit and back to his car. As he drove away from the site, he called Gram, who recommended her doctor, a man who generously offered to meet them at the emergency room. Dr. Sands actually beat them to the E.R., and Summer, who'd once fallen off a stage in Manhattan and had waited hours in a New York E.R., was both appreciative and amazed to be treated so quickly and expertly in such a small hospital. Most of all, she was grateful to Zach for staying with her.

When a team of nurses stepped inside the treatment room and asked him to leave, Zach demanded to know what they planned to do.

"Dr. Sands wants her to disrobe for an examination, so we can make sure we don't miss any of her injuries."

"But it's only my ankle that hurts," Summer protested.

"Hopefully you're right. But this is our protocol. We have to be sure."

Summer reached for Zach's hand. "Would you…"

So, he stayed beside her, gallantly turning his back when they handed her a hospital gown and she began to undress. But once, when she moaned, he turned. She saw his quick flush and heard his gasp before he averted his gaze from her body.

Her stomach fluttered. Funny that it hadn't occurred to her to be embarrassed that he should see her almost naked. She simply wanted him beside her.

When the professionals finished checking her body and stooped to examine her ankle, she cried out in pain.

Zach was at her side, pressing her hand to his lips. "Hang in there. We'll be home before you know it."

Home. How sweetly the word buzzed in her heart. She squeezed his fingers and held on tight, feeling illogically reassured.

He was right. In less than an hour she was back at Zach's house, propped up on his couch by plump pillows, surrounded by his remotes, her script and her favorite snacks.

Strangely, after the hospital, there was a new easiness between them. Gram and Tuck had stopped by to check on her, and after they departed, Zach remained attentive, never leaving her side for long. He said he wanted to be nearby in case she needed anything. She found his hovering oddly sweet and realized it would be much too easy to become dependent on such attentions.

When the sun went down, he cooked two small steaks and roasted two potatoes for their dinner while she watched from her chair at the kitchen table. They had their meal with wine and thick buttered slices of French bread out on the back veranda.

Again she marveled that a man who must be used to servants knew his way around in a kitchen. She didn't mind in the least that he hadn't thought to prepare more sides. The simple meal was perfect even before the three deer reappeared to delight them.

Later, when she was back on the couch again and he'd finished the dinner dishes, he pulled up a chair beside her. Pleased that he hadn't gone up to his room, she declared the steak delicious and thanked him for his trouble.

"I'm not much of a cook," he said. "Eggs, steak and toast. That's about it."

"Don't forget potatoes. Yours were very nice. Crispy."

"Right. Sometimes I can stick a potato or two in the oven and sprinkle them with olive oil and salt. I have a cook in Houston, but I don't like eating at home alone. So, mostly I eat out."

"Me, too. Or I do take-out. Because I don't have time to cook."

"I imagined you in ritzy New York restaurants, dining on meals cooked by the world's best chefs, eating with famous movie stars."

When his expression darkened, she suspected he was thinking of Hugh.

"Not all that often. Fancy meals take time to eat…as well as to cook and serve," she said, avoiding the topic of Hugh. "And fans pester you for autographs. Besides, there's nothing quite like a homemade meal, is there?"

"You used to want to be an actress so badly. What's it like now that you've succeeded?"

"It's nice, but I work almost all the time. Even when I have a job, I'm always auditioning for the next part. When I sign on with a show that isn't in New York, I travel and live out of a suitcase. One minute it's a crazy life, full of parties and friends, then it gets pretty lonely. You can't hold on to anything because it's all so ephemeral. The friends I make within a cast feel closer than family for a while. Then they vanish after each show closes," she admitted.

"But when you sign with a new show or film you have a new set of friends."

"Yes, but as I get older, I see that, despite the bright lights, a life without stability isn't nearly so glamorous as people think."

"It's what you wanted."

She sighed. "Be careful what you wish for. I guess I took my real life for granted. Lately, I've realized how much I miss family…and roots."

"What does that mean?"

"My job is so all-consuming that I…I haven't been good at relationships. I'm Southern, like Gram. She sees my single state as a failure, and lets me know it every chance she gets. Her dream for me was marriage to a handsome husband. I was supposed to have two children, a boy and a girl, and live happily ever after in a cute house surrounded by a white picket fence."

He smiled. "But you, being a modern woman, aren't into such an outdated, traditional formula for happiness. Strange, that it can still exert such a hold over a female as wise as your grandmother."

"You're right, of course. I just wish I could make her understand that I have everything I set my heart on. I'm grateful for what I have, for what I've achieved. So many people would give anything to be me."

She was saying the same truths she'd lived by for years, but, for some reason, the words felt hollow tonight.

Zach didn't say anything.

She'd never imagined having such an ordinary, simple,

companionable evening with him, and she found herself enjoying it more than she'd enjoyed anything in a very long time. When they'd been kids, they'd been friends before they'd been lovers. They hadn't fallen in love until after he'd graduated and she'd been entering her senior year.

Now, as an adult, she spent so much time working on her image and her brand, so much time learning various roles, and never very much time being herself. What would it be like to have a lifetime of such evenings with a man like him? To take them for granted?

She sighed. That wasn't who she was now. She had her career, a bright future—and it was on the stage and screen.

"What about you?" she whispered. "You're successful. Are you happy?"

"Like you, I'm not unhappy," he muttered thickly. "I, too, have everything I always thought I wanted…except maybe for…" He shot her a look that was so intense it burned away her breath.

"For what?"

"It doesn't matter," he growled. "Not even billionaires can have it all. Not that we don't pretend that we can, with our fancy cars and homes and yachts." Frowning, he sprang to his feet and then glanced at his watch. "But you're injured, and it's late. You must be tired. Besides, Sands prescribed that painkiller. I'm afraid I've been very selfish to keep you up so long."

She didn't want him to go. "No. I'm barely injured, and you've waited on me hand and foot…. And I just sat there and let you."

"Well, I won't keep you any longer."

"But I really do want to know…about you," she whispered.

"Let's save that boring tale for later," he said, cutting her off. "Who knows—maybe you'll get lucky and never have to hear it." He picked up her crutches. "Why don't I help you to your room?"

Feeling stunned and a little hurt by how abruptly he'd ended their pleasant evening, she got to her feet. As she stood, her uncertain eyes met his. But he wouldn't hold her gaze.

Suddenly, she again felt awkward at the thought of their sharing the house for another night. Stiffening, he handed her the crutches and then backed away.

"I hate these things," she said as she placed the crutches under her arms.

"It's a minor sprain. The doctor said you might even be off them as soon as Tuesday."

"I hope so. Thanks again for tonight. When you convinced me to come here for the weekend, I never thought…we would have this kind of evening or that I could enjoy simply being with you so much."

"Neither the hell did I," he admitted in a stilted tone, still not looking at her. "Believe me—I had a very different kind of weekend in mind."

"Well, you've been very nice."

"Good night, then," he muttered, his voice sounding so furious she realized he'd had more than enough of her company.

He'd blackmailed her because he'd wanted revenge. He'd wanted sex. Had this evening, with its simple pleasures, bored him?

She felt hurt and rejected, just as she had last night.

Six

Zach knew he wouldn't be able to sleep for a while, so instead of undressing for bed, he poured himself a glass of scotch. Then he strode out onto the balcony where the humid air smelled of honeysuckle, jasmine and pine.

Damn those bewitching blue eyes of hers and her pretty, sweet smile that made him want her so badly he hurt.

Why hadn't he taken Summer as he'd intended? Why hadn't he punished her? Usually he came on strong with women. What the hell was wrong with him this weekend?

Next week she would be with Hugh, making love to him—at least on film. And probably offscreen, too. Not that her relationship with Jones should be any concern of Zach's. Still, he burned every time he thought about her with that egotistical phony.

Their first night here she'd seemed so vulnerable and uneasy. Then today, when she'd fallen, she had taken his hand and begged him to stay with her. Her fingers and wrist had felt so slim and fragile in his much larger hand. What kind of man forced his presence on a woman who seemed so defenseless and in need of his protection?

Still, Zach wasn't so noble that he could forget the glimpses he'd seen of her breasts and her creamy thighs. He wanted to kiss those breasts, tongue all the warm, succulent places between her thighs. He knew what she'd done in the past, how close she'd come to nearly destroying him—but for reasons he didn't understand, he continued to balk at using her sexually.

No longer did he want to expose their relationship to the press for public consumption.

This weekend had backfired. Damn it.

The sensitive male was a new role for him.

She'd beaten him.

To save his own ass, tomorrow he'd tell her their deal was off and send her packing.

Then he'd do the smart thing: return to Houston and forget her.

The next morning, when Summer awoke, her ankle was so much better she could almost walk without limping if she used one crutch. When she went into the kitchen she discovered that Zach had already cooked and eaten breakfast. She looked down at his dishes in the sink and realized he was avoiding her.

Rolling the scrambled egg and bacon he'd left for her into a tortilla, she walked outside and saw him swimming laps in his pool. When she waved, he got out.

As he dried off, it was all she could do not to stare, even though he wore swimming trunks.

His eyes were guarded as he strode up to her. "How's the ankle?"

"Much better," she whispered, lowering her lashes.

"Good. Bob is standing by to fly you to L.A. So, whenever you're ready, just call him. I know you've got work, and so do I, so I won't keep you."

He was so remote and cool that her acute disappointment and hurt felt like withdrawal, which was ridiculous.

"What about next weekend?" she whispered, her voice catching. "Do you still want to see me?"

Zach sucked in a breath. "Like you said, maybe spending the weekends together wasn't such a good idea. So—you won." His voice was cold, revealing nothing.

He slung a towel across his shoulders and turned away, dismissing her as if she were of no importance to him.

"Are you mad at me?"

"Yeah. Mad at myself, too."

"Zach…"

"You have your real life…in the theater. And I have mine. I think we should just cool it."

He was right, of course.

"Or maybe not," she said huskily as she focused on his profile. "I want to know why you blackmailed me and then changed your mind, why you were so nice last night and are so cold today."

"Maybe I started thinking about what happened fifteen years ago and don't see this going anywhere positive."

He wasn't making sense. Last week he'd wanted to punish her. And now… What did he want?

"What if I disagree?" she whispered. On impulse, she leaned forward on her tiptoes and kissed his rough cheek tentatively.

When he jerked away as if burned, she beamed. "I enjoyed last night, you see. Too much. And I thought maybe you did, too…just a little. You were sweet."

"Sweet?" He almost snarled the word.

She smiled gently. "And I thank you for what you're doing

for Tuck, too…taking him out to the tech school and all…
especially after what he did to you."

"Forget it," he snapped.

"What if I can't?"

"Soon you'll fly to L.A. to film those love scenes with
Jones. Don't waste your charm or blatant come-on sexuality
on me. Save it for him."

"I don't care about him."

Not believing her, he scowled.

"I don't."

When she edged closer and held her hand to his face, Zach
froze. At the first light touch of her fingertips on his warm
throat, he shuddered. When he tried to wrench away, her
hands came around his neck so she could hold him close.
She had no idea what she was doing or why she was doing
it, she only knew she didn't want to part from him so dis-
passionately, when something new and wonderful was beginning in her heart.

"Can't you at least kiss me goodbye," she whispered, too
aware of her taut nipples pressing against his hard, bare chest.

"Not a good idea," he growled.

"You sure about that?" She rubbed her hips against the
hard ridge of his erection, sighing as her body melted against
his.

On a groan, he reached for her, gripping her with strong,
sure arms, pulling her close, like a man who was starving
for her.

She was starving, too, starving for the intoxicating sensu-
ality of his mouth claiming hers. He tasted so good, so right.
For fifteen years, she'd wanted this and denied it. Why should
she fight it now? Moaning, she kissed him back.

His savage grip crushed her. His hungry passion ignited
unmet needs. Murmuring his name feverishly, her fingertips
ran through his thick, inky hair.

"All weekend I wanted this," she whispered. "Wanted you. Wanted to touch you, to kiss you…to be in your arms…even though I tried to tell myself I didn't. Friday night I lay in bed, wanting this more than I'd ever wanted anything. And last night after we talked, I craved it even more, craved it so much I felt like I was about to burst. Then you went upstairs, and I felt so lost and alone in that bed. I—I couldn't sleep for hours. You told me you'd make me want you, and you were right."

"You shouldn't say these things."

"I don't understand any of it and yet…it's the truth."

"Hell," he muttered. "This isn't some damn role you've got to understand. Life's messy and chaotic and doesn't make a lick of sense most of the time. Like now. Like last night. I decided you're the one woman I should have nothing to do with. And yet here I am…."

"Tell me about it," she whispered. "You're definitely bad for me, too."

When his mouth took hers again, his desperation and urgency made her dizzily excited.

"This is crazy," she whispered as her fingertips glided across the damp hair on his bronzed flesh. "I didn't want to come this weekend, and now I can't bear to go."

"I don't want you to go, either."

"Punish me like you swore you would. Make love to me," she whispered.

The next thing she knew, he was lifting her, kissing her wildly as he carried her up the stairs, into the house and then down the hall to her room. Locking the door, he drew her down to the bed.

In no time, she stripped, but even in her rush, she enjoyed the striptease, for never had she played to a more fascinated audience. He lay on the bed watching as she undid her blouse in the shadows. Button by button, her slim fingers skimmed downward. He held his breath, his eyes burning when she threw her blouse aside and unhooked her bra.

"You are exquisite," he rasped when she slid her lacy panties down her thighs. Vaguely she was aware of him rustling with a foil wrapper. Then, reaching for her, he lay down beside her and buried his face in the curve of her neck.

She let her head fall back, offering him her breasts. "You're pretty okay yourself."

His lips traced the length of her throat. He tasted first one nipple and then the other until they beaded into damp, pink pearls. She trembled with an enjoyment she couldn't hide, which she could see excited him even more.

When his lips found hers again, she fell back against the pillows and opened her mouth so his tongue could slide inside.

"Strip for me," she whispered. "I want to see you naked."

"Wicked girl."

Grinning, he ripped off his swimming trunks. Her breath stopped. He was huge and gorgeous, magnificently virile. While she watched approvingly through the screen of her lowered lashes, he tossed his trunks into a far corner.

Reaching toward him, she slid her hand over his manhood, circling it so that he inhaled sharply. While she touched him, he caressed her most secret, delicate folds with blunt-fingered hands, teasing her sensitive nub of flesh until her breath came hard and fast and she wanted him inside her more than anything.

But he refused for a while longer, teasing her with his mouth and hands while she grew hotter and wilder.

How had she lived without him all these years?

Squeezing him, she rubbed in an urgent, methodic way until he groaned and gathered her close. She heard the sound of a foil wrapper again. Then he slid the condom on and, much to her delight, positioned the head of his shaft against her damp entrance.

Murmuring her name, he hovered there, kissing her hair, her brow. Only when she arched her hips upward in sensual invitation did he slide all the way inside. For a moment, he stopped and simply held her so they could savor the sensation of their joined bodies.

"Zach," she pleaded.

His hips surged. She cried out as he drove himself home.

Their eyes met and held. With her hands, she cupped his face and kissed each of his cheeks and then his nose.

He sighed, as if relieved of some immense weight. Then, all too soon, some primal force took over.

How she loved lying underneath him, staring up at the breadth of his bronzed shoulders, at his black hair that dripped perspiration onto his gorgeous face as he pumped. She felt on fire. With every thrust he claimed her, and she surrendered to him as she had as a girl, completely, irrevocably, giving him every shattered piece of her heart.

Thus did he sweep her away to emotional and sensual peaks she'd never known before. Crying out in the end, she held on to him, feeling lost and yet found again as he exploded inside her. In a blinding flash, she saw that he had always remained at the center of her heart.

For a long time she lay trembling quietly beneath him. Then she kissed his damp eyelashes and eyebrows. *I love you,* she thought. *I always have. This is what has been missing.*

If I have everything else and lack this, I can never be complete.

Only gradually did she grow aware of how wonderfully heavy he was on top of her. When she opened her eyes and looked up at the hard angles of his handsome face, she saw that he was staring down at her with a brooding intensity that frightened her.

"You've got to go soon, so you can cram for those damn scenes with Jones." Frowning, he kissed the tip of her nose.

"Yes," she replied drowsily without the least bit of enthusiasm. "I think you just sapped all my ambition to be a movie star. I just want to stay here with you."

He nipped her upper lip a little firmly…as if to snap her out of her languid mood. "But that's not who you are, is it? You said your career is what completes you, not relationships. And with my uncle not there to help me anymore, I've got a helluva lot to do in Houston. So…"

No sweet words. Nothing. Just those two parting kisses.

A chill swept her. Had she been wrong about their sex being spiritual as well as physical? Had it just been revenge for him after all? Now that he'd had her again, was he done?

"And next weekend?" she murmured, deliberately keeping her voice light. "Do we meet again?"

"I'll call you," he said slowly, but there was no conviction in his voice. Her heart sank as he stroked her neck absently. "Like I said, we both have a lot on our plates."

"Sounds to me like maybe I'm off the hook. For good behavior?"

"Maybe," he admitted.

"Okay, then. I get it."

He stared at her, sucked in a breath, but didn't reply.

She rose, reached for her clothes and began to dress hurriedly.

So what if he wasn't going to call? She'd served her time, so to speak. Now he wouldn't press charges against Tuck.

Logically, she knew that it was probably best if this thing between them ended here. For her, sex with him had been too intense, too all-consuming for her to have a light affair. He would break her heart all over again if she wasn't careful. No smart adult should let herself become involved with a man she'd loved and obsessed over for years.

But she wasn't feeling logical. She was feeling sensually

and emotionally aflame after his lovemaking. The whole world seemed aglow. He seemed a part of her, her other half.

Naturally, she wanted to see him again, to lie in his arms like this again. She felt she'd lose a vital part of herself forever if she couldn't. Which meant he'd completed his mission, by using sex as a weapon to punish her.

He'd won.

Seven

On her flight to L.A., try as she might, Summer found it impossible to concentrate on her script. Hurt simmered inside her because of Zach's coolness at their parting. Thus, the minute the jet's wheels slammed against tarmac, she turned on her phone, desperate to check her messages.

She swallowed when she found only a single text from Hugh.

can't meet u. nominated sexiest man n known universe 2day. jerk leaked information about hot scenes n dangerous man. horde of paparazzi @ my bldg.

No sooner had her plane rolled to a stop in front of a private hangar than a herd of photographers stampeded her jet.

Great. I'm on my own. This is what I deserve for letting the world think even for one minute I was ever serious about Hugh.

Bob stuck his shaggy head out of the cockpit and said, "Not to worry. I've already notified security."

When she finally left the jet, with a security detail, paparazzi on motorcycles chased her limo all the way to her hotel. Apparently, Hugh's premiere had been well-received by critics and the public, so for now he was the hottest talent in La-La Land.

Welcome to Hollywood, she thought as she bolted herself into her hotel room.

When room service arrived with her breakfast the next morning, Summer found a weekly tabloid tucked under her door along with a note from her agent. The tabloid's banner headline read: Sexiest Man In The Universe Teams With Reputed Lover, Broadway Actress Summer Wallace, To Shoot Super Sexy Love Scenes. The article beneath the headline made her feel cheap and tawdry, especially after her weekend with Zach.

Summer Wallace upset legions of fans this weekend when she failed to attend the premiere of *Kill-Hard* on the arm of rumored lover, Hugh Jones, star of the film. Instead, the actress tiptoed into the city late last night. It's no secret their fans can't wait for a sneak peek of their favorite couple out on the town together this week. Or better yet, a sneak peak of those love scenes in *Dangerous Man*. We hear they're going to be sizzling.

Her week got crazier, but what made her *feel* crazier was that Zach never called or texted.

When she was on the set, Summer didn't know if it was the soul-stirring sex she'd shared with Zach or Hugh's sulky attitude toward her after she'd told him she'd reconnected with Zach over the weekend, but filming intimate moments with Hugh was awkward. She was tense, Hugh impatient and their director, Sam, who called for endless takes, apoplectic.

It didn't help her mood that every male employee in production made up some pretext to show up on the set to leer. During the most intimate scenes, she felt as if she was betraying Zach. Even though he'd dismissed her and had shown no inclination to see her again, she worried about what he'd think of the finished film. Not that she or Hugh had to strip for the camera—in fact, she had a clause in her contract that protected her against nudity.

By day two she felt as if she was playing Twister with a sullen, male octopus. Whatever spark had ever existed between Hugh and her was absolutely dead. The only way she endured her scenes with Hugh and managed to respond in character was to remember how she'd felt when Zach had touched her or kissed her.

She wanted Zach, but his silence made her that wonder if her longing was one-sided. At night, when she was alone in her hotel room, hoping Zach would call, she felt lost and lonely and under more pressure than ever.

By Thursday, they were forced to film late into the night. Just when she thought the endless, excruciating takes on that satin bed would never end, Sam yelled it was a wrap. He was thrilled with the rushes.

"You were fantastic, Summer," he said. "Gorgeous in every shot. Every man in America will envy Hugh."

For the first time in her career, she didn't care about that. She just wanted to be with Zach. Even though it was pretty obvious Zach didn't feel as she did, Sam's praise reawakened her concerns about how Zach might react to the movie.

Relieved to be finished, Summer headed back to her hotel. While she was showering, her phone rang. She grabbed for a towel and then her cell. She could see from the number that it was Zach.

"Hi," Zach said as she pulled the towel around her dripping body. "How's the ankle?"

His voice sounded so hard and cold, she wondered why he'd even called.

"Actually, I'm not on crutches anymore. So, it's great...." Her voice died into nothingness.

"Glad to hear it. So—you won't sue me," he murmured drily.

She held her breath, waiting, hoping his mood would lighten, hoping he'd called to say he wanted to see her again.

"I called to say I decided not to let you off for good behavior after all."

"Oh." She stopped, stunned, wondering where this was going and whether his motive stemmed from the need to punish or the desire to be with her.

"There's a ground-breaking ceremony tomorrow—Friday night—at my construction site. My PR people think I need a date, and they think you'd be the perfect one.... You being a celebrity and a hometown girl. Since you still owe me, I decided to call. You'll need to dress up and look beautiful— movie-star beautiful."

So this wasn't about them; this was about his work.

"But you've already broken ground. I mean... I fell in that hole, didn't I?" she said softly, hoping he would admit to feeling more for her.

"Won't happen tomorrow night because I'll be holding on to you all night long. Good for my image."

Her hopes and his tension warred in the silence that hung between them. She was a big girl. She should be used to men wanting her only for publicity.

"The whole town will be there," he said. "So, a fringe benefit of this appearance will be having the gossips around here see that you don't view me as a threat. I know this is late notice, but you do owe me."

"Of course, I'll be your date," she whispered.

When he didn't say anything, she realized anew how tense he was. How could he have made love to her so passionately and then have turned so cold? It was as if he'd turned off a switch and now disliked her more than ever. How could she have been so wrong about what they'd shared?

To keep him from hanging up, because some tiny part of her believed she hadn't been wrong, she said, "So—how've you been all week?"

"Fine." Again his voice was too abrupt.

"Work went okay?"

"The usual challenges. And your scenes with Hugh? How did they go?" As always, when discussing the subject of Hugh, his tone hardened. Which was strange—he'd been so aloof since they'd slept together. Why would he care?

Maybe she should explain about how grueling and unsexy the work had really been. Maybe she should tell Zach that because of him, she'd ended it with Hugh. But she didn't want to discuss Hugh, not when Zach was in his present dark mood. Not over the phone.

"Sam, our director, says he's happy. I'm…I'm just glad the week's over. After Bonne Terre, it felt like the four longest days of my life…because I…I missed you."

She willed him to say he'd missed her, too, to say anything…. When he didn't, she chewed at the edge of a fingernail.

"Zach…"

"Hmm?"

She took a deep breath. Why was it so impossible to talk to him now when it had been so easy the night after her fall?

"Never mind," she finally said. "I'll see you tomorrow."

"Tomorrow," he repeated sternly. "Bob will call you and

set a time and place to pick you up." He hung up after an impersonal goodbye that left her feeling emotionally dissatisfied.

If only he'd sounded the least bit eager to see her.

He'd called, hadn't he? He'd demanded that she spend another weekend with him.

Maybe she'd given up on them too soon when she'd been younger. She didn't want to make the same mistake a second time.

"There's no such thing as bad publicity." That's what Zach's PR guys said. They loved that somebody had stolen the hot love scenes from Summer's new movie and plastered them all over the internet.

Zach disagreed. Tension fisted around his lungs as he studied the stolen clips of Summer with Jones. She was so gorgeous he couldn't breathe. Even though she was lying beneath another man, just the sight of her sparkling eyes, tremulous lips, breasts and silken hair got his pulse thudding violently. In an instant, he remembered her looking at him exactly that way and how nauseatingly vulnerable he'd felt when he'd realized there was no way he could make love to her again without surrendering his heart. In one stolen weekend, she'd gotten through every careful barrier he'd spent years erecting, which made her too dangerous to fool around with.

Since there was no way he was ever giving her his heart again, he'd sent her packing.

But that hadn't stopped him from wanting her.

Hell. She'd plunged him back into hell. That's what she'd done.

Within minutes of starting the clip, he'd seen more than he'd ever wanted to see of Summer on those satin sheets. Did she have to moan under that egotistical actor just as she had when Zach had made love to her last weekend?

She was just acting.

Or was she?

Maybe she'd been acting in Bonne Terre, in Zach's bed.

It didn't matter.

He damn sure hadn't been acting. He'd been wildly upset that he'd felt so much more than lust for her; furious that he'd experienced the same shattering, soul-deep bond he'd felt for her as a kid.

He knew too well the destructive power of those emotions, so he'd known what he'd had to do. She'd acted hurt when he'd dismissed her, and that had gotten to him, too, but then she was an actress.

He'd lived without her before. He could do it again.

But then, when he'd been missing her the most, his PR guys had come up with the idea to invite her to the ground-breaking, to put a positive spin on an old story by dating her.

His PR guys had handed him an excuse to see her again. So, he'd broken his vow to himself and called her. He'd told himself it was business; it would only be for one night; they'd be in public. He had no intention of sleeping with her again. He'd be safe.

But he'd been lying to himself. He'd called her because he wanted her.

Damn it, he wanted her so badly he couldn't think rationally. Even as he'd willed himself to forget her and move on, he'd spent the week fantasizing about her lips, her wide eyes, her sweet, responsive body. He'd remembered the same soft expression on her face that he'd just seen captured on film.

He'd been suffering serious withdrawal from his weekend with Summer Wallace.

Zach wished to hell he could cancel her flight. But it was too late for that now. She was already in the air.... Probably an hour away. Bob had said they would run into bad weather west of Louisiana. The last thing Zach wanted was to distract Bob when he was flying during a storm.

He knew it would be a mistake to see her again. Even though his PR guys were even more adamant that he court her after the internet clips were released, Zach wanted to make the smart move and avoid her.

He hated the way she tore him in two. Hated the way he'd felt so out of control, during sex and ever since.

He clenched a fist. He knew one thing for sure. Tonight, after the ground-breaking, he would end it for good.

Eight

Eight

As soon as Zach's jet landed on the narrow tarmac nestled between tall pines outside of Bonne Terre, Summer bent over her phone and frowned. She saw dozens of texts and voice-mail messages from Sam and several other producers of *Dangerous Man,* but none from Zach. Gram and her agent had left messages, too. What was going on?

First, she called Sam, who began ranting about pirated scenes and a lunatic Brazilian hacker, before she could even say hello. He spit out words so fast she could only catch half of what he said.

"But how could this have happened?" she demanded after she finally understood the gist. "And what are you going to do about it?"

"Somehow the kid hacked into my laptop, that's how, damn it," Sam yelled. "I've got firewalls. She's fifteen! That little hacker gave away everything. For nothing! Just 'cause she's got the hots for Hugh. She's cost us millions. Maybe cost me my job. She's denying it, of course, but we've got her IP address."

After more of the same, Sam finally wound down and hung up.

Oh, God, had Zach seen the video? With grim foreboding, Summer listened to Gram's message.

"Everybody's been telling me about some love scenes you're in.... What's going on? Call me!"

Of course, Zach had seen them. Taken out of context, the scenes might look pornographic and might compromise the integrity of the movie, not to mention her integrity as an actress. Summer felt violated, but her main concern was how Zach would interpret those scenes.

With a heavy heart, she listened to Gram's second message.

"You swore to me you weren't going to take off all your clothes. And what about Zach? Everybody says you're his date tonight. Call me."

She hadn't been nude. A double had been used in the only nude shot.

Press coverage had caused tension at home before. Why couldn't Gram learn not to believe all the lies that were printed about celebrities to sell newspapers?

It would be nice to have understanding and support from those who loved her and really knew her. But, no, those closest to her were as easily manipulated by the press as everybody else.

Feeling very much abused and in no mood to explain herself to anyone—not the town or even Zach—she shut her phone off and buried it in the bottom of her purse.

Thibodeaux House was so dark she could barely see it among the trees when Bob dropped her in the drive.

As she was heading up the walk, he called after her. "Hey!

Zach just sent me a text. He'll be here at six to pick you up for the ceremony."

Fumbling with the keys Bob had handed her, she let herself into Zach's shadowy house and unset his alarm.

Had Zach seen the pirated scenes? Did he think the worst of her?

Of course, he did. And he was furious, no doubt.

Carrying her bag, she went to her room and threw herself on the bed. There she lay, hugging herself, as she listened to the birds and the creaks of the old house as the light went out of the sky. She knew she should get ready, but she felt too weary to move.

Finally, after what seemed an eternity, she heard Zach's car on the gravel drive. She ran to the window and watched him walk grim-faced toward the house.

The front door opened and slammed. He strode briskly into the kitchen. When she heard his heavy tread on the stairs, she sat up warily. He hadn't even bothered to check on her.

As if he read her mind, he stopped. She held her breath during that interim before he headed back down the stairs.

Finally, he rapped his knuckles on the door.

"Come in," she whispered brokenly.

He flung the door open and stared at her across the darkness, his blazing eyes accusing her. When he flipped on the light, she sat up, brushed her fingers through her hair.

"Not ready I see." His voice was hard and clipped.

"I was tired," she whispered.

"I can well imagine." His black eyes glittered coldly.

"I didn't know what to wear…. Or if you'd still want me to go with you…."

"Not go when everybody in Bonne Terre is so anxious to see you?" he said in a low, cutting tone. "Not that you left much of yourself to the imagination."

"I can explain…."

"I'm sure—but why bother? Besides, my PR guys are thrilled. They say all your internet coverage is great for Torr Corporation."

He walked over to the luggage rack and unzipped her suitcase. After rummaging through her clothes, he yanked out a low-cut, ruby-red gown that a personal shopper had bought for her in L.A. before she'd known about the pirated love scenes.

"Wear the red. Perfect choice," he said. "You'll look the part your legions of fans expect you to play. And you'll be gorgeous beside me, which is all my PR people care about."

But what did *he* care about? Whatever it was, it was devouring him alive.

"Zach, I haven't seen the videos, so I don't know exactly what you saw…. But I was acting."

"Save it! I'll be back down in a minute!"

"Please—I can explain…."

"Sorry. I don't have time for one of your offscreen Oscar performances. Although you're good—very good. And you were even better last week—in my bed."

He slammed the door in her face and was gone. As she listened to him stomp up the stairs, her heart constricted so tightly she was afraid it would shatter into a million tiny pieces. So, he didn't care how she felt at all.

"You'll get through this," she whispered to herself. "You've gotten through worse."

But had she? She'd never gotten over him…. Or their precious baby.

Don't think about that. You'll go crazy if you do.

Zach didn't speak to her on the drive over, and he looked so grim and forbidding she decided it was wise to give him time.

She had done nothing wrong. She'd done her job. Actors acted. She hadn't made love to Hugh for the camera. Her character had. She didn't even like Hugh. It wasn't her fault someone had stolen the video.

Something told her Zach's mood went deeper than jealousy.

The glow that hung over the trees ahead of them brightened as they neared the construction site. When they reached their destination, Zach parked and helped her out of the car. She drew in an awed breath.

The construction site looked nothing like it had last weekend. Transformed into an enchanted fairyland, it was lit by a thousand lanterns. White tents covered dance floors and a dining area. Champagne was being served by a dozen bartenders. Warm laughter and music drifted through the happy crowd. A podium had been set up in front of a thousand chairs.

No sooner had he stopped his Mercedes than reporters and photographers surrounded them.

Taking her icy hand, Zach led her into the thick of the paparazzi where they were blinded by flashes.

His expression fierce, Zach gave the screaming horde a brief statement and posed beside her for more pictures. Then he'd had enough. She hardly knew how he managed it, but with a wave of his hand, his own people led them past the press and into a cordoned-off area where the music and laughter died. For a full minute, she clung to Zach's arm, while he braved this fresh crowd gaping at them with stunned expressions.

Before those prying eyes, she began to tremble, feeling the same guilt she'd known fifteen years ago when these same people had thought the worst of her and Zach.

"Easy," Zach whispered against her ear as he placed a protective hand over hers. Then he signaled his contractor and the band, and the music resumed.

We've never done anything wrong, she thought. *We were wronged.*

Slowly, people turned away and began talking once more. Still, even though Summer held her head high, she felt their lingering interest too acutely; just as she felt the steely tension emanating from Zach's hard body beside her.

Never had she been more conscious of having a spellbound audience. During the politicians' speeches and the ceremonial breaking of the ground with shovels, people couldn't stop staring at her and Zach.

She couldn't let their stares matter. All that mattered was Zach.

Maybe he was furious at her. Maybe he felt utterly betrayed. Never once did he leave her side, but perhaps he was putting on a show for the public. Would he make such an immense effort to show his support merely for publicity reasons?

He even danced with her beneath the softly lit lanterns and moonlight, holding her close, swirling her about while all she wanted was to run home and have him to herself so she could explain.

Instead, he forced her to brave the curious, fawning crowd, forced her to stay until all the important guests and photographers had departed. Only then did he whisper in her ear, in a tone that chilled her to the bone, "The crowd has lost their appetite to devour you. Time for us to go home, sweetheart, and start our weekend."

Once they were out of the area that had been cordoned off from the paparazzi, the horde chased them to his Mercedes.

A microphone was shoved in her face. "Is Torr your man now?"

"No comment," snapped Zach as someone snickered.

"When do you plan to make up your mind, Summer?"

Summer felt a jolt as Zach shoved a reporter aside so he could open her door.

A flash went off in her face, blinding her as Zach raced around the hood.

He jumped behind the wheel. "Get your head down. There are cameras everywhere."

"I thought this was what your PR guys wanted."

"Yes, they're probably thrilled."

A moment later, he sped out of the parking lot with the pack tailing them. Inside his Mercedes, which was lit by the headlights of the paparazzi, Zach was fiercely silent behind the wheel. So fierce, she thought his anger had built during the opening ceremonies. She didn't dare say a word during that endless drive through that tunnel of trees to his home.

No sooner were they at his house than the photographers circled them, snapping photographs and yelling questions again.

Zach put his arms tightly around her, shielding her face, and escorted her inside.

"I can see that after this, I'm going to have to build a wall and hire guards to protect my privacy," he muttered once they were in his living room and had drawn the drapes.

"What did you expect, when you asked me to come here as a publicity stunt?"

He double-bolted the front door and turned on her.

"Okay. I got what I deserved—in spades. The PR junket is over. Tomorrow I want you gone. They'll soon forget."

"No, you and I know they never forget."

"Well, I intend to forget. Bob will fly you wherever you want to go. My only request is that you and your bags are on the front porch at 8:00 a.m. That's when I told Bob to pick you up. Do you understand?"

She nodded. "Why won't you even let me explain?"

"I'm sure you could explain your way out of hell itself, but I'm not interested in hearing it."

"What about Tuck?"

"I won't press charges."

"You just want me gone? Out of your life?"

"That about sums it up."

"Zach, please—"

"Save it for your true loves—the stage and the press." He turned on his heel and headed to his room. When his door slammed, she sagged against the wall as he banged about upstairs.

"But they're not my true loves," she whispered. "Not anymore."

In fact, sometimes, such as now, being an actress felt like hell. She was a human being, a woman, whose privacy had been invaded and whose work had been exploited to serve as lurid entertainment for a mass of strangers on the internet. They'd hurt her, but it was Zach, and his refusal to hear her explanation, that ripped her heart out.

An hour later, Summer felt worse than ever as she closed her laptop after having viewed the pirated clips.

The integrity of the film had been compromised by allowing those provocative scenes to be viewed out of context. She felt used and abused as a woman, as well.

She did look wildly enthralled in the videos, but those hadn't been her real emotions.

After the connection they'd shared last weekend, she'd worried about Zach's reaction. Maybe she should have explained what was involved in filming sex on-screen for a major motion picture before she'd left for L.A. She should have made it clear that it was work, hard work…. That it was far from a sensual experience. But Zach had been so cold and forbidding.

Well, she had to talk to him now; had to do whatever was necessary to make him listen…. To make him understand that they had a bond worth fighting for. She wasn't about to leave him again without doing so. That's what she'd done fifteen years ago.

Her heart was beating too fast as she pulled on her robe and headed up the stairs. In her anxious state, it seemed that every stair creaked so that he had plenty of warning to throw the bolt against her.

Much to her surprise, when she twisted the knob and leaned against the door, it opened.

She saw the bottle of whiskey on the table beside the bed. A crystal glass glimmered in his clenched hand as he stood by the window.

"Zach, I'm not going until we talk…."

He whirled. "What do you want now?"

"You. Only you."

"Get out, damn you."

"You'll have to throw me out, because I'm not leaving on my own. Not until you let me explain."

"There's no need."

"You're being unfair…like Thurman and the people of Bonne Terre were to you fifteen years ago."

"And you!" he said. "You were the star of that public farce, too!"

His words felt like blows.

"I was sixteen. Thurman had been running me so long, I didn't know what to do."

"Except stand by him and sell me out."

"I—I never intended to hurt you. The whole thing just got out of control. All I know is that I don't want to lose you again."

She pushed her robe off her shoulders, indifferent as it slid down her arms and pooled on the oak floor. She stood before him in a shimmering, transparent nightgown.

"Last weekend you made me feel so special when you made love to me. I hoped it might be a new start for us," she whispered, feeling fearful because he was so cold and determined to shut her out.

"Did you now? Well, there is no new start for us. There never was, so put your robe back on and get out."

Even as his harsh tone ripped through her, she stepped farther into the room, shut his door and then locked it. She was shaking when she flipped off the light. "You'll have to make me," she said softly, refusing to lose her courage.

"Don't think I won't." Slamming his glass down on the windowsill, he stormed across the room and seized her by the shoulders. "Listen to me—this ends now!"

She put her arms around his waist, lifted her eyes to his, then laid her head against his chest and clung.

He stiffened.

"Please! Don't do this," she begged, even though she felt desperate that he might push her away. "Last weekend…being with you…meant everything…. Don't let the press's distortions destroy us."

"Stop it," he rasped even as he shuddered from her nearness.

Her breath caught. She could tell he wanted her every bit as much as she wanted him, but he was fighting his emotions. Maybe because he didn't trust them, or her.

"I can't. Not until you hear me out. When I saw you at Gram's that first day, all those weeks ago, something started between us again. At least it did for me. Maybe it never died. I didn't want to admit it. I had my career, and that was enough. Then you kissed me… And then we made love. Now none of what I had before you is ever going to be enough. I…want you so much. So very much. Even though I live a crazy life that leaves no time for relationships, I want you."

"What about Hugh?"

"I told you—there's nothing between Hugh and me now except for a little chemistry on the screen and whatever fantasy lingers in fans' minds. We never really dated. I became involved with him after Edward, my boyfriend, walked out on me publicly. I knew the press would focus on Hugh instead of my failure with Edward because Hugh loves media attention and encourages it. It seemed less invasive because it was false. Now I see I shouldn't have used him like that."

"Those love scenes between you two were pretty hot. When I saw you on those satin sheets, looking up at him the same way you looked up at me, something snapped."

His face was closed; his eyes had gone flat and dark. She could tell there was a lot he wasn't telling her.

"I…I can't even begin to imagine what you felt. I only know that if I saw you give another woman that special smile or look, I'd feel betrayed. Foolishly, I thought I'd be able to explain about the love scenes before you saw them…since *Dangerous Man* won't come out for nearly eight months." She paused. "I'm afraid I was thinking about you, when I was with Hugh in front of the camera."

"I don't much like hearing that." His black eyes impaled her from beneath his dark brows.

"I know it was wrong, but I was turned off by Hugh and my selfish, seductive character. It was the only way I could get the work done…. So, in a way, I did use you…use us…. But it's hard for an actress not to use parts of herself to make a role convincing. Our tools are our own emotions."

"Does the acting ever stop?"

"Yes. Now. This is me, and I'm begging you to give me—to give us—another chance."

Terrified, feeling naked to the soul after asking this of him, she inhaled a long breath and waited as he considered what she'd said.

"I don't know," he said finally, but the anger had gone out of his voice. "Since I was nineteen, when everything I read about us was distorted and used to hang me, I've worked hard to keep my private life private. There were, of course, always those reporters who wrote new stories about what I'd supposedly done to you, but mostly my life was a private affair.

"I've never dated a famous actress before. Frankly, I never wanted to. But here you are—a bomb that's gone off in my life. If we date, your career, with all its fuss, is going to take some getting used to."

"I know. I'm sorry about that."

"I thought I had my life under control. It was simple. It was all about building and developing and making more money. Then I lost Uncle Zachery. And I saw your tear-streaked face and kissed you on Viola's porch."

"See—your work is not so different from my roller-coaster career. Until that kiss, I lived for interesting parts and good reviews and felt like death when some critic said I couldn't act."

"I don't like feeling out of control—or in your control."

"That's understandable because I hurt you before," she whispered.

"I don't want this…you…us," he growled. "You're bad for me."

"Not according to your PR guys," she whispered with a smile.

Zach took a deep breath. For a moment, she was terrified that her little joke would backfire, that he was still going to send her away. She wouldn't have blamed him.

But he smiled. "I should never have listened to them."

"Were they really the only reason you called me?"

"Point taken. No… But I wish I could say they were. Then maybe I could resist you."

"That's not the wisest course," she whispered.

Very slowly, his arms gentled upon her shoulders. Wrapping her closely against him, he drew her to his bed and pulled her down onto the mattress beside him. For a long time they just lay together in the darkness growing comfortable in each other's presence.

His nearness calmed her and made her feel safe again.

Then he rolled on his side and began to stroke her lips, her ears, her neck—and lower.

"All night, at the ground-breaking, I was so miserable… because I knew you were going to send me away again." Her words were muttered shatteringly against the base of his throat, her hands clinging to his shoulders.

His hand traced the length of her spine.

"I thought that this second chance was over before we'd even begun to understand what we feel," she continued.

"I damn sure wanted it to be over. You're like a dangerous drug, and I'm an addict."

His hands were smoothing her tumbled hair out of her eyes. His lips kissed her brow lightly. Then he pulled her fully against him, so that she was pressed against his long, hard length. Again—he felt so right.

While he petted her hair, she poured out the details of her past week in a jumble—the male members of the crew jamming the set to ogle her, a dissatisfied Sam shouting commands, the alienation she'd felt every night in her lonely L.A. hotel room when she'd longed for him to call.

"I know people think I have a glamorous life, but sometimes it just feels lonely. One minute I'm onstage admired by thousands. Then I'm home alone—or vilified in the press." She buried her lips against the warm hollow of his neck. "Edward couldn't stand my crazy life, and I don't think you will be able to stand it, either. I'm good at acting, at fantasy onstage. But so far, ever since we parted fifteen years ago, I've never been able to hold on to anything real."

"Just promise me you won't act when you're with me," he said roughly.

She nodded.

"I don't want to look at your face and wonder if you're

using an emotion you felt for someone else to make something work for us."

"I'd never do that."

"Okay, then." His mouth fastened on hers with a passion that soon spiraled out of control. He stripped her, stripped himself and flung their clothes on the floor. Then he mounted her, his knees wide. Straddling her thighs, he cupped her breasts.

She ran her hands down his lean torso. How she loved the way his body was hard and warm; how every part of him was gorgeous.

He breathed in rapid pants, and she was just as hot for him.

He kissed her with such desperate urgency she could only imagine he felt as she did. A foil wrapper rustled. Then, with his condom in place, he thrust inside her, each stroke deeper and harder than the last. She clung, arching her pelvis to meet his. Relentlessly, he took her higher and higher until, at the end, he clutched her close. When he shuddered and ground his hips against hers, she cried his name again and again, her release glorious.

For a long time afterward, their bodies spent, they clung. An hour or so later she awoke to find herself still wrapped in his arms. Never had she felt closer to anyone.

This is where I belong, she thought, refusing to consider the secrets she still hadn't told him.

Some time later he began to kiss her with a feverish need that fueled her own desire into an instant blaze. He licked his way down her slim body, exploring secret feminine places until she felt she was so hot and tremulous even her bones might melt.

Don't stop, she thought. *Don't ever stop....*

After she recovered from the most shattering climax of her life, he made love to her again. Then they napped and made love again, and maybe again. She lost count.

Needs she'd never experienced before made themselves known. Their bodies spoke to each other in a dark, sweet language only they understood. They said things and did things they'd never done before. Things they could only do now because trust was building between them.

They played erotic games, with tied hands and blindfolds. Sometimes their love was rough, but mostly it was gentle. For an endless time, Summer lived in a sensual universe she shared only with Zach. It was nearly dawn when she drifted to sleep in his arms once again.

She felt changed, as if she'd been reborn within the dazzling magic of his love.

At eight o'clock sharp, his phone and doorbell rang at the same time.

They sprang up groggily, laughing when they realized it was morning.

Zach grabbed for his phone, cursing when it wouldn't stop ringing.

"It's Bob! How the hell could I have been so crazy as to ever tell him eight?"

She giggled. "You wanted me gone, remember."

"Strange how that seems a lifetime away."

He spoke much too curtly to Bob then, who said he was surrounded by paparazzi.

"Poor guy," she said after he hung up.

"I'll apologize. But later. He's too busy keeping the screaming horde at bay." Zach's gleaming eyes met hers sheepishly. "Now that we're up, we might as well make the most of it."

"First, I'm going to go downstairs and take a shower, brush my teeth...present a more civilized—"

He laughed and grabbed her hand, preventing her from squirming across the sheets and running downstairs. "I don't want civilized! I want the wicked wanton I had last night all over again, only wilder."

"Not possible."

"I'm going to prove to you that you're wrong. You're going to stay right here where you belong. Under me. In my arms."

Unable to deny him anything in that moment, she lay back and waited for him to again turn their world into a fiery wonderland that was theirs alone.

Nine

Nine

Summer Wallace Steps Out With Billionaire Zach Torr!

"What the hell do you think you're doin', boy?"

Nick slapped a newspaper with the two-inch headline onto Zach's desk, covering the blueprint he'd been studying.

When Zach looked up, Nick began to read him the article in a low, sarcastic voice.

"It seems the thirty-one-year-old actress known for her light comedy roles has revamped herself. Shortly after pirated film clips from *Dangerous Man* exploded all over the internet, Wallace was seen on Torr's arm at the ground-breaking ceremony for his new casino. The couple has a scandalous history. She once charged Torr with—"

"What is this? Read-aloud time?"

Zach wadded the paper and pitched it into the trash. "I've seen it already. Read it already."

And he'd been sickened to have the most beautiful thing in his life described in such cheap terms.

"You said you saw her again for the publicity, yes? Was her two-day sleepover a publicity stunt, as well?"

"That's my business, and hers—not yours! And certainly not the damn newspapers'!"

"Then date another woman."

Zach's voice was meticulously polite. "Look, I intend to. In the future. Right now…I'll be seeing more of Summer."

No way in hell could he give her up now.

"Tell me you've got more sense than to start up with her again. You know as well as I do that she's a liar to the core of her rotten soul, yes? You had to sneak around with her in high school because her step-daddy thought you was trash. Then look what they done to you, those high-and-mighty folks, first chance that they got."

Zach remembered too well. He still wasn't sure about what had been real back then between him and Summer. Hell, he wasn't sure what was real now. But he wanted to find out.

"People don't change, boy. She's probably stepped on a lot more folks to get where she is. You gonna end this or not?"

Or not.

Since he couldn't reassure Nick, Zach fixed his gaze on the blueprint. The tension between them built until Martin knocked on the door of the trailer.

"Pete's here," Martin said. "He thinks he sees a way to get what you want done and not go over budget."

"Great." Zach turned on Nick. "I'm busy as hell. I've got things to do here. The costs on a project in Houston are going through the roof, so I've got to fly home ASAP. You and I— we'll catch up later, okay?"

"I'm not finished here, no. That little gal proved what she was fifteen years ago, yes. All that she ever worries about is what's good for her. She don't care about you. She never did. She never will."

Flushing with dark embarrassment to have interrupted his boss's personal conversation, Martin backed out of the trailer.

Zach's face grew stony. "Look, Nick, I've dated a lot of women since Summer. Can't a guy fool around?"

"Not with her, you can't, no. You're not just playing with fire. She's nuclear."

Zach clenched his fist around his pencil, letting go of it right before it snapped. "You're right. You're right."

"Which is why you're madder than hell, yes."

"Stay out of this, Nick."

Grabbing the blueprint, Zach stormed past Nick and out of the trailer.

"No! No! No! Earth to Miss Wallace!" Paulo, Summer's stage director, was bouncing up and down as he bounded toward her, his face purple.

"You still haven't got it! Quit thinking about your personal love triangle and listen to me!"

Summer blinked first. Then she blushed. She was sick of the ceaseless teasing she'd had to endure due to all the news stories.

"Sorry." Rubbing her forehead, she fought to concentrate on what Paulo was saying.

Paolo was actually a very insightful, inspiring director, one of the rare ones who really understood actors. Still, it wasn't easy for her to take direction. She was too worried about her fragile new start with Zach and about how she would tell him about the baby. She was concerned about how all the media attention impacted him, as well. Again, the sex had been glorious. Again, she'd felt she'd shared everything with him in bed. But once they'd separated and the stories about them had hit full force, he'd erected the old walls between them.

So, she was no closer to feeling the time had come for her to confide in him.

He'd called her once, texted her twice. All three times her heart had leaped with joy. Even as his husky, but oh-so-controlled tone had made her remember all the thrilling things they'd done to each other—against the wall, on the floor, in the bed, on the chair—she'd sensed his emotional withdrawal.

In Bonne Terre, after their night together, she'd felt so close to Zach. He'd seemed easy, open. But now he was unreachable. Really, she couldn't blame him. He wasn't used to life in a fishbowl. He'd said he'd hated the stories that had linked them for years.

Rehearsals were difficult during the best of times and trying to give birth to a character could be exhausting. Summer's head, back and feet ached from the effort. Distracted by Zach and the media storm, she'd found the rehearsals this week to be sheer torture.

She would think about him and break character, lose her bearing. Another actor would say a line, and she would just stare at them, lost. The entire cast was out of patience with her, as she was with herself.

She needed to get a grip before she sabotaged the show completely. At night, when she was alone in her apartment eating takeout, her obsession was worse.

She would try to imagine living with Zach as an ordinary couple in a house with a garden and a picket fence, try to envision holidays with Gram and Tuck, dinners with friends, shared vacations, dark-haired children that looked just like Zach.

But, always, her vision would pop like a bubble as an inner voice taunted her.

Zach has his life and you have yours. You're still keeping your secrets. He values his privacy, and you can never have total privacy. So—just enjoy what you have now.

An affair such as theirs couldn't last long, not with her secret eating at her and the world interfering and them living so far apart, not with each of them working at all-consuming careers. Added to those obstacles, there would be no way for her to leave New York on the weekends once her show started.

She thought of Gram, who was always pressuring Summer to marry and have children, who now called constantly to express her pleasure at Zach's renewed visitations and to express her concerns about how their story was playing out in the media and around Bonne Terre.

"You are running out of time for children," she would say. "He isn't."

"Gram, please…don't!"

Gram's advice added unbearable pressure to Summer's already fragile situation.

Until Zach, Summer had focused only on her career. Now when she thought of the possibility of little darlings and a more private life, she felt an eager wistfulness.

What if Zach wanted children but saw her career and all that went with it as obstacles too large to surmount? Since he was a man, he could simply enjoy her for as long as it was convenient and then move on. He could choose a woman young enough to bear his children.

An urge to see him again and to make love to him—to claim him in all the imaginative ways he'd taught her—filled her.

By Thursday night, when he hadn't called her again, she finally weakened and picked up the phone.

"I've missed you," she whispered the minute he answered, fighting to keep the tension out of her voice.

Oh, why did I say that of all things?

"I missed you, too," he admitted, his tone polite.

"I'm sorry about all the press coverage."

He said nothing.

"I saw where you were besieged in your Houston office."

"I didn't realize you were so famous." He didn't sound happy about it.

"Hey, you're the handsome billionaire. I think your money and your looks are as big a draw as I am. It's a huge part of the fantasy reporters are trying to sell."

"Oh, so now it's my fault, too," he mused, but his voice had warmed ever so slightly. "When I couldn't get into my building downtown for all the reporters, I wondered why the hell I'd ever gotten myself into this mess. It seems so cheap... what they write about us. Maybe we should take a break until all the fuss dies down."

When he fell silent after dropping that bomb, her breath caught painfully. For a long second, the wound from his words seemed too hurtful to bear.

"Zach, I...I hope you don't really want that. I know the press is a major hassle right now, and I'm truly sorry. But once my show starts, I'll be too swamped to travel. You'll get busy with other projects, too.... And then we'll...drift apart...." Her voice cracked on a forlorn note.

"I've lived in the spotlight for years. It won't always shine this brightly or be this invasive. I swear."

"That's reassuring," he said in a smart-aleck tone that somehow cheered her.

"My PR people spend a lot of time manipulating my brand. It's all so false. The person you read about in those stories is not me. It's this pubic person, the actress. The real me often feels lost in all the hubbub.

"But there is a difference. Last weekend, after the ground-breaking, was wonderful and true. I've never been happier in my whole life."

"Me, too," he admitted slowly.

"So, will you give us another chance?"

"Sweetheart, who am I kidding? Don't you know by now,

that no matter how much I hate the press, I'd go crazy if I didn't see you again—and very, very soon. I need you, even though I hate needing you. But that doesn't kill the need. It's fierce, unquenchable."

She drew in a long, relieved breath because she felt the same way.

"I'm new to this, too," she whispered. "I haven't dated anyone outside the business before. Maybe we should only worry about how we are together…so that those on the outside don't matter quite so much. What we have shouldn't be about them or what they think. It should be about us. I want this piece of my life to belong to me and to you and to nobody else."

He was silent for a long time. "We do live in the real world, you know, an intrusive world."

A world that would devour them all over again if it learned all their secrets.

"I know. But I want to try to keep our relationship a personal matter. There are things I need to share with you…. Personal things I've been afraid to share…."

"You sound very mysterious all of a sudden."

"I can't talk about it over the phone. So, about tomorrow… Do we still have a date?"

When he hesitated for a heartbeat, he put her in an agony of suspense.

"I can't wait," he admitted in that low, husky tone she loved.

Friday afternoon came at last, and she rushed to LaGuardia in a chauffeured car with a single bag. Hours later, when his jet set her down on a deserted airstrip several miles from the one Bob usually used outside Bonne Terre, she saw him— and no press—waiting beside his Mercedes at the edge of the dark woods. A wild joy pierced her.

Stepping off the plane, she told herself to play it cool. But at the bottom of the stairway, she cried his name and flew into his arms.

"I missed you so much," she admitted ruefully as she flung her arms around his neck.

He pulled her to him, folded her close.

"You smell so good," she whispered.

He slanted a look down at her and smiled. "So do you."

Feeling the fierce need to taste him, she pulled his mouth down to hers. Then he kissed her with a wonderful wild hunger that turned her blood to fire, the ferocity in him matching her own. Suddenly, it didn't matter that he'd barely contacted her last week or that he'd had so many doubts about their very public relationship. Even the unbearable weight of her secret felt a tiny bit lighter on her heart. There was truth in his kiss, in his touch, a truth he couldn't hide.

"I brought you something."

Soft white flashed in the darkness as he handed her a bouquet of daisies.

"They're gorgeous." She jammed her nose into the middle of their petals and inhaled their sweetness. "Simply gorgeous. I love them."

"It's a cliché gift."

"I don't care."

"You've got gold dust all over your nose now."

"Pollen, they call it," she whispered as she dabbed at her nose and giggled. "All gone?"

"Not quite." He dusted the tip of her nose for her.

Then he wrapped his arms around her and held her close in the shadows of the trees. After another kiss, this one brief and undemanding and tender, he said, "Let's go home, sweetheart."

The press corps waiting for them at his pillared mansion were held at bay by a team of security guards, so Zach drove around back where they could run inside without having to face questions.

Locking the door of the little sitting room where they'd entered, he pulled her into his arms and kissed her hard. So urgent were his kisses as they skimmed her lips, her throat, her breasts. She began to tremble violently. Then he lifted her skirt and found that soft place in between her thighs.

"You're not wearing panties, I see."

His tongue made contact and she gasped.

"No...."

She was wet and breathless and dying for more as he peeled off the rest of her clothes.

"Am I bad?" she whispered as he undid his belt and began tearing off his jeans and shirt.

"I like bad."

When they were naked, he shoved her against the wall and held her close. "Wrap your legs around me, sweetheart."

When she complied, he put on a condom and ground himself into her, scraping her back and shoulders against the wall in his eagerness. She didn't mind. She cared only for him as he rode her fast and hard. Arching her pelvis to meet his thrusts, she cried out. Again, he took her to that strange, wild world that was theirs alone. Clinging to him fiercely, her heart pounded in mad unison with his.

Afterward, their bodies drenched in perspiration, they sank to the floor with their arms still wound around each other.

"I don't know if I can ever stand up again," Summer whispered breathlessly.

"Not to worry, sweetheart. You don't have to."

He lifted her and carried her through the house to the bed in the room she'd used that first weekend. Then he lay down beside her and stared at her hot, damp body gleaming in the moonlight.

When she was with him like this, she felt almost sick with

pleasure and terror of losing him. She thought about her secret and how he might react when she confided in him. How, when could she tell him?

The long, lonely years without him had taught her what loss felt like, and she dreaded anything coming between them again. But something would. All it might take was her confession about the baby.

She'd been young when she'd loved him before. People like Thurman, who'd been wrong in all the advice they'd given her, had told her she'd been lucky to have lost their baby girl, lucky a lowlife like Zach was out of her life, lucky that she could start over. They'd said she would meet someone else, someone respectable, have another baby, that all would be just fine.

She'd learned better. Thurman had been wrong about almost everything, but he'd been especially wrong about how she felt about losing Zach's baby and about losing Zach himself. Yes, she had her career, and she'd enjoyed national, even international, acclaim. But never once in all those years had she felt this alive.

Zach was special. When she'd been a foolish, naive girl, he'd lived in a shack. He'd been considered beneath her by the kids at school, and she'd still thought he was the one. Until Thurman and his cohorts had twisted and turned their love into something ugly and sordid and had driven them apart.

Now Zach rolled over, took her hand and interlocked his fingers with hers. When he looked at her, her blood beat with a mixture of desire and fear. When she kissed him, she realized she was going to take the easy way out…at least for now. They could talk in the morning. The happiness she felt was simply too precious to risk.

That night they made love several more times, but early Saturday morning, when they might have talked, Zach had to go to the site because his contractor had encountered a new challenge. Then he wanted to see Nick. He said they'd had a minor quarrel earlier in the week and he wanted to make things right on his way home.

"I hope you didn't quarrel about me."

His eyes narrowed, and she knew that they had.

"I see. Okay, then," she agreed, feeling a little relief at the reprieve, deciding it was probably best for him to handle Nick as he saw fit. "You'd better stop by. Last week I was terrible in rehearsals, so I really need to go over the script."

But no sooner was he gone than her whirling emotions centered on her secret and him and she was unable to concentrate. Her need to confess made her as uncertain as a young girl in the throes of first love, and she could do nothing except worry about what Nick might say against her.

Hours passed. Unable to focus, she stared at the daisies and her script.

Her phone rang. When she saw it was Gram, she answered it, glad of the distraction.

"I've got some news. I was calling to invite you and Zach over to dinner. I could tell you then."

"I'll ask Zach…. See what he says." *If they went out to dinner, it would be more difficult to find the perfect moment to confess.*

"Tell Zach I'm cooking chicken and Andouille gumbo, crawfish étoufée and a shrimp salad. Oh, and those chocolate-chip cookies he loves so much. Maybe after dinner we could play Hearts."

When Gram hung up, Summer remained as unfocused as ever, even as she comforted herself that it was all right not to work, that sometimes procrastination was part of any actress's process.

Finally, Zach's car roared into the drive out back. Jumping up, breathing hard, she ran to a tall window where she stood until she saw a reporter. Only with the greatest effort did she tiptoe back to the table, pick up a pen and sit down before her script. But when Zach walked through the front door and called to her, she answered with her next breath.

"In here! Working!" She giggled at that last.

He strode inside the kitchen and kissed her. "Sorry it took so long. I hope you got something done."

"I tried," she said evasively.

Her frustration must have shown because he ran his knuckles up the curve of her neck. "Sounds like somebody needs a holiday."

"Right.... It's your fault I couldn't work. I *was* thinking about you the whole time you were gone."

"Ditto." He swept her into his arms and devoured her mouth in a dizzying kiss.

As eager as he, she tore off her clothes while watching him do the same. They ended up making love on the kitchen table—but only after she'd removed the precious daisies for safekeeping.

"Oh," she said, while they were dressing afterward. "I almost forgot and Gram would have killed me...."

"What?"

"She said she had something to tell us, and she invited us over for dinner tonight."

"It must be nice, having family to share things with," he said.

She realized it was, even if Gram had her own ideas about how Summer's life should be and never stopped pushing for her own agenda.

"I take it that's a yes," she said.

Zach would never know exactly at what point that night he knew for sure that no matter what she'd done in the past, no matter what the masses believed, Summer was the one woman who was essential to his happiness. Nothing spectacular happened; it was simply a very special evening.

To elude the paparazzi, he had a pair of doubles drive away in his Mercedes so he and Summer could slip out the back to the dock and take his airboat. As they sped along the glassy water, laughing like children, the sun glowed like gold in the cypress trees, turning the bayou into a gilded ribbon of flashing darkness and light.

Summer's hair whipped back from her pale face, and her heavily lashed blue eyes shone every time she glanced at him as if she were as exhilarated by his nearness as he was by hers. She wore a navy dress with tiny white buttons and held the filmy skirt down with hands pressed against her knees.

Why had he thought he couldn't get beyond their past and her fame? Despite the betrayals, when they were together, he forgave her everything and felt as comfortable around her as he had as a kid. Upon reaching Viola's rambling old plantation house, he followed Summer around the yard as she stooped in the tall grasses to pick wild violets for the dinner table while amusing him with tales about her funniest roles. In turn, he talked about all the various disasters that could befall a construction project.

"I can't believe a giant crane costing millions can actually topple over," she said, sounding amazed.

"Yes, we were so lucky nobody was killed, we didn't even care about the money."

They smiled and laughed together. Holding hands, they carried armfuls of violets into the house, which was redolent with the smell of Cajun spices. Together they looked for a vase and finished setting the table while Tuck followed them around like a lost puppy.

"Tuck's very good at looking like he's doing something when he isn't," Summer whispered when steaming dishes needed to be carried to the table and her brother chose that moment to say he had to go to the bathroom.

"He'll grow up. You'll see."

"We keep hoping...."

Zach enjoyed the simple dinner party. When Viola started tapping her crystal goblet filled with ruby-red wine, Zach felt Summer tense beside him.

"Careful, Gram. Mama's crystal," she chided.

Gram shot her a look. "I'm always careful with dear Anna's crystal. I was only trying to get your attention, dear." She took a deep breath. "And now that you're all listening—I have something to tell you, something I couldn't be more thrilled about." Her sharp blue eyes sparkled like a naughty child's.

"Oh, no, now what have you gone and done?" Summer asked.

In the flattering candlelight and in her soft gray dress with those sharp, mischievous eyes dancing, Viola looked years younger than her age.

"Well, your Gram has bought herself a condo in Plantation Alley."

"Without even telling me," Summer said, shocked.

"I told you I was thinking about it, didn't I? It was such a good deal. I had to snap it up. Besides, you're never here, dear. If you lived closer, maybe I'd form the habit of confiding in you."

"Well, I'm here now," Summer said. "I've been here all weekend."

"I wouldn't dream of disturbing you, child," her grandmother replied innocently, slanting a pointed glance at Zach. "And you didn't drop by...not till I invited you."

"Zing," Summer murmured in Zach's ear.

"Stop whispering, you two! I want to hear everything that's said at my table."

He squeezed Summer's hand.

"Do you want to hear about my new condo or not?" Viola asked peevishly.

"We want to hear," Summer soothed.

Viola brought them a folder that contained a colorful brochure spelling out the amenities of the complex as well as a contract and a copy of the deposit she'd put down. Then she described the condo she'd bought in detail. Several of her friends already lived in the complex, so she'd have lots of company for playing Hearts. The clincher was that Silas approved. He simply adored the cozy window with the view of the bayou where he could sit and watch birds.

"The girls and I sort of thought that if we lived in the same complex we could look after each other, call one another every day, you know."

"The girls are her Friday Lunch Bunch," Summer explained. "They eat together every Friday at a restaurant another friend owns. That's where they hatch their mischief, which mainly has to do with thinking up schemes to meddle in my and Tuck's lives."

"We do not!"

Zach picked up the contract and scratched a few things out, added a sentence or two, explaining why he'd made the changes.

"I'm not sure I understand," Gram said.

"Just take this to Davis first thing Monday. Tell him I sent you. He'll take care of you."

Gram nodded. "It has three bedrooms, so there'll be room for you and Tuck to stay anytime."

"Well, that's a relief. I'm glad you're not kicking me out," Tuck said.

"You won't have to move out on your own, until you're ready, dear. And, Zach, you're always welcome. Silas is so fond of playing Hearts with you."

"Gram! I'm sure Zach's had enough of Silas's opinions for one evening," Summer teased.

"Well, who's going to speak for him, since dear Silas won't speak for himself?"

"Exactly," Summer said.

Tuck hadn't said much during dinner, but he'd come to the table with his hair combed and had answered all Zach's questions about his classes. The small changes in him pleased everyone since he was mildly enthusiastic for a change.

The gumbo and spicy étoufée were delicious.

All in all, it was one of those rare, pleasant evenings, a family evening, the kind of evening Zach hadn't experienced since his Uncle Zach's death. He felt like he belonged—with Summer, with all of them. Suddenly, the past and its pain didn't matter quite so much.

Suddenly, he wanted nothing more than to start over with Summer.

Realizing that thanks to Tuck's misbehavior, they had already started over, Zach took Summer's hand, turned it over in his own, drew it to his lips. For a second he caught a haunted expression in her eyes, but when she flashed him a dazzling smile, he forgot where he was. He would have planted a quick kiss on her cheek if he hadn't caught a very pleased Gram watching his every move. Not in the habit of public displays of affection, he let go of Summer's hand in the next instant.

When dinner was over, they retired to the card table where Gram's three guests conspired to let her win more than her fair share of the games.

"It was a perfect evening," Gram said after they'd helped her clear the table. As they stepped out onto the porch, the black, misty darkness was filled with the cloying scent of honeysuckle and the glorious roar of cicadas. They were saying their goodbyes, and Summer's beautiful face was aglow beneath the porch light.

He loved her, Zach realized.

Love. He hated the word. He'd sworn never to fall under its dark power again, but here he was, lost in its grip. After everything she'd put him through, it was stupid of him, terrifying for him, but he wanted to claim her—to marry her.

When her beaming grandmother read the emotion in his eyes, she closed the door and wisely left them alone. Like a fool, the minute they were alone, he wanted to get down on bended knee in the damp St. Augustine grass and propose.

Luckily, he caught himself, opting to proceed with caution. If this new relationship with Summer was to work, he'd need to reorganize his business, his entire life. He'd need an office in Manhattan for starters. That was okay. He'd worked all over the world; he could work anywhere.

He would have his people contact several knowledgeable Realtors in Manhattan. He'd tell them he wanted to shift the focus of Torr Enterprises, that they were to start searching for opportunities in the northeast. He'd buy Summer a penthouse with a view of Central Park.

Not that he would want to live there all year. But surely she'd meet him halfway by living in Houston or even Louisiana for at least part of the year.

As they sped home across the black, glassy waters of the bayou, Zach seemed quieter, more withdrawn, and yet content.

Their speed wasn't as fast as it had been earlier, since it was dark now and there were patches of ground fog, but there was no way she could speak to him over the roar of the airboat.

Arriving home without incident, she watched as Zach secured the boat quickly and efficiently with the easy expertise of a man who knew exactly what he was doing. Nick had taught him all of that, she thought.

Then Zach pulled her close, and they walked across the lawn holding hands in the moonlight with no paparazzi to spoil the exquisite, shared moment.

He paused beneath the long shadows of the live oak trees to kiss her. She thought his kisses were different somehow, sweeter, and they filled her heart with joy.

Everything felt so right, so perfect—the way it had felt when they'd first fallen in love. It was as if they'd reclaimed their lost innocence and faith in one another. For the first time in years, it was easy to imagine them belonging to each other forever. A knot formed in her throat as she thought about the little girl she'd lost. She had to tell him. But when?

For Summer the evening had been magic. It had been nice to bring Zach to Gram's, so nice to share this man she cared about with her family, especially since her controlling stepfather used to force her to sneak out to see him.

Summer had learned not to stand up to Thurman. It had seemed smarter to maneuver around him. Still, she'd felt like a spineless wimp not taking up for Zach. But if she had, Thurman would have gone ballistic. He would have stopped at nothing to destroy her relationship with Zach.

The only reason Zach had stayed in Bonne Terre that year after his graduation was to wait for her.

Her memories merged with her present need to find a way to tell him about the baby. But when he pulled her close and slanted his hard mouth over hers beneath the shadows of the oak, she sighed and wrapped her hands around his neck to better enjoy the kiss.

Time stopped. There was nothing but the two of them. Their bodies locked as they surrendered to each other in the magical pine-scented darkness. There was no Thurman to stop them now.

She could have kissed him forever, but she began to feel him, hard and swollen, pressing against her thighs. She opened her eyes and met the burning urgency of his gaze.

When he spoke, his voice was rough. "Let's get the hell inside."

Quickly, he took her hand and they ran to the back entrance. When they were in the house, and he'd locked the door, he kissed her again even more fiercely than before. Then he lifted her into his arms and carried her up the stairs into the enveloping darkness of his bedroom.

"Now, where were we, sweetheart?" Zach demanded as he set her on his bed. His eyes were intense as he began to undo the tiny white buttons on her dress.

"I can't believe you want to make love to me after a big old dinner like that."

"Well, I do. We played cards for an hour, didn't we? Besides, do you have a better idea?"

"We could sit outside on the upstairs veranda, enjoy the moonlight and talk...maybe about the past." *About our baby....*

"The past...." He frowned. "I'm in much too good a mood to want to go there. Trust me. We're better off making love, enjoying what we have now. We deserve some happiness."

"But aren't we hiding from things we need to think about and resolve?"

"You expect me to care about what's over and done with, when you're so damn beautiful I hurt?"

But she felt so close to him right now, close enough to tell him everything.... Even tell him about the baby. It would take more than a single conversation, she knew. But she felt a profound need to share everything with him. He had to know the worst.

She wanted him to listen, to hold her, to forgive her, to

grieve with her and then to make love to her. Had she been wrong about their special bond tonight?

He grazed her lips with his mouth with such infinite tenderness he soon sparked a wild conflagration.

But he was a man, and he was aroused. So, now wasn't the time to talk after all.

They could not get their clothes off fast enough. Then they took their time exploring each other. He took his turn kissing and touching her, and then she broke away and started kissing him everywhere, her tongue running down his body until she found his manhood, which was thick and engorged.

She took him into her mouth. He was too close to the edge to endure this for long. Soon he moved on top of her and slid inside.

That was all it took for her to explode.

He thrust deeply and then shuddered, too.

Afterward, as they lay in the darkness, while he held her close, she gathered her courage again. "Wouldn't you feel better if you knew exactly what happened to me and why I might have failed you years ago?"

"What?"

Perspiration glistened on his brow as he rolled over to brush his hand through her tangled hair. "I can't believe you're bringing that up again. Now."

"I just think we should talk. It's a perfect time, after our lovely evening."

"No. Let's not tarnish tonight."

He sat up so he could stare down at her. "Look, I'm not blaming you for the past any longer, if that's why you want to talk about it. On Viola's porch that first day we reconnected, I felt this terrible lingering sadness in you. It made it impossible for me to continue blaming you for everything. That's all the explanation I need about the past. I hurt you, too. I know that."

"But…"

"It's over. I'm trying to forget it. I suggest you do the same."

"But there's something I really need to share.…"

He ran a finger around the edges of her lips and shushed her. "Don't ruin what we have right now. It's too special. I want to hold on to it. We can talk later. I promise."

When she frowned, he pulled her close and kissed her.

But he was so adamant, and she wanted this time with him so much, she let him have his way. So, when she left on Sunday, she still hadn't told him about what happened in New Orleans.

"Why don't I come see you next weekend, for a change?" he said as he put her on his jet. "It just so happens I have a few things to do in New York."

"That would be wonderful."

"I'll come up on Thursday, rent a suite at the Pierre and take you anywhere you want to go."

"So, you intend to spoil me hopelessly?"

"Absolutely."

"Lucky me."

"No. Lucky me," he said as he kissed her.

Ten

Something was different about Zach, and Summer wasn't sure what it was.

Their first three-day weekend together in New York was not as intimate as their previous weekends in Bonne Terre. But that was to be expected under the circumstances. He had business affairs to attend to and she the theater. Only at night could they make time to be together.

If his purpose in coming to the city had been to impress her with his grand lifestyle, he succeeded. His gilded suite was spectacular. Limos followed by the paparazzi whisked them to fabulous dinners and nightclubs where he knew people, some of them beautiful women.

"Zach has a thing for blondes," Roberto, one of his top executives, whispered in her ear while Zach conversed with a beautiful woman during a business dinner.

"Good thing I'm a blonde, then," she quipped.

For the first time since their reunion, Zach hadn't shared

details about his current project. She wondered exactly what he'd done all day while she'd rehearsed. When they were alone later, she grilled him.

"Where were you all afternoon? What business exactly do you have to do here?"

"I'm tweaking an important project."

"Tweaking?"

"I'll explain everything when it's all in order."

"Does this project concern me?"

"I said I'll explain later."

"You're not bored with me and chasing another woman already? Another blonde?"

"Good Lord, no! Whatever gave you that idea?"

She refrained from throwing Roberto to the wolves for one ill-advised remark. "Oh…nothing. Forget I asked."

"There's no other woman for me, and there never will be."

"You're a billionaire. You could have anybody."

"Strange as this may sound, that's not true. Believe me, I have had plenty of time to discover that there's no substitute for the real thing. You're the real thing."

Something twisted near her heart. "Oh. Am I? Tell me more…."

But that was all she could get out of him other than a quick kiss on the tip of her nose.

He was hiding something. *Just as she was.*

The next weekend as Zach stood in a glamorous penthouse that had seventeen gloriously imagined rooms with high ceilings and tall windows, he thought of Summer's cozy apartment. Was the penthouse too much? Would she like it? Women could be very particular about their homes. Maybe he should show it to her before he bought it, but he was too impatient.

She could call the marble and gold vulgar and rip it out if

she didn't like it, he decided. She was too creative not to find a way to make it hers. The location was too stupendous to pass on, and he needed a place like this to impress the business people he dealt with.

All week Zach had been in a fever to ask her to marry him. Every time they'd talked, the question had been at the forefront of his mind. The pressure to wait until he had the ring selected and the penthouse bought and his new offices acquired and a contractor to remodel Thibodeaux House was making him feel explosive.

She'd looked so haunted when she'd tried to talk to him about the past. Was he rushing into this because he knew he should wait?

What if she said no?

Zach opened a glass door and walked out onto the terrace. The air was cool and crisp. Central Park was ablaze with riotous fall colors forty stories beneath him.

"I told you the penthouse was fabulous and the view lovely," the Realtor gushed behind him. "Now do you believe me?"

"I had to make sure," Zach said. "It's a deal, then." He turned and shook the woman's perfectly manicured hand. "Send me a contract."

She grinned brilliantly. "I like you so much."

"Roberto Gomez will be handling this for me."

"Yes. I've already had several emails from him. Charming man. It's been a pleasure...."

Zach nodded, turned on his heel and strode toward the elevator. He had a long day ahead of him and no time to waste.

He'd arrived in Manhattan a day early this weekend to approve his future office space in Lower Manhattan and the penthouse that his most trusted people had selected. Summer didn't expect him until tomorrow.

He was staying at the Pierre. She'd liked the suite there so much last weekend, he'd rented it again.

In the elevator, he slipped his hand into his pocket and touched the small, black-velvet box.

Tomorrow, at the Pierre, when they were alone, he would offer her a glass of champagne, get down on his knee and hand it to her.

When he got off at the bottom floor, his excitement about the gorgeous penthouse and his new offices and the ring was so great he wanted to share his news with her. Why wait until tomorrow to propose when he felt so sure this afternoon?

Why not go to the theater and propose to her now? He knew she was in rehearsals and that they hadn't been going well. He knew he shouldn't bother her. Still, he wanted to see her. He wanted to hold her. Most of all he felt an urgent need to propose to her. He was afraid if he waited, somehow he'd lose her again.

He pulled out his phone and studied his calendar. Calling Roberto, he told him to cancel the rest of his meetings.

Then he stepped into his limo and ordered his driver to take him to her theater.

Bad idea, he thought. But he couldn't stop himself.

Summer raced to her dressing room during a break in rehearsals to return her agent's calls, of which there were three. She hoped the call wouldn't take long because she wanted so badly to call Zach.

Carl answered on the first ring. "You're an angel for getting back to me so fast."

"What is it?"

"Hugh Jones is in town. Just for the day. The PR people from the studio want to set up a short interview for the two of you."

"When? Where? I'm really busy."

"They had a hard time talking Jones into it as well, but they've got him to agree. So—say in an hour. In your dressing room."

"Impossible. Things for the show aren't going well, and some of the production's big investors are here giving Paolo a hard time. He's pretty insane."

"The studio has already talked to Paolo. He's fine with it."

"What?"

"The interview won't take more than fifteen minutes. There was so much buzz about your scenes with Jones that…"

She shut her eyes. That buzz, as Carl termed it, had nearly destroyed her relationship with Zach. Except for the fact that she hadn't found a way to tell him about the baby, things were going so well for them right now. She didn't want to stir up another round of press interest, and Hugh was a hot button she didn't want punched until Zach truly trusted her and their relationship was on less fragile ground. Until she'd told him about the baby….

"The movie isn't coming out for months. I don't see why I have to do an interview with Hugh this afternoon."

"Well, the PR department makes those calls, not us. Their team thinks it's essential to keep up the momentum."

Translation: they wanted hordes of paparazzi questioning the true nature of her relationship with Jones and continuing to chase her and take pictures of her with Zach. The PR department wanted her face and name out there, so she'd be a draw. They didn't care that by linking her to Jones, they drove Zach crazy. To them, this was just another juicy story.

She had to protect her relationship with Zach at all costs.

"Sorry!" she said and ended the call. But no sooner had she hung up than Sam rang her.

"You signed a contract agreeing to do promotion. Paolo's okay with it, so what's your problem?" Sam read her the clause in her contract. It didn't take a genius to understand his thinly veiled threat. They could sue her if she didn't do as they commanded.

Feeling queasy and a bit shaky, which had been happening a lot lately, especially in the mornings, she hung up and called Zach's cell.

But his phone went to voice mail. She didn't want to leave this kind of news in a message. When she called him repeatedly, and he still didn't answer, she began to feel sick with worry. She had to tell him about this interview before the paparazzi caught up with him and peppered him with questions he was not prepared to answer.

On the way to the theater Zach's limo got caught in traffic beside a flower stall, so Zach whipped out and bought two dozen roses from the elderly flower seller. The perfect buds were so bright in the sunlight they blazed like flames, but they burned no brighter than the towering emotion in his heart.

Inside the limo, their scent was so overpowering he set them aside. When the driver braked, Zach leaned forward, staring at the sea of vehicles surrounding them, cursing vividly when a truck cut in front of them.

Damn it. He sat back against soft leather and forced himself to try to relax. But he couldn't. He was out of control, which he hated. He was impatient to see Summer, to take her in his arms and beg her to love him. To ask her to make a life with him.

He could walk iron without breaking a sweat. So what was so terrifying about baring his soul and asking the woman he loved to marry him?

When his cell phone rang, Zach answered it automatically.

"You bastard!"

"Hello, Thurman."

Zach hadn't heard the other man's voice in years. Funny, that he recognized the cold, dead tone instantly.

"You think you're so smart, that you know everything, but you don't. You're a gambler. I'd bet money Summer hasn't told you what she did in New Orleans...."

The hair at the back his nape rose. "What the hell are you talking about?"

"Why don't you ask Summer?"

Thurman laughed nastily and hung up.

When Zach jumped out of the limo at the theater with a conflicted heart, a dozen reporters leaped toward him, hammering him about Summer as their flashes blinded him.

His expression turned to stone as he stormed past them into the auditorium, slamming the door on their idiotic clamor.

Zach was remembering how vulnerable Summer had looked every time she'd tried to talk to him about the past. What hadn't she told him? What did Thurman know that Zach didn't?

He knew exactly where Summer's dressing room was since she'd given him a personal tour last weekend, so he wasted no time on his way through the crowded corridors. Backstage was like a maze, but he didn't stop, not even when actors, who were milling about, tried to greet him.

He wondered why everyone was on break. Maybe this meant Summer would be free to talk to him. He wouldn't have to wait.

When he found the door with her name on it, it was closed. He banged on it impatiently.

What he wanted was beautiful golden Summer with her long-lashed eyes to open the door and blush charmingly when she saw him. He wanted to take her in his arms and then set a time for a private talk. This time he would listen to whatever she had to tell him. Then he would tell her how much he loved her and ask her to be his wife.

What he got was Hugh Jones and a photographer.

The reporter didn't miss a beat when he saw the chance for a shot of the two men together.

When the flash went off twice, Zach turned on his heel. No way could he face the press when he felt so conflicted privately. Then Summer was behind him, her voice nervous and high-pitched.

Instead of smiling, her blue eyes were wide with panic and guilt. "Zach, what are you doing here?"

Logically, he knew he shouldn't have interrupted her on such short notice, but he wasn't feeling logical.

"Making a damn fool of myself. Again."

"Zach, no.... Wait! Listen!"

She'd gone pale, and her hand shook as it tugged at his sleeve. He felt sorry for her, so he let her pull him into the dressing room beside hers and listened impatiently as she whispered to the young actress inside it. "Can we please talk here for a few minutes?"

"Sure. Anytime." Moving like a dancer, the girl, who was thin as a rail, got up languidly, picked up the magazine she'd been flipping through and left in a swirl of silken yellow skirts as she winked at Zach.

"We were just doing an interview for *Dangerous Man.* That's all. My agent called me less than an hour ago or I would have told you.... I had to do it. Because I signed a contract saying I would. I tried to call you, but you didn't answer."

"I understand. I was on the phone." *With Thurman,* he thought, frowning.

"No, you don't understand. I can see that. You look furious...."

"I said I believe you're doing an interview, and I do. But before the press is through with this story, nobody else will. I can't help wondering if this will always be the way we have to live—with the press playing up your nonexistent relationships with other men and making me look the fool."

He knew he wasn't being totally honest. He felt too raw to be completely open with her. He'd come here to propose, and then Thurman had called and stirred up all his old doubts about her.

"Zach, I want you in my life. I do…. What are you doing here a day early?"

He shouldn't have surprised her like this. He felt vulnerable, as if his heart was on his sleeve, and suddenly he didn't want her to know about all the plans he'd made. Now wasn't the time to ask her about New Orleans or to propose.

"It doesn't matter. I'm leaving."

"I wish you'd stay."

"Well, I'm not sure I want idiots second-guessing every stage of our relationship when I feel…" He stopped, torn.

"When you feel…what?"

"Nothing."

"Zach, what's wrong?"

"Maybe I'm not in the mood to share you with everyone in the known universe. So, I'd better go, so you can finish the damn interview. The entire crew and cast is waiting on you, right?"

She swallowed. "Talk to me, Zach. Please talk to me."

Her eyes were so earnest maybe he would have, if a red-faced Paolo hadn't burst into the room, shattering the moment.

"Sorry to interrupt, but Sandy said you were in here. You did say fifteen minutes. How much longer is this damn interview going to take?"

"Sorry. We haven't started yet."

"Why the hell not?"

"It's my fault, but I'm going," Zach said.

"No!" she cried, grabbing him.

Paolo shot him a look of disgust before he turned and left.

"I'm beginning to realize how demanding I am," Zach said. "You see, I'm the kind of guy who expects his wife to put him first sometimes…like now, even when I know it's a very bad time for you."

"Your wife…. Did you say *your wife?*"

"I came over here because I had something very personal to say to you…. Something very important, to me at least. Now I see that you have a lot more to deal with than my concerns."

"Zach, did you come over here to ask me to marry you? Because I will."

He didn't want to ask her now, like this. He was beginning to think he shouldn't ask her at all. Instead of answering her, he said, "On the way over here I got a phone call. From Thurman."

"Thurman?" She went very white.

"He told me to ask you about New Orleans. He insinuated that you've been keeping something important from me. Is that true?"

"Oh, Zach…." Her eyes misted with guilt-stricken anguish. Her hands were shaking. "I…I tried to tell you in Louisiana. I want to talk about it. Truly I do, but not now. I have rehearsals, the interview…and you're too upset."

"It doesn't matter," he said.

He saw now that he'd been a stupid, emotional fool to be in such a rush to marry her. They both had huge, time-consuming careers; their past had haunted them for years; the press wouldn't leave them alone. Was there room for love and marriage with so many distractions, responsibilities and conflicts?

"Maybe neither of us has time for a marriage," he said.

"That's not fair. This is just a very bad time for me. What if I happened to drop in on you, when you were in the middle of a negotiation and forty people were waiting on your decision?"

"That's the point, isn't it? I've just realized there's not room in a marriage for two huge egos and two big careers…along with everything else that's between us. I don't like goodbyes, Summer, so I'll just make a quick exit."

"You're not telling me everything," she said, grabbing his arm to keep him in the room.

"I could say the same thing to you, couldn't I, sweetheart?"

The last thing he saw was her ashen face as she staggered backward, knocking a wig stand over as she sank down onto her friend's couch. Her big blue eyes glimmered with unshed tears, and she looked white and shaken. It tore him up to realize he'd hurt her again.

But maybe there had always been too much between them for a relationship to ever work. Maybe he'd let their chemistry blind him. Had he been rushing into marriage because he hadn't wanted to stop to think about the realities?

On his way out of the theater, he pitched the perfect red roses in the first stinking trash barrel he saw. Then he stepped through the throng of reporters and into the hushed silence of his luxurious limo.

"Take me to LaGuardia Airport," he said.

Eleven

Summer Wallace Dumps Billionaire For Movie Star.

Summer felt sick to her stomach as she sat up straighter in her bed to turn the page of the newspaper.

She'd tried to phone Zach, but he wouldn't take her calls. She had to tell him about their lost little girl even if the timing was awful and the news killed whatever remaining tenderness he felt for her.

"When will the thirty-one-year-old actress make up her mind…."

There was an awful picture of Zach and Hugh together. Two more shots showed Zach entering the theater with roses, and there was one of him looking furious as he dumped the gorgeous bouquet on his way out.

Why did the headlines always have to mention her age and remind her that her biological clock was ticking? Why did every headline have to remind her that Zach would never marry her? That she would never have his darling black-haired children.

She felt a rivulet of perspiration trickle down her back. Then a hot sensation of dizziness flooded her. Cupping her hands over her mouth, she lurched to her feet and ran to her toilet where she was violently ill.

When she was able to lift her head, she opened the window and gulped in mouthfuls of sweet, fresh air. Then she put the toilet lid down and sat, holding her head in her hands.

The episode of nausea was the third she'd had this week. Since her stomach was often queasy during rehearsals and she'd been so busy, she hadn't really thought about it. Until now.

"Oh, no," she whispered as comprehension dawned.

Slowly she arose and stared critically at the reflection of her white face in the mirror.

She was pregnant. Since she'd been pregnant before, she should have recognized the signs. Her breasts were swollen, and her period was late. She had the oddest cravings at the strangest times. Like that other night when she had to have a corn dog and a tomato and a pickle and nothing else would do. She felt lethargic, different.

Great timing. Just like last time.

Zach had left her. And she hadn't even told him about their little girl yet. He wouldn't be happy to learn the truth about their past, nor would he be overjoyed that they were going to have another child.

Then there was the not-insignificant detail that she was starring in a play that was going to open in less than three weeks. One where her character was not pregnant and the director and cast were on the verge of a collective nervous breakdown if things didn't start coming together soon.

Zach had been swimming laps in his pool behind Thibodeaux House for an hour, so it was time to get out.

He wanted to forget Summer, to go on with his life. So, he'd ignored her calls; ignored the pain he felt at her loss.

He would get through this. He would. Not that it would be easy.

As he toweled off, he heard furious shouts and scuffling out front.

At first he thought it was the press and paid no attention. They'd been stalking him all week, ever since they'd caught him with Jones the day of the interview. Then he recognized the hateful voice.

"Let me through, damn it," Thurman Wallace yelled at Zach's security team. "I've got something to say to Torr, and I won't go until I say it."

Pulling on a shirt without bothering to button it, Zach strode to the front of the house. "Let him in," he said.

When Wallace stepped through the gate, Zach smelled the hot stench of liquor on the man's breath.

"Say your piece and leave, Wallace."

"You think you're something, don't you, you arrogant you-know-what, coming back here, to my town, getting everyone on your side because you're rich…. Taking up with Summer again…. Using her like a…"

"Watch your language. Say your piece. Then get the hell off my property."

"It wasn't all me, wanting to bring those charges. You think she wanted you back then, but she didn't. She thought you were trash, same as I did."

"Shut up about her."

"If she'd cared for you, why did she kill your baby?"

"What the hell did you say?"

"You got her pregnant. I had to send her to New Orleans before she started to show so nobody around here would know about her and ruin my good name."

"I don't believe you! Get out of here before I throw you out!"

When Wallace didn't move, Zach started toward him. "Get out of here now, or you'll be sorry!"

Wallace took one look at Zach and ran for his life.

Zach sank to his knees and thought about a younger Summer, pregnant and alone in New Orleans. Whatever she'd done, he'd never believe she'd deliberately killed their baby. But she hadn't told him about it, had she? So, how could he trust her?

All doubt that he had made the right decision in leaving her vanished.

The sudden certainty hurt.

God, how it hurt.

Billionaire And Actress Had Secret Baby!

The ugly headline screamed at Summer, shattering her heart into a million tiny pieces.

Gram had warned her about the awful story that Thurman had sold to the tabloids. In spite of the warning, Summer was still shaking as she laid down a wad of cash for all the newspapers on the rack at the tiny grocery store a block from her apartment.

Folding them, she plunged them into her bag, put her sunglasses back on and ran outside where she dumped them in the first trash bin she saw. It was a hollow gesture since there were hundreds of thousands on similar racks all over the country. Everybody would see them when they were in the check-out lines.

How could Thurman be so filled with hate? How could he have sold such a personally heartbreaking story? She felt brokenhearted, betrayed and mortified at the same time. But most of all she hurt for Zach. This was no way for him to discover the truth.

Until now, she'd held on to a fragile hope that Zach might be missing her as much as she missed him, and that given time, he would change his mind and come back to her.

Thurman's story extinguished all such hope.

She felt like weeping, not just for herself, but for the baby she was carrying.

Then a reporter sprang out of nowhere and called her name. When she turned, he took her picture.

"Gram, I've got to talk to Zach."

A week had passed since Thurman's story had hit the stands. Zach was still refusing to take her calls. His secretary was impatient whenever Summer called his office and left a message. So she'd called Gram, hoping for her help.

"But I thought that he and you…that it was…over," Gram said.

"It is," Summer said softly. "I've called him so many times, and he won't talk to me. But that's not the worst. Gram, I'm pregnant. I don't know how it happened…because we were always careful."

"It was meant to be," Gram said in her know-it-all way.

"No," Summer replied, knowing Gram couldn't be right. "What this means is that in spite of everything that's wrong between us, I've got to talk to him."

"Nick told Moxie Brown, who told Sammy, who told me that Zach has fired the contractor he'd hired to remodel that old Thibodeaux place and has put it up for sale. Nick said that big gambling boat of his is arriving at the end of the week. So, Zach's coming to town to inspect it."

Summer let out a breath. Finally, she'd caught a break. Once the play opened, she'd be doing eight shows a week. It would be very difficult for her to take time off. Paolo would pitch a fit, but maybe she could sneak in an overnight trip home.

She couldn't make the same mistake she'd made the first time they'd broken up, when he'd put up roadblocks and she'd given up on telling Zach the truth about their little girl.

She had to see him one last time—to tell him face-to-face about the baby they'd lost and this precious baby that she was carrying.

Their baby.

Summer barely glanced at the chain-link fence covered with No Trespassing notices meant to keep out the press. And her. Nor did she take note of the large sign over the gate that blared in big red letters, No Admittance. Employees Only.

Hunched over, with a pink pashmina covering her hair, Summer rushed past a uniformed man.

"Ma'am, you can't go in there. Ma'am…"

Running now on her ice-pick heels, Summer ignored the burly individual in the hard hat and brown uniform as she sped toward the dock where Zach's magnificent floating gambling palace was now secured.

"Ma'am!"

What luck! There he was.

Every muscle in her body tensed. Then she forced herself to let out a breath.

Holding a clipboard and pen, Zach stood in the middle of a dozen men. His stance, with long legs spread slightly apart, reminded her of a large cat who looked relaxed but was coiled to spring. His face was hard, and he was talking fast. The other men, their heads cocked toward him, held clipboards and pens, too. Those standing beside him were frowning in frustration as they wrote furiously in an effort to keep up.

"Zach," she cried, pink heels clattering as she ran farther out onto the dock.

She wore a soft pink dress. The bodice clung and its skirt swirled around her hips. Once he'd accused her of dressing to be desirable. Well, today she'd given it her best shot. She'd gone shopping and had deliberately picked a sexy dress for this confrontation.

All the men stopped talking at once. She let her pashmina slide to her shoulders.

Jaws fell. Zach spun, then hissed in a breath at the sight of her. Even though his eyes went icy and hard, she'd seen the split-second spark of attraction her appearance had caused. She'd caught him off guard in front of his men, exposed his vulnerability, and she knew he hated that.

Grief that he was hers no longer, that she couldn't run into his arms, slashed through her like a knife.

He didn't look as sure or confident as he had the last time she'd seen him. His face was thinner; his eyes shadowed.

"Get her out of here," he ordered, his frigid voice radiating antagonism.

"Sorry, Mr. Torr. Ma'am, I'm gonna have to ask you to leave," the burly man said behind her.

She had only seconds before she'd be forced to go.

"Zach," she cried. "I've got to talk to you."

"Too bad. I'm in a meeting." Slamming on a pair of dark glasses, he turned away.

The burly man grabbed her arm and began to tug her gently in the direction of the exit. "Please, ma'am…"

Frantic, she struggled to free herself. "Zach… You've got to listen to me."

The man's grip hardened. "Come on, ma'am."

"Zach! Please!"

His face tight and determined, Zach tapped his pen against his clipboard and continued to ignore her.

She didn't want to tell him like this—not when he was

surrounded by other people. She didn't. But what were her choices?

"Zach, I'm pregnant!"

Zach had selected the elegant office onboard his ship as a place where they could be alone, but the space felt cramped and airless to Summer as Zach subjected her to a thorough, intimate appraisal. Never had she found his arresting face more handsome, but when she searched its hard, angular planes for a trace of sympathy, she found none.

His eyes were so intense and cold, they made her feel almost faint with grief.

"Zach..." For a second, everything in her vision darkened except his face, which blurred in swirling pinpricks of light.

His hard arms reached for her, steadied her, led her to a chair, where she gulped in a sweet breath of air.

"Are you okay?" he demanded.

"I—I'm fine."

He stood over her, watching her carefully to make sure.

"Zach, I didn't want to tell you the news like that...in front of your men...when you were so furious. But I had to tell you face-to-face. I didn't want to leave a message with your secretary, or for some reporter to accost you with questions because I was having our child."

"Oh, really? You didn't bother to tell me the last time you were pregnant. Are you eager to share this child with me since I've got money now? And when do you intend to tell the press, so as to heighten your box-office draw? Frankly, I'm surprised you didn't bring the hounds with you today."

Again Zach's eyes had become emotionless. She felt as if her heart were freezing and dying. It was as if, instead of her, he saw some cruel, cunning stranger.

She took a deep breath. "No... Why would I... You can't, you can't believe I'm that low."

"You're wrong."

"I want to protect our baby. And I have my own income, I'll have you know. So, money is the last thing I need from you."

"I'll set up an account and do what's necessary. But the less I see or hear from you, the better. In the future, my lawyers will talk to your lawyers. I'll want to see our child rather frequently, I'm afraid. As you know, I'm sorely lacking in close family. And as I distrust the mother, I'll need to be as big an influence in his life as possible if he's to have a fighting chance. And I repeat, I will see to it that these matters are arranged so that we meet as infrequently as possible."

"I—I know how you must feel…finding out the way you did…about our first baby. You must think me truly awful…."

"No! You don't know how I feel! You couldn't possibly imagine."

For a moment his hard face was expressionless. Then he shook his head. "You don't understand me at all."

"I know I didn't stand up for you the way you wanted me to when my stepfather brought charges against you. You thought I went along with him, but I didn't. I loved you. I still do."

"Don't use that four-letter word. You say it too easily. All it's ever been for me is a one-way ticket to hell."

"Zach, I was sixteen…pregnant…terrified…of him and of the accusations, of all the ugliness. I was so confused. Hysterical, really."

"It doesn't matter anymore," he said in a weary, defeated tone.

But it did matter to her, fiercely. She'd thought she'd learned to live with her regrets, then he'd come back into her life and made her love him again. Being with him right now, when he was so distant, knowing that he was shutting her out forever, made her want to confess everything, to finally share all the regrets she'd carried alone for so long.

She'd organized a funeral for their first baby, had attended
it by herself in the rain. Her mother, who would have come,
had been too ill to leave Bonne Terre. Gram had been caring
for Summer's mother, and Tuck had been too young to be of
any comfort. Summer had stayed in the cemetery until she'd
been drenched, until the last clod of dirt had been thrown,
until a compassionate grave digger had plucked a single white
rose from the funeral wreath she'd bought and handed the
dripping blossom to her.

"Press this in that Bible you be carrin', *cher.* And go home.
You can't do any good here. The little one, she's in heaven
now."

Summer had placed angels on the grave.

Somehow she swallowed her tears when she came back
to the present. "I went to Houston when I was nearly five
months along. I tried to talk to you, to find you, but you
wouldn't see me."

"Because I knew you were manipulating me."

"But I tried to tell you about the baby. I really tried."

"Not hard enough apparently. You could have told somebody else…. My uncle, maybe. He would have gotten the
message to me. But you didn't."

"I was out of money. I wasn't feeling so well. I—I thought
it was no use, so I went back to New Orleans. I—I lost the
baby the next week. I was all alone. I wanted you so desperately. I never wanted you with me more."

A muscle in his carved cheek jerked savagely, but when
he spoke, his voice was low, contemptuous.

"You didn't do anything deliberate to bring about that unhappy event, did you?"

"What?" His words hit her like a blow. Once again his
face swirled in blackness. If she'd been standing, she would
have fallen. Only with the greatest effort did she manage to
catch her breath.

"No." The single word was a prayer asking him to believe her. The single tear that traced down her cheek spoke the truth.

Not that he could see the truth, blinded as he was by his own fury and sense of betrayal.

"You damn sure know how to deliver a line." His low voice was hoarse. "I'll give you that. You need to remember that little trick for the stage, sweetheart. It was very effective."

"Okay. I understand," she whispered. "You'll never trust me again. Or forgive me."

"You've got that right. The sooner we finish this conversation, the sooner we can get on with our separate lives. I said I'd help you with the baby, and I will. You don't look well. I want you to take better care of yourself this time. Cut back on your schedule. You can't possibly do eight shows a week. I'll pay for the best doctors...anything you need. And I want to be there when you deliver. Not for your sake, but for the baby's."

She nodded, feeling crushed at his efficient tone.

"I love you," she murmured. "I'll always love you."

"Then I'm sorry for you because it's over between us. I consider myself a stupid fool for getting involved with you again. Usually I'm smart enough to learn from my mistakes. Nick tried to warn me you were nuclear. He was right."

"I'm so sorry I've caused you so much pain...."

"Sorry never cuts it, does it?"

Ravaged, she stood up. Then turning from him, she fled.

Outside, the sunlight in the trees was as dull as old pewter, and she was deaf to her favorite song playing on her car radio.

She didn't want to go back to New York and work onstage, work with people. She wanted to curl up somewhere in a dark room and cry.

Then she remembered Gram's tin of chocolate-chip cookies on the shelf above her fridge. She would go back to Gram's and confide in her. Her grandmother would take Summer in her arms as she had after Summer had lost Zach, her mother and her little baby girl, and, for a brief spell, she'd feel better. Then she'd stuff herself on her grandmother's cookies until she fell asleep.

Slowly, she'd gather enough courage to go through the motions of living. She'd pack her suitcase and set her alarm. Tomorrow she'd dress and drive to the airport. Then she'd return to her lonely apartment and get back in her old routine and try to forget Zach all over again.

It wouldn't be possible, but she'd try just the same.

The memory of her soft, pale face with those unshed tears tore at him.

"I can't do this. Take over for me," Zach growled as he slammed his clipboard down on a table inside the casino.

Roberto and his men watched silently as Zach stalked past them, the rows of slot machines and then the gaming tables. Outside, the air was thick and oppressive with the scent of rain. He looked up and saw threatening black clouds moving in fast. A fierce gust ripped across the bayou.

Perfect weather, he thought, as the first raindrop pelted him.

No sooner had he slammed the door of his Mercedes, started the engine and roared out of the parking lot, than it started pouring. Not that the rain kept him from whipping violently across the narrow bridge and skidding onto the main road. A truck honked wildly. Brakes squealed as it surrendered right-of-way.

Zach took his foot off the accelerator. No use killing some innocent motorist. Summer damn sure wasn't worth it.

It was going to take a long time for his love, or rather the illusion of who he'd believed she was, to die again.

Maybe forever.

She'd looked so damn pretty in that soft pink dress that

had clung to her slim body, and so desperately forlorn with those damp blue eyes that had shed that single spectacular tear at exactly the right moment. She'd shredded his heart all over again. It would probably thrill her to know she'd nearly had him believing what he saw and felt instead of what he knew to be true.

His gut had clenched, and his heart had thudded violently. He'd wanted to grab her, pull her close, soothe and console her, kiss that tearstained cheek and those beautiful, pouting lips…just one last time. He'd wanted it so much he'd almost lost control.

Then he'd remembered she was an actress, who'd dressed to entice him, who'd played her role perfectly despite her vows never to act when she was with him.

He remembered all her lies of omission about the baby. What part of their relationship had ever been true? What was he to her? Another circus act in the three-ring show she put on for her adoring fans? Did she need a man in her life to complete the picture of her as America's number-one sweetheart? Acting was a highly competitive career. What sin wouldn't she commit to stay on top?

He thought of all the magazine-cover stories he'd seen about actresses with their adoring babies and husbands. Were any of those heartwarming stories truthful? Weren't they all just fodder for fools like him, who, deep down, wanted to believe the dream?

Had anything she'd said today been real?

Whether it was or not, she'd damn sure shattered his heart and sent him to hell and back all over again.

Twelve

One week later

Zach moved silently through the long shadows of the tall spreading oaks near Viola's house, stepping past Silas, who looked like a black-and-white fur ball as he napped under the pink blossoms of his favorite crape myrtle bush.

The dazzling pink flowers blurred, and suddenly Zach saw Summer instead of the worthless feline: Summer with her heart in her eyes, Summer looking lovely and too sexy for words in that ridiculous pink confection of a dress.

Damn her. As the image dissolved, he experienced burning, agonizing loss.

Frowning, he approached Viola's screen door warily.

Why was he even here? He had a plane to catch. It wasn't as if he had to show up at her request. Hell, these days he ignored most invitations, and he had every reason to ignore Viola's. Why was he putting himself through this?

Because she'd sounded so fragile when she'd summoned him. Because he genuinely liked her. Because she was family now, in spite of everything Summer had done. Viola would be his son's great-grandmother. Because she was hurting nearly as much as he was that the dream wouldn't come true.

Viola's bossy cat trotted toward the screen door and rubbed his tail arrogantly against Zach's jeans. Then he sank a claw into the screen as he waited to be let in.

Viola welcomed them both. Silas, who sprang inside first, she gave a can of tuna. Zach, she gave a plate of chocolate-chip cookies and a glass of iced tea that she'd flavored with mint from her garden.

He didn't have time for tea or cookies, but he was loath to say so. Viola had a strange power over him.

When he saw the empty shelves and all the boxes stacked against the walls in every room, in an effort to make polite conversation, he asked when she planned to move to her new condo.

"I'm taking my time. I can only do an hour or so of packing each day before my back starts howling. Tuck's not much help, bless his lazy soul, not even when I pay him. Slow as molasses. Drops things, he does. And Summer's not going to rent out this old place after all. Because of the baby…." She said that last with reverence as she lifted her sharp gaze to his.

When she didn't avert those piercing eyes that saw too much, his heart sped up to a tortured pace.

"She's feeling quite sentimental about the old place. Said she's going to keep it for herself and the baby, so the baby will grow up loving it as much as past generations have before her. That's nice, don't you think?"

Her? Funny how Zach always thought of their kid as a boy. A little boy with golden hair and bright blue eyes. But it could be girl, couldn't it? A beautiful little girl who looked like Summer, who'd break his heart because he loved her so.

Viola noted his empty plate. Usually, she hopped up to re-fill such a plate. But not today.

"I'm afraid there aren't any more cookies. You see, Summer ate practically all of them the other day...stuffed herself on them, the poor dear. Not a good thing really, in her condition. She has to get into all those costumes, too, you know. But she was so down before she left. Kept eating one after another, couldn't stop herself. Until I took the plate away and froze the remaining cookies for future guests. And here you are."

"Why did you ask me to come over here today, Viola? I have a plane to catch, meetings in Houston...."

"You poor dear, with your big, important life. You know, you don't look any better than she does. I can see that, despite your tough exterior, this is just as hard on you as it is on her."

Zach froze. "Did *she* put you up to this?"

"Who?" Viola's eyes were suspiciously guileless. "Put me up to what?"

Those innocent eyes, so compelling in her wrinkled face, seemed to search his soul in the exact way that Summer's sometimes did. But unlike Summer, Viola's deep compassion for him was genuine.

"Zach, is this really what you want? You two are going to have a child. Summer's brokenhearted, and I think you love her, too. I think you always have and always will."

He felt the ice that encased his heart melting beneath the brightness of her sweet, determined gaze, but his face remained a mask.

"Zach, you have the baby to think of. When parents don't live together, it's the child who suffers most. The family's broken. That's what happened to Summer when her father walked out on Anna. Look at poor Tuck, how he's still struggling. A baby needs to be part of a close, loving family."

"Unfortunately, we can't all have the ideal family," he muttered. "I was on my own after my mother left my father, and then my father remarried a younger woman, who threw me out after he died."

"So, then you know how it feels. Do you want your baby to suffer the way you did, when you could so easily prevent it?"

Easily?

Again, he asked himself why he'd come here. It was hard enough to let Summer go without this fragile old lady, whom he liked, trying to pry his innermost secrets from him. Summer was wrong for him. Period.

He'd believed in the dream, but it had all been a lie. Summer was the ultimate liar. And even if it weren't for that calamity, even if she were the lovely illusion he'd believed in, he couldn't live with the press pouncing on them every time one of them had so much as a conversation with another attractive person. He didn't want his marriage to be a feast for public consumption. He wanted a real marriage—a private, personal bonding of two souls—not some mirage of perfect love that would heighten Summer's popularity.

"I don't need this," he growled as he stood up.

"Sit back down," Viola commanded in her bossy way.

Strange that, in his hopeless mood, he found her firm manner oddly comforting.

Slowly, he sank back into the chair, Summer's favorite chair, which happened to be his favorite, too.

"I may be a pushy old lady, who doesn't know half as much as she should, but I know you two belong together."

"Not anymore. Too many things have happened. The past…our first baby…all the lies. I don't want everything we do to be magnified by the media."

"Summer is a wonderful girl, and you know it! Thurman was a real stinker. Hasn't he cost us all enough? As for the press—why do you care so much about what other people think?"

"It's not that simple."

"I say it is. I say maybe you're too proud, too arrogant. And maybe, despite your bluster, you're something of a coward."

He scowled at her.

"I know this because I've been guilty of the same thing at times. When anything bad is written about Summer, my friends all tease me. I don't like it. I feel put down and ashamed. But they're jealous, you see, of her success. Not that any of them will admit it. But don't they just love it when unkind words are written about Summer or an unflattering picture of her is taken? I fall for their bluster every time and blame Summer. Either she sets me straight or I get my bearings back on my own. All the negative stuff is backward praise in a way. People see how wonderful she is and want a part of her. It's up to me to stay centered and put her first and everybody else last—where they belong."

"We've got an ugly past to live down, as well."

"When you've lived as long as I have, you learn you can live anything down."

"Look, our lifestyles just aren't compatible."

"Then modify them. Maybe it won't take as much give on your part as you think. When two people who are right for each other come together, the most insurmountable obstacles can be conquered."

"I've gotta go."

"My, but you're stubborn. It's probably one of the reasons you're so successful. You stick to what you decide to do, and do it. But in this case, you're wrong. You're making the biggest mistake of your life."

"Usually, I go with my gut. This time, though, I made an intelligent decision, based on past and present experience—that's all."

"Maybe you should stick with your gut."

"Not smart. She's too good of an actress. She throws off my instincts."

"Has this all been about revenge, then—about you wanting to get even with her for what happened fifteen years ago?"

"Hell, no."

"Well, too bad, 'cause you'd sure be even with her if it was. You really hurt her this time. I haven't seen her like this since she failed to carry your first child. It seems so unfair that here she is pregnant again, you both have a glorious second chance, but you're walking out on her like before. You just about killed her last time."

"I don't need this."

"I say you do. When you were in jail, Thurman found out she was pregnant and sent her away to New Orleans to have your baby. He didn't want you or anybody else to know about the baby because he was afraid it might sway public opinion in your favor. There were people, even back then, who sided with you and didn't like the way Thurman was using his pull to rush the due process of law.

"Did you know Summer tried to contact you shortly before she miscarried?"

"You're not telling me anything I don't already know."

Viola ignored his protest. "Summer was inconsolable when she couldn't find you. Finally, she felt that she had nowhere to go but back to New Orleans, and that's where she lost the baby. Summer had the saddest little funeral for that child. Not that I could go. I was too busy tending to my dying daughter. When Summer finally came home to stay, she was different, changed.

"Then Anna, her mother, died. Summer blamed Thurman for everything that had happened, for the end of her mother's remission, for losing you, for the death of the baby. She said she couldn't live in this town with her memories, so she broke away from all of us and went to New York. That's where she took bit parts while going to college in her spare time. I sent money. She worked herself to the bone in an effort to forget you. But she never could."

"I had my own problems back then."

The ancients and the wise say a man can learn the greatest truths of the universe in an instant. Suddenly, that was true for Zach. No sooner had he said those bitter words than his perspective shifted dramatically. All the pieces of the story he had imagined to be the truth about his love affair with Summer arranged themselves in a new and different order with a new and different meaning.

Had he been hurt and too bitter to consider what Summer had gone through? He had. And he hadn't known the half of it. When she'd sought him out in Houston, how coldly he'd rejected her.

Just as he was rejecting her now.

All that had ever mattered was their love for each other. If they'd kept their focus on that, no one could have touched them.

The pain he felt was staggering. He'd hurt Summer terribly, more than Thurman ever had. Because he'd been stubbornly focused on his own grievances. And blind to hers.

The image of that single tear trickling down her beautiful face tugged at his heart. Why hadn't he listened to his instinct and drawn her close and kissed her tears away?

"I've said my piece, so you can go now," Viola said as she laid a gnarled hand on Silas, who purred in her lap.

For a long moment, Zach sat where he was, stunned. Without Summer beside him, he faced nothing but long years of emptiness. He would fill up his days with work, but the nights would be long and lonely. There would be no one to hold him in the darkness. No one to care about his failures or share his successes. He would be forever diminished without her love.

And he was throwing it all away.

"You have a plane to catch, don't you?"

"Thank you for the cookies and tea," he muttered mechanically, like someone in a dream.

He stared at the spot on the porch where he'd kissed Summer as a girl. She'd been so blushingly shy and lovely. When he'd kissed the woman in that same spot fifteen years later, she'd been hurt and defiant and in denial, but he'd seen into her heart and had fallen in love with her all over again.

He loved her.

He wasn't going to stop loving her just because he willed himself to do so. His love for her was the truest and strongest part of him. By sending her and his child away, he faced the death of everything that would ever matter to him.

He had to make this right.

He needed Summer and their child.

Damn the press. Why hadn't he seen that he should put her first, instead of his own damn ego? She'd carried his child and lost it while her mother had been gravely ill. The thought of her alone and pregnant again was excruciatingly unbearable. If anything happened to her or the baby because of his horrible cruelty, he would never forgive himself.

He had to take care of them. He had to find a way to protect them from the press instead of blaming Summer for the made-up headlines. And when he couldn't protect them, he'd endure the media coverage…. If only Summer would forgive him and take him back.

Thirteen

It was raining outside the theater, pouring. Not that Summer cared.

Opening nights were all about families and friends. Thus, her dressing room and bathroom overflowed with vivid bouquets of flowers, embossed cards from the greats and the near-greats and telegrams, as well. Everybody she remotely cared about was packed inside these two tiny rooms with her. Everybody except Zach, the one person who mattered most.

As she waited for her place to be called, her grandmother and brother sat to her left on her long couch, while her dresser, hairdresser and agent sat to the right. It was a tight squeeze, but Summer needed their support desperately because Zach wasn't here.

She still felt raw and shaken from their breakup, and she'd kept people with her constantly so she wouldn't break down when the press asked their prying questions.

She kept telling herself she needed to accept that he was

gone so she could move on from this profound pain, but some part of her refused to believe he was out of her life forever. She kept hoping against hope for a miracle. He would relent and forgive her…. And love her. She wanted this miracle more than ever, and not solely because she was carrying his child.

That's why she was barely listening to the buzz around her, why she couldn't stop staring past Gram toward the door, why she couldn't stop hoping the door would open and she'd find him standing there. If only he'd walk in, take her in his arms and say everything was all right.

Then, only then, would she be whole and happy again. She didn't want to get over him. She simply wanted him in her life, in her baby's life, every day for the rest of her days. She wanted to wake up to his face on the pillow and go to sleep with the same vision, and she couldn't seem to get past that heartfelt desire. So for days—or was it weeks, she'd lost count—she'd lingered in a dreadful suspended state of suffering.

She was an actress, so she hid her pain with brilliant smiles and quick laughter, but those who knew her weren't fooled.

Suddenly, there was a roar in her ears, and she felt faint.

Summer closed her eyes and wished them all gone. She needed some alone time before the places were called to get her mind off Zach and onto her character, but everybody else was drinking champagne and having way too good a time to leave the couches.

Suddenly Paolo stormed into the dressing room. His expression was so serious when he yelled for everybody to be quiet that the uproar died instantly. He motioned for them all to leave, and because of his imperious manner, Paolo got what he wanted. They fled.

Normally, she would have thought his actions meant her reviews were bad and he'd come to tell her this bitter truth, but tonight she couldn't stop thinking about Zach long enough to care.

Paolo took her hand, squeezed it fiercely. "*Bella!* I came to tell you your reviews are sensational! The critics loved you in the previews! They adore you! We've got a hit!"

"You're sure?"

"I'm sure."

"Oh."

"Is that all you can say?" he thundered, quite put out at her lack of enthusiasm.

"I'm thrilled. Of course, I'm thrilled," she whispered dully as the overture began and places were called.

She was hardly aware of the music or of Paolo as she rose.

Paolo kissed her cheek and shoved her toward the door. "Go out there and break a leg."

She was on her way out the door when she remembered her secret ritual on opening nights. Walking swiftly to her dressing table, she flung open a drawer and removed the white-leather volume with fading gilt letters on its covers. She opened it and pressed her lips gently against the withered, yellowed rose.

Then she replaced the cherished volume and ran.

Lightning lit the sky. Thunder reverberated almost instantly.

Then all was dark again as torrents of rain slashed the jet.

Inside, Zach jammed his cell phone into his pocket impatiently and began to pace the length of the plane. He should have been in Manhattan hours ago, before Summer's play even started. He'd taken a box seat. He'd planned to be in it when she came onstage. He'd never make curtain call now.

He went to the liquor cabinet and grabbed a bottle of scotch. Splashing it into a glass, he drank deeply. Then he fumbled in his other pocket to make sure the tiny, black-velvet box was still there. He'd told himself to get rid of the ring, but he hadn't. Had he known even then that he couldn't live without her?

Pulling the ring out, he lifted the lid. The enormous engagement diamond shot sparks at him as he imagined himself slipping it onto her beautiful hand. If only, she'd have him after he'd pushed her away.

He hated this feeling of being in limbo, on edge, vulnerable. Only his need for her could reduce him to this.

What if Summer said no?

"Stop!" Zach said when he saw Summer's name blazing in red neon atop a brightly lit marquee.

Grabbing the dozens of red roses he'd bought her, he got out of the limo in the middle of traffic and made a dash across the street for the theater.

Brakes squealed. Horns honked. Cabbies cursed him. A reporter yelled his name and took his picture. But he didn't care.

Maybe he could still catch her grand finale.

When he opened the doors of the theater, he heard the roar of applause and a thousand bravos.

They loved her!

His heart swelled with joy and admiration. He loved her, too, and he was nearly bursting with pride at all she'd accomplished. No wonder so many people craved the details of her life. They saw her as a princess in a fairy tale, and they wanted a place in the dream.

He remembered when she'd wowed everybody in Bonne Terre in her high-school production of *Grease*. Zach had believed in her dream then. He had wanted her to succeed, and now she had.

He was running down the center aisle of the orchestra section when she walked onto the stage in a glittering gold gown to take her final curtain call. At the sight of her, so slim and stunningly lovely, the crowd went even wilder, yelling her name along with more bravos.

There must have been two thousand people in that theater, and they were packed to the rafters.

She bowed gracefully as people stood cheering.

Zach waved and called her name, but she couldn't hear him over the roar of her audience.

Everyone began to throw roses at the stage.

This was her moment. He stopped and waited, allowing her to shine.

There would be time later to take her in his arms, to tell her how sorry he was he'd hurt her, to swear to her he'd never do it again, to beg for her forgiveness. He'd tell her he wanted to marry her so he could spend the rest of his life making it up to her.

The past didn't matter. Her fame didn't matter. Only she and their baby and the life they would make together was important to him.

Blinded by the stage lights and feeling a little faint, Summer took another deep bow. When she straightened, she raised her hands and blew kisses as the audience continued to clap.

They stomped and screamed louder, so she bowed a final time.

This time when she straightened she heard a man on stage right call her name.

His voice shuddered through her, or did she only imagine him there?

Hoping, she turned and was overjoyed to see a tall man in a dark suit holding the biggest bouquet of roses she'd ever seen.

"Zach," she whispered, not really believing what she saw, as she took a faltering step toward him. She sucked in a breath. "Is it really you? Or am I dreaming? Oh, please, God, don't let me be dreaming!"

Then he came nearer, and his dear face with all those hard angles came into focus, and she saw that his eyes were warm and filled with love. He smiled sheepishly, but he dazzled her just the same.

"Oh, Zach. You came. You really came. I wanted you here so much. You'll never know...how much."

Handing her the huge bouquet of red roses, he swept her into his arms and kissed her.

Dozens of flashes exploded. The crowd roared, loving him, loving her, loving them together because their fairy tale had come true.

She couldn't believe he'd come tonight, that maybe he still loved her. But then she could believe it because his kisses took her breath away as did the tears shining in his beautiful, dark eyes.

"Forgive me," he whispered. "Love me.... Please love me again or I'll die."

"Oh, Zach.... With all my heart," she replied. "Always. And forever."

Although the corridor outside Summer's dressing room was noisy, Summer was aware of nothing except Zach, who was on bended knee, looking up at her, his expression fierce, almost desperate, as he clutched her hand.

"Tell me you weren't playing a part for the crowd when you promised to love me out there, sweetheart."

"I wasn't."

"I wouldn't blame you if you were. I deserve that...and worse."

"I've loved you since I was thirteen. I never stopped loving you. I never will."

"I never stopped loving you, either. I'm sorry I was so brutal when you came to Louisiana to tell me about our baby. You were so beautiful in pink, so damned beautiful, so sad...."

And I deliberately hurt you. Maybe because I felt so much and was determined to ignore those feelings. Gram called me a fool for not listening to my gut and a coward for pushing you and your love away, and she was right."

"It's okay. It's okay." Gently Summer cupped his rugged face in her hands. "It's okay. I understand. I do."

"To ever think you weren't worth whatever it costs to make our life together was the second biggest mistake of my life. The first was that I should have stood by you fifteen years ago instead of blaming you for not standing by me. I've always been a selfish, egotistical bastard."

"I should have done better by you, too."

"We can't go back," he said. "Or control the events of the past. We can only control how we view them."

"And the press? You really think you'll be able to stand all the fuss?"

"I don't care what the world thinks about me or you. Whatever we have together is true. It is the strongest force in my life…. Stronger even than my ambition, stronger than any lie the vicious press can write or say. I haven't given a damn about work since we've been apart. Nothing matters to me as much as you and our child. Nothing. I can't change the past, but together we can change our future."

She'd waited so long to hear such words from him, to feel loved by him so completely. Happiness overflowed in her heart.

"Will you marry me, then, Summer Wallace? Will you honor me by becoming Mrs. Zach Torr?"

"What? And give up my stage name?" she teased.

He pulled a black-velvet box out of his hand and opened it. The diamond sparkled with a vengeance.

But her eyes shone even brighter as she stared down at him. "Oh, my! You could persuade a lot of girls with a rock that size."

"You're the only one I want, and you didn't answer the question."

"That's because I'm still in shock. But, yes. Yes!" she cried as he slid the ring onto her finger. "Yes!"

"Then kiss me, Summer. This time I won't complain about an Oscar performance."

She laughed as she pulled his face up to hers and pressed her lips to his and did just as he commanded, for a very long time. Only it wasn't a performance, it was true and real.

She'd always been true and real. He would never doubt her again.

"Mrs. Zach Torr," she breathed in an awed tone when he finally released her.

A single tear traced down her cheek. Only this time it was a tear of joy.

Summer had never had more fun at a cast party than she was having tonight with Zach beside her and his ring glimmering on her left hand. At the same time she couldn't wait to steal away from the lavish affair, so she could spend the rest of the night with her fiancé.

But they had forever, didn't they? Or at least as long as they both should live.

Because they'd known the reviews would be good, the producers were out to impress. They'd rented a fabulous ballroom at the top of one of New York's most prestigious hotels. The food was excellent; the champagne vintage. She had to stay awhile because she was the star.

When Hugh crashed the party unexpectedly and began garnering more press than anybody else, she tensed, whispering to Zach that she'd tell the show's producers to make him leave.

Zach pressed a fingertip to her lips. "Let him stay, sweetheart. I don't care. The press can write whatever they want about the three of us."

"You really don't care?"

"I swear it. Don't worry about me. Introduce me to the bastard. I'll even pose with him. Go do what you have to do. Work the crowd. Let the photographers take the appropriate pictures of you with your cast and producers. Because the sooner you do, the sooner we can leave and have the rest of the night for each other."

She listened to his sure, calm voice, which didn't hold the faintest trace of jealousy, and felt as if she'd come home. At last.

Happiness filled her. So much happiness, she couldn't speak.

"Oh, Zach."

He pulled her into his arms. For a long moment, as he held her close, she realized that this was her new life, their shared life. He was part of all she was, just as she would be part of all he was. No more scandals stood between them.

They would be together forever.

Epilogue

The stairs creaked as Summer carried Terri, who was bundled in pink blankets and asleep, up to the nursery. But she couldn't put her beautiful, dark-haired little girl in the crib. The baby was too soft and warm and cuddly, and every minute Summer held her was too precious.

The joy-filled days passed so fast. Summer had given herself a year off for maternity leave, and already four months of it were gone. So she sat in the rocker and began to sing to her little girl while she stared out at the pines that fringed the house that had belonged to her family for more than a hundred years.

Summer loved the time she and Zach spent in this old house, the time when they left their nannies and servants in their larger residences in Houston and New York, and they could be together with Gram and Tuck.

Downstairs Gram was cooking a dinner for all of them, so the house was fragrant with the rich aroma of Cajun spices.

Nick had supplied Gram with shrimp, and she'd promised them all, including Nick, a big pot of gumbo.

Nick, who adored Terri so much he'd even made a place in his heart for Summer, would be joining them.

Summer heard Zach's Mercedes in the drive. Then the screen door banged behind him. Would that man ever learn to shut a door quietly when it was nap time?

"Summer!" Zach hollered.

"Up here," she called down to him softly and was relieved when he didn't yell again. Much as she adored Terri, like any other new mother, she counted on having a breather when her little darling snoozed.

Zach strode silently into the room and knelt beside them. Reaching out his hand he touched Terri's cheek. In her sleep, the baby smiled. Then she grabbed on to his little finger, and he gasped.

The baby's pale fingers with their little fingernails were so tiny and perfect; his tanned ones so large and blunt.

"Can I hold her?" he whispered.

Summer nodded, lifting their daughter into his arms. She got up so he could have the rocker.

"She's got me. I'm afraid I'll never be able to be stern and say no to her," he whispered. "I'll spoil her rotten."

"Well, we won't have to discipline her for a while."

Summer's eyes pooled with tears of happiness as she watched her two raven-haired darlings—her rugged husband and their trusting and innocent baby daughter.

She wished she could hold on to this moment.

The past would always be a part of them, especially the loss of their first daughter. But love filled Summer's days now with all its richly rewarding experiences. Marriage. Motherhood.

Life was so wonderful, she was determined to savor every sparkling moment of her shared happiness with Zach.

"Come here," he whispered as he got up to put their baby in her crib.

Turning to Summer, he took her in his arms and pressed her tightly against him.

"I love you," he said.

He told her that every day, and she never tired of hearing it.

She was glad that love was no longer a four-letter word he equated with hell. She was glad their love had become the guiding force in his life.

As it was in hers.

* * * * *

SEDUCED BY
THE PLAYBOY

PAMELA YAYE

Chapter 1

Demetri Morretti yanked open the door of the sleek, ultra-modern WJN-TV building and stalked inside the bright, bustling lobby. The station was abuzz with activity, the mood was cheerful, and everywhere Demetri turned were young, well-dressed people. Some were drinking coffee in the waiting area, others were yakking into their cell phones, and a few were snapping pictures in front of the life-size bronze statue.

Keeping his head down, and his pace brisk, he strode past the reception desk like a man on a mission. And he was. He'd driven across town to issue a warning to Angela Kelly, the female broadcaster with the lying lips, and wasn't going to let anything stop him. His left shoulder was killing him, throbbing in pain from his neck to his elbow, but he kept his smile in place as he continued through the sun-drenched lobby.

Demetri was about to breeze past the security desk but saw the robust-looking security guard eyeing him and thought better of it.

As he approached the circular desk, he caught sight of the gigantic oak clock. Demetri was surprised to see that it was already eleven-thirty. He was supposed to be meeting his team of his agent, his manager and his no-nonsense publicist for lunch at their favorite uptown pub. But when he remembered last night's episode of *Eye on Chicago*, Demetri decided nothing was more important than confronting the broadcaster who'd slaughtered his name on national television. This was the second time Angela Kelly had taken a cheap shot at him, and he was sick of being the butt of her jokes. This was a detour he had to make— one his manager couldn't talk him out of no matter how hard he'd tried.

"Hey, man, what's up?" Demetri said, greeting the guard with a flick of his head. "I'm here to see Ms. Angela Kelly."

"Now's not a good time."

"This won't take long. I just need a few minutes."

"Do you have an appointment?"

Demetri shook his head. "No, but—"

"But nothing." The guard waved him off with his beefy hand. "Come back at the end of the day. I might be able to squeeze you in then."

"I can't. I'm busy."

"Doing what? Panhandling?"

Taken aback by his comment, Demetri glanced down and inspected his attire. He'd left the house without shaving and wore dark, stubbly hair on his chin, but he didn't look *that* bad, did he? He'd showered and wore his new signature Gucci cologne, and his black Nike warm-up suit didn't have a wrinkle in sight. *I look good,* he decided, squaring his shoulders. *This dude needs to have his eyes checked.*

"You cats from the Ninth Street homeless shelter are driving me nuts," the guard complained. "You're always coming in here begging to see Ms. Kelly just because she volunteers down at the center, but enough is enough. She's too nice to tell you bums to get lost, but I'm not, so get lost!"

Demetri raised his eyebrows for two reasons. One because the security guard thought he was down on his luck, and two because the man spoke about Angela Kelly in glowing terms, as if she were a saint. Demetri found it hard to believe that the mean-spirited newscaster volunteered with the homeless. It had to be a front. Something she did to look good, to boost the ratings of her TV show. Demetri considered leaving, and tracking her down at the shelter up the block, but quickly decided against it. He was going to talk to Angela Kelly today, and the gruff security guard with the unibrow was going to lead him straight to her.

"I'd appreciate if you could help me out," Demetri said, glancing around the lobby for any signs of the enemy. "It's important that I talk to Ms. Kelly *before* she goes on the air."

"Are you deaf? I said to come back later." Glowering, he bared his crooked, coffee-stained teeth. "Scram before I toss you out myself."

Demetri took off his dark aviator sunglasses and flashed his trademark grin. The one that had landed him a seven-figure deal with Sony, Crest toothpaste and a dozen other multimillion-dollar companies. "Now, is that any way to talk to the Athlete of the Year?"

The guard's eyes flew out of his head. "Holy crap! You're Demetri Morretti!"

Leaning forward, Demetri pressed a finger to his lips and spoke in a conspiratorial whisper. "Keep it down, man. I don't want anyone to know it's me."

The guard raced around his desk, cap in hand, a giddy expression on his wide face. "I've been a fan ever since you signed with the Chicago Royals, and I haven't missed a home game since!"

Demetri nodded. "Thanks, man. I really appreciate the support."

"My friends are going to trip when I tell them I met you! We watch your games every week and even drove a thousand miles to see you play in..."

Demetri stood patiently, waiting for the guard to quit rambling about last year's All-Star Game. Unfortunately, this happened several times a day. And although he was out for the rest of the season due to his bum shoulder, there were fans out there who still treated him like a champion. Everyone else had turned on him, and the last thing Demetri needed was more bad press. That was the main reason he'd come to tell Angela Kelly to back off and stop the station from airing the last installment of her *Athletes Behaving Badly* series.

"Can I have your autograph?" the guard asked, snatching a piece of paper off the desk and shoving it under his nose. "No, no, forget that. Can I take a picture with you?"

"I don't know. That depends on whether or not you're going to take me to Ms. Kelly."

"Anything for you, Mr. Morretti. Right this way."

Grinning from ear to ear, he hustled Demetri through the lobby, past the reception desk and down a long, narrow corridor. The scent of freshly brewed coffee filled the air. Offices and conference rooms were on either side of the hallway, and Demetri could hear conversation, laughter and the distant sound of the radio.

The guard stopped in front of a door with the letter *A* marked on it. "This is where Ms. Kelly tapes *Eye on Chicago*." He wore an apologetic smile. "Sorry, Mr. Morretti, but I'm going to have to ask you to switch off your cell phone before we head inside. I know it's a pain, but those are the rules."

"I figured as much, so I left my cell in the car." Demetri slid his hands into his sweatpants. That wasn't the only reason. His phone had been ringing off the hook ever since he signed his contract extension last week, and he was sick of the incessant calls from his relatives. Everyone needed money for something—to pay his or her mortgage, for tuition, to get a second boob job. If not for his mother's heartfelt pleas, he would have cut his mooching family members off a long time ago.

A siren blared behind him, and his burly escort cursed under his breath.

"I can't believe that stupid alarm is going off again," he grumbled, whipping his walkie-talkie out of his pocket and rattling off a series of security codes. "I'll be right back, Mr. Morretti. Hang tight."

"Take as long as you need, man. I'm not going anywhere."

The security guard took off down the hall, mumbling to himself in Portuguese. Demetri waited until his escort disappeared around the corner, then calmly opened the door of Studio A. People in headsets, clutching wooden clipboards, rushed around the room. He slipped inside the darkened studio with the stealth of a burglar.

The studio was spacious, and the air was thick and hot. He heard a woman speaking and instantly recognized the low, sultry voice. It was the same voice he'd heard in his dreams. The one that had teased and tormented him last night.

After watching *Eye on Chicago* the previous night, and seeing his past transgressions in high definition, he'd stormed into his home gym, fuming mad. But it didn't matter how many push-ups he did or how much weight he lifted because he still couldn't get Angela Kelly's voice out of his head. Or her blistering jabs. *Demetri Morretti is an overrated, overpaid athlete with no class... His off-field behavior has not only disgraced the Chicago Royals organization, but his teammates and fans... If I was the league commissioner, I'd give Morretti the boot, once and for all.*

Demetri clenched his hands into fists. He wanted to punch something, wanted to unleash the anger shooting through his veins. Another workout was definitely in order. He was tense, more fired up than a boxer on fight day, and those deep breathing exercises his conditioning coach had taught him weren't working. They never worked. These days, he was more stressed than ever, and getting injured during the preseason had only made matters worse.

Now stepping out from behind the curtain shielding him, Demetri slid up against the back wall. Standing perfectly still, he zeroed in on the raised stage. Seated behind the V-shaped glass desk was the studio's most popular broadcaster—Angela Kelly. The stunning twentysomething Chicago native with the girl-next-door appeal. Her beauty was jaw-dropping, as breathtaking as a Mediterranean sunset, and at the sight of her dazzling smile his mouth went bone-dry. Everything about her was chic and sophisticated. Her fuchsia blazer and shorts, her silky black hair, the way she spoke and moved. Angela Kelly looked well put together, as if she'd just stepped out of hair and makeup, and she spoke with such exuberance that the entire studio was filled with her positive energy.

And Demetri Morretti hated her on sight.

"Thanks for watching this week's edition of *Eye on Chicago*," Angela Kelly said, staring straight into the camera and wearing her brightest smile. "Make sure you tune in next week for the conclusion of my *Athletes Behaving Badly* story. Until next time, stay safe."

"That's a wrap, people!" the cameraman yelled. "Great job, Angela. You really outdid yourself this week. Faking tears as you read the intro was a nice touch."

"I wasn't faking," Angela said, unclipping her microphone and resting it on the desk. "Watching those clips of teenagers rifling through the garbage was heartbreaking."

"Sure it was." The cameraman winked and then patted her on the back. "I'll see you on Friday. We're filming two segments back-to-back, so make sure you bring your A game."

"I'll bring mine if you bring yours!"

The cameraman chuckled and then strode off the sound-stage.

Angela slid off her chair, adjusted her blazer and ran a hand through her perfectly flat-ironed hair. Spotting her boss, Salem Velasquez, at the back of the room, she swiped her clipboard off the raised glass desk and stepped off the set. This was her chance to talk to Salem—alone—about the proposal she'd submitted last week for her new three-part series. Angela was determined to win her boss over. If she wanted to be taken seriously in the journalism community, she had to continue pursuing meatier news stories. Stories that would impact the world and change lives. Stories that she could be proud of. After eight years of covering celebrity gossip, Angela was ready for a change. She was ready for the big leagues. And if she wanted to be the station's lead broadcaster by the time she turned thirty at the end of the year, she had to start pushing the envelope.

"Angela-wouldn't-know-the-truth-if-it-slapped-her-in-the-face-Kelly," a male voice said from behind her. A tall, hooded figure, decked out in all black, slid in front of her.

Angela stepped back with a yelp. "What the hell?" she snapped, touching a hand to her chest. Narrowing her eyes, she studied the lean, muscled stranger. His baseball cap was pulled low, past his eyebrows, a thick Nike hoodie covering his head, and his hands were tucked in the pockets of his sweatpants. His head was down, and his shoulders were bent. The man looked sinister, like the villain in a comic book, but he smelled heavenly.

"I need to have a word with you."

"I'm sorry, but I'm going to have to ask you to leave. This is a closed set, and no one…" Angela's voice faded when the stranger took off his hoodie. Her clipboard slipped out of her hands, falling to the floor with a clatter.

"I'd say it was a pleasure to meet you, but I'd be lying, and I'd hate to make a second trip to confession this week."

Angela felt her eyes widen and her knees buckle. Not because she was surprised by the dig, but because Demetri Morretti—the reigning bad boy of Major League Baseball—was standing in front of her, live and in the flesh.

Her thoughts were running wild, but her gaze was glued to his handsome, chiseled face before her. Dark eyebrows framed his brown eyes, a thin mustache lined his thick lips, and his wide shoulders made him seem imposing, larger-than-life. The half Italian, half African-American star athlete was a force to be reckoned with on the baseball field. And even though he was casually dressed in workout clothes and had a very present five-o'clock shadow, he was still smokin' hot.

His skin was a warm caramel shade of brown and so smooth and flawless-looking, Angela suspected he had weekly facials. Demetri Morretti was a pretty boy if she'd ever seen one, but she didn't think for a second that he was soft. Angela had read enough about the thirty-two-year-old superstar to know that he was a spoiled, ridiculously rich athlete who pushed around anyone who got in his way.

Recovering from the shock of seeing Demetri Morretti in her studio, Angela hit him with an icy glare. "Tapings aren't open to the public," she said tightly. "And since you're not an employee of the station, I'm going to have to ask you to leave, Mr. Morretti."

"I will, as soon as you go on the air and issue an apology to me and my family."

Angela almost laughed in his face but caught herself before a snicker escaped her mouth. No use antagonizing him. According to published reports, Demetri was impulsive, a hothead of the worst kind, and there was no telling what he'd do in the heat of the moment.

"My mother is very upset about the lies you told about me on your show, but I assured her you'd apologize once you realized the errors of your ways."

"Apologize for what? Speaking the truth?" Angela rolled her eyes to the ceiling. She didn't tell Demetri about the countless hours she'd spent reading articles and sports blogs about his background and twelve-year baseball career. The headlines about the gifted shortstop were damning and more salacious than a CIA prostitution scandal. There were reports of bar brawls, drunken Las Vegas parties and explosive run-ins with rival baseball fans. She'd found so much "dirt" on Demetri Morretti, and the other players featured in her story, she'd had enough material for a three-part series. And the viewers were eating it up. Her show had slayed the competition in the ratings last week, and everywhere she went people were talking about her *Athletes Behaving Badly* story. It was a hot topic, one that viewers couldn't seem to get enough of.

"Don't mess with me, Ms. Kelly, because when it's all said and done, I *will* get my way."

Angela's toes curled in her five-inch black pumps. She couldn't believe his nerve. Demetri was rotten to the core, a man of such extraordinary arrogance, Angela didn't know why she was even talking to him. "You might be able to throw your weight around the clubhouse," she began, meeting his hostile gaze, "but it's not going to work here. I double-checked the facts and have taped interviews with eyewitnesses to back up my report."

"Your report was full of lies. It was nothing more than a smear campaign done by a bitter, angry woman who got dissed and dismissed by her ex-boyfriend."

Angela's breath caught in her throat. Her face must have registered surprise, because a grin that could scare a mobster broke out across Demetri's lips.

"Your ex plays for the L.A. Jaguars," he continued. "And he was nice enough to share all of the dirty details of your relationship with him."

Fear blanketed her skin. Licking her dry lips, Angela cast a nervous glance around the studio. She spotted her colleagues at the other end of the room, perusing the snack table, and sighed inwardly. Angela wasn't proud of her past, and the last thing she wanted was for her colleagues to find out about all the wild and crazy things she'd done while living in L.A. It was hard enough being the only woman of color at the TV station, and she didn't want to give the other broadcasters another reason to resent her. Not that they needed one. They thought she was too young to host *Eye on Chicago,* unqualified to work at the station and skating by on her looks. "Who I've dated is none of your business, and furthermore, my personal life has absolutely nothing to do with my *Athletes Behaving Badly* story."

"You see, Ms. Kelly, I did a little digging of my own and discovered that you've dated a lot of professional athletes," he said, stroking his jaw reflectively. "And from what I hear, several of them dogged you out *bad.* That's why you did that story. To get back at the guys who dumped you and to stick it to anyone who plays pro sports."

"That's ludicrous." Lifting her head, Angela arched her shoulders and looked him dead in the eye. She wasn't going to be Demetri Morretti's punching bag. Not now. Not ever. "This conversation is over. Please leave."

"I will, Madame Gold Digger, as soon as you—"

"Gold digger?" Angela repeated, splaying her hands on her hips.

"Did I stutter?"

"I don't know any gold diggers who put themselves through school or who volunteer twenty hours a week at various local shelters, do you?"

Angela saw a bolt of surprise flicker across Demetri's face, but bragging about her volunteer work made her feel small, as if she'd just insulted all of the families she worked with. But her unexpected confession clearly stunned the baseball star, and Angela was determined to use this leverage to her advantage. "I have nothing against you or any of the other athletes mentioned in my story," she said, meaning every word. "I did the piece to warn young women about the perils of pursuing professional athletes and—"

"To stick it to your ex-lovers," he tossed out, mirroring her rigid body stance.

Angela made her eyes thin. "Maybe instead of coming down here and harassing me, you should have gone to the clubhouse to practice."

"What are you trying to say?"

"I saw your last game before your shoulder injury. You jumped every pitch, your timing was way off, and your swing looked lifeless."

Demetri flexed his jaw muscles. He was well aware of his batting slump, and the problems with his swing, but he didn't need anyone—especially a newscaster—reminding him. "There's nothing wrong with my game."

"Oh, but there is. Ask your coach. Ask your teammates. Hell, ask the fans."

"I didn't come down here to get batting tips from a reporter with no conscience," he said, folding his arms. "I came to issue a warning. Go on the air and apologize, or I'll—"

"You'll what?" Angela jeered, cutting him off. "Hurl a beer bottle at me like you did to that poor college kid in Newark? Or get one of your flunkies to rough me up?"

His nostrils flared, and the corners of his lips curled into a scowl. Demetri stepped forward, and when Angela jumped back, she bumped into one of the towering black light stands. A sharp pain stabbed her leg, but it was the menacing gleam in her adversary's eyes that made her knees quiver.

"I'm not going to touch you, Ms. Kelly." Demetri's voice was calm, but his tone was colder than ice. "But if you don't go on the air and apologize, I'll sue you, your boss and this damn station."

Chapter 2

Angela felt a cold chill snake down her back. Swallowing the lump in her throat, she discreetly dried her damp palms along the side of her fitted Chanel shorts. Since part one of her series aired two weeks ago, she'd received scores of hate mail. Several athletes had taken to Twitter to express their anger, but no one had shown up at the station threatening litigation—until now. It wasn't the first time Angela had ruffled someone's feathers, and usually she wouldn't give a threat a second thought. But the way Demetri was staring at her, with his head cocked and his eyes narrowed, made her stomach coil into a suffocating knot.

"So, what's it going to be?" Arms folded, he tapped his foot impatiently on the floor. "Are you going to issue that apology, or are we going to have to hash this thing out in court?"

Angela swallowed hard. Demetri sounded serious, looked serious, too, but she didn't believe him. Not for a second. He was too busy getting into bar fights, throwing wild parties at his Chicago mansion and drag racing in his Maybach to show up in court.

"You're not going to win this, so you might as well give up now."

"Get out," she snapped, pointing at the studio door. "And don't come back!"

"I'll leave, as soon as I get that apology."

Angela glowered but said nothing. What could she say? "Leave or I'll call security"? The baseball star was trespassing, but the security guards weren't going to throw a future hall-of-famer off the property.

"I don't want to play hardball with you, Ms. Kelly, but you leave me no choice. Your report was biased and unfounded. Not to mention full of outright lies."

When Demetri took another step forward, infringing upon her personal space, she imagined herself smacking the broad grin off his face. But instead of acting on her impulse, Angela faked a smile. It was time to try a different approach because arguing with Demetri Morretti was getting her nowhere. "I'll give some thought to what you said, and someone from the station will contact you by the end of the week. Okay?"

Demetri clapped his hands. "Well done, Ms. Kelly. Nicely played. For a second there, I actually believed you were a rational human being."

"Well, at least I'm not a—"

Angela felt a hand on her shoulder and broke off speaking. She turned to her right, and groaned inwardly when she saw her producer, standing beside her, wearing a concerned expression. And worse, everyone in the studio, from the voluptuous makeup artist to the bearded engineer, was now staring at her, with wide eyes and open mouths. How much had her colleagues heard? And why were all of the men in the studio shooting evil daggers at her?

"Welcome to WJN-TV, Mr. Morretti. I'm Salem Velasquez, one of the head producers."

Wearing a tight smile, he nodded and shook the hand she offered.

"If you have a few moments, I'd love to speak to you in private."

"Great. The quicker we resolve this issue the better."

"Please follow me. My office is right this way." Salem motioned to the studio door, and Demetri fell in step beside her.

Angela stayed put. She didn't want any part of this meeting, and she had better things to do than listen to Demetri

Morretti whine about her report. Anxious to return to her office, she turned around and stalked off in the opposite direction. She needed to vent, and her best friend, Simone, was the perfect person to talk to.

"Angela!"

Angela stopped dead in her tracks. Her heart was hammering in her chest. The sharpness of Salem's tone and the booming sound of her voice made Angela break out in a nervous sweat.

Glancing over her shoulder confirmed her worst fears. Now her boss *and* the surly baseball star were glaring at her. The air in the studio was suffocating, so thick with tension, Angela felt as if she was going to faint. And the way Demetri was staring at her—all serious and intense—made her skin prickle with goose bumps.

"You will be joining us."

"Oh, of course," Angela lied, nodding her head. "I was just going to…to…to…"

"Whatever it is can wait. Get in my office. Now."

I'd rather ride a unicycle naked down the Magnificent Mile, she thought, dragging herself across the studio and past her gawking coworkers.

"Please, Mr. Morretti, have a seat," Salem said, gesturing to one of the padded chairs in front of her large oak desk. "Make yourself comfortable."

The small, cramped office was overrun with bookshelves, knickknacks, and the scent of cinnamon was so heavy in the air, Angela's stomach grumbled. It had been hours since she had breakfast, but the thought of eating made her feel queasy. So did the way her boss was smiling at Demetri Morretti. He was the enemy, a man bent on destroying her, and if Salem didn't toughen up and quit making eyes at him, they'd both be out of a job.

"Thanks, but I'd rather stand."

"Very well." Salem sat down in her leather swivel chair and clasped her hands together. "I understand that you're upset about Ms. Kelly's *Athletes Behaving Badly* piece, but I stand behind the story and what was reported. All of our stories are vigorously researched, and we pride ourselves on double-checking every fact and every report."

"No one from your station contacted me or my team."

"I assure you, Mr. Morretti, my assistant phoned your publicist for a statement."

He crossed his arms. "I would like you to provide the name of the person who called and the time and date the call was placed."

Nodding, Salem picked up her pen and made a note on one of the open file folders on her desk. "That's not a problem. I can forward the information to you later today."

Angela raised her eyebrows but didn't speak. She stood at the back of the room, beside the door, and watched the exchange between Salem and Demetri with growing interest. Maybe her boss was going to come through for her after all. Salem's eyes were glued to Demetri's lips, but she sounded confident and looked in control.

"There are two sides to every story, but your report only focused on one side. The side filled with lies. As a result, my character and integrity have been compromised."

What integrity? Angela thought, clamping her lips together to trap a curse inside. *You're a hothead who can't control his temper!* She thought back over every second of her argument with Demetri. And when she got to the point where her boss showed up, Angela decided that was the most humiliating moment of her life. She'd been reprimanded in front of her crew, then ordered into her boss's office to speak to the enemy. Even more troubling, Salem was being nice to him. A little too nice. Her body was angled toward him, and she hadn't stopped smiling since they entered the office. If Angela didn't know better, she'd think Salem had a crush on

Demetri, because the only time she'd ever seen her boss this happy was when she received her annual Christmas bonus.

"If your assistant had contacted me, I would have been here."

"Really?" A quizzical look covered Salem's face. "But it's been widely reported in the media that you don't do interviews."

"You shouldn't believe everything you hear."

Angela wanted to gag. Demetri was lying and making it look easy. He hadn't done an on-camera interview in years, and according to reports, his publicist had to preapprove the questions. The baseball star was a recluse, a man who liked to be alone, who kept to himself. Except when he was getting into bar fights or humiliating waiters and service staff.

Angela looked him over, slowly. Demetri Morretti was a man of great presence, with more natural charisma than an A-list actor. That was probably why people overlooked his bad behavior and made excuses for him. But Angela wasn't one of his crazed fans or easily seduced by ridiculously rich athletes. She decided right then and there that she wasn't going to let Demetri Morretti disrespect her again.

"You seem like a very nice lady, Mrs. Velasquez," Demetri began smoothly, favoring her with a smile that warmed his entire face, "and I don't want to sue you, but if Ms. Kelly doesn't apologize publicly for slandering my name, I will."

Silence filled the air and stretched on for several long minutes.

"I have an idea." Salem's voice was filled with excitement and she practically bounced up and down on her chair. "Why don't you come on *Eye on Chicago* and do an exclusive sit-down interview with Ms. Kelly this month?"

No, no, no! Angela wanted to scream out in protest, but shot evil daggers at Demetri instead. He was bad news, someone she had to stay far, far away from. He was a rich, cock-sure athlete who thought he could push her around, and she had absolutely no desire to have him on her show. Not tomorrow. Not next week. Not ever.

"No, thank you. I'm not interested."

"What if we gave you the questions beforehand? You and your team could even add a few of your own. We never do that, but I'm willing to make an exception for you, Mr. Morretti."

"No way!" Angela hollered, the words bursting out of her mouth. "He shouldn't get preferential treatment just because he's a—"

Salem's eyes thinned. In an instant, Angela's jaw locked and her tongue seized up.

"I don't trust reporters." Demetri cast a glance at the back of the room. "Not even the ones who look sweet and innocent. They're the worst kind."

Angela ignored the dig. *Sticks and stones, Morretti. Sticks and stones.* There was nothing the surly baseball player could say to hurt her. Life was good. Great. For the first time ever, her show was on top of the ratings, and next weekend she was covering the grand opening of Dolce Vita.

The posh three-story lounge was the first of its kind in Chicago, and Angela had been looking forward to the event for weeks. Because of her busy schedule, Angela hadn't hung out with her girlfriends in weeks. And since they would be in attendance at the star-studded launch, she was excited about catching up with them and eating some award-winning Italian food.

"If you'll both excuse me," Angela said, gripping the door handle. "I really have to go."

Salem shook her head, and Angela dropped the door handle as if it were a roasted stone. Her boss spoke to Demetri in a soft, soothing voice, but her eyes were glued to Angela. "I want to hear your side of the story, and I bet America does, too."

"I know I don't," Angela grumbled. Her colleagues would

probably jump at the chance to interview Demetri Morretti but the thought of interviewing him, under the bright studio lights, made Angela feel queasy. The camera captured everything—every pause, every nervous glance, every awkward movement—and she feared her nerves would get the best of her and she'd drown on live TV. Add to that the fact that she had to worry about keeping Demetri *and* his ego in check. Angela didn't like him, didn't trust him and had a feeling he was up to no good. He'd embarrassed her once in front of her crew, and there was no doubt in her mind he'd do it again. *What if he outsmarts me on my show?* she thought, swallowing hard. *What if he makes me look like a fool on national television?*

"This would be your opportunity to finally set the record straight," Salem continued. "And imagine what the press could do for you, your team and your charity foundation. It's a win-win situation for everyone involved, and…"

Angela tuned her boss out. Catching sight of her reflection in the wall mirror, she straightened her shoulders and cleaned the scowl off her face. There was nothing she could do about the hatred in her heart, though. Angela was fuming, her pulse pounding violently in her ears.

Her gaze bounced around the room and landed on Demetri. It was easy to see why fans disliked him. Charming one minute, acerbic the next. Former coaches, rivals and the media criticized him for his conduct on and off the field, and after having the misfortune of meeting Demetri for herself, Angela believed the criticism was due. She only wished he wasn't so good-looking. He gave her chills—the ones that started in her toes and shot straight to her core—and it was impossible to ignore his raw masculine energy. Everything about him was a turn-on.

"I'll give it some thought." Demetri took his sunglasses out of his back pocket and slid them on. "My publicist will be in touch."

"That sounds great, Mr. Morretti. I look forward to hearing from her."

"Thanks for your time, Mrs. Velasquez. Have a nice day." Demetri nodded, then turned and strode out of the small, cramped office.

"Angela, I know you're upset because I ordered you into my office, but I had no choice," Salem said, her facial features touched with concern. "You were losing control."

"Of course I was! Demetri Morretti is a complete jerk!" Gesturing to the door, her eyes narrowed and her lips pursed, she raged, "Who the hell does he think he is?"

Salem picked up the latest copy of *People* magazine off her desk and held it in the air. "The sexiest man alive, that's who!"

"I wonder who he had to bribe to get on the cover."

"You're kidding, right?"

"No, Demetri's a jerk, and in my opinion there's nothing sexy about him."

Salem snatched her phone off the cradle and started dialing.

"Who are you calling?" Angela asked, frowning.

"My optometrist." She was wearing a straight face, but her tone was rich with humor. "I'm booking you an emergency appointment."

"Why? My eyes are fine."

"No, they're not." A smirk lit her glossy, pink lips. "There's definitely something wrong with your vision *and* your hormones because Demetri Morretti is the finest man on the planet!"

Chapter 3

The moment Demetri entered MVP Sports Bar & Grill and smelled fresh garlic wafting out of the open kitchen, his mouth began to water. Located a half block from Skyline Field, the sports bar was insanely popular among young and college-aged sports fans. Every time Demetri stopped inside the restaurant bar, the staff gave him a hero's welcome.

"Demetri, my man, so good to see you!" The manager, a portly man with a double chin, grabbed his hand and gave it a hearty squeeze. "How are you doing?"

"Good, Mr. De Rossi. How's the family?"

"My sons are growing up fast and getting in all sorts of trouble." Chuckling, he bent down and pointed at his receding hairline. "The kids are the reason I'm losing my hair, and the little I have left is turning gray!"

Demetri laughed heartily. The fellow reminded him of his dad, right down to his wrinkle-free pants, buffed leather shoes and thick Italian accent. Shooting the breeze with the jovial bar manager always put Demetri in a good mood. And after the tongue-lashing he'd received from Angela Kelly at the station, he needed something to laugh about.

"I just put your calzone in the stove," he said, patting Demetri on the shoulder and steering him toward the dining room. "I'll bring it out as soon as it's ready."

"Thanks, sir. I appreciate it."

Spotting his staff sitting in one of the cushy, padded booths, Demetri acknowledged them with a nod of his head.

Nichola Caruso, his savvy, no-nonsense publicist and personal assistant, waved, but his manager and agent were too busy on their cell phones to notice he'd arrived. Every Friday, he met with his team at MVP Sports Bar & Grill, and because Nichola rented out the entire restaurant, they could eat and talk in peace. Demetri didn't have to worry about paparazzi snapping pictures of him with barbecue sauce on his face or crazed fans hitting him up for autographs or cash. "If it's not too much trouble, can I have a basket or two of bruschetta?" Demetri patted his stomach. "I'm starving, and I bet the guys finished what was on the table."

"No problem. I'll whip up a fresh batch for you."

Demetri thanked him again and strode into the lounge. Dark wood paneling, vintage sports memorabilia and plush burgundy couches created a sophisticated decor. The tall, oversize windows provided a tranquil view of downtown Chicago and plenty of warm sunshine. It was the perfect weather for gardening or reading out on the deck, and as soon as Demetri finished his meeting, that was exactly what he was going to do.

"Sorry I'm late, but the I-94 was backed up for miles," Demetri said, taking off his hoodie and chucking it inside the booth. Sitting down, he snatched a menu off of the table and flipped it open. "Did you guys order already?"

His agent, Todd Nicholas, answered with a nod of his head. Buff, with blue eyes and tanned skin, he looked like the quintessential all-American boy. "I have a meeting across town in an hour, but I couldn't leave here without having Chef Sal's delicious lasagna. I've been craving it all week."

Demetri stared longingly at the barbecue chicken wings and licked his lips.

"Want some?" Nichola picked up the basket and offered it to him. "Go ahead, Demetri. They're all yours."

"Are you sure? I know how much you love Sal's wings."

"I'm sure. I shouldn't be cheating on my diet anyway."

Demetri plucked a wing out of the basket and took a big bite. "Thanks, Nichola. I can always count on you to give me just what I need."

"Just make sure you remember that when my birthday rolls around in August!" she said, swiveling her neck. "I want shopping money *and* Porsche Cayenne in pink just like Mariah Carey!"

Demetri released a hearty chuckle. Small and petite, with a short, funky haircut, Nichola looked more like a high school student than a Princeton graduate. A friend of his family for years, he'd hired her as a favor to his father, Arturo, and in the twelve years Nichola had been working for him, he'd never once regretted his decision.

"You're moving a lot better today." Nichola wore a concerned expression on her face, but her tone was upbeat and bright. "How's the shoulder?"

"Not bad. It's only been a couple weeks since the surgery, but my surgeon and physiotherapist are pleased with my progress."

"Is that where you were this morning? At your doctor's office?"

Demetri glanced to his right. His manager, Lloyd Kesler, may have needed a haircut, and an extreme fashion makeover, but when it came to negotiating deals, he was the best in the business. "No, I've been around. Just maxin' and relaxin'."

"Around, huh? Doing what?"

"You know, this and that." Demetri continued eating the barbecue chicken wings. They were onto him. He was sure of it. He couldn't do anything without this terrible threesome finding out, but he wasn't going to let anyone make him feel guilty for confronting Angela Kelly. The television newscaster had it coming to her. Or at least that was what he told himself when guilt tormented his conscience.

"Why are you giving me the third degree for being a couple minutes late?" Demetri said, choosing to stare at the mounted flat-screen TV instead of at his chubby, high-strung business manager. "I said I was sorry, man, so let it go. It's no big deal."

Nichola and Todd exchanged a worried glance, one he'd seen a million times over the years they'd all been working together, but it was Lloyd who spoke.

"You disregarded my advice and went down to WJN-TV station, didn't you?"

Demetri shrugged. "So, what if I did?"

"I told you I would handle it."

"You were taking too long," he said, shrugging his shoulders once more.

Nichola pointed a finger at him. "You went down to the TV station dressed like that?"

"What's wrong with my clothes?"

"Nothing if you're a street sweeper!" she quipped, laughing. "Why didn't you wear a suit? You look gorgeous in Armani, and you have the entire fall collection in your closet. I should know. I hung everything up when it arrived last week."

Demetri opened his mouth but quickly closed it. His team wouldn't understand. Every time he left the house, he felt as if there were a giant bull's-eye on his back, but with sunglasses, a baseball cap and workout gear on, no one recognized him. He could go about his business without pushy fans or sports reporters breathing down his neck. "To be honest, I didn't think much about what I put on," he lied.

"Well, you certainly fooled me." Todd snickered as he draped an arm along the back of the oversize booth. "I didn't recognize you when you walked in, and I've been your agent for more than a decade!"

"I didn't even know you owned sweatpants." Nichola's short strawberry-blond curls bounced all over her head as she laughed. "I thought you were a delivery guy!"

Good—my disguise worked, Demetri thought.

"I'm scared to even ask what happened down at the studio."

Lloyd looked stiff, like a statue in a wax museum. His eyes were narrowed so thin, Demetri couldn't see his pupils.

"What did Ms. Kelly say when you confronted her?"

A picture of the titillating newscaster flashed in Demetri's mind, and despite himself, a grin tickled his lips. "What *didn't* she say? The woman reamed me out, and at one point things got so heated, I thought she was going to give me a Chi-Town beat down!"

Todd chuckled and then said, "I really wish you hadn't gone over there, Demetri. You're supposed to be focusing on rehab and restoring the strength in your shoulder, not…"

Demetri's eyes wandered in the direction of the open kitchen. He spotted the waitress sashaying toward him, bread basket in hand, and licked his lips in hungry anticipation. When their eyes met, she stumbled and her legs buckled out from underneath her, sending the bread basket into the air. Dozens of buttered rolls shot across the shiny tiled floor.

Everyone at the table laughed, except Demetri.

"Are you okay?" Demetri slid out of the booth, clasped the waitress's forearm and slowly helped her to her feet. "You didn't hurt yourself, did you?"

"No, no, I'm okay…just *really* embarrassed."

"Here," he said, bending down. "Let me help you clean up."

Demetri gathered the discarded rolls, tossed them into the wicker basket and handed it back to her. "Be careful. These floors are slick," he warned, offering a reassuring smile. "I almost fell flat on my face the last time I was here!"

"I—I—I am *so* sorry, Mr. Morretti. It's my first day on the job, and I wasn't expecting to see you seated there."

"Baseball players have to eat, too, you know."

The redhead giggled. "Sorry again. I'll be right back with your order, Mr. Morretti."

"Call me Demetri. And good luck with the new job."

Smiling from ear to ear, she dashed back through the dining area and into the open kitchen.

"Don't forget the rolls!" Todd hollered, cupping his hands around his mouth. "And hurry up, tootsie! We don't have all day."

"Relax, man. She's new."

"Finish telling us about what happened at the station," Lloyd demanded, leaning forward in his seat. "I hope you kept your cool, because the last thing you need is any more bad press."

"Oh, I was as cool as an alley cat. Can't say the same for Ms. Kelly, though."

Nichola glanced up from her salad bowl. "You let her ream you out?"

"I let her rant and rave for a few minutes, and then I said my piece."

Todd gulped. "It sounds like your conversation was anything *but* peaceful."

"You can say that again," Lloyd mumbled, shaking his head.

Demetri finished chewing the food in his mouth and then continued. "I told Ms. Kelly if she didn't go on the air and apologize, I was going to sue her."

"You know that would be a waste of time and money, right? Not to mention—"

"Todd, I don't care," Demetri snapped, using a napkin to clean the sauce off his sticky fingers. "I'm sick of the media taking cheap shots at me and my family. If I don't take a stand now, the abuse will never end."

Nichola agreed. "I'm with you, Demetri. I think you should sue Angela Kelly. She's a bully, and you're not the only celebrity she's bad-mouthed on her show."

Demetri shot his publicist a grateful smile. He could always count on Nichola to go to bat for him. She went above and beyond her job description, made sure his day-to-day life ran smoothly. She kept the gold diggers—in his family and on the streets—at bay during the regular season so he could concentrate on his game. Nichola was more than just his publicist; she was a real, true friend.

"Once we finish up here, I'll give the station a call and see what they're willing to do."

"Don't bother, Lloyd. I met with the producer of Ms. Kelly's show, and she invited me to come on and do a live one-hour interview—"

"That's great!" Lloyd cheered, pumping his fist in the air. "You can set the record straight about all those crazy rumors floating around on the internet and plug your sponsors."

"And your charity work," Todd added. "That will get you the sympathy vote."

"I'm not doing the interview."

"What?" Lloyd made his eyes wide. "Why not?"

Nichola jumped in. "Because Angela Kelly's a vulture! She looks all nice and sweet, but she's cutthroat. Last week, she interviewed the pregnant girl on *NFL Wives,* and by the time the interview was done, the chick was in tears!"

"Yeah, probably because she felt guilty for screwing her sister's husband." Lloyd made a disgusted face. "I represent her ex, so I know the scoop. Trust me, she's no wallflower, and those tears weren't real. That woman was just playing it up for the cameras."

"Back to the matter at hand," Todd said, stealing a glance at his gold Rolex watch. "Demetri, please reconsider doing the interview. Angela Kelly isn't going to double-cross you. And just to make sure she doesn't try to pull a fast one on us, I'll be on set watch—"

Demetri cut his agent off midword. "Still not interested. Drop it."

Todd held his hands up high in the air like an unarmed man surrendering to the police. "All right, all right, you're the boss. I won't mention it again."

"Good." Demetri leaned back in the booth and calmly

addressed Nichola. "I want you to call Salem Velasquez at WJN-TV and politely decline her offer."

Nichola gave a thumbs-up sign. "I'll call her when I get back to the office."

The food arrived, and their discussion came to an abrupt halt.

Picking up his utensils, Demetri bowed his head and said a quick word of grace. He was starving, but he ate his food slowly, savoring each tasty bite. The conversation turned to his weekly agenda, his newest sponsorship deals and the upcoming Caribbean cruise he was planning for eighty-five of his family members and friends. He traveled with his family every year, and every year, the trip caused Demetri enormous stress. Thankfully, Nichola was overseeing all of the pertinent details of the three-week vacation in August and keeping his most unruly relatives in line.

"There are a few things I need to run by you." Nichola set aside her salad bowl and retrieved her iPad from her designer purse. "As you know, the Demetri Morretti Foundation is having a Fourth of July extravaganza this summer, but so far I've only heard back from a handful of celebrities. You're going to have to call some of your superstar friends and extend a personal invitation."

"Nichola, why can't you do it?"

"Because I'm not the slugger with the golden arm. You are!"

Everyone chuckled.

"We're doing it real big this year," Nichola declared. "We're having magicians, flamethrowers, a dunk tank and even circus performers. To keep everything on track, I booked celebrity event planner Claudia Jeffries-Medina. And award-winning photographer Kenyon Blake will be on hand to capture every heartfelt moment."

"It sounds like the Demetri Morretti Foundation is throwing one hell of a party!" Todd said with a grin.

"The more press we get to cover the event the better." Nichola rested a hand on Demetri's forearm. "I'm going to need you to be nice to the media from here on out. No more arguments with Angela Kelly or anyone else who rubs you the wrong way."

I'd let that sexy newscaster rub me the right *way all night long.* Demetri shook his head in an attempt to remove the insane thought from his mind. Angela Kelly was the enemy, a woman who took great pride in humiliating him, and he wasn't even remotely interested in her.

Then why are you thinking about all the wicked things you'd like to do to her in bed? his inner voice jeered.

"Demetri, if you want this event to be a success, you'll have to be that fun, personable guy we all know and love."

"It's hard to be in a jovial mood when perfect strangers are snapping pictures of me in the bathroom and the paparazzi is trailing me around town."

Nichola wore a sympathetic smile. "Just remember this event is for a good cause. Last year, we raised over a half a million dollars for the foundation, and this year I'm hoping to triple that number."

Her words made Demetri grin, filling him with pride. That was what it was all about. Making a difference in someone's life. Being famous definitely had its good points, and now, thanks to his new multimillion-dollar contract, he could help even more children in need. "Thanks for overseeing everything," he said, feeling bad for snapping at her earlier. "As usual, it sounds like you have everything under control."

"Now," Todd said, "all we need are some celebrity faces to give the event star power!"

"Speaking of star power, I received dozens of letters from local area schools this week." Nichola took a stack of envelopes out of her purse and showed them to Demetri. "Are you interested in speaking at any of these functions?"

Demetri thought for a moment. As far as he knew, he had

nothing planned for the month. But if he went to the career-day events, there was a good chance someone would tip off the media, and he'd arrive to find a mob of fans and paparazzi. This was a main reason Demetri avoided public events. Because of his wealth, and the poor choices he'd made in the past, he was an easy target, and these days he couldn't go anywhere without some young punk looking to start a fight. "Tell the organizers I can't make it, but send each school a check."

"For the same amount as last year?"

"Double it."

Lloyd's jaw hit his flabby chest with a thud. "B-but, Demetri, that's over two hundred thousand dollars to each school. A million dollars total."

"I know, Lloyd. I did the math."

"I'll ensure your accountant sends out the checks today," Nichola said, typing furiously on her iPad. "And I'll make sure to tip my source at the *Tribune* about your *very* generous donation to five inner-city schools."

"No, don't. It's nobody's business how much I give." Demetri's expression turned serious. He'd learned early on in his career it was better to leave some things private. He didn't want anyone—especially his relatives—to hear how much he gave to charity. He could almost hear the outlandish things they would request if they knew. "Keep it quiet, Nichola. The less people who know the better."

"But it would be great press," she argued. "And a touchy, feel-good story even someone like Angela Kelly would love!"

At the mention of the newscaster's name, he remembered their heated argument that morning at the studio. He told himself to stop thinking about Angela Kelly, to forget they'd ever met, but he couldn't get her pretty brown eyes and her toned, curvy shape out of his mind.

After leaving the television station, he'd returned to his car and turned on his cell phone. Instead of reading his newest text messages, he'd opened the internet and searched her name, clicking on the first link that popped up. He read Angela Kelly's bio, then watched an hour's worth of her most popular interviews. Most of them were with celebrities— actors, singers, professional athletes and supermodels. But Angela was so engaging, and witty, she looked like a star in her own right. There were dozens of pictures of her, at various events in and around town, and in each photograph she looked like a million bucks *and* had a different date.

What's up with that? Demetri quickly told himself he didn't care. And he didn't. His mother had always warned him against falling for pretty money-hungry types. And from the day he was drafted in the major leagues, gold diggers had been throwing themselves at him left, right and center. Feisty, headstrong women—like Angela Kelly—where by far the worst type.

Tasting his wine, he hoped the savory drink eased his troubled mind. Demetri closed his eyes and saw Angela Kelly glaring at him. He gave his head a hard shake. He had to quit wondering how many guys she was dating and if she had a lover, because after today he had no intention of ever seeing her again—unless it was in civil court.

Chapter 4

Angela stormed inside her best friend's kitchen, dumped her purse on the granite countertop and paced the length of the room, gesturing wildly with her hands. "I'm so angry I could scream!"

"Well, please don't," Simone Young said, glancing into the living room. "The boys just fell asleep, and if you wake them, I'll kill you."

Angela blew out a deep breath and counted to ten. On the drive over from the WJN-TV station, she'd relived every second of her argument with Demetri and the subsequent meeting with her boss. It didn't matter which way Angela looked at it—she felt cheated. As if Salem had thrown her under the bus.

"Now, what's got you all riled up?" Simone closed the dishwasher and then leaned against it. Rubbing a hand over her baby bump, she cocked her head to the side and frowned. "Did that sleazy sportscaster proposition you again?"

"No. Worse."

"I can't imagine anything worse than being propositioned by a guy who drives a lemon *and* still lives at home with his mama!"

A giggle tickled the back of Angela's throat. Leave it to Simone to make her laugh in the midst of a crisis. That was why she'd driven across town in rush hour to see her. They'd been friends ever since meeting on the University of Chicago campus ten years ago, and Angela loved Simone like a sister. The busy wife and mother could make her forget her

problems, even if just for a few minutes. And now more than
ever, Angela needed her advice. "Hakeem's not that bad. Just
annoying. I can handle him."

"I'm all for keeping the peace at work, but I would have
spoken to HR about his unwanted advances months ago."

"And have everyone at the station turn against me? No,
thanks. The lead anchor hates me, so the few friends I have,
I'd like to keep."

"Do you want a cup of ginger tea?"

"Yeah, but put some vodka in mine."

Simone opened the cupboard, took out two ceramic mugs
and waddled over to the kettle. "I swear, Angela, sometimes
you're just too much."

"What? I need some alcohol to steady my nerves. I've had
the day from hell!"

"Girl, please. You work at a TV station and tape your show
in a warm, cozy studio." Simone handed Angela a mug, then
sat down at the table in front of her laptop and social-work
case files. "Come down to my agency, and I'll show you what
a bad day *really* looks like." Sliding her hands around her
mug, Simone raised it to her mouth and took a sip. "I'm trying not to let anything stress me out," she confessed, gazing
down at her belly, "but it's hard being pregnant, taking care
of my family *and* doing my job effectively."

"God, I am such a bad friend! I came barging in here
and didn't even ask how your doctor's appointment went
this morning." Angela took the seat across from Simone and
squeezed her hand. "How are the babies doing?"

Her grin lit up the kitchen. "They're good. Gaining weight
and kicking me like crazy!"

Angela listened to Simone recount every detail of her ul-
trasound appointment and, for a split second, wondered what
it would be like to be pregnant. Back when she was a naive
nineteen-year-old, madly in love with her college sweetheart,
she'd had dreams of getting married and raising a family. But

after countless arguments about her career, he'd dumped her via email and moved on to greener pastures. *Younger, thinner pastures,* Angela thought, recalling the day she'd bumped into her ex and his new girlfriend at the mall. Her ex had foolishly thought he could control every aspect of her life, and although it stung to see him with someone else, Angela knew she was better off without him.

The whole male species, actually.

Since moving back to Chicago six months ago, Angela had been playing the field and loving every minute of it. She never went out with the same guy twice, and although she'd earned a reputation of being a heartbreaker, she had no intention of ever settling down. She'd leave getting married, having babies and watching cartoons to her love-struck girlfriends.

"So what's going on with you?" Simone asked. "What's got you all worked up?"

"Demetri Morretti showed up at the station today and demanded that I go on the air and apologize to him," Angela said, the words tumbling out of her mouth in one long gush. "Can you believe it? I mean, really, who does he think he is?"

"Well, you did call him a spoiled, immature athlete on national television…"

"None of this would have happened if the security guards had been doing their job," she continued. "They should be fired."

"It was bound to happen, Angela. You couldn't avoid Demetri Morretti forever."

"I knew some of the players were upset, but I never expected Demetri to show up at the station. I almost fell over when I saw him, and when he started in on me, I lost it." Angela shook her head at the memory of their heated confrontation. "It was horrible, Simone. We were yelling and arguing and dissing each other."

"I know. I saw *and* I heard."

"You saw and you heard what?"

"Your showdown with Demetri. The video was posted online about an hour ago."

"Online?" she repeated, shaking her head. "As in on the internet?"

"Yup. Sexy Chicago Newscaster Goes Off on Baseball Superstar, and since it's gone viral, it's received thousands of hits." Simone slid the laptop in front of Angela, clicked on the appropriate link and said, "See for yourself."

Angela gasped when she saw her image on the screen. "H-h-how come Demetri looks all calm, cool and collected and I look like a raving lunatic?" she stammered, unable to believe her eyes. In the heat of the moment, Angela felt as if Demetri was attacking her, but that hadn't been the case at all. He was chill, at ease, and his tone was so soft, she could barely hear what he was saying. Unfortunately, she heard her curt, clipped tone loud and clear.

"I'm going to be the laughingstock of late-night television!" she wailed.

Simone put her hands on Angela's shoulder. "Girl, it's not that bad."

"You're right. It's worse."

"Look on the bright side—"

"There isn't one."

"Yes, there is." Simone tapped the computer screen. "You're working the hell out of your new Chanel shorts suit, and all those sessions with your personal trainer are definitely paying off because your booty looks good!"

"You're not helping, Simone."

"And as usual, you're being overly dramatic."

"No, I'm not." Angela cringed when she heard the note of despair in her voice, but she couldn't help the way she was feeling. Being secretly recorded unnerved her, but having the video posted online, for the whole world to see, made Angela want to curl into a ball in the middle of the kitchen floor. "I want to be taken seriously as a journalist, and this whole episode with Demetri is only going to set me back."

"Or it could catapult you to stardom, and you could end up with your own reality show!"

Angela gave her best friend a blank stare.

"What? Throwing a tantrum on camera has worked for dozens of other stars. I don't see why it can't work for you."

"Why would someone waste their time uploading this stupid video on YouTube?"

"Probably just for kicks. People post all sorts of wacky things online these days."

Angela winced and then dropped her face in her hands.

"Sorry, girl. That's not what I meant."

"But that's exactly how I look. Wacky," she admitted, swallowing a sob. "I bet Demetri posted the video to get back at me, to make me look like a fool."

"You think so?"

Angela gave it more thought and considered exactly what had transpired between them that afternoon. "I don't know. He had no way of knowing what would happen, but I wouldn't put it past him. He's surly and bitter, and this sort of thing is right up his alley."

"So, what happened after your boss ordered you into her office?"

Angela told Simone an abbreviated version of her terse ten-minute meeting with Salem. She admitted being so wound up after her argument with Demetri, she couldn't concentrate on what her boss was saying. But she did vividly remember Salem inviting the baseballer on her show. "I can't believe Salem invited him to appear on my show!"

"I don't understand why you're mad. Having Demetri Morretti on your show will send your ratings through the roof!" Simone said, throwing her hands up in the air. "For some reason, people love to hate that guy, and since he hasn't done a sit-down interview in years, viewers will tune in. I don't even like baseball, but I'd definitely watch!"

"I'd rather have a mime on my show than Demetri Morretti."

"No one said you had to play nice, Angela. Do the interview *your* way," she advised. "Put him in the hot seat. Ask tough questions. That's what viewers want to see. Good, hard interviews with today's hottest stars."

Nodding her head slowly, she considered her best friend's advice. Angela knew if she grilled Demetri Morretti on air, her boss and everyone in the production team would be licking their chops. "Simone, you're brilliant!"

"I know. That's what I keep telling my husband, but he doesn't believe me!"

The women laughed.

"I better get started on dinner." Standing, Simone gathered her case files and dumped them into her briefcase. "Marcus will be home soon, and I still haven't seasoned the chicken."

Angela watched her girlfriend, moving anxiously around the kitchen, and was glad she didn't have to rush home to cook dinner for a man. *If I ever get married, my husband will cook for* me, she decided.

"You didn't touch your tea," Simone said. "Do you want me to reheat it?"

"Sure, and don't forget the vodka this time!"

Simone raised her eyebrows.

"What? I'm stressed-out," Angela argued, feeling the need to defend herself. "I want *Eye on Chicago* to do well so I can move on to bigger and better things, but I hate the thought of having Demetri Morretti on my show. The guy's creepy."

"Yeah, creepy *fine*," Simone quipped, ambling over to the microwave. She put the mug inside and hit Start. "I read in *Forbes* magazine that his new mansion is so big, he needs a helicopter to get him from one end to the other!"

Angela's eyes strayed back to the computer. For some

reason, she couldn't stop thinking about Demetri. He had a dreamy look and such a compelling presence, he could give a perfectly healthy woman asthma. Long after he'd stalked out of her studio, Angela was still thinking about how good he smelled, how broad his shoulders were and how sexy he looked in his workout gear.

"The guy is so frickin' hot, actresses and pop stars are constantly fighting over him!"

Scowling, Angela took the mug Simone offered her and cradled it in her hands. "I don't see why. He's a pain in the ass. And rude, too."

"Girl, don't hate. Demetri Morretti is the hottest thing in sports right now and for good reason. He's guest starred on a slew of TV shows, hosted *Saturday Night Live,* and he's been on the cover of dozens of magazines, as well."

Angela raised an eyebrow and studied her best friend closely. "For someone who doesn't like baseball, you sure know a lot about the guy."

"It's not my fault. My husband's a sports addict, and he thinks Demetri's mad cool," Simone explained, opening the fridge and grabbing a bag of mixed vegetables. "They've worked out together a few times at Samson's and really hit it off."

"Why didn't you say anything?"

"Girl, please, with all I've got going on I can barely remember what day of the week it is, let alone who Marcus trains on a daily basis."

"The fifteenth can't come fast enough," Angela said, slumping down into her chair. "I'm really looking forward to us hanging out and cutting loose. It's long overdue."

Simone glanced up from the marble cutting board. "We have plans for Friday?"

"Ah, yeah. We're going to the grand opening of Dolce Vita, remember?" Angela shot her friend a funny look. "I'm covering the event for the station, but I should be done and ready to party by eight—nine at the latest."

"Sorry, girl, but I can't go. Marcus has the weekend off, and he's taking me away for a few days," she explained, a girlie smile exploding onto her face.

"What are you going to do with the boys?" Angela asked. "Cart them off to your mother-in-law's house again?"

"You know it!"

The friends laughed.

"I never dreamed Gladys and I would be close, but ever since I got pregnant, she's gone out of her way to help me," Simone confessed. "She never follows the boys' schedule, but she'll babysit at a moment's notice and always encourages me to take time out for myself."

Angela concealed a grin. "I'm glad you and Gladys worked out your differences, because you're *really* going to need her help when you get pregnant with baby number five and six!"

"No way. After I have these girls, I'm done. It's your turn to be barefoot and pregnant."

"I'm not having children, remember?"

"Why not?" Wrinkling her nose, her lips pursed, she placed a hand on her hip. "You're great with my boys and the kids at the shelter love you. Even the teenagers. And everyone knows, teenagers hate everybody!"

"That's different. The kids at the shelter don't have anybody else."

"Good with kids is good with kids. It doesn't matter if they're yours or not," Simone argued. "You can have a career *and* a family, Angela. It doesn't have to be one or the other."

"It does for me."

"That's because you're a perfectionist with implausibly high standards."

"And proud of it," Angela said. *I'm going to make it to the top and no one is going to stop me,* she decided, as an idea began taking shape in her mind. Tomorrow, she'd tell Salem she was on board to do the interview and submit a list of fake questions. Questions she had no intention of asking Demetri Morretti on the air.

A smirk tickled her lips. By the time Angela was finished with the baseball star, he'd be toast, and she'd be the talk of the town. And one step closer to sliding into that lead-anchor chair. Angela was going to take the news world by storm, and she wasn't letting anyone—especially a sly superstar athlete with a chiseled physique—get in her way.

Chapter 5

"**Y**ou need to change your name to Trouble," a voice boomed, drowning out the hip-hop song playing inside Samson's Gym, "because everywhere you go, trouble seems to find you!"

Demetri cast a glance over his shoulder at his former teammate and workout buddy T. J. Nicks. Unable to hold the weight any longer, Demetri dropped the barbell on the floor and plopped down on the workout bench.

Samson's Gym, a state-of-the-art fitness center frequented by pro athletes, college students and moneyed professionals, was usually packed, but this morning there was only a handful of people working out. An older man, who looked as if he was on the verge of collapse, was lifting weights a few benches over, but he was so focused on his routine, he was oblivious to the world. And that was how Demetri liked it. As long as he kept his head down and didn't make eye contact with anyone, no one would recognize him and he could work out in peace.

"I haven't seen you in a minute," Demetri said, swiping his towel off the side of the workout bench and wiping the sweat off his face. "What's up?"

"You tell me."

Shrugging a shoulder, he readjusted his baseball cap. "Nothing much."

"Are you sure? From what I hear, you've been a very busy boy."

"You saw the video?"

A grin fell across T.J.'s dark, narrow face. "Sure did. One of my boys emailed it to me. I almost died laughing when that gorgeous newscaster from WJN-TV called you a spoiled, overgrown kid who needed a time-out!"

Demetri chuckled, though at the time, when Angela was giving him a verbal smackdown, he didn't feel like laughing. He hadn't felt like lashing back at her, either. Maybe because his eyes were glued to her lips, and her scent was a bold, exotic fragrance that aroused his senses. One week after his infamous showdown with Angela Kelly, and he was still thinking about her. Demetri loved his mom, but he blamed her for his present state of mind. If she hadn't called him last night from Italy and reamed him out for disrespecting Angela at her studio, he wouldn't be thinking about the sexy TV newscaster now. He didn't know why Angela had someone record their conversation, and post it online, but he intended to ask her. Demetri didn't care what his mother said. He wasn't a bully. Angela Kelly was a liar who had it coming to her.

"Are you here to work out or gossip?" Demetri asked.

"Both. You know ribbing you is the highlight of my day!" Chuckling, T.J. bent down and retied the laces of his white sneakers. "Why aren't you working out at your home gym? Having it renovated again?"

"No, I needed a change of scenery."

"Shoot, if I had a home gym like yours, I'd never leave the house!"

Demetri picked up his titanium sports bottle, unscrewed the lid and took a long drink of water. T.J. was a good friend, and he'd never put Demetri's business out on the street, but he wasn't going to tell him the truth. The real reason he was there, at seven o'clock in the morning, was to talk to Angela Kelly. Thanks to the owner of the gym, Demetri knew what days and times Angela worked out with her personal trainer. To ensure he didn't oversleep, he'd set every alarm clock in his house and asked his personal assistant to phone him just in case. Now he was at the gym, waiting for her to make an appearance. He only hoped this time when they spoke, she wouldn't go off on him.

"How is rehab going?" T.J. asked, striding over to the free weights and selecting a set of dumbbells. "Think you might make it back in time for the play-offs?"

"I hope so, but I doubt it. It kills me not being out there with my team, but my surgeon wants me to take the rest of the season off, and I'm not going to disregard his advice. The last time I did, I ended up tearing a ligament in my knee, and that hurt like a bitch."

"I hear you, man. What's next on your circuit?"

Yawning, Demetri stood and stretched his hands lazily above his head. "I'm going to do a couple laps around the track, then cool down in the sauna."

"Really? You look like you're about to fall asleep." T.J. wore a quizzical look. "Why are you here so early, anyways? You never get out of bed before noon."

Demetri thought fast and said the first thing that popped into his mind. "I'll be tied up the rest of the day, so I decided to get my training out of the way now."

Eyes wide, T.J. dropped the dumbbells back on the rack and gestured to the cardio room. "Dude, guess who just strode up in here looking like my next baby mama. Angela-sexy-as-sin-Kelly!" he hollered, eagerly rubbing his hands together. "I've met a lot of gorgeous girls, but that honey takes the cake. She's hot, successful and crazy-smart."

"Sounds like somebody has a crush," Demetri teased, poking fun.

"Who doesn't? She's one of the baddest chicks around!"

Demetri wore a blank face. He didn't want his friend or anyone else to know that he was feeling Angela Kelly. He had a knack for picking the wrong woman, and the TV newscaster was everything he *didn't* want in a girlfriend. From now on, he was staying away from fame-loving, celebrity-obsessed types. His ex, a wildly popular R & B singer with a good-girl image, had gone to extraordinary lengths to keep their relationship a secret. But Demetri was through with secret phone calls, ducking out back doors and clandestine meetings in hotel rooms across town. He'd just have to fight his attraction to Angela Kelly, because hooking up with the feisty, headstrong sister was asking for trouble. "She's all right," he said with a shrug. "Too prissy for me, though."

"All right?" When T.J.'s jaw dropped, his tongue fell out of his open mouth. "Man, please. Angela Kelly is a dime piece and you know it!"

Spotting Angela inside the cardio room, Demetri admired her shapely physique. He liked to see tall, athletic women in bright, figure-hugging workout clothes. He loved how the TV newscaster's yellow shirt and fitted leggings showed off her curves.

Demetri told himself to look away, but his eyes were glued to Angela's big, beautiful backside. And when she bent over and touched her toes, all the blood drained from his head. Swallowing hard, he gulped down the rest of his water.

"Quit frontin', man." T.J. leveled a finger at him. "You're hot for Angela, too, just like every other guy in Chi-Town. You're just scared of getting shot down."

Demetri shook his head. "She's not my type."

"Yeah, right!"

"If I wanted Angela Kelly, I could have her, but I don't, so—"

"No offense, bro, but she's *way* out of your league."

Now Demetri was the one with wide eyes. "I'm not trying to brag, T.J., but I'm one of the highest-paid athletes in baseball," he said, feeling the need to defend himself. "Money is no object, man. You know that."

"Yeah, but you know how you are with your money."

"No, I don't. How am I?"

"Cheap, cheap, cheap," he chirped, shielding his mouth

with the back of his hand. "You signed a blockbuster deal a few months back, but you live like a struggling college student!"

"I'm not cheap. I just don't believe in wasting money." Demetri stepped out onto the track. "I have no intention of blowing through my earnings and being broke in ten years."

"Is that why you force your personal shopper to clip coupons and comparison shop?"

"No," he argued with a laugh. "My mom ordered her to!"

Chuckling, the men jogged the length of track at a smooth, fluid pace.

"Word on the street is that Angela only dates rich guys," T.J. explained, his tone matter-of-fact. "You know, men who can wine her, dine her and pay her expenses."

Demetri frowned. He found it hard to believe that Angela Kelly was a kept woman. She didn't strike him as the kind of girl who'd expect a man to support her, but what did he know about women? If he knew more about the species, he wouldn't keep getting played. All of his ex-girlfriends were more interested in his celebrity status than having a real, meaningful relationship with him. And at thirty-two, that was exactly what Demetri was looking for. He knew he was a great catch and he wanted to catch a great woman. Someone who would be there when his career ended and the endorsement deals dried up. His teammates told him he was lucky to be single, but Demetri didn't agree. He envied the guys who got off the team bus and had their wives and children waiting for them. One-night stands left him feeling empty inside, and contrary to what his older brothers, Nicco and Rafael, told him, a warm, curvy body didn't make everything better.

"You dumped the last girl who demanded you buy her a mansion in Bel Air, and that Hawaiian chick for stealing your underwear and selling them on eBay, so there's no way you and Angela Kelly would ever work out."

"Good, because I'm not interested in her," he tossed back.

"But if you were, you could do her, right?"

Demetri wet his lips with his tongue. The thought of sexing Angela, on his custom-made bed, with soft jazz music playing in the background and scented candles flickering around the room, made a slow, lazy smile break out across his mouth. "No comment."

T.J. raised his eyebrows. "Oh, so you think she'd be putty in your hands?"

An explicit image of Angela—naked and rocking her shapely hips against his erection—flashed in Demetri's mind, derailing his thoughts. He couldn't shake the picture from his mind, and when they jogged past the cardio room, and Demetri saw Angela performing squat thrusts, his erection came to life. "I never said that, T.J."

"It was implied."

"Angela Kelly is just like every other girl. Willing to do whatever it takes to bed a baller so she can enjoy his status *and* his checkbook."

"Care to make a friendly wager?" T.J. stuck his hands into his track pants, took out a few hundred-dollar bills and waved them under Demetri's nose. "A thousand bucks says you don't get past first base with that sexy TV newscaster."

"Knock it off, man. We're not in grade school, and betting about women is juvenile."

"Scared you're going to lose, huh? You should be. Angela Kelly is a hard nut to crack."

Demetri believed him. The newscaster was a fiery, passionate woman with a sharp tongue, and there was nothing soft or genteel about her. His eyes trailed her around the cardio room, and when she hopped off the treadmill and toweled off, Demetri knew it was time to make his move. "Be right back," he said, spinning around and jogging backward. "See you in five."

"Where are you going?"

Demetri wore a crooked smile. "To settle a score."

* * *

"I—I—I think I'm dying." Gasping for air, Angela fanned a hand in front of her face and slumped against the wall like a sack of potatoes. "Everything hurts, even my butt, and I didn't sit down once during our session!"

"That's because plyometric workouts engage all of the major muscle groups in the body." Her personal trainer, a stocky man with thick dreadlocks, patted her on the shoulder. "You did awesome today, Angela. Way to go pushing yourself through that last rep of weights."

"Great—tell that to the E.R. doctor when he wheels me into the operating room."

"I'll see you on Thursday."

"If I don't die between now and then." Too tired to wave, she closed her eyes and breathed deeply through her nose. It was the first time all week she hadn't thought about her run-in with Demetri Morretti or her problems with her brother, Rodney. But now that her treacherous hour-long training session was over, all her troubling thoughts came rushing back. Demetri had posted a scathing message about her on his blog, and all morning she'd been fielding calls from the media. Angela wanted to report the news, not *be* the news, and it annoyed her that she'd become a hot topic.

Her legs felt like rubber, but she staggered over to the water fountain, one aching step at a time. Placing her bottle underneath the spout, she pressed the lever and leaned against the wall. Angela stared out onto the track. Her gaze wandered aimlessly around the gym before landing on a fit, muscled specimen in a sleeveless Chicago Royals T-shirt and knee-length shorts.

For the second time in minutes, Angela let out a deep-seated groan. Her eyes ate up every inch of the stranger's towering frame. The square jaw, the rack of his shoulders, his bulging biceps. Since high school, she'd had a weakness for strong, athletic guys, and Mr. Man was definitely her type. All lean and rugged, he looked like the kind of guy who could fix the leaky faucet in her kitchen *and* rock her world in the bedroom.

Angela felt ice-cold water flow down her hands and snapped out of her thoughts. Releasing the lever, she tucked her water bottle under her arm and dabbed her wristband over her damp cheeks. She glanced over her shoulder, to ensure no one had witnessed her reaction, and there, standing a few feet away, was Demetri Morretti. *Damn.* He was the same guy she'd been drooling over on the track seconds earlier.

Angela sucked in a breath. Her pulse soared, and her heartbeat drummed so loud in her ears, she couldn't think. Physically active and fit her entire life, she'd never had any problems with her heart, but every time Demetri Morretti was around, it throbbed, skipped and beat out of control. Like right now.

"Good morning," he said, tipping his baseball cap at her. "Can we talk?"

His voice was husky and matched his gruff disposition. He looked angry, and pained, as if someone had just beaten him in an arm wrestle.

"I think you said enough the other day at the TV station, don't you?"

"I'm sorry I barged into your studio."

"You should be."

"You're right, and I shouldn't have stepped to you like that, either. It won't happen again."

His gaze probed her eyes, one terrifying second at a time. Admitting he'd made a mistake couldn't have been easy, and Angela found herself moved by the sincerity of his tone. But not enough to forgive him for what he'd written about her on his blog yesterday.

"I was hoping we could start over."

"Let's not and say we did," Angela quipped.

"I knew you were going to make this hard for me."

She puzzled over Demetri's words but decided not to question him. Angela had zero interest in patching things up with the conceited baseball star but knew better than to argue with him in public again. There was no telling who was watching. Or secretly taping them. And the last thing Angela wanted was another video of her screaming at Demetri Morretti to mysteriously surface online. "I don't have anything to say to you."

"If anyone should be holding a grudge, it should be me," he said, pointing an index finger at his chest. "Because of you, I'm the most hated athlete in America."

"Don't kid yourself, Morretti. Your reputation was in the dumps long before my *Athletes Behaving Badly* story."

"Well, your report certainly didn't help."

"Neither did your six-game batting slump."

His face, like his voice, was stern and tense. "I didn't come over here to argue. I came here to apologize for what happened the other day."

"You have some nerve. First, you post a nasty message about me on your blog—"

"My blog?" Demetri looked puzzled, as confused as a driver who'd exited a store and forgotten where he'd parked, but when he spoke, his words were measured and his speech was slow. "I don't blog or Tweet or post online messages. My publicist manages all of my social-media accounts."

"But the blog is in your name."

"I know," he said with a shrug of his broad shoulders, "but I'm not much of a computer person. I prefer talking to people face-to-face, *especially* beautiful TV newscasters."

Angela felt a smile claim her lips but washed it off. She wasn't ready to forgive and forget what Demetri had done, but she believed he didn't write his blog. It didn't sound like something a guy would write. Most celebrities didn't post online messages or respond directly to fans, but the smart ones were wise enough to preapprove what their handlers put on the web. But obviously Demetri Morretti was too busy getting into bar fights to care. "A guy could get in a lot of trouble letting other people speak for him."

"No one speaks for me. I speak for myself."

"Could have fooled me." Her confidence kicked in and stamped out the unruly butterflies flittering around her stomach. "You're just full of surprises this morning, aren't you? Next, you'll be telling me you didn't have someone record our argument and post it online."

"I didn't. Actually, I thought *you* did."

"Are you kidding me?" Angela gave a bitter laugh. "Why would I post a video that made me look crazier than the Joker?"

His scowl fell away when he chuckled. It was the first time Angela had ever seen or heard Demetri laugh, and she liked the sound. Immensely. Angela caught herself and quit giggling. He was the enemy, a man bent on destroying her, not someone she could trust. She'd never been a play-it-safe kind of girl, but whenever Demetri was around, her guard went up.

"Let's call a truce," he suggested, offering his right hand. "You stop bashing me on your show, and I'll promise not to come back to your studio. Deal?"

Angela paused. She was ready to bury the hatchet, but when she remembered his Facebook post—the one that said *Talentless newscasters who sleep their way to the top shouldn't throw stones*—she came to her senses. Her gut instincts told her Demetri was behind the post. Had to be. He was the one who hated her, not his stupid flunkies. "Sorry," she said, wearing an innocent face. "I don't make deals with the devil."

Then Angela spun around and stalked into the ladies' changing room.

Chapter 6

Angela stepped inside her two-bedroom town house, immediately seeing the enormous framed photograph hanging in the foyer, and smiled to herself. It didn't matter how long her day was—one look at the picture of her and her friends sipping cocktails on a Fiji beach, and her frustrations melted away.

Dumping her keys on the front table, she dropped her work bag on the floor and kicked off her leather pumps. Entering her living room and seeing her chic home furnishings filled Angela with pride. *My swanky bachelorette pad deserves a spread in* Home Decor *magazine,* she thought, collapsing onto her cozy red velvet couch. Her house was inundated with bright colors, unique artifacts she'd scored from her travels abroad and cute, cozy furniture. Purchasing her first home, in a neighborhood she loved, was one of Angela's greatest accomplishments. On warm, sunny days she loved to sit on the porch and chat with her neighbors.

But not today.

Her run-in with Demetri Morretti yesterday morning at Samson's Gym consumed her thoughts and weighed so heavily on her. It was all she had been thinking about. Stretching her legs out in front of her, she allowed the sunshine streaming through the windows to quiet her mind. The tree-lined street was overrun with kids. They were riding bikes, splashing in puddles and doing cartwheels across their lawns. On any other day, their shrieks of laughter would draw her outside to cheer them on, but tonight Angela didn't have the energy to move.

Unzipping her tweed blazer, she shrugged it off and chucked it at the end of the couch. After work, she'd stopped by Simone's house for dinner, and after two hearty servings of vegetable lasagna, and a couple of strawberry wine coolers, she was stuffed.

Picking up the remote, she pointed it at the TV and hit the on button. Angela flipped channels, in the hopes of finding something funny to watch, something that would take her mind off of her troubles. Angela spotted the clip of her arguing with Demetri playing on a rival news station and pounded the sofa cushions with her fists. "I can't believe WQK is showing this stupid video again!" she raged, her chest heaving with anger. "Those jerks!"

Sitting in her living room, watching the video for the umpteenth time, Angela wondered how she could spin her showdown with Demetri into an even bigger news story. Not one that had people pointing fingers or laughing at her. Rather, a story that would drive more viewers to check out her weekly show.

As the clip played, Angela found herself admiring Demetri's long, lean frame. He looked as cool as a gun-slinging cowboy, and although he was glaring at her during the entire video, there was no disputing the baseballer's striking good looks. With his smooth skin and dark, striking eyes, Demetri Morretti could land a role in any big-budget Hollywood movie. And it would be a guaranteed smash hit at the box office.

Angela heard the telephone ringing on the table behind her but decided to let the answering machine pick it up. She wasn't in the mood to talk. It was probably one of her single girlfriends calling to ask about Demetri Morretti, and Angela was sick and tired of hearing the man's name. In the past week, the video had received thousands of hits, and according to Simone's husband, it was still making the rounds of the local radio stations and was a hot topic on *Sports Chicago.*

Angela released a deep sigh. By now, anyone who didn't live under a rock had heard about her showdown with Demetri Morretti. And even though Angela knew the story made sensational headlines and would drum up free publicity for her show, she was embarrassed over the way she'd acted. In the video, she was loud and brash and looked completely out of control. That wasn't her. In all her years of working in television, Angela had never gone off on a guest, never lost her cool. But there was something about Demetri Morretti that brought out the worst in her. And that scared her. What if he agreed to do her show and she lost her temper again? Would she even have a show when the dust cleared?

Angela heard her cell phone buzz, and she fished it out of her nearby purse. She scanned the screen for the number and released a deep sigh when she saw the Denver area code. It was her dad, calling from the road. He never called to chit-chat, and was an avid sports fan, so she knew he was phoning to find out if she'd lost her damn mind. "Hey, Dad," she said, faking a cheerful voice. "How are you doing?"

"Angela, what happened with Demetri Morretti?"

So much for easing into the conversation, she thought, raking a hand through her hair.

"Dad, it was nothing."

"It sure looked like a whole lot of something to me."

Biting the inside of her lip, she racked her brain for a plausible explanation for why she'd gone off on baseball's biggest star.

"Quit stalling, baby girl, and tell me what happened."

At his words, Angela smiled. Her father, Cornelius Kelly, had raised her and her brother single-handedly. He had never once complained or bad-mouthed her absentee mother. And when her mother died from a drug overdose, it was her dad who helped her overcome her grief. A proud daddy's girl, Angela grew up doing all the things her father loved. To this day, Angela consulted her dad before making any major decisions and lived for the afternoons they spent jogging around Millennium Park, watching their beloved Chicago Royals play or barbecuing at her childhood home. Her dad was a truck driver who worked long hours for crummy pay, and as soon as Angela became lead anchor at WJN-TV, she was going to pay off his bills and buy him a new car.

"Demetri Morretti showed up unexpectedly at WJN-TV."

"And," Cornelius prompted.

"And when he confronted me over my *Athletes Behaving Badly* segment, I lost it," Angela confessed, forcing the bitter truth out of her mouth. "I know the athletes mentioned in the story are upset, but I never expected Demetri Morretti to pop up at the studio, demanding an apology. Seeing him threw me for a loop."

"Morretti didn't put his hands on you, did he?"

"God, no!" she hollered. "If he had, I would have slugged him!"

"That's my girl!"

"Dad, I'm…" Angela struggled with her words. Swallowing, she pushed past her emotions and spoke from her heart. "Dad, I'm sorry if what I did embarrassed you. I got caught up in the moment, and—"

"I'm not mad at you, baby girl. I'm damn proud!"

"You are?"

"Of course. It's about time someone stood up to Demetri Morretti, and I'm glad that my smart, beautiful daughter was the one to do it."

Angela sat up straight. "You really mean that?"

"I sure do!" His strong voice boomed through the phone. "It's not your fault you lost your temper. Demetri Morretti provoked you, didn't he?"

Angela stayed silent. She wasn't going to defend Demetri Morretti—he was the enemy—so instead of correcting her dad, she vented her frustration. "Dad, you should have heard him! He was making demands and ordering me around like I was one of his flunkies," she complained. "And get this— he said if I don't go on the air and apologize, he's going to sue me."

"Tell him to bring it on! I'm not scared of him!"

A giggle fell out of her lips. "Dad, you can't fight Demetri Morretti—"

"I will if he disrespects you again."

"Don't worry, Dad. I can handle him."

"Baby girl, he's a bully. You can't take him on by yourself."

"I won't." Angela thought for a moment and considered what she could do to make the whole ugly issue with Demetri Morretti go away. "I'm thinking maybe I should ask the station to cancel the last segment of my *Athletes Behaving Badly* story."

"Why? I've watched all of the shows online, and I think it's one of the best pieces you've ever done."

"You think so?" she asked, stunned by her father's words. "You don't think I was too hard on the athletes featured in my story?"

"Hell no! They're all rich, spoiled stars who've had multiple run-ins with the law."

"Well, everyone except Demetri Morretti."

"Yeah, but he's the worst of the bunch. Talk about an overpaid, overhyped star. He had a lousy season, both on and off the field. If I was the GM of the Royals, I'd cut him loose."

"A lot of people feel that way."

"And for good reason. Remember the last home game we went to? Fans were so pissed, they started tossing things onto the field and screaming obscenities."

Frowning, Angela thought back to that day. She didn't remember any of that happening. But at the time, she imagined that she would've been too busy eyeballing Demetri Morretti to realize what was going on around her. In the midst of developing her *Athletes Behaving Badly* segment, she'd decided to use the time to scope out the players featured in her story. But when the stadium announcer called Demetri to bat, Angela ditched her iPad. There was something about the baseball star that excited her, something about his energy that turned her on. Her dad was sitting next to her, chatting away, but Angela hadn't heard a word he'd said.

Her eyes had been glued to number seven.

Demetri's uniform was crisp and clean and outlined his ripped forearms and firm butt. He had universal sex appeal, and when he took to the field, the women in the crowd went wild. Sitting there, in her plastic red seat, Angela felt something stir inside her. Something profound. Her attraction to him was so intense, it consumed her entire body.

Angela shook off the memories of that blustery fall day in September. *I'm attracted to Demetri—so what?* she decided. *I'm attracted to a lot of men, and just because I've fantasized about him a time or two doesn't mean I want him. Because I definitely don't.*

"Stay away from Demetri Morretti," Cornelius advised. "He's always been a loose cannon, and since injuring his shoulder during training camp, he's only gotten more volatile. There's no telling what he'll do the next time you two cross paths."

"Relax, Dad. He's not *that* bad."

"I just want you to be safe."

Angela smiled to herself. It didn't matter how many people online bashed her show. She would always have her dad's love and that meant the world to her. "I know, Dad, and don't worry. I will be."

"While I have you on the line, there's something else I'd like to discuss with you."

"Let me guess—you want me to get you some more Harlem Globetrotter tickets, right?"

"No, the ones you gave me last week were more than enough."

Angela heard her dad pause, then release a deep sigh, and immediately knew something was weighing heavily on his mind.

"Your brother called today."

"From where?" she quipped, rolling her eyes. "The Cook County Correctional Center?"

"Angela, don't joke about things like that."

"Why not? That's exactly where Rodney and his gang-banger friends are headed."

"This thing between you and your brother has gone on long enough," Cornelius said. "When are you going to forgive him and move on?"

"Dad, I moved on a long time ago."

"Then why won't you take his calls or respond to his messages?"

Because I've washed my hands of him. Angela didn't want to hurt her dad, and if she spoke the truth, he'd be crushed. "Dad, every time I think about what Rodney did to me, I get angry all over again, so let's talk about something else."

"No one's perfect, Angela. Everyone makes mistakes!"

"I know," she conceded, "but Rodney's mistakes always end up costing me thousands of dollars and a trip to the county jail to bail him out."

"He's only twenty-one. He has a lot of growing up to do—"

"Dad, quit making excuses for him. When I was in college and my scholarship fell through, I didn't go out and steal from my family. I got a job and worked damn hard." Angela felt a pang of guilt but pushed past it. Her dad didn't need to know the truth about the job she'd taken her freshman year. No one did. It was her little secret—one she was taking with her to her grave. "I busted my butt to make my dreams come true, and so can Rodney."

"I'm not condoning what your brother did, but I think

you're being too hard on him. He's the only brother you have, your flesh and blood, and he needs you now more than..."

Angela didn't have the strength to argue with her dad. Not after the day she'd had. And not about her wayward sibling, Rodney. Her brother was a full-time criminal who could outsmart the cops any day of the week. Over the years, she'd become accustomed to making excuses for his poor choices. But when he'd stolen her debit card and withdrawn five thousand dollars from her account, she'd cut him off for good. Angela missed having her kid brother around, missed shooting hoops with him in her dad's backyard and firing up the grill, but she'd never forgive Rodney for betraying her. "Dad, I'm tired," she said, anxious to end the phone call. "I'm going to turn in."

"Okay, I understand. You've had a long day."

"I'll talk to you tomorrow."

"Angela, please give some thought to what I said."

"I will," she lied. As she clicked off the phone and rose from the couch, she decided to put her problems with Rodney out of her mind. She had an interview with Demetri Morretti to prep for, and after their argument yesterday morning at Samson's Gym, Angela knew she had her work cut out for her.

After taking a quick shower, Angela got into bed, turned on her laptop and logged on to the internet. Once she checked her email and updated her Facebook page, she began typing "safe" interview questions. Questions she planned to submit to her boss but had no intention of asking Demetri Morretti on the air.

Excitement pumped through her veins. It didn't matter if they taped the episode next week or next month, because when the time finally came for her to sit down with the reigning bad boy of Major League Baseball, she'd not only have the upper hand, but she'd also be laying the groundwork for a promotion.

By the time I'm done with Demetri Morretti, he won't know what hit him!

Chapter 7

"Hold the elevator!"

Angela stuck her foot out to prevent the elevator doors from closing, and when Salem rounded the corner and hustled inside, she couldn't help but laugh. "The one time I decide to sneak out early, I get caught! Talk about rotten luck!"

Salem laughed, too. "Where are you rushing off to? Got a hot date tonight?"

"Nope, I'm getting a mani-pedi done up the block at Glamour Girlz."

"Mind if I join you? My gel nails are a hot mess."

"Sure. Why not? We can finally finish discussing my proposal."

"*Or,*" she said, drawing out the word, "we can gossip about our coworkers!"

Twenty minutes later, Angela and Salem were sitting in the café adjacent to Glamour Girlz. Since the salon was packed, and there was an hour-long wait, Angela suggested they grab a cup of coffee to pass the time. They were the only people in the café, and once seated at a corner table, Salem sank down in her padded leather chair and kicked off her pumps.

"God, I've been wanting to do that all day," she confessed, shrugging off her black two-button blazer. "Those shoes were cutting off my circulation."

Angela glanced under the table and gazed longingly at the multicolored peep-toe heels. She'd been coveting them for months, and had the perfect dress to wear them with, but because Rodney had pilfered her bank account, she wouldn't be making any trips to the mall anytime soon. "Those shoes are hot."

"I know, huh? I love my Louboutins, but after giving several studio tours, and running around the station all day, my feet are on fire!"

"I've been there too many times to count." Angela wore a sympathetic smile. "Sometimes it sucks to be a woman."

"Says the young, gorgeous newscaster who has men lining up to date her."

"Yeah," Angela conceded, rolling her eyes to the ceiling. "Broke, lazy types who want me to be their sugar mama!"

The women laughed.

Crossing her legs, Angela picked up a menu and scanned the day's specials. The Espresso Bar was a quaint spot with oak tables, fake flowers and framed paintings that looked as if they'd been done by three-year-olds. But Angela didn't come to the café to admire the decor; she came for the desserts. The Polish-born chef made the best pastries in the city. Cakes so rich and creamy, patrons ordered them for breakfast. When the waiter arrived to take their order, Angela felt no guilt in ordering a slice of chocolate *sformato* to go along with her cappuccino. She needed something sweet to give her fuel for the rest of the day.

"I might have to skip that manicure," Salem said, tapping the face of her watch. "It's getting late, and I have plans with my husband tonight."

"Are you guys going to the Cadillac Palace?" Angela wasn't a fan of the theater, but she loved connecting with viewers, and opening night of *Les Misérables* was sure to be a star-studded affair. "I'll be there with the crew, covering the event, and I think fans of *Eye on Chicago* are going to love getting an up-close view of what happens backstage."

"I really want to go, but my husband got tickets for the Vultures game."

"But you hate hockey."

"Yeah, but he loves it. And if I want him to go with me to the Enrique Iglesias concert next month, I have to suck it up and go cheer on the home team."

Turning her face toward the window, Angela touched a hand to her mouth and patted back a yawn. "Excuse me."

"Late night?"

"No, early morning." Swallowing another yawn, she dabbed her teary eyes with her fingertips and smiled sheepishly at her boss. "I had another session with my trainer this morning, and he worked me so hard, I hurt in places you wouldn't imagine!"

"Well, keep it up because all your hard work is paying off. Hey, think your trainer can whip me into shape? I'd love to drop a few pounds by my fortieth birthday."

Angela made a sour face. "Salem, you don't need to lose a single pound. I have handbags that weigh more than you!"

The waiter arrived and, after unloading the food from his tray, bowed chivalrously at the waist. "Enjoy your desserts, ladies. If you need anything else, don't hesitate to ask."

Angela watched Salem slice into her raspberry cheesecake and giggled when her boss moaned out loud. *Now's the perfect time to talk to Salem about my new proposal,* she decided, sipping her coffee. *She's high on sugar and caffeine — there's no way she'll blow me off!*

"I really enjoyed reading the proposal you turned in last week."

Inwardly, Angela cheered, but outwardly she remained as calm. "You did?"

"Yup, all nineteen pages!" A grin spread across her face. "One of these days, we're going to have to sit down and discuss a shorter, more succinct approach, though."

"I'm just glad you liked it. I worked on it for weeks."

"I know. It showed." Salem reached for her mug and took a sip of her chamomile tea. "You always do a great job on your proposals, but you really outdid yourself this time. Once

I started reading, I couldn't stop. Your report was *that* compelling."

Angela felt as if she were going to burst. Happiness filled her, and she was so overcome with excitement that she wanted to reach across the table and hug her boss. "Salem, thank you so much. I really appreciate this opportunity and I promise not to let you down."

Salem coughed, then pushed a hand through her long, wavy locks.

"I can't wait to get started. Would it be okay if we met tomorrow morning to discuss—"

"Angela, your proposal was outstanding, and the sexual harassment of female soldiers in the military is a story that needs to be told, but I can't approve it."

"Why not?" The question shot out of Angela's mouth before she could stop it. "I don't understand. You just said you loved my proposal."

"I do, but the story's all wrong for *Eye on Chicago.*"

"But the victims are Chicago natives and decorated war veterans, as well."

"I'm not trying to hurt your feelings, Angela, but viewers don't give a rat's behind about human-interest stories," she said with a shrug of her shoulders. "These days, all people care about is which celebrities are dating and who was caught with his pants down—*literally.*"

Plastering a smile on her face, one she hoped concealed her profound disappointment, Angela stirred her spoon furiously around her coffee mug.

"Online celebrity videos get millions of hits every day, but human-interest stories get little to no press," she continued, her expression contrite. "This is the first time *Eye on Chicago* has been number one in the ratings, and if we want to stay on top, we have to keep giving the viewers what they want."

"And what's that?"

"Scandalous, salacious stories featuring their favorite entertainers. People like…"

Angela sat frozen, with her eyes lowered and her lips pursed, listening to Salem go on and on about hot topics and future celebrity guests. She heard her cell phone buzz but didn't dare take her BlackBerry out of her purse. Although Angela was angry that Salem had shot down her proposal, reading her messages right then would be rude.

"Viewers have an insatiable appetite for celebrity gossip, and whenever you interview a ditzy actress or troubled athlete, fans tune in by the tens of thousands."

"I know," Angela agreed, "but we've been doing essentially the same show for the last nine months. I think it's time we shake things up and—"

"Hold that thought." Salem whipped her iPhone out of her jacket pocket and checked the screen. "This will only take a minute."

"No problem. Take as long as you need."

"Hello, Salem Velasquez speaking," she said, pressing her phone to her ear. Pushing away from the table, she hopped to her feet and strode toward the ladies' room.

Angela looked down at her dessert and pushed the plate aside. She didn't feel like eating. And if she thought her boss would understand, she'd grab her stuff and head home.

Staring aimlessly out the window, Angela watched as pedestrians drifted up and down the street. A guy wearing a Chicago Royals jersey and tattered jeans stood at the bus stop smoking a cigarette. The number seven was marked on the bottom of the shirt, and the initials *DM* were on each capped sleeve.

Those initials, of course, belonged to Demetri Morretti, the face of Grey Goose, Nike and a dozen other international companies. These days Angela couldn't go anywhere without seeing his handsome face splashed across a billboard, the side of a bus or a glossy magazine.

Her thoughts returned to last Friday and the exact moment she spotted Demetri Morretti at Samson's gym. Time stopped when their eyes met. Angela had been so stunned to see him that she had become hot and flustered. She'd dated a lot of men over the years but she'd never felt a spark with anyone. Never experienced that indescribable magic she saw in movies or read in romance novels. But every time she saw Demetri Morretti, Angela felt as if she was going to pass out. The man made her quiver. And tingle in the most delicious places. And that was reason enough for her to stay far away from him.

"Sorry I took so long." Salem plopped back down in her seat and rested her cell phone on the table. "That was Demetri Morretti's publicist, Nichola Caruso."

Angela's stomach lurched. She already knew what this was about and quickly racked her brain for a way out. She thought of telling her boss about her run-in with Demetri at the gym but decided against it. Salem would want to know details, and Angela didn't feel like rehashing her ten-minute conversation with the surly baseball star.

"I've got bad news," Salem said. "Morretti refuses to do your show."

Relief flowed through her. Angela wanted to scream for joy but kept her feelings to herself. Angela didn't want to look like a fool in front of her crew or her viewers and was secretly thrilled that the baseballer had turned Salem's offer down.

"You know what this means, right? He'll probably go ahead and sue us."

"I doubt it. Morretti's all talk." Angela wasn't scared of being sued, and she'd read online that defamation lawsuits were likely to be dismissed.

"You're probably right. It's not the first time someone's threatened to sue the station, and it won't be the last." Salem tapped her fingernails absently on the table. "I'm sure his legal team will talk him out of it. Suing us would be a waste of time and money."

Angela picked up her fork, sliced into her cake and tasted the dessert. Her head tilted to the side as she savored the moist, rich flavor. A smile tickled her lips. All wasn't lost. This wasn't over. One way or another, she'd find a way to convince Salem to approve her proposal. She had to. Her future was riding on it.

"I'm more upset about him not doing the interview than anything."

Angela gave a dismissive shrug of her shoulder and took another bite of her cake. "You win some, you lose some, I guess."

"This isn't over," Salem announced. "We're going to get Demetri on *Eye on Chicago* if it's the last thing we do."

"We? Count me out. I couldn't care less…" Catching the surprised look that crossed her boss's face, Angela broke off speaking and cleared her throat. "What I meant was, we've had really great guests this year, celebrities who actually *like* giving interviews, so why even bother with someone as grouchy as Demetri Morretti?"

"Because he's the hottest thing in sports right now!"

Attempting to play dumb, Angela made her eyes big and wide. "You think so?"

"Uh, yeah. Where have you been?"

Busy writing proposals no one gives a damn about, Angela thought, stabbing her cake with her fork. Were her colleagues right? Had she been hired because of her looks and not because of her talent? The truth weighed heavily on her, but before she could get Salem's take, her boss dropped another bombshell.

"Talk to Demetri tonight when you see him at Dolce Vita. And by 'talk,' I mean do whatever it takes to get him on your show."

Angela stared openmouthed at her frizzy-haired boss.

"Get him alone, away from his entourage, and work that Angela Kelly charm," she advised. "And this time, no yelling or screaming at him, okay?"

Angela's cheeks burned like fire. Ever since her argument with Demetri went viral, everyone from the cameramen to the engineers had been teasing her. Salem thought the video was great press and had even spoken to their computer tech about uploading the clip to the station website. But Angela was dead set against it and had talked the tech guy out of posting it.

"We have to strike while the iron's hot, and since your showdown with Demetri, the whole city's been buzzing about you *and* your show."

"How do you know Demetri will be at Dolce Vita tonight?" Angela asked. "The guy's a recluse who rarely goes to parties or local events anymore. And when he does, he never stays more than ten or fifteen minutes."

"Dolce Vita is his brother Nicco's brainchild, and Demetri has attended restaurant openings from Tokyo to Dubai." Salem looked determined. "Angela, I want Demetri Morretti on *Eye on Chicago* during sweeps week—"

"Then why don't *you* talk to him?" Angela heard the edge in her voice and rephrased the question. "You're the producer of the show, and if you called him up and talked to him about an appearance, it would carry more weight."

"I would, but Demetri's not sweet on me. He's sweet on *you.*"

"No, he's not. He hates my guts, and the feeling's definitely mutual."

"*Hate* is a strong word," Salem said, raising her eyebrows. "Especially for two people who have insane chemistry like you guys do."

"Chemistry?" Angela shook her head and the thought clear out of her mind. "You must be confusing us, because the only thing Demetri Morretti and I have in common is mutual disgust and animosity for one another."

"There's a thin line between love and hate…" she sing-songed. "And trust me, when it comes to you and Demetri Morretti, the lines have already blurred."

"No, they're not. I know exactly where I stand. He's not my type, I'm not even remotely attracted to him, and to be honest, I think he's obnoxious."

"Oh, drop the act already! You're not fooling anybody, Angela."

"What act?" Angela fussed with the silver necklace draped in front of her purple V-neck sweater. "I don't know what you're talking about."

"Sure you don't." Salem studied her closely and then wagged an index finger at her. "Just admit it. You're attracted to Demetri Morretti, just like every other woman in America. Hell, the man gives me butterflies, too, and I'm a newlywed!"

Angela had zero interest in talking to Demetri again, but she couldn't dismiss her boss. Not after all Salem had done for her. They were friends, the only two women of color at WJN-TV. And Angela could always count on her producer to go to bat for her. But that didn't mean she was willing to throw herself at Demetri Morretti. There were just some things Angela couldn't do, and begging him to appear on her show was one of them.

"Salem, I'll do anything to make *Eye on Chicago* a success, but I'm not a miracle worker. Demetri isn't going to talk to me, let alone agree to be on my show."

"I think he will." Her smile was coy. "His personal chef is in my yoga class, and yesterday she mentioned that Demetri's foundation is having a Fourth of July extravaganza for hundreds of children and their families."

"Okay," Angela said, slowly drawing out the word.

"Maybe if you agree to cover the event, he'll agree to do your show."

Angela wished she shared her boss's optimism, but she didn't. "I doubt it."

"Then try talking to his publicist, Nichola Caruso," Salem said while signaling the waiter for the check. "There are rumors circulating that they're lovers, and apparently, she can persuade Demetri to do anything."

"I bet." Angela had heard the rumors about Demetri and his publicist and didn't doubt for a second they were true. She'd seen pictures of them eating at five-star restaurants, shopping on the Magnificent Mile and cruising around in one of his many sports cars. Athletes got a kick out of sleeping with their staff, and the internet was saturated with intimate photographs of Demetri and his female employees. "I'm not trying to be difficult, Salem, but how do you expect me to persuade Demetri to be on my show when he obviously doesn't want to?"

Salem winked. "You're a smart girl. You'll think of something."

"That's just it. I don't think I can!"

"You do want *Eye on Chicago* to stay on top of the ratings, right?"

"Yes, of course, but—"

"Good," she said curtly. "Then quit arguing and go get me that interview."

Chapter 8

Touted as the hottest restaurant lounge in the city, Dolce Vita Chicago offered world-class food. Its stylish rooms were draped in plush black silk, and its terrace was decked out in cozy furniture, vanilla-scented candles and hanging lights that bathed the space in a soft blue light.

"Let's head upstairs," Angela suggested, addressing her three-man crew. The restaurant was crowded, packed from wall to wall with Chicago's brightest stars. The air was saturated with the scent of expensive perfume and fine Italian cuisine. "I spotted a famous blogger head into the VIP area, and I'd love to get him on camera. He always has something outrageous to say!"

"My lower back is killing me," the cameraman complained, sliding the camera off his shoulder and resting it at his side. "I need a break."

"Another one?" Angela glanced at her thin silver watch. "But it's only been thirty minutes since your *last* break."

The lighting technician spoke up. "Yeah, but we put in four long hours at the Cadillac Palace, and the music was so loud, it gave me a headache."

Angela smelled alcohol on his breath and knew his last bathroom break had involved a trip to the bar. She had warned him not to drink on the job, but instead of calling him out in front of the rest of the crew, she reached for the Tylenol inside her purse. "Want some?" she asked, presenting the bottle in her hand.

Shaking his head, he stared down at his sneaker-clad feet.

"I need a five, too." The sound assistant took a pack of cigarettes out of his pocket. "Climbing up and down those steps holding our equipment was no walk in the park, Angela."

I managed just fine, she thought, nixing an eye roll. *And I'm wearing stilettos!* "Let's go strong for the next hour and then finish up. Once we get some shots from the roof and I do another quick round of interviews, we can call it a night."

"Or we can call it a night now." The cameraman wore a grin. "It'll be our little secret."

Angela shot him down. "No way. We have takes to redo, and—"

"We're not redoing any shots, Angela. I told you, everything looks fine."

"'Fine' isn't good enough, Mac. The footage needs to be perfect, and those clips we shot earlier aren't fit to air," she told him, refusing to back down.

"I don't have the energy to refilm." The cameraman opened his mouth wide and yawned so loud, he startled a couple standing nearby. "Are you forgetting that we put in a full eight-hour shift today at the station?"

Angela didn't like his condescending tone, but she didn't lose her cool. "I've been up since four-thirty this morning, but you don't hear me complaining."

"Yeah, getting gussied up in hair and makeup is *real* tiring work." Snickering, the cameraman bumped elbows with his colleagues. "Anytime you want to swap jobs, let me know!"

"One interview and then we'll take another quick break."

"Break first, interview second." The lighting technician watched a buxom waitress sashay by and licked his thin chapped lips. "I'm going to the bar. I need some, ah, water."

Angela crossed her arms. This was why she hated working with this crew. They complained about everything, took countless breaks and had the attention span of a toddler in a toy store. "Ten minutes, guys. That's it."

Their eyes lit up with boyish excitement.

"Let's meet in the lobby at..." Angela paused to glance down at her watch, but when she looked up, her crew was gone. Peering around the lounge, she watched the trio make themselves at home at the sleek circular bar.

"There you are! We've been looking all over for you!"

At the sound of her girlfriend's high-pitched voice, Angela spun around. Her friends Remy Foster and Farrah Washington were dressed to kill in short, flirty dresses and wearing huge matching smiles. "I'm so glad you guys could make it!" Angela said, throwing her arms around them. "It's been forever since we hung out."

"Who you tellin'? It's been so long, I forgot what you looked like!" Remy joked. "Let's go grab a booth. I need some champagne."

Angela raised an eyebrow. "Champagne? Why? What are we celebrating?"

"The fact that we're the sexiest chicks in here!" Striking a model pose, Remy raised her chin and slid her bejeweled hands up and down her thick, voluptuous shape. "I'm killing them in this dress. Every guy in here is checking me out, *especially* the married ones!"

Laughing, the three friends linked arms. A waiter arrived, and as he escorted them through the dining area, Angela spotted several famous faces partying in Dolce Vita. A Grammy Award–winning rock group and a movie icon and her latest boy toy were seated on a black velvet couch, posing for pictures and downing body shots.

"Can I start you gorgeous ladies off with something from the bar?" the waiter asked, his head cocked and his pen poised to write on his notepad. "Some cocktails, maybe?"

"For sure!" Remy picked up a menu and scanned it. "We'll have a round of peach Bellinis and an appetizer basket with a double order of calamari."

"Coming right up!" The waiter nodded and then ran off.

"I wonder what's keeping Simone?" Farrah took her cell phone out of her purse. "I expected her to be here by now. She's always on time."

"Simone's not coming," Angela said absently, scanning the bar for her camera crew. They were nowhere to be found, but Angela hoped when she was ready to resume filming, they'd be ready to work.

"Are Jayden and Jordan okay?" Farrah wore a concerned face. "They didn't catch that nasty stomach bug that's been going around, did they?"

Shaking her head, Angela abandoned her search for her crew. "No, the boys are fine. Marcus whisked Simone away to St. Bart's for the weekend, and trust me, ladies, the girl's on cloud nine!" Angela laughed. "She called a couple hours ago to let me know they arrived safely *and* to brag about sitting next to Hugh Jackman in first class."

Farrah snorted. "Why are we friends with her again?"

"Because she's one hell of a cook!" Remy hollered. Throwing her arms around her girlfriends, she hoisted her cell phone in the air and shrieked, "Say 'cheese'!"

Remy snapped picture after picture and then uploaded the images on her Facebook and Twitter accounts.

"Remy, do you have to do that now?" Farrah asked, raising her voice above the noise in the dining room. "We came down here to have a good time, not to watch you play on your phone all night."

"Of course I have to load the pictures now. I want all my friends *and* frenemies to see how much fun I'm having at Dolce Vita!"

Three waiters, carrying trays topped with enough food to feed a family of ten, swiftly entered the dining room. Stopping in front of the booth, they unloaded their trays on the raised mahogany table. "This isn't our order," Angela said, waving her hands out in front of her. "We ordered a round of Bellinis and an appetizer basket. That's it."

"Shhh, girl." Putting an index finger to her crimson-red lips, Remy jabbed Angela in the side with her elbow. "Don't say anything. We're about to get free food."

"This is courtesy of Demetri Morretti," the blue-eyed waiter said. "After you finish eating dinner, he'd like you and your friends to join him in the VIP lounge."

"Tell him we'll be there in ten minutes." Remy grabbed a champagne flute and giggled. "Thanks, fellas. Everything looks delish!"

A fourth waiter arrived, carrying the largest bouquet of yellow tulips Angela had ever seen, and he handed it to her. "These are for you, Ms. Kelly."

Angela sat there, dumbfounded. She couldn't think or speak and was glad Farrah had the presence of mind to thank the waiters and give them a generous tip.

"Thank you," the headwaiter said. "We'll be back shortly with the second course."

Farrah frowned. "The second course? Just how many courses are there?"

"Seven," the waiters said in unison.

"Wonderful! Thanks, guys!" Remy said, shooting them a wink. "Hurry back!"

"Wow, look at all this food," Farrah gushed, her eyes big and wide. "And there's still more to come. Demetri Morretti must *really* like you."

Remy shrieked. "Girl, you better go up to the VIP lounge and give him some! Hot, rich guys are hard to find, and if I were you, I'd do Demetri Morretti and *do him well!*"

Her friends erupted in laughter.

"Aren't you going to read the card?" Farrah asked, pointing at the bouquet.

Angela's face flushed and her body stiffened. She then plucked the tiny white card out of the lavish bouquet. "'To the most beautiful woman in the room,'" she read out loud, as if puzzled over the words. And she was. The last time she had seen Demetri they'd argued, and now, less than a week later, he was sending her yellow tulips. Her favorite flower. "'I look forward to spending the rest of the night with you and your gorgeous friends.'"

"I thought you and Demetri hated each other?"

Angela stumbled over her words. "W-we do."

"Then why did he send over flowers, dinner and three bottles of Cristal?"

"I don't know, Farrah. Maybe he gets off on being insulted."

"There's gotta be more to this story than you're telling us," Remy insisted. "You had wild, passionate sex with Demetri in your office, didn't you?"

"Of course not! I'd never do something like that."

Remy hollered, "I would!"

"Come on," Farrah pleaded. "Tell us what's really going on between you and that gorgeous man. We're your girls, remember?"

As they ate, Angela told her girlfriends about what had happened with Demetri at Samson's Gym and her conversation at the Espresso Bar with her boss. "Salem practically ordered me to speak to him tonight," she said, staring down at the flower bouquet. "I wasn't going to, but now it looks like I have to. Demetri's obviously in a good mood, so I'm going to see if I can get him to reconsider the interview."

"What are you going to do if he shoots you down again?"

"He won't turn her down," Remy said. "Angela's got this in the bag."

Farrah glanced up from her plate. "Wow, you sound confident. What makes you so sure she'll convince him to do her show?"

"Because once this chick gets an idea in her mind, there's just no stopping her!"

"That's true," Farrah agreed.

Overcome with confusion, Angela sat there, trying to figure out what Demetri Morretti was up to. This had to be yet another sophisticated ploy to deceive her. Or was it? Could the flowers have been a generous peace offering and nothing more? She shook her head, quickly pushing the later thought from her mind.

Lowering her face into the bouquet, Angela closed her eyes and inhaled the sweet, fragrant scent. Angela loved flowers and was a sucker for elaborate romantic gestures. This was easily the nicest thing anyone had ever done for her. Dolce Vita was overrun with celebrities—rich, glamorous types whom legions of people envied—but she was the only woman who'd received flowers. And even more shocking, they were from a man who hated her!

"Are you still in a funk because that TV newscaster dissed you on her show?"

Demetri didn't have to look over his shoulder to know his brothers were behind him. He was standing in front of the oversize window in the VIP room, surveying the scene down below, when Nicco and Rafael sidled up beside him. They stood well over six feet tall, both with a full head of wavy black hair. Dressed in their casual white suits, they could easily pass for Hugo Boss models.

Nicco and Rafael were always ribbing him because he was the youngest, but tonight Demetri wasn't in the mood for their teasing. "No, I'm straight. Forgot all about it."

"Then why are you over here crying in your drink?" Nicco broke into a hearty chuckle. "You look pitiful, bro, and you're bringing down the mood in my bar. Get it together, man. Crying is bad for business!"

"Shut up, Nicco. You don't see me cracking on you for crashing your Maserati *again.*"

He shrugged his shoulders. "Hey, man, accidents happen."

Rafael wore a coy grin. "Maybe next time you'll keep your hands on the wheel and *off* your girlfriend's double Ds."

"What girlfriend? I'm single."

"What happened to the Playboy Bunny from Nepal?" Demetri asked.

"She dumped me. Said I had trust issues."

"She's right! You do!" Rafael and Demetri shouted in unison.

"We're not talking about me. We're talking about you." Nicco pointed a finger at Demetri. "You need to chill out and quit stressing. Who cares what the media says about you?"

"I do. I'm sick of people dogging me out."

"I'm not surprised. You've always been sensitive."

Demetri raised his chin and straightened his bent shoulders. "I'm not sensitive."

"Yeah, you are," Rafael insisted with a curt nod of his head. "You're the sensitive one, Nicco's the stubborn one, and I'm the cool, laid-back one who keeps you both in check."

The brothers chuckled.

"Want me to talk to this Angela Kelly woman for you?" Nicco asked, hiding a self-incriminating grin. "I'll tell her to quit bad-mouthing you on her show, and if that doesn't work, I'll storm into her studio, and… Oh, wait, you already did that!"

Rafael playfully slapped Demetri's shoulder. "Ignore him, D. I saw Angela Kelly in the lobby a few minutes ago, and she's a stunner. If she had gone off on me like that, I'd be crying, too!"

"She's here? Are you sure?" Nicco asked, glancing wildly around the VIP room. "I personally thanked all the members of the media for coming tonight, but I definitely didn't run across anyone from WJN-TV."

Rafael slowly swept his gaze through the main-floor bar and lounge. "There she is! In the corner booth across from the kitchen."

"I hope you never witness a crime, because you'd suck at describing the perp!" Nicco gestured to the crowd with his glass. "Could you be a little more descriptive? There are dozens of beauties in the lounge, and I still don't have a clue who she is."

"Five-nine. Honey-brown skin. Killer curves." Demetri's hungry gaze slid down Angela's trim, fit body. "Little black dress. Gold accessories. Nude pumps."

"Damn, bro, can you see what's *under* her dress, too?"

The brothers erupted in laughter.

"Now I see why you're bummed," Nicco said with a frown. "Angela Kelly's gorgeous, easily the sexiest woman in here tonight."

I know, and I can't get her out of my mind! Demetri dragged a hand over his face. Since their run-in last week at the gym, he'd thought about Angela nonstop. After arriving home, he had called his publicist and ordered her to delete her blog post about Angela. He then spent the rest of the afternoon watching old episodes of *Eye on Chicago* online. The more he watched, the more intrigued he was about the fresh-faced beauty. And reading her online blog had given him an idea. When the waiter presented her with the lavish flower bouquet, her face lit up, and Demetri knew he was one step closer to earning her forgiveness.

"I'll be right back," Nicco said, adjusting his collar. "Since I'm the owner of this fine establishment, I'm going downstairs to introduce myself to Angela Kelly."

"I bet that's not all you're going to do," Demetri grumbled. The thought of his brother stepping to Angela made his temperature rise. He didn't want anyone, especially a smooth talker like Nicco, putting the moves on Angela. Not when he was trying to make peace with her.

That's not all you're trying to do, jeered his inner voice.

"Be careful," Rafael warned. "If you piss her off she'll crucify you on her show!"

Nicco gave a hearty chuckle. "I know. That's why I'm

going to welcome her to Dolce Vita and tell the waiters to give her the star treatment."

Rafael cocked an eyebrow. "And get her number, too, right?"

"A man can never have too many beautiful women in his life…"

"Hey, guys!" Nichola said, her smile bright and her tone filled with enthusiasm.

Rafael gave her a one-arm hug. "Are you having a good time or is this guy making you work the room?"

"I'm having a blast. The lounge is packed with celebrities and the food is crazy-good!" Nichola pointed a finger at the bar. "Demetri, I need you to do a quick interview with the guy from *Sports Chicago*. He's been waiting to talk to you for the last hour, and he's starting to get antsy."

"Go do your interview," Nicco said. "I have some business to attend to anyways."

"We'll hook up later, bro!"

His brothers strode off, leaving Demetri alone with his publicist. Demetri didn't want to talk to the guy from *Sports Chicago* or any other press about his shoulder injury. Not tonight. He wanted to hang out with his friends and talk to Angela Kelly—alone, in private. At the thought of her, he sneaked a glance over his shoulder. He watched Angela exit her booth, with her girlfriends in tow, and wondered where she was rushing off to. Sailing through the lounge, the gorgeous trio left a trail of mesmerized, wide-eyed men in their wake.

"If you do this interview, I won't bother you for the rest of the night."

He raised an eyebrow. "Promise?"

"Don't be silly. I can't do that!" Giggling, she waved off his comment with a flick of her hand. "It's my job to keep your name in the press and get you free publicity, remember?"

"I know. I know. That's what you keep telling me." Removing the cap on his water bottle, Demetri nodded at the portly reporter, sitting alone at the end of the bar. "Let's get this over and done with so I can get back to having fun."

"That's the spirit! Let's give a great interview and land a cover story!"

Chapter 9

"I can't find them anywhere!" Arms folded, her teeth clenched in suppressed rage, Angela searched frantically around the lounge, hoping to find her crew among the well-heeled diners. She wondered if the lead anchor had a hand in this. The lead anchor, a distinguished older man with refined mannerisms, was always trying to embarrass her, and this was just the sort of thing he'd put the guys up to. "How am I supposed to interview the season-two winner of *The Song* if I don't have a cameraman?"

"We're wasting precious time," Remy complained, tapping one of her sandal-clad feet impatiently on the floor. "Time we *should* be spending in the VIP lounge partying with Demetri Morretti and his rich baller friends."

"I'm not here to party, Remy. I'm here to work."

"But your crew bailed on you! As I see it, you're done for the night."

Angela took her cell phone out of her purse. She didn't want to bother Salem on her night off, but her boss had a right to know what was going on. Angela dialed her number and it went to voice mail. She left a message and then searched the dance floor for any signs of her crew.

"I didn't get dolled up to stand around doing nothing," Remy complained. "I'm going to the VIP lounge to meet some men. Are you coming or not?"

Angela couldn't help but laugh. There was never a dull moment when the man-crazed makeup artist was around.

When they reached the entrance of the VIP lounge and her friends squealed with joy, Angela cracked up. Guests were mingling, posing for pictures, and the blonde female DJ was forcing dancers into a gyrating frenzy. Two brunettes, wearing itty-bitty dresses and blinding smiles, stood at the door offering glasses of champagne and an eyeful of cleavage.

When Angela stepped inside the lounge, the first person she saw was Demetri Morretti. He looked handsome and cool. Like the kind of man she usually lusted after. It was the first time Angela had seen Demetri without his baseball cap on, and his short textured hair gave him a mature look. He was standing at the back of the room, chatting with his publicist and a slim man with a straggly ponytail.

Watching him, Angela decided that the editors at *J'* magazine were right. Demetri Morretti *was* the best-looking man on the planet. Hands down. None of the other men featured in the magazine even came close. He was immaculately groomed, and his casual white shirt, leather jacket and blue jeans fit his toned, ripped physique perfectly. He was fine in every sense of the word and had the sexiest set of lips Angela had ever seen. But his best feature was his eyes. They were dark, filled with intrigue and framed with long eyelashes. Demetri Morretti was a chick magnet, and Angela noticed everyone—from the pop singer to the mayor's daughter—blatantly check him out.

"Oh, my God! Nicco Morretti's here!" Remy grabbed Angela's forearm and gave it a hard squeeze. "Girl, you have to introduce me."

"Me?" Angela touched a hand to her chest. "Why me? I don't even know the guy."

"Yeah, but his younger brother is crushing on you, bad."

"Forget it, Remy. Every time I introduce you to someone, I end up regretting it."

"Come on. Be a good sport," she begged, her voice shrill. "You don't want to stand in the way of true love, do you?"

Farrah burst out laughing. "True love? Ten minutes ago,

you were dirty dancing with a Sony music producer, and now Nicco Morretti is your one true love?"

"Girl, you'd be in love, too, if you knew how much his net worth was!"

In her peripheral vision, Angela saw Demetri stride out of the lounge with his cell phone at his ear and a frown on his lips. Her eyes followed him out of the room and down the long, narrow hallway. He looked upset, but Angela wanted to speak to Demetri alone—without his entourage listening in—and knew this was her best chance to have some one-on-one time.

"Do you guys mind if I step outside for a minute?" Angela asked, her eyes glued to the window. "I need to speak to Demetri, but I won't be long. Ten, fifteen minutes, tops."

Remy smirked. "Don't hurry back on my account. There are more than enough ballers here to keep me busy!"

Angela found Demetri outside the VIP lounge, leaning against the far wall. His head was back, his eyes were closed, and his hands were hanging loosely at his sides. He was the picture of calm, and seeing him like this—all relaxed—made Angela wonder if she'd made a mistake following him out into the hall. Deciding she had, she spun around on her heels, anxious to return to the VIP lounge and her friends.

"I like your perfume."

At the sound of his voice, Angela turned and faced Demetri. He was standing in the middle of the hallway, staring right at her. Intently. Then, after a long, terse minute, he broke into a wide, disarming smile. One that put her on high alert.

"How was dinner?"

"Amazing," she gushed. "Thanks for everything. The flowers, the food, the champagne. Everything was delicious."

"I'm glad to hear it. Are we cool now?"

"That depends. Are you still planning to sue me?"

"I need you to stop dissing me on your show, Angela. It kills."

She waited for Demetri to chuckle or break out into a grin, but when he didn't, Angela knew he was serious. Dead serious. That stunned her. Demetri was a rich bad-boy athlete who settled disagreements with his fists, so why did he care what she thought of him? His sensitivity was endearing, a complete surprise, and Angela found herself even more intrigued by him.

"What's it going to take to squash this beef between us?" he asked.

"You could do my show."

"I don't do interviews."

"Why? Scared the questions will hit too close to home?"

"I'm not scared of anything." Demetri's gaze was as intense as the tone of his voice. He appeared stern, like a corporal, and spoke through clenched teeth. "I've been double-crossed too many times to count, and I don't have the stomach for lies and bullshit anymore."

Pausing reflectively, Angela took a moment to consider his words. "That's not what I'm about, Demetri. I'm not going to trick you or humiliate you on my show, but I will ask you tough questions. Questions my viewers are dying to know the answers to."

"So, if I come on your show you'll stop gunning for me?"

"I'm not gunning for you," she said, shaking her head.

"You called me an immature, overpaid athlete who cares more about winning bar brawls than a baseball championship."

Angela winced. Those weren't her words. Sure, they'd come out of her mouth, but her *Athletes Behaving Badly* piece had been tweaked, cut and rewritten by the producers. On the day of taping, she'd dutifully read the teleprompter and was so busy trying to nail the segment in the first take, she hadn't given a second thought to what she was reading. But Angela couldn't tell Demetri that. He wouldn't understand. Not after she'd criticized him for not writing his own blog.

"Maybe you're right. Maybe I was a bit harsh," she conceded, pinching two fingers together. "But if you come on my show, I'll give you the opportunity to set the record straight. That's forty commercial-free minutes to plug your endorsements, your charity and give a shout-out to your ten million followers on Twitter."

Demetri raised an eyebrow. "Ten million? Is that a lot?"

"Most athletes don't even have half that number, so I'd say you're doing okay."

"As long as I have more followers than my brothers I'm happy!"

They shared a laugh.

"Please reconsider doing my show," Angela said, hoping to capitalize on their truce.

"Fax the questions to my publicist, Nichola Caruso, and we'll look them over."

"No way. If we're going to do this, we're going to do it my way." Hearing the bite in her tone, she cleared her throat and took a moment to gather her thoughts. Convincing Demetri to come on her show was a daunting task, but Angela was up for the challenge. Every time Demetri smiled or stared deep into her eyes, her heart fluttered in her chest. "I want us to have an open, honest conversation, not a scripted interview with you and your team calling the shots."

"You're one tough cookie, Ms. Kelly."

"I'm a Chi-Town girl," she quipped. "What do you expect?"

Demetri shot her an amused look. "Can I have your number?"

"Why? So you can prank call my house?"

"No, so we can discuss this further," he explained, stepping forward and sliding his hands into his pockets. "Maybe we can get together tomorrow and iron out the details."

"I can't. I already have plans."

"With your boyfriend?"

"Don't have one. Don't need one," she singsonged. "I volunteer at the food bank on Saturdays. You should come. We could always use more volunteers."

"I just might."

"Sure you will."

"Why is that so hard to believe?"

"Because you're Demetri Morretti, baseball player extraordinaire," she said, raising her voice. "These days, celebrities don't do anything unless it's a planned photo op, and I hate to disappoint you, Demetri, but there won't be any fanfare at the food bank."

"Don't need any." He took his cell phone out of his jacket pocket and handed it to her. "Can you enter all of the necessary information in here?"

Angela knew Demetri wasn't going to show, but to humor him she took his cell phone and entered the details. They were on good terms—for now—and until he agreed to do her show, she was going to be on her best behavior. But once they taped the interview, all bets were off.

"I'll be there at nine o'clock."

Laughing, she slid his cell phone back into his front pocket. "I'll have to see it to believe it." Anxious to get back to her friends and away from the gorgeous baseball player, Angela spun around and waved a hand high in the air. "Good night, Demetri. Thanks again for dinner."

"Hold up."

Capturing her forearm in his palm, he slowly drew her toward him. Their faces were close, their bodies touching. The air was thick, saturated with the scent of his desire. His rich, refreshing cologne made Angela feel light on her feet.

"Not so fast, beautiful. We're not done talking."

Angela swallowed. Her mind was spinning, and her flesh was scalding hot. She didn't trust herself to speak, not with the way she was feeling inside, but managed to croak out a response. "I have to get back inside. My girlfriends are waiting for me."

"But you haven't given me your number yet." He drew his gaze from her lips to her eyes and ran a hand down the length of her arm. "How are we supposed to get to know each other if I have no way of reaching you?"

Angela stared at him openmouthed. *He's joking, right?*

Standing chest to chest with Demetri Morretti in the darkened hallway was asking for trouble. Angela knew it. Felt it. But she didn't move away. Not when her legs were shaking uncontrollably and her feet were glued to the floor. Angela started to speak but struggled with her words. His smile was so sweet and wild, outrageous thoughts attacked her mind. Scared Demetri was going to kiss her or worse, she stepped back. Right into the wall. Now she was stuck, trapped with nowhere to go and nowhere to hide.

How in the world did we get here? Angela wondered, licking her lips. A week ago, Demetri was plotting her demise, and now he looked as though he wanted to kiss her. More shocking still, she wanted to kiss him, too.

Checking her thoughts, she ordered her horny body to get under control. Nothing good could come out of fooling around with Demetri Morretti, and Angela wasn't willing to ruin her career or her reputation for one night of carnal pleasure.

"You have the perfect look for TV, you know."

Angela blinked. "I do?"

"You come alive in front of the camera." He spoke in a whisper, one that made shivers dance along her spine. "You have an incredibly sexy voice and perfect diction."

"Perfect diction?" A nervous giggle fell out of her mouth. "I've heard a lot of crazy pick-up lines over the years, but that one's a first."

"Pick-up lines are whack. I prefer to speak from the heart." Her heart stood still when he touched her cheek. "What would your publicist think if she knew you were out here flirting with me?"

Lines of confusion wrinkled his forehead. "It's none of her business."

"But you're lovers."

"I'm single. Have been for over a year."

"I saw a video of you guys on *Entertainment Tonight*," she said, unable to conceal the note of accusation in her voice. "You looked awfully cozy in Maui with her last week."

"Are you keeping tabs on me?"

Angela couldn't think of a witty comeback and knew if she spoke, her feelings would betray her, so shook her head instead.

"Nichola's like a sister to me. There's nothing going on between us."

"You're not friends with benefits?"

"I don't believe in that. Not my speed."

Angela threw her head back and let out a laugh. "Yeah, right! Athletes are the biggest players on the face of the earth, and when it comes to deceiving women, they have no conscience."

"I've never been a player. Now, my brother Nicco is a different story." A grin crimped his lips. "He loves chasing women and doesn't have a faithful bone in his entire body."

"And you do?"

"Most definitely."

"So, all those tabloid stories about you dating various Hollywood starlets are lies?"

"There's only one woman I'm feeling right now. She's a tenacious TV newscaster with bright, beautiful eyes and a gorgeous smile, but unfortunately, she thinks I'm a complete jerk." Demetri bent his head low and dropped his mouth to her ear. "Don't know if I can change her perception of me, but I'm going to try. Starting right now...."

Then Demetri covered her mouth with his lips.

Stunned, Angela felt her eyes widen and her breath catch in her throat. She couldn't describe the feelings that washed over her when their lips touched. The urgency and hunger of his kiss overwhelmed her. His caress was tender, his hands soft, and his lips were the best thing she'd ever had the pleasure of tasting. Using his tongue, he parted her lips and eagerly explored every inch of her mouth.

Loud, heavy footsteps reverberated around the corridor. A bulb flashed, flooding the hallway with a harsh, bright light. Pulling away from Demetri, Angela covered her face with her hands and turned her body toward the wall.

"Get out of here!" Demetri shouted, sliding in front of Angela. Shielding her with his body, he pointed a finger at the grizzly-haired photographer snapping pictures with his high-powered camera. "Scram, or I'll shove that camera down your throat!"

Two bouncers, in black muscle shirts and jeans, appeared at the end of the hallway and snatched the photographer up by his jacket collar. "This clown must have snuck up here through the bathroom window," one said. "Don't worry, Demetri. We'll take care of him."

The bouncers dragged the photographer into the elevator, and the doors slid closed.

"Angela, are you okay?

"Yeah, I'm fine." She touched a hand to her lips, to the exact place where Demetri had kissed her. His soft caress, along her bare arms, caught her off guard. Slowly, he turned her around. Her breath came in quick, shallow gulps. Not because she was scared but because she was overcome with desire and wanted nothing more to pick up where they'd left off.

"You're shaking." Demetri took off his jacket and draped it over her delicate shoulders. "Don't worry. Those pictures will never see the light of day. The bouncers will confiscate his camera, then toss him out into the back alley."

Angela released an audible sigh. "That's good to know."

"Let's head back inside. You look like you could use a drink."

"No, you go ahead. I need to use the ladies' room."

"Then I'll wait right here."

"Demetri, that's really not necessary."

"It is to me." A smile dimpled his cheeks. "Go on. I'll be patiently waiting right here."

As he watched Angela walk down the hall, his gaze slid along her hips and her long, toned legs. And when she slipped inside the ladies' room, he released a long, slow whistle. He couldn't believe it. He'd kissed Angela Kelly—the woman who'd slandered his name on national TV. He was so hungry for her, he wanted to call it a night and head back to his place. In a moment of weakness, his desire for the provocative newscaster had overruled his logic, and he'd acted on his impulse. Angela Kelly was a spitfire, a woman full of contradictions and surprises, and he was interested in learning more about her. A lot more.

He slumped against the wall and rubbed a hand over his face. He felt as if he'd been struck upside the head with a foul ball, and the more he tried to censor his feelings, the stronger his desire for Angela Kelly grew. His brain went into overdrive, entertaining one outrageous thought after another. Thoughts of sleeping with the enemy.

Now it's a whole new ball game, he decided, casting a glance at the ladies' room.

And that excited him.

Chapter 10

The Cook County Food Bank was a large brick building bordered by broken-down houses with rusted for-sale signs. When Angela pulled into the parking lot and saw the litter on the ground, she made a mental note to speak to the director about hiring someone from the Ninth Street shelter. The participants in her employment-readiness class were desperately looking for work, and one of them would do a good job keeping the area spick-and-span.

Exiting her car, she spotted Farrah on the other side of the lot and waved in greeting.

"Hey, girl," Farrah said, heaving her tote bag over her shoulder. "I wasn't expecting to see you until the afternoon."

"Why? I told you I'd be here bright and early."

"I know, but when I left Dolce Vita, you and Demetri were still going strong."

"We were talking, Farrah. Just talking," Angela stressed.

"More like gazing and flirting and touching!" Her eyes twinkled and her smile was tinged with amusement. "I saw you guys all hugged up on the couch. And at one point, Demetri was even holding your hand. Don't try and deny it. I saw it with my own eyes."

A smile appeared across Angela's mouth as the memory of last night played in her mind. Fast-forwarding past the interviews she'd done and the argument with her crew, she mused over the hot, tantalizing kiss she'd shared with Demetri—the one that had stolen her breath. It was two minutes of heaven, the most electrifying and passionate kiss she'd ever experienced. After returning to the VIP lounge, she'd sat with Demetri in a quiet corner, talking and laughing. At the end of the night, long after the restaurant had closed, he'd walked her to her car and given her another long, slow kiss. One that kindled her body's fire and unleashed her desires. But Angela couldn't tell her friend that. "My boss ordered me to get Demetri on my show, so I have to be nice to him until he signs on." To convince herself, and Farrah, she gave a shrug of her shoulders. "It was nothing."

"It sure *looked* like something."

Ignoring the dig, Angela followed Farrah up the rickety wooden steps.

"When are you seeing him again?"

"Hopefully, he'll agree to do my show, and we can tape the interview by the end of—"

"No one cares about your show," Farrah said, flapping a hand in the air. "I want to know when you and the sexiest man alive are going on your first official date."

"Farrah, it's not like that."

"Oh, yes, it is! You want Demetri so bad that lust is literally oozing from your pores!" Farrah's head cocked to the side, and she reached out and patted Angela's stomach. "Before you know it, you'll have a little bun in the oven and be planning a lavish summer wedding!"

Angela slapped her hand away. "You're worse than Remy!" she said, shaking her head in disbelief. "She demanded to be my maid of honor *and* begged for Nicco Morretti's address and cell-phone number all in the same text!"

The women cracked up.

"Would you hurry up and open the door? I'm roasting out here," Angela complained.

Farrah rummaged around in her oversize gold purse. "Sorry, girl, I can't find the keys. I know they're in here somewhere but…"

Loud music pierced the morning air. Fully expecting to see a group of teens cruising down the block in a lowrider, Angela glanced over her shoulder. She watched dumbfounded as a sleek, black Lamborghini turned into the food-bank parking lot.

Her eyes widened. Feeling her knees give way, she grabbed the railing to keep from falling headfirst into the bushes. *No way! It can't be!*

Angela inspected the posh sports car. It had tinted windows, diamond-studded rims, and when it rolled to a stop, the engine released an audible purr.

"Someone got lost in the wrong part of town," Farrah quipped, pulling her keys out of her purse. "Nice wheels, though, huh? Wonder how much drugs he had to sell to afford it."

Before Angela could answer, the driver's-side door lifted in the air, and Demetri slid out. Farrah gasped, dropping her keys to the ground as a hand flew to her open mouth.

"Oh, my God!"

Angela shared the same thought. Shock filled her. Not because she was surprised to see Demetri strolling through the parking lot, but because of how ridiculously handsome he looked. *It should be illegal for a man to be that fine,* she thought, admiring his casual street style. He had the confidence of a runway model and the requisite body to match. She only hoped Demetri didn't try to kiss her again, because resisting him required superhuman control, and whenever he was around she became helplessly weak.

Angela ran her eyes down the length of his body. Clad in his trademark Chicago Royals baseball cap and sunglasses, he strode through the parking lot carrying a box of doughnuts in one hand and a tray of coffee in the other. His light, refreshing cologne carried on the breeze, and his boyish grin was dreamy.

"Good morning, ladies."

Desire burned inside Angela, but she gathered herself and returned his warm greeting. "Hey, Demetri. What's up? I wasn't expecting to see you this morning."

"Why not? I told you I'd be here, and here I am."

His grin was wide and disarming. It was meant to charm, to remind her of the special moments they'd shared at Dolce Vita. And it did.

"We should get inside. There's a lot to get done today, right, Farrah?"

Her friend didn't speak. She just stood there, staring wide-eyed at Demetri.

Angela scooped the keys up off the ground and pushed them into Farrah's hands. But she didn't move. To rouse her friend from her trance, she poked her in the side with her elbow. "Come on, Farrah. Time to go inside."

"Huh?" Farrah blinked, then gave Demetri a puzzled look. "I don't mean to be rude, Mr. Morretti, but what are you doing here?"

"Call me Demetri," he said smoothly. "Angela invited me. She said you were short on volunteers, and since I had nothing to do today, I figured I'd come down and help out."

"You're here to volunteer?"

"If that's okay with you."

"Yes, yes, of course."

Demetri raised the coffee tray in the air. "I brought breakfast. If there isn't enough for everyone, I can zip back over to Dunkin' Donuts and grab some more."

"We're the only ones here so far, so that's more than enough." Farrah unlocked the door and disabled the alarm. "Welcome to the Cook County Food Bank. Please, come in."

Demetri climbed the steps and strode down the sun-filled hall behind them.

"Demetri Morretti didn't come down here to volunteer," Farrah whispered, clutching her friend's forearm. "He came here to see you!"

"I don't care." Angela unzipped her jacket. "I told you. I'm not interested in him."

"For real? You're not just saying that."

"All I care about is Demetri doing my show."

Farrah licked her glossy lips. "Good—then can I have him?"

"I don't care what anyone says," announced a tall, full-figured woman, slamming a can of kidney beans on the table. "*The Song* is rigged! And so was the last presidential election!"

Demetri chuckled. Over the past hour, he'd sorted and shelved nonperishable food items and listened in fascination to the spirited discussion the other volunteers were having. The only person who didn't join in the conversation was Angela. But Demetri suspected it was because she was too busy packing backpacks and not because she was being antisocial. He had never, in all his life, seen someone work as hard as her. She checked and double-checked the names on her list, ensured every backpack had the same number of school supplies and had taken the time to write each child a handwritten note.

"Son, you're moving too slow. You've gotta keep up."

Demetri tore his gaze away from Angela and addressed the slim, gangly man with an unkempt beard. The supervisor either didn't know who he was or didn't care. Both suited Demetri fine.

"Sorry, sir, but I'm going as fast as I can." To prove it, he scooped up the cans in his cardboard box, dropped them on the shelf and lined them up in a straight, neat line. He felt a twinge in his shoulder but smiled through his pain. "How does that look?"

"Fine, but at the rate you're going, we'll be here all day. You've only unloaded three crates in the last two hours, but Mr. Sullivan, who's thirty years your senior, has done eight!"

"Really? Wow! Good for him." Demetri chuckled, but when the supervisor crossed his fleshy arms, he halted his laughter. The man looked as if he was about to blow, and since Demetri didn't want to get tossed out of the Cook County Food Bank, he quickly unloaded the rest of the items in his crate. He was here to give back to the community *and* spend quality time with Angela, and he couldn't afford to piss anyone off—especially the ill-tempered supervisor. "I'll work harder from now on, sir. I promise."

"If you don't pick up the pace we'll be here all day, and I have plans with my old lady tonight," he said, hoisting a sack of potatoes onto the top shelf and dusting the dirt off his wide, fleshy hands. "What did you say your name was again?"

"Just call me D."

"D., you should go help Angela and the ladies and leave the sorting to us."

Demetri gestured to the black flatbed truck parked in front of the storage-room door. "There's still a lot of groceries to unload, and I'd hate to leave you hanging, sir."

"Go. I insist." The matter decided, the supervisor rested a hand on Demetri's shoulder and steered him across the storage room. "Angela, this fine young man is going to help you and your team for the rest of the morning."

Angela kept her eyes on the ribbon she was tying into a large, elaborate bow.

"Angela's a little intense," the man said, lowering his voice. "But she's the best volunteer here. Don't worry, son. You're in good hands."

Demetri didn't doubt it. Angela did it all and made it look easy. He'd been watching her on the sly for hours and marveled at her humility in serving others. Her physical beauty was striking, but he was attracted to her mind more than anything.

Sunlight poured through the window and cast a bright glow around Angela. Dressed in a belted blouse and tights, her hair cascading down her shoulders, she looked like a beautiful brown angel. And she was. After seeing her cheerfully answer the phones, pack dozens of food hampers for single mothers and clean the freezer from top to bottom, he realized Angela Kelly was an unstoppable one-woman show.

And he wanted her more than he'd ever wanted anyone.

Where the hell is Nichola? he wondered, stealing another glance at his watch. He'd called her hours ago, and she'd promised to be at the center by noon. It was twelve-thirty, and he still hadn't seen any sign of her.

Taking his cell phone out of his pocket, he checked for missed calls or texts. He had dozens of texts but none from Nichola. He considered calling her again, but when he spotted the elderly woman in the peach blouse giving him the evil eye, he shoved his cell phone back into his pocket. "What needs to be done?" he asked.

"Nothing. I got this. Just relax."

"Angela, I'm here to help, so let me."

Her eyebrows were furrowed, and she looked worried. "Englewood Elementary School was severely damaged during the thunderstorm we had a few weeks back, and the students were left with practically nothing. This project is near and dear to my heart and I want the backpacks to be perfect."

"I know, and don't worry. I'm not going to screw anything up," he said, rolling up his shirtsleeves. "Just tell me what you want me to do, and I'll do it."

Angela gestured to the wooden table to her left. "Put a box of crayons, a ruler and a spiral notebook in each backpack." She wore a sheepish smile, one that caused her eyes to sparkle like diamonds. "Thanks, Demetri. As usual, I've fallen way behind, and Mr. Crews is mad at me."

"I bet. That brother doesn't play," Demetri said, wearing a wry smile. "He should enlist in the U.S. Army. He'd make one hell of a drill sergeant!"

They shared a laugh. As they worked, they talked about the weather, movies they were anxious to see and the Fourth of July extravaganza his foundation was throwing.

"Angela, I'd love if you and your friends could come," Demetri said, glancing at her. "The event is for a great cause, and all the money raised will go toward sending disadvantaged kids to private school and junior college."

"When is it, and where is it being held?"

He thought hard but drew a blank. "I can't remember."

"Are you actually involved in the organization or just the face?"

"Just because I don't run to the papers or post it on Facebook every time I make a charitable donation doesn't mean I don't give."

"Million-dollar checks are wonderful, Demetri, but the greatest thing you can give a kid is the gift of time. They'll probably never remember what toy they got from your foundation, but they'll never forget the time they spent with their hero."

"I never asked to be a role model."

"Well, you are, and it's time you started acting like it."

Demetri folded his arms. "What's that supposed to mean?"

"Whether you like it or not, you're the face of the Chicago Royals franchise and idolized by practically every kid in this city," she explained, hurling a box of crayons into a pink Hello Kitty backpack. "Quit bellyaching about how it sucks to be famous and use your stardom for good. Read to schoolchildren, play ball in the park with neighborhood kids and, for goodness' sake, get to know the families who use the services offered by your foundation."

Demetri stood there, stunned by her criticism and the harshness of her tone. He felt small, and guilt troubled his conscience. It wasn't every day he got put in his place, and Angela's words stung. "I'm not a bad guy."

"I never said you were," she countered, "but the next time you're tempted to complain about the media hounding you or have a pity party in your twenty-room lakefront mansion, remember all the Chicago kids who look up to you."

Silence fell between them. For the next hour, Demetri worked side by side with Angela but didn't say a word. Not because he was mad, but because the tension in the room was high, and he didn't know what to say to break the silence. Her words stuck with him, played over and over again in his mind. Was Angela right? Was he a spoiled, rich athlete who did nothing but complain? Had he allowed the trappings of success and fame to make him bitter?

"Lunch is ready!" Farrah announced, sticking her head inside the storage room and waving her hands wildly in the air. "Y'all get in here and eat before my gumbo gets cold!"

A cheer erupted from the group, and everyone sped out the door.

"Aren't you going to eat?"

"I will, after I finish the rest of the backpacks." Angela stood and walked up the aisle. Slowly and carefully, she searched the shelf for more boxes of cartoon character–themed fruit snacks. "Go ahead and eat, Demetri. I bet you're starving. You've been working hard all morning."

"Not as hard as you."

Angela's shoulders tensed when Demetri moved to stand directly behind her. He was so close that she could hear him breathing.

Turning around, she pressed her back flat against the shelf. Her eyes settled on his lips. Desire swept over her, mercilessly battering her inflamed body. Angela had to find a way to withstand the heat in order to overcome the power he held over her.

Conversation and laughter flowed out of the kitchen, reminding Angela that they weren't alone, that one of the other volunteers could walk in at any minute.

"We need to talk."

"We're talking now."

"Are you mad at me?"

His words floored her. "No. Why would I be mad at you?"

"Because I've been a terrible role model for Chicago kids."

Angela wore an apologetic smile. "You came down here to volunteer, not to listen to me gripe. I'm sorry. It won't happen again."

Demetri touched a hand to her waist, and her heart stood still.

"Don't censor yourself around me. I find your honesty refreshing."

"Then why did you barge into my studio two weeks ago and threaten to sue me?"

"To get your attention," he said smoothly.

Angela wasn't buying it but didn't argue the point. To keep from staring at Demetri, she fixed her eyes on the storage-room door, watching to make sure no one was coming.

"We need to finalize the details of the interview, and the sooner the better."

"Yeah, right, the interview," she said, tearing her gaze away from the door. "Why don't you come by the station one day next week?"

"You had me banned from the building, remember? And besides, I'd prefer something less formal and more relaxed."

"Um, okay. What did you have in mind?"

Demetri moved closer, lowered his voice. "Dinner, at my place, tomorrow night."

"I already have plans."

"Break them."

"I can't," Angela said, shaking her head. "My dad has been looking forward to the Harlem Globetrotters show for weeks, and I promised I'd meet him and my brother."

"I'd hate to piss off Pops." He gave a hearty chuckle. "All right, let's do lunch instead."

"I'll have to check to see if my producer's available," she explained. "Salem normally doesn't work weekends, but I have a feeling she'll make an exception for you."

"Mrs. Velasquez is not invited. It's an intimate lunch for two."

Playing with her necklace gave Angela something to do with her hands. Something that wouldn't get her in trouble. But when Demetri stepped forward, she braced her hands against his chest, which was what she'd been itching to do from the moment he'd barged into her studio.

"I'm going to make you an authentic Italian meal and you're going to love it."

"No," she corrected, "your personal chef is going to cook, and you're going to pass the food off as your own!"

Demetri shook his head. "I don't need to. My dad taught me and my brothers how to cook at a very young age, and I can really throw down in the kitchen."

I bet you can throw down in the bedroom, too.

"I can't stop thinking about that kiss."

"Really? I forgot all about it."

A grin broke out across his face. "Is that right?"

"Yeah, it was terrible. The worst I've ever had."

"Then I'll have to redeem myself."

A warm sensation fell over Angela when Demetri crushed her lips with his mouth. Angela had no control over what happened next. At least that was what she told herself as their hands stroked and caressed and fondled each other.

Lust consumed her. Fully. His kiss was magic, and his touch shot a thousand bolts of electricity up her spine. Overwhelmed with desire, and the adrenaline coursing through her veins, Angela boldly kissed him back. But she didn't stop there. She pushed a hand under his shirt and stroked the length of his chest. His pecs were firm, his biceps were smooth to the touch, and his rock-hard abs were as perfect as she had imagined.

Caressing his powerful upper body turned Angela on. They stood there, in the middle of the aisle, pawing each other. Her body trembled, hard and fast, as his lips, tongue and hands aroused her.

Angela closed her eyes, savoring the moment. She couldn't believe it. She was standing in the food-bank storage room, kissing Demetri Morretti. It was their second kiss in two days, but this one was more passionate, more urgent and so damn erotic her panties were drenched with desire. When Demetri slid his tongue into her mouth and teased her own, she released a loud, savage moan.

"Demetri, where are you? It's showtime!"

Angela jumped back. Her heart was beating in double time, and her thoughts were a scattered mess. Her eyes scanned the room, searching for the owner of the shrill, high-pitched voice. Demetri's publicist pranced up the aisle with a cameraman and fashionably dressed entourage in tow. They were holding gigantic shopping bags and frantically snapping pictures with their cell phones.

Resting a hand on her chest, Angela took a moment to compose herself. Her heart was beating so fast, so out of control, she feared she was having a heart attack.

"Smile," Nichola shouted, clapping her hands. "This is being broadcasted live!"

Then a thin, blond man pointed a camera at them, and for the second time in twenty-four hours, Angela was sure she was going to die of embarrassment.

Chapter 11

"**G**et that camera out of her face." Demetri slid into the cameraman's line of vision and covered the camera lens with his hands. "Shut it off now."

"Sorry, Mr. Morretti. I didn't mean any harm. I was just doing my job."

The guy lowered the camera to his side, and Angela sighed in relief. Glancing down at her clothes, she ensured nothing was unbuttoned or unzipped and adjusted her ivory blouse.

"Demetri, relax." Nichola dumped her shopping bags on the nearest table and rushed over, all smiles and giggles. "This is Jay, your new personal videographer."

"My new what?" Gritting his teeth, he threw his hands out at his side and glanced around the room. "Nichola, what is all of this?"

"What? You told me to buy school supplies and bring them to the Cook County Food Bank, so here I am. Just like you asked."

"Yeah, but I never told you to bring a cameraman and a huge entourage."

"I know. That was my brilliant idea," she said proudly. "We've already filmed the fans and interviewed the food bank director, Mr. Crews. He's quite the character, huh?"

"Fans? What fans?"

Nichola strode over to the window and gestured outside. "Those fans," she said, pointing at the crowd gathered in the parking lot and spilling out onto the side streets. "Don't worry. I brought your security guys in to keep an eye on your Lamborghini. If anyone gets too close, they'll bring them down with ease."

Angela watched Demetri shuffle over to the window. He looked like a man who had the weight of the world on his shoulders. She actually felt sorry for him and wished she could do something to help. He'd come down to the food bank to volunteer, but all his publicist cared about was turning his good deed into a sensational news story.

"Why are there so many people here? I didn't tell anyone I'd be at the food bank."

"That was me again," Nichola said, giggling. "When you called, I posted the info on all the social-media sites, and your fans came out to show their support. Isn't that wonderful?"

"No, Nichola, it's not."

"Of course it is! Think about all the great press you're going to get and how you being here will draw attention to the needs of the food bank."

Curious about what items Demetri's publicist had bought, Angela moved over to the table and peeked inside the shopping bags. There were thousands of dollars' worth of school supplies, and when Angela saw the netbook computers and electronic dictionaries, she let out a shriek.

"This is awesome! Now we have enough school supplies to make backpacks for every student at Englewood Elementary!"

"Angela, are you sure? I'd hate for you to run out of supplies again."

"I'm positive. Thanks so much, Demetri. This is very kind of you."

He shook his head. "Don't thank me. I didn't do the shopping. I just footed the bill!"

"I don't think we've met. I'm Nichola Caruso, Demetri's publicist and personal assistant." Draping her long, thin arms through Demetri's, she leaned casually against his shoulder. "I keep this guy in line, and I love every second of it!"

"I'm Angela Kelly. It's a pleasure to meet you."

"Nichola is a huge fan of your show," Demetri said. "She watches it every day."

"Not every day. Just when there's nothing else on." Her smile was thin, as fake as her spray tan, and when she squeezed Demetri's forearm, her breasts jiggled under her low-cut designer top. "We better get going. I don't want us to be late."

"Late for what? I don't have anything planned today."

"We're visiting sick kids at the children's hospital this afternoon," she explained. "They're expecting us at one o'clock sharp."

Demetri released a deep breath. "Okay, I'll go, but the camera guy isn't coming."

"Of course he is! Why do you think I hired him?"

"No cameras, Nichola."

"Why not?"

"Because this visit to the children's hospital isn't about me. It's about those courageous kids and their families. Pay the videographer and send him home."

"Okay, okay, he won't film you at the hospital," she agreed. "But I'm not sending him home. Jay's flying with us to L.A."

"What's in L.A.?"

"You're making three nightclub appearances tonight, and in the morning you're shooting a Got Milk? commercial."

Demetri stared at Angela, and a smile fell across his lips. "Cancel it. I have plans tomorrow afternoon. Plans I'm not breaking."

"But, Demetri—"

"Nichola, this is not open for discussion. Reschedule it for another day or cancel it altogether. I don't care either way."

"Fine. You're the boss," she said with a shrug. "We'll be waiting outside."

The group shuffled out of the room, wearing long faces, and the storage-room door closed with a bang. When the room was clear, Demetri faced her. "Angela, I'm sorry. I asked

Nichola to drop off some school supplies, but I had no idea she'd bring a cameraman and ten of her closest girlfriends to use as human props."

"Demetri, you don't need to apologize. And thanks again for all of the stuff."

"I could come back when I finish at the hospital and help you finish the backpacks."

"I'll be fine. If I need help, I'll just ask one of the other volunteers."

"No, you won't!"

Angela laughed. "So, I like things to be perfect. Sue me!"

"You have to learn to relax and live in the moment." He drew a hand down her cheek. "I love when the unexpected happens. Don't you?"

"Yeah, as long as it isn't taped and posted on YouTube!"

More laughter filled the room.

"I'm looking forward to our lunch date tomorrow."

"I'll be there at twelve o'clock sharp."

"Of course you will." A grin pinched his lips. "You're always on time, you always play by the rules, and you do everything just right. I'm hoping your good qualities will rub off on me, because according to the media, I'm a screwup who does everything wrong."

His words gave Angela pause. There was something in his tone that troubled her, that made her feel guilty. Her gaze moved over his face. He didn't look like the terse, surly athlete who'd stormed her studio weeks earlier. Instead he appeared sensitive and vulnerable, and there was nothing cocky about that.

"I'll call you later to give you my address."

"But you don't have my phone number."

"Yeah, I do. I've had it for weeks. Got it from your station manager."

"Then why did you ask me for my number last night at Dolce Vita?"

"Because I wanted to see if you were feeling me." He grinned. "I'm glad you are."

He bent down, kissed her on both cheeks and then turned and strode out of the storage room.

Angela sashayed through Woodfield Mall with a smile on her lips and glitzy shopping bags in her hands. Slipping on her diamond-studded sunglasses, she sailed through the sliding glass doors and out into the warm spring night.

The air smelled of tobacco, but despite the putrid odor, her stomach released a loud, audible growl. Angela had been so busy trying on clothes and fretting over how she looked in each outfit, she'd forgotten to eat lunch. But after countless trips between the clearance racks and the fitting room in her favorite store, she'd finally found an outfit to wear for her lunch date tomorrow with Demetri. And not just any old thing. A dress that would make the man drool all over his Chicago Royals jersey.

Angela shook her head, and the thought, out of her mind. "It's not a date. It's a business lunch," she told herself, unlocking the trunk of her car and dumping her purchases inside.

Anxious to get home and pair her dress with the right shoes and accessories, she slid into the front seat of her car and started the engine. Hearing her cell phone ring, she rummaged around in her purse until she found it.

"Hello?" she said, putting her cell phone to her ear seconds later.

"Angela, it's Salem. Sorry I didn't get back to you last night. That lousy hockey game went into triple overtime, and my husband wouldn't leave!"

Angela laughed. "It's no problem. I understand."

"How did everything go at Dolce Vita?"

You don't want to know, she thought, releasing a deep sigh. But instead of ratting out her crew to her boss, she said, "Everything went great. We did a ton of interviews, got some amazing shots from the roof and taped a group of college kids singing the show's theme song!"

"Everything went okay? Really? That's not what Phil and the guys said."

"What?" The word blasted out of Angela's mouth. "What exactly did they say?"

"They said you went to the ladies' room and never came back!"

"No. They. Didn't." Angela was gripping her BlackBerry phone so hard, she was surprised it didn't shatter into a million pieces. "They're lying! That's not what happened!"

"Okay," she said slowly, "so why don't you tell me what really happened, because Phil's version of events was just too fanciful to believe."

Slumping back in her seat, Angela recounted every moment of the previous night—except for the kiss she'd shared with Demetri and the time they'd spent alone together in the VIP lounge. Thoughts of Demetri kept Angela from firing up her car, driving to the station and kicking Phil's country ass. How dare he double-cross her! Was he in cahoots with the lead anchor or just trying to make himself look good? "Wait until I see Phil on Monday," she thought aloud. "I'm going to make him wish we'd never met!"

"Slow your roll!" Salem laughed. "Leave Phil and the rest of his crew to me. I have something extra-special in store for them."

A sigh of relief escaped Angela's lips. "I'd never bail on an assignment," she said, shivering at the thought. "I'm so glad you believe me, Salem. It means the world to me."

"Of course I believe you! You're one of the most diligent and hardworking newscasters I've ever met."

Angela smiled, but inside she was still fighting mad.

"I've got good news and bad news. Which do you want first?"

"The bad. I'll forget all about it when I hear the good news."

"I presented your proposal this morning at the producers' meeting, and the team hated it. They said the topic was too dark and heavy for *Eye on Chicago.*"

Angela's shoulders sagged in defeat. To ward off tears, she pressed her eyes shut and bit the inside of her cheek. She felt as if she'd been kicked in the stomach. The pain in her chest was so sharp, she could barely breathe.

"They want to keep the show fun and current," Salem explained, her tone loud and exuberant. "We want you to play it up for the cameras and flirt even more with your male celebrity guests. That's your niche, Angela! That's where you shine!"

Strangling a groan, Angela slumped back in her seat, feeling deflated and defeated. She was more than just a pretty face, and she had the education to prove it. Working for WJN-TV was a dream come true, but Angela was sick of having the same argument with her boss. Viewers tuned in to see her on Thursday nights—not the show's producers—so why was she letting *them* tell *her* what to do?

"What's the good news?" she asked, unable to hide her disappointment and anxious to get off the phone.

"Earl is having hip surgery next month, and he'll be out six to eight weeks."

"That's too bad. I hope everything goes okay."

"How do you feel about filling in for him?"

Angela shot up in her seat. "Seriously? You want me to do the live morning show?"

"Yeah, I think you'd be great," she said with a laugh. "I already know you'll be on time. You're always the first one at the station!"

"Howard will never go for it. He hates having female co-hosts."

"Don't worry. We go way back. I can handle him."

"Do you think the head-ups will go for it?"

"They already have!"

Angela squealed like a teenage girl on a roller coaster. "Really? No way!"

"Once they heard that you'd scored an exclusive sit-down interview with Demetri Morretti at his Lake County estate, they were putty in my hands."

"But…Demetri hasn't agreed to be on my show."

"Not yet," Salem quipped, "but he will. I have complete faith in you."

"I'm glad one of us does." Angela felt her smile fade and her excitement wane. Resisting the urge to scream in frustration, she took a deep breath and channeled positive thoughts. None came. All she could think about was how her good mood had been shot to hell. First, her crew lied about her and then her boss fabricated a story about her show to impress the studio heads. What else could possibly go wrong today?

"Stay close to your phone, Angela. I might need you to cover the hot-dog-eating contest out at Six Flags this afternoon."

It's true, she decided, shaking her head. *Bad things do happen in threes!*

"I have to run. The in-laws are coming over for dinner, and I'm still in my bathrobe."

"Okay. Talk to you later."

"Oh, and, Angela, one more thing." Her tone grew serious. "The next time Demetri Morretti shows up at the food bank, text me immediately, because *that's* breaking news!"

Chapter 12

"Are you sure you don't want me to stay?" Nichola asked, climbing down the front steps of Demetri's Lake County estate and joining him in his Mediterranean-style garden. "Angela Kelly's a piranha in Gucci pumps. You might need backup."

"Go home, Nichola. I'll be fine." Demetri pointed his silver watering can at the terra-cotta pots and moved slowly down the row of leafy plants. He wanted his publicist to leave so he could go inside and get ready for his date in peace. It had been months since he'd invited a woman to his house, and he wanted everything to be perfect—the food, the ambience, his appearance. Angela was in a league of her own, and Demetri knew if he wanted to make headway with her this afternoon he had to bring his A game. "Have fun at your sister's bachelorette party."

"I have a bad feeling about Angela Kelly coming here."

"Don't worry. It's all good. We made a truce."

Nichola's eyes thinned and shrunk into a glare. "You're not interested in her romantically, are you?"

"Who, me?" Demetri coughed to clear the lump in his throat. He didn't want anyone—especially his brothers—to know he was interested in Angela. In part because he knew they'd laugh him out of the room. He was attracted to the very woman who had dissed him on national television, and more shocking, he'd been thinking about her nonstop since they'd kissed at Dolce Vita. *If that isn't crazy, I don't know what is!* he thought, shaking his head.

"This is a business lunch," he said. "We'll talk, and then she'll be on her way."

"And you're sure you don't want me to stay and run in-terference?"

"I'm a grown man. I don't need anyone to hold my hand or fight my battles," he said, trying to keep the lid on his frustration. "And besides, Angela Kelly isn't a threat. I can handle her."

"Speak of the devil…"

Demetri glanced over his shoulder. When he saw Angela exit her navy blue jeep, the fine hairs on the back of his neck shot up. Wide-eyed, he watched her glide up the mosaic-tile steps with the grace of the First Lady. Her walk was poetry in motion. Mesmerized, he stood beside the decorative oak bench, speechless. Angela's belted mustard dress showcased her curves, and her ankle-tie pumps gave her a sexy bad-girl edge. Her classy, sophisticated look was a home run, and he was so aroused by the sight of her mouthwatering shape, his brain turned to mush.

Smiling brightly, Angela waved as she approached. Her long, black hair flapped wildly in the light spring breeze, drawing his gaze up from her hips to her beautiful oval face.

Demetri felt the urge to run, to sprint full speed ahead to-ward her. It was impossible to be around Angela and not feel good. Yesterday at the food bank, they'd talked and joked and laughed with ease. He'd felt like his old, jovial self, like the person he used to be before the media started gunning for him and his injuries began piling up.

"Welcome to my home." Taking her hand, Demetri leaned in and kissed Angela on each cheek. It was a standard Italian greeting, but there was nothing innocent about the surge of blood flow he felt below his belt. He wanted to take Angela in his arms and tease her soft, moist lips with his mouth, but for now holding her hand was enough. "You're early. I wasn't expecting you for another half an hour."

"It's raining in the city, and the streets are crazy, so I decided to leave early," she explained. "Surprisingly, I made it here in record time."

Nichola appeared, like a puff of smoke, scowling in earnest. She looked Angela up and down but addressed Demetri. "I'll see you tomorrow," she said, her voice terse. "Don't forget, the rep from Rolex International will be here at one to discuss your new signature line."

"I won't forget. Have a good time with your girls tonight."

"I will, but if you need anything, just call. It doesn't matter how late." She gave a curt nod and then hustled down the steps to her white sports car.

Angela was glad to see Demetri's publicist go. Not because she wanted to be alone with him, but because there was something about the petite strawberry blonde that unnerved her.

"Perfect timing," Demetri said, squeezing her hand. "I was just finishing up in the garden."

"You garden?"

"I love it. Being outside and working with my hands is very therapeutic. If not for the helicopters buzzing around here all day, I'd probably sleep on the lawn!"

"A baseball star with a green thumb? Who would have thought?"

Demetri chuckled. "I'm no Martha Stewart, but I'm getting there."

The estate was as calm as it was scenic and dotted with dozens of trees, flower beds and white stone structures. The soothing sound of rushing water added to the tranquillity of Demetri's ten-thousand-square-foot home. The fragrant scent of jasmine was heavy in the air.

"Wow, your garden has everything. Fruits, herbs, vegetables, even colored tulips…" Angela broke off speaking and pointed at the gazebo. "The flowers you sent me at Dolce Vita came from your garden?"

"Yeah, I handpicked them." His smile was proud. "I read on your blog how much you love tulips, so I figured I'd make you an original Demetri Morretti bouquet."

His words stunned her. There was more to him than bar brawls and drag racing. "What were you doing poking around on my blog?" she asked, her tone playful. "You weren't trying to hack into it, were you?"

"No, I was doing some research." He winked and gave her hand a light squeeze. "Do you mind waiting inside the living room while I run upstairs to change?"

"You don't need to change. You look great." Angela immediately wished she could stick the words back in her mouth. But it was true. He looked handsome in his white, cuffed shirt and khaki shorts, and when a wide, boyish grin broke out across his lips, Angela knew she'd said too much.

"I'm glad we didn't meet up at a restaurant or bar," he said, still smiling. "Because I'd have to beat the guys off of you with my lucky baseball bat!"

Angela's mouth dried. His words floored her, and when he gave her another peck on the cheek, goose bumps erupted over her skin. It was bad enough Demetri was still holding her hand, but now she had to contend with the tingles pricking her flesh, too.

"Let's eat. Everything's set up on the patio for us."

"Lunch can wait," Angela said. "First, you have to give me a tour of this stunning estate."

Demetri chuckled. "It would be my pleasure. Just let me buzz one of the groundsmen and ask them to bring up a golf cart."

"Can we walk instead?"

"Are you sure? It's almost two acres."

"I'm sure. It's gorgeous out here, and since I skipped my

morning session with my trainer, I could really use the exercise."

Angela heard her cell phone ring but ignored it. Rodney had been blowing up her phone all day, but she didn't feel like talking to him. Or seeing him, either. Her dad had invited him to the Harlem Globetrotters show, and Angela would rather skip the game than listen to her brother's tired apologies. "How long have you lived here?"

"Seven years. I have a condo near the Royals training facility, but I spend most of my time here. It's peaceful out here and I love being near the lake…"

As they strode around the grounds, discussing all of the unique features of his lavish, custom-made home, Angela felt herself start to relax. Flirting and laughing with Demetri was exhilarating, and she loved his fun, playful mood. It was hard to believe this was the same guy who'd stormed into her studio weeks ago and threatened to sue her. But it was. And although Angela was anxious to finalize the details of their interview, she sensed that now was not the right time and decided she would broach the subject during lunch.

"I saw your report from Club Eclipse last night," Demetri said, leading her past the greenhouse. "Every time I turn to WJN-TV, you're on it. Do you work twenty-four seven?"

"No. I have days off just like everybody else."

He raised an eyebrow and wore a teasing smile. "And what do you do on these supposed days off?"

"I go to the movies, peruse used-book stores and go club hopping with my girls. You know, the usual single-girl stuff!"

Demetri chuckled. "So, you're not seeing anyone special right now?"

"No one worth mentioning."

"You like kicking it with athletes."

"No," she corrected, "I like sports. There's a big difference."

He wore a confused face. "Care to elaborate?"

"I'm a tomboy in a skirt, and guys love that I don't mind getting down and dirty."

Angela laughed when Demetri's jaw fell open.

"I grew up playing sports, fishing and going to auto shows with my dad and younger brother, so naturally I get along really well with guys," she said with a shrug.

"Your mom didn't mind you playing with G.I. Joe instead of Barbie?" he teased.

"She was never around, and when she died five years ago, I grew even closer to my dad." Angela didn't want to talk about her mom or the pain of never really knowing her, so she moved the conversation along. "I enjoy activities the average woman doesn't, and men like that." She paused. "And for the record, I don't pursue men. They pursue me."

"But you've dated an athlete in every major sport."

"No, that's not true. I've never dated a hockey player or a soccer star." Angela wore a cheeky smile. "But I'm still young. There's plenty of time for that."

"Not if things go the way I hope." Desire twinkled in his eyes and warmed his rich, smooth baritone. Demetri slid a hand around her waist and hugged her to his side. "You must be starving. How about some lunch?"

When they reached the sprawling multilevel patio, which was handsomely furnished with tan couches, circular tables and a stone fireplace, Demetri pulled out her chair. Once she was seated, he filled her glass with Chianti and her gold-rimmed plate with lobster and pasta.

"This is some house," Angela said, admiring her lavish surroundings. The estate was unlike anything she had ever seen. She was blown away by the sheer size and grandeur of the twenty-room mansion. "Do you live here alone?"

"Not if I can help it!" Demetri chuckled. "My younger cousins crash here a few nights a week, and my parents and brothers stay with me whenever they're in town."

"Wow, that's different."

"That's the Italian way. My family means everything to me, and without them I'm nothing." He paused to taste his wine. "My happiest memories are with my relatives, and even though they can be a pain in the ass sometimes, I love when we all get together and hang out."

"Is that why you're taking eighty-five family members with you on vacation?"

Demetri nodded. "I've been planning these trips since my rookie season, and each trip is better than the last. We're going on a Caribbean cruise in August, and I'm real hyped about it."

"I love my dad, but I couldn't imagine traveling with him for a week, let alone a month!"

"Then you should consider joining us. All of your travel expenses will be covered, and for three weeks you won't have to worry about a thing."

"Demetri, that's crazy." Angela draped a silk napkin onto her lap and picked up her gold utensils. "I can't go with you and your family overseas. They probably hate me for trashing you on my show, and besides, we barely know each other."

"I know a lot about you."

"Sure you do," she teased. "You've been secretly stalking me for weeks. I knew it!"

A knowing smile crossed his lips. Lowering his fork, he studied her closely. "You graduated from the University of Chicago with a degree in communications, you hate musicals, you're addicted to coffee and designer shoes, and the only movie to ever make you cry is a French film called *A Kiss in Paris.* And not because you thought it was a great love story, but because the acting was so bad!"

Angela groaned and covered her face with her hands. "You read the first entry in my blog? The one way back in 2004?"

"No," he said, correcting her. "I read *every* entry."

"Now I'm really embarrassed. That means you saw all my

pictures in my video diary. I had terrible hair when I was in college and no fashion sense whatsoever."

"No, you didn't, and you looked great in your volleyball uniform." Demetri winked and pointed his fork at his chest. "I made your Hot 100 List that year, so you know I'm happy!"

"I typed that blog while I was watching your rookie game, and every time you came to bat, I got goose bumps," she confessed. "You were amazing that night, Demetri."

"My rookie season was the best year of my life."

"Was? Don't you still love playing baseball?"

"I'm getting old, and—"

Angela cut him off. "Old? You're only thirty-two!"

"Yeah, but I've been in the league since I was twenty." He chewed his lobster slowly and then took a long drink of wine. "If I just had to play ball, I could deal, but the paparazzi, the crazed fans and the constant demands on my time are taxing. I'm not complaining or bitching about how unfair life is, but sometimes the glare of the spotlight is just too bright."

Angela nodded. "I've heard other celebrities say the same thing. From the outside looking in, it seems like you have the perfect life, but I guess things aren't always as it seems."

"You can say that again." He wore a wry smile, but his voice betrayed his true feelings. "I love this estate, and it has a ton of cool stuff in it, but sometimes I feel like a caged animal. There are so many places I can't go, so many things I can't do anymore unless I take my security, and sometimes it's just not worth the hassle."

"What do you miss doing?"

"Little things, like going to the movies, surfing at Montrose Beach or taking the L line up to the field and—"

"Liar!" she shrieked. "You do *not* miss riding the smelly, crowded L train!"

"You're right. I don't. Bad example."

Laughter bubbled out of Angela's lips, and Demetri smiled.

And when he served dessert several minutes later, and she broke out in a cheer, he had a good hard chuckle.

"I love strawberry gelato," Angela cooed, spooning some into her mouth and savoring the cold, refreshing taste. "I could eat a whole tub. And I have!"

"Do you like to play pool?"

"Of course. Who doesn't?"

"Practically every woman I've ever met!" Demetri chuckled. "After we finish dessert, we should go inside and hang out in my media room. We can play pool, listen to music and…"

Hearing her cell phone ring, Angela discreetly slid a hand inside her purse and rummaged around for her BlackBerry. When she saw her brother's name pop up on the screen, she hurled her cell phone back into the bottom of her purse.

"Your phone's been ringing off the hook all afternoon." Demetri wore a pensive expression on his face. "Someone must want to reach you bad."

"Yeah, probably to ask for another loan," she grumbled, rolling her eyes to the gray, overcast sky. "I wish Rodney would quit blowing up my phone and lose my number altogether."

"Rodney? Who's that? An ex-boyfriend or something?"

"Yuck." Angela wrinkled her nose. "Rodney's my kid brother."

"And you guys don't talk?"

"Not anymore."

Demetri sat straight in his chair. "Why not?"

"I'd rather not talk about it."

"Did he put you in harm's way?"

"No, of course not. Rodney would never hurt me." Angela sucked her teeth. "Lying and stealing is right up his alley, though."

"Angela, you should try to work things out with your brother. He's your flesh and blood. Don't ever forget that. Friends come and go, but family is forever."

"I'm so mad at Rodney, I don't want anything to do with him ever again."

"Forgiveness isn't forgetting or condoning bad behavior, Angela. It's a gift to yourself."

His words gave her pause, struck a chord with her.

"For years, I was mad at the world and everyone who had ever betrayed me, but ever since I started reading the teachings of eastern philosophers, my attitude's changed for the better." Leaning forward, Demetri took her hand in his and gave it a light squeeze. His touch was gentle, not what she'd expected, but welcome.

"Forgiveness is a gift you give to yourself, because once you forgive the person who hurt you, you're free of the hurt, anger and resentment that's been eating you up inside."

Scared her emotions would get the best of her and she'd dissolve into tears, Angela looked up into the sky. A curtain of dark, thick clouds eclipsed the sun, and the air held the scent of rain. Angela didn't know when the weather had taken a turn for the worst, probably somewhere between dessert and her third glass of Chianti, but she'd been too busy chatting to notice. "What you're saying makes sense, Demetri, but it's hard to forgive someone who keeps hurting you. Rodney's twenty-one, but he still acts like a teenager," she complained. "It's time he quit running the streets and did something productive with his life instead of stealing from me."

"It sounds like he's going through a rough time. You should be there for him."

"And let him rip me off again? No way."

"Haven't you ever done something you regretted? Something you wish you could undo?" he asked softly. "I know I have. Too many times to count."

"I've made mistakes, but I've never intentionally hurt anyone."

Yeah, but if your dad knew how you paid for your uni-

versity tuition, he'd be deeply ashamed, said a small voice in her head.

Angela stared down at her dessert bowl. She didn't want to think about her freshman year in college or the job she'd reluctantly taken after her scholarship had fallen through. Those memories belonged in the past, hidden in the deepest corner of her mind. Her father would never forgive her if he knew what she'd done, and she couldn't bear to disappoint her dad. Not after all the sacrifices he'd made for her over the years. "Let's talk about something more interesting," she said, anxious to change the subject, "like you being a guest on *Eye on Chicago.*"

He lifted the wine bottle and tipped some into her glass. "I checked my schedule, and I'm free on May seventeenth. Does that work for you?"

"I'll make it work!"

Thunder boomed, and streaks of lightning lit up the sky.

"We better get inside before it starts to—" Demetri broke off speaking and jumped to his feet when raindrops pelted his face. "Follow me!"

Angela swiped her purse off the nearby chair and grabbed Demetri's outstretched hand. Moving as fast as her high-heel-clad feet would take her, she sprinted across the patio, through the French doors and into the kitchen.

Scared she was going to drip water on the white marble floor, Angela stood perfectly still on the mat in front of the back door. The main floor was as wide and as long as a football field and decked out in the best home decor money could buy. Soaring columns, dark velvet drapes and leather furniture gave the room a strong masculine feel, and the burgundy color scheme was striking.

"I'll be right back," Demetri said. "I'm going to go grab some towels."

Shaking uncontrollably, Angela rubbed her hands over her

shoulders. Her hair was a tangled mess, her dress was stuck to her wet body, and water was oozing from her high heels.

A loud crash drew her gaze to the side window. Outside, the wind battered the plants hanging on the porch. It was raining so hard, Angela couldn't even see the pool. To stop her teeth from chattering, she clamped her lips together and rocked slowly from side to side.

"Sorry I took so long." Wearing a concerned face, Demetri wrapped the fluffy, white towel he was holding around her shoulders and drew her to his side. His scent had a calming, soothing effect on her. Closing her eyes, she rested her head on his chest. His shirt was damp, but Angela felt warm, cozy and safe.

"I could stay here with you forever like this," he murmured against her ear.

Me, too, Angela thought but didn't dare say. *This feels so right.* You *feel so right.*

"Are you okay?"

"I'm fine. It was just a little rain."

"I'm not talking about the rain."

Angela's eyes fluttered open, and when his dark, predatory gaze slipped over her flesh, her stomach muscles tightened. Demetri was trouble. Assertive. Confident. Determined to have his way. And Angela wanted him. More than she'd ever wanted anyone before.

"You had several glasses of Chianti with lunch."

"Demetri, I'm not drunk."

"Are you sure?" he questioned, cupping her chin and cradling it in his palm. "I don't want to take any chances."

"I'm far too responsible to ever drink and drive—"

"You're not leaving."

"I'm not?" Angela gave him a puzzled, bewildered look. "Then why are you worried about how much I had to drink?"

Lowering his mouth, he brushed it ever so gently against

her lips. "Because when you wake up in the morning, I want you to remember every sinfully wicked thing that's going to happen tonight."

Chapter 13

"That's it, baby! Right there! Right there!" Angela panted, gripping Demetri's head with her hands and pulling his long, nimble tongue deeper inside her. Collapsing against the mound of silk pillow cushions, she tossed and turned, wiggled and withered beneath him. His touch was electric, made her body hot and wet all over. "Damn, baby…"

His hands traveled to her breasts, reverently cupping each one. Demetri was good with his hands. No, great, the best. He kissed her nipple slow and tender with his soft, warm mouth. Angela felt her eyes roll in the back of her head. Her breathing became labored, difficult. She tried to the best of her ability to think straight. She didn't remember how they'd gotten to the master bedroom or even which floor they were on. The past hour had been a body-tingling ride, one filled with sensuous highs, delicious French kisses and so much grunting and groaning, they sounded like wild animals.

But that was exactly how Angela felt. Wild, brazen, out of control. And it was the best feeling in the world. Demetri brought out the beast in her—the naughty, erotic side she didn't even know she had. And tonight Angela didn't care about being perfect or looking perfect. All she cared about was pleasing Demetri.

Rain smacked against the bedroom windows, and although the blinds were open, the master suite was bathed in darkness. The perfume of their desire filled the air. The scent was so powerful, Angela got drunk off its fragrance. Out of sorts, the room spinning around her, she closed her eyes and stroked Demetri's broad, muscular shoulders. He knew exactly what she wanted and gave it to her. His hands knew where to go, what to do, and every flick of his tongue was more urgent and hungrier than the last.

Angela moaned his name over and over again. She couldn't help it. Without a doubt, he was the sexiest, most skilled lover she had ever had. Lying on Demetri's custom-made bed in nothing but her jewelry should have terrified Angela, but it didn't. He'd undressed her slowly with a look of admiration in his eyes. And by the time he carried her over to his king-size bed, she was desperate to make love to him. Lust filled her. Made it impossible to think, to breathe. She wanted him to touch her, to stroke her, to feel every inch of his erection inside her.

"Demetri," she whispered, her tone a breathless pant. "Come here."

He joined her at the front of the bed and wrapped his arms around her.

"We'll cuddle later. I need you inside me. *Now.*"

"Not yet, Angela. There's no rush. We have all night…." Nuzzling his chin against the curve of her ear, he whispered, "I'm going to love you like you've never been loved before, and when you come, you're going to feel the strongest emotion you've ever felt."

Well, I'll be damned, she thought, overwhelmed by the rush his words gave her.

Longing for the taste of his lips, Angela draped her arms around his shoulders and pressed her lips hard against his mouth. Demetri reeled back against the headboard. It was a deep, passionate kiss—one that put Angela in the mood for hard, fast sex. His lips tasted like wine, his kiss was as exhilarating as his touch, and his whispered promises touched the depth of her heart. Tilting her head to the side, she swirled her tongue around his mouth. She licked and sucked the tip of his tongue as if it were coated in chocolate syrup.

Demetri placed light kisses down her cheeks and along the side of her neck. Using his lips and hands to make sweet love to her flesh, he covered every inch of her body in fervent kisses and tender caresses. Using the tip of his tongue, he licked from her nipples to her stomach to the insides of her thighs. His hands traveled the length of her waist, and the finger he slipped between her legs to stroke her clit only fanned the flames.

Demetri stroked her butt with his hands. His touch made her ache for more—more sucking, more teasing, more grinding. Angela loved the way he was making her feel and couldn't get enough of his kiss. But tonight she wanted to be in control of her pleasure. She wanted to please Demetri, wanted to erase every other woman from his mind, and Angela knew just what to do to make it happen.

She eased herself onto Demetri's lap. Stroking his shoulders, she watched in anticipation as he opened his side drawer, took out a condom and rolled it onto his long, thick erection. Angela licked her lips. This was it. The moment she'd been waiting for, the moment she'd been dreaming about for weeks.

Demetri pressed a hand to her cheek and stared deep into her eyes. "Are you sure about this, Angela? I don't want you to have any regrets."

"My only regret is waiting this long."

He brushed his nose against hers, and she let out a giggle.

"Quit teasing me, Demetri. I want this, and I want you."

"I'm just making sure."

Angela couldn't tell Demetri the truth, that she'd been fantasizing about him ever since he'd stormed into her television studio. Scared of where their attraction would lead, she'd told her friends, her boss and anyone else who would listen that she wasn't interested in the baseball star. But Angela couldn't deny how his touch made her feel. She felt alive, as if she were spinning upside down on a Ferris wheel. Being with Demetri was the ultimate rush, a shot of adrenaline that blew her mind. He did it for her. Made her hot, revved her engines.

And when Demetri slid his erection inside her, shivers ripped down her back. Pleasure filled her, drenched her skin like the raindrops pelting the bedroom windows. Gripping the headboard, she rotated her hips at a pace that intensified her need. Demetri whispered soft words against her ears as he nipped at her earlobes and the side of her neck. Seemingly knowing what turned her on, he cupped her breasts, then teased and sucked each erect nipple into his open mouth.

Angela moaned and screamed in ecstasy. She was losing it, coming apart at the seams. She felt exhilarated, as if she'd been shot a hundred feet in the air. A moan escaped out of her lips. Then another. Her heart was pounding, racing, dribbling like a ball. Angela never imagined a man could be this giving, this unselfish in the bedroom. Feeling tears fill her eyes, she blinked them away and bit down on her lip. Demetri ran his lips along her arms, playfully nipping and licking her warm flesh.

Angela pushed her breasts into his face, stuck her nipples into his mouth so he could have another taste. Reverently, he kissed and stroked each breast. Throwing her head back, she moaned to the high heavens. This was euphoria. The most thrilling and erotic moment of her life. Nothing compared to making love to Demetri. Nothing. Not a five-figure raise. Not a free swag bag from the Grammys. Not even meeting her idol, Diane Sawyer, at last year's Emmy Awards.

"I knew from the moment I saw you that you were the one."

A grin pinched her lips. "Was that before or *after* you threatened to sue me?"

"I was never going to sue you. I just wanted to get your attention."

"Well, *Mr. Athlete of the Year,* you certainly did that."

"Angela, I've fallen hard for you." His voice deepened,

grew thick with feeling and emotion. "You're the only woman I want. The only woman I need."

Angela stared at Demetri. His gaze was intense, locked in on hers, and he wore a dreamy, lopsided smile.

"I knew the second I walked into your studio that I was done. I tried to fight our attraction, tried to ignore it, but the harder I tried to get you out of my mind, the more I thought about you, fantasized about you and dreamed about being inside you."

I know exactly how you feel. Angela rubbed her hand along his shoulders and chest. Everything about Demetri turned her on. His voice, his scent, his sensitivity, how he tenderly caressed and kissed her. He was different. *This* was different. Tonight was about more than just sex. Her heart was in it, her soul and her mind, too. And for as long as she lived, she'd never forget how amazing it had felt when he'd kissed her for the very first time.

"I'm a hundred percent ready to commit to you, Angela. Not for a day or a week or a month, but forever." He placed his palms against her cheeks and kissed from her eyelids to her earlobes and back again. Love showed in his eyes and covered the length of his face. "Give me the opportunity to spoil you, to love you, to cook for you…"

His words left her wide-eyed and tongue-tied. Demetri had a brusque exterior and walked around with a chip on his shoulder, but inside he was a softy. The reigning bad boy of professional baseball wasn't an arrogant jerk; he was a deeply sensitive man who wore his heart on his sleeve, and each caress and kiss made her feel like a cherished jewel.

"You are absolute perfection," he praised. "You're the sassiest, most vibrant and engaging woman I've ever met. And did I mention sexy as hell?"

"I am pretty wonderful, aren't I?"

In one swift motion, Demetri flipped Angela onto her back

and pinned her hands above her head. "Yes, baby, you are, and don't you ever forget it."

Stretched out, lying face-to-face, with their bodies meshed together, Angela felt at home in Demetri's arms. He slowly slid his erection inside her, one delicious inch at a time. Clamping her legs around his waist produced the most exquisite sensation. Quivering, shaking, trembling all over, she fought to stay in the moment and in control. As Demetri loved her, he shared his heart. He spoke about their future, about all the wonderful places he wanted to take her and activities he wanted them to do. His earnest, heartfelt confession blew her away.

"You have no idea how amazing it feels being inside you...."

Angela loved everything Demetri was doing and saying. Using her fingernails, she tenderly stroked his shoulders and the length of his back. She held him, snuggled close as he quickened his pace. Angela showered kisses on his lips, along the slope of his jaw and the front of his neck. Her heart opened and filled with unspeakable love. This wasn't just a night of carnal pleasure. It was a reawakening of her soul and her entire being. There had been a hollowness in her heart for years, but tonight, in Demetri's bed, in his arms, she felt whole. But Angela didn't tell Demetri that. She never talked about her feelings and didn't really know how to. Besides, telling him the truth would only complicate things, and their relationship was already complicated enough.

Demetri hiked her legs in the air, spread her wide open. And three deep, powerful thrusts later, his climax hit. His muscles strained; his body tensed. Angela pressed her lips together to trap a scream inside, one she was sure would shatter every window in the estate. She felt as if she were outside herself, in a different world. A world filled with passion and desire and love. Demetri was a tender, gentle lover who told her she was strong and beautiful and special. Pleasing her was his only priority, and his words aroused and excited her. Never had she felt such love, such compassion in a lover's touch, and when her orgasm struck—knocking the very breath out of her—Angela knew she'd never be the same again.

Chapter 14

Demetri stared at the silver breakfast tray, realizing he'd forgotten the fruit, and strode back over to the stainless-steel fridge. He had to hurry. Angela was still sleeping in the master bedroom, and he wanted to be back upstairs with breakfast waiting on the deck before she woke up. Sunshine splashed through the open windows, and the glass chimes, hanging on the patio, tinkled as the wind whipped through the backyard.

Demetri smiled to himself. He felt exhilarated, on top of the world. As if he'd just smashed a fastball out of Skyline Field. Angela had put it on him, and not just in the bedroom. They had a deep connection, one he'd never experienced with any other woman before. Just the thought of her made him break out into an ear-to-ear grin.

As he sliced the pineapple and arranged it on the gold-rimmed plates, he relived every moment of their evening together. The long stroll around his estate, eating and chatting outside on the patio, that explosive kiss that rocked his world. He thought about their passionate lovemaking and the long, heartfelt talk they'd had afterward.

"Relationships are too complicated," she'd said, her tone matter-of-fact. "That's why I play the field and leave having husbands and babies to my girlfriends."

"I used to think that way, but things changed when I turned thirty. I started wanting a wife and a family of my own."

"My ultimate goal is to become an international news correspondent, not to have more kids than Octomom," she said with a laugh. "And I'm my working my butt off to make it happen."

"News correspondents get the toughest, most dangerous assignments," he'd pointed out, tightening his hold around her waist. Without makeup and designer clothes on, Angela looked like a fresh-faced college student, and Demetri loved how it felt having her in his arms. "They travel all over the world and are away from their friends and family for long stretches of time."

"I know. That part sucks, but I want to cover the stories shaping and impacting the world."

"Dating across three continents could be challenging."

"Challenging? It would be impossible. I suck at relationships, and besides, no guy would ever put in the time or effort to make it work."

"I would." Demetri put a lot of thought into what he said next. He didn't want to scare Angela off, but he had to tell her what was in his heart. "As long as we're honest about our feelings and put each other first, we can survive anything, Angela. Even international time zones."

He felt her body tense. "Demetri, you're a great guy and last night was amazing, but that's all it was. One night. I'm not looking for anything serious."

"Are you sure about that?" Demetri lowered his mouth and slowly brushed his lips across hers. She giggled, which made him smile. "I think we'd make a great team."

"We want different things. You want a family, and I love the single life."

"No, you don't. That's just a cover you use to keep people away."

Lips pursed, she turned away and stared out into the darkness. "That's not true."

"I think it is."

"Well, you're wrong."

Feelings of guilt and regret quickly consumed him. He'd

said too much, pushed too hard, and now her wall was back up. To smooth things over, Demetri kissed her cheek, the tip of her earlobe and then her shoulder blade. "I've been in lust a lot, and like a few times, but I've never fallen this hard or this fast for anyone," he confessed. "You're special to me, Angela, and I want us to be exclusive."

"Demetri, that's crazy. We just met!"

He started to speak, but Angela spoke over him.

"Let's just see what happens. No pressure, no expectations, no promises, okay?"

"Is there someone else?" Demetri heard the tremor in his voice, but there was nothing he could do about it. He couldn't stomach the thought of Angela being with another man and didn't want to share her with anyone else. "Are you sleeping with other men?"

Angela slid a hand down his chest, gripped his erection and stroked it until it came to life. "Why would I need someone else when I have all this?"

Then she whipped off the blanket, climbed onto his lap and rode him until he climaxed.

Demetri thought about the bubble bath they took afterward. While stretched out in the tub, they chatted about his baseball career, his ongoing rehab for his injured shoulder and the stress of being a celebrity. Angela didn't talk much, but she did answer all of his questions honestly. Demetri knew she had a string of ex-boyfriends, guys she'd dumped as soon as things got serious, but he wasn't a hit-it-and-quit-it type of man. And deep in his heart he knew Angela was the one. The only one. The right one. He wouldn't push her, though. He couldn't risk Angela shutting him out. Not when he wanted her to be his girl.

The phone rang, pulling Demetri out of his thoughts. He checked the number on the screen and then hit the speaker button. "Hey, Nicco, what's up?" he asked, glancing at the video screen. His brother's eyes were bloodshot, and his rumpled suit looked as though it had seen better days. "You look like hell. Lost big at the casino again, huh?"

"No, a bunch of punks broke into the restaurant near Miami Beach and trashed the place." His voice was hoarse and sounded as if he had a cold. "There's over fifty thousand dollars' worth of damage, and the new security system I had installed last week was destroyed."

"Damn, bro, I'm sorry. What did the cops say? Do they have any leads?"

"Nothing yet. They promised to keep me posted, but I'm not holding my breath."

"Do you want me to come out there? I could fly down this afternoon."

"You sound just like Rafael. He's in Madrid on business, but he's ready to come down here and lead the police investigation himself!"

The brothers laughed.

"That's what we do. We stick together." Demetri leaned against the counter. "Just say the word and I'm there."

Nicco shook his head. "You can't come to Miami. You're filming your new Nike commercial with Rashawn 'The Glove' Bishop this week, remember? Rashawn and his wife, Yasmin, were at the restaurant a few nights ago, and he sounded real excited about it."

"It can always be rescheduled."

"Don't bother. I won't be around anyways. I'm going to Argentina for a few days."

"What's in Argentina?"

"You mean besides babes, sunshine and a guaranteed good time?" Nicco chuckled. "How are things in Chi-Town? Not still tripping about that Angela Kelly broad, I hope."

At the sound of her name, a grin exploded across Demetri's face. He glanced up at the ceiling, thoughts of their night together at the front of his mind. Angela was the closest thing to perfection, the only woman he'd ever met to stop him dead in his tracks. She knew who she was and what she wanted. And that was damn sexy. He'd been with a lot of women and thought he'd seen it all when it came to the bedroom, but nothing compared to making love to Angela. He loved the sounds she made in bed, loved how she screamed and lost control. And the force of her orgasm always triggered his own. They'd made love three times last night, but just thinking about her juicy, pink lips made him hunger for another taste.

"Damn, bro, what's going on? You're smiling like a kid in a candy store!"

"I guess you could say Angela and I finally came to a mutual agreement."

Nicco straightened in his chair and moved so close to the LCD screen that Demetri could see the dark worry lines under his hazel eyes. "Did this *agreement* involve getting buck naked and going at it on your pool table?" he asked, wetting his lips with his tongue. "Come on, D. Fess up. I want to know all the dirty details."

"I'll bring you up to speed next time you're in town," Demetri said smoothly. Angela was special to him, and he didn't want to discuss the intimate details of their relationship with his brother. At least not yet. "Have a good one, Nicco. Take it easy."

A sly grin claimed his lips. "Trust me, bro, I intend to. I have a thick, curvy honey waiting for me in my bedroom as we speak."

That makes two of us, Demetri thought, grinning, *but my girl's more than just a pretty face. She's the total package, and I'll move heaven and earth to make her mine.*

Angela tiptoed out of the master bedroom, closed the door behind her and glanced down the hall. It was empty. No maids, no Demetri in sight. Spending the rest of the day in bed with Demetri was tempting, but Angela knew it was time to go. The party was over, and she didn't want to overstay her welcome. Besides, she had to meet her father at noon and didn't want to show up in rumpled clothes and with tangled hair. She owed her dad an apology for skipping the Globetrotters game last night and hoped he'd had fun with Rodney. Angela checked her watch. If she hustled, she could make a quick pit stop at home for a shower and a wardrobe change.

Clutching her purse to her chest, she headed down the hallway, careful not to make a sound. Angela didn't know where Demetri was, but she sensed it was the perfect time to make a clean getaway. He was probably hiding out in his media room, anxiously waiting for her to leave. There would be no terse exchanges or awkward goodbyes, and if she was lucky, she'd make it out of the house without seeing any of his staff or family members.

Her heart pounded as she crept down the staircase and through the grand sun-drenched foyer. Angela had a hand on the doorknob and a foot out the door when she heard Demetri call her name. Guilt pricked her heart and burned her skin with shame. She turned around, fully prepared to repeat the lie she'd rehearsed while upstairs getting dressed. But when she saw Demetri standing in the kitchen, holding a silver tray in his hands, she swallowed the fib.

"Where are you rushing off to?"

"Who, me?" Angela wanted to kick herself. *Of course he's talking to me!* They were the only two people in the foyer, and worse, he was staring right at her. "I'm going to get out of your hair. I bet you have appointments and interviews and a million other things to do today."

"I have nothing planned, besides spending the day with you."

A smile pinched her lips. It was hard being this close to Demetri, impossible to withstand the heat of his gaze and his boyish grin. Her feelings were all mixed up, and her hormones were raging out of control. If her body got any hotter she was going to faint.

"I made breakfast," he said, holding up the silver tray. "Do you like waffle paninis?"

"Waffle what? I've never heard of it."

"Then you're in for a treat because I made you an authentic Italian breakfast."

Angela stood in the doorway, her eyes wide and her mouth open. This was not what she'd expected to find when she came downstairs. Demetri Morretti had cooked for her—again. He stood there staring at her with such warmth and affection that she didn't have the heart to disappoint him. "Okay, I'll stay for breakfast," she said, closing the front door, "but after we eat I really have to go. I have, um, things to do."

"Do you mind if we eat in the living room? My favorite show is about to start."

"You're a big fan of *The Girls Next Door,* aren't you?" Angela teased. "I knew it."

"No, today's the start of celebrity week on *Family Feud,* and my old teammate is on."

"I love that show," Angela said with a laugh.

"What are we waiting for? Let's go watch the Feud!"

Entering the living room, Angela admired the dark couches, marble structures and the entertainment unit filled with the latest high-tech gadgets. But what stunned Angela were all of the towering built-in bookshelves. The estate had a two-story wine cellar, a bowling alley and a game room twice the size of her house, but Angela never dreamed Demetri would have more books than the Chicago public library. "You like to read?"

"Not like, *love.*" Demetri put the silver breakfast tray down on the glass coffee table. "If you think this is nice, wait until I show you the reading room."

"The reading room? Sounds intriguing. I'd love to see it."

"Right now?"

"Sure. Why not?"

"But what about breakfast?" His expression was thoughtful. "We were up late last night. Aren't you hungry?"

"No." Angela hid a self-incriminating grin. "I hope you don't mind, but I helped myself to some of the snacks in the mini bar."

Demetri chuckled. "As long as you didn't eat the last Snickers bar, we're good."

"Now you tell me!" Angela giggled.

He slipped an arm around her waist and led her down the hall. "This is my favorite room in the house," he said, entering the spacious, wide den. "I spend more time here than anywhere else."

The room was filled with padded chairs and antique reading lamps. Angela ambled over to one of the shelves and drew her index finger along the books in the row. Demetri owned all of the greats—Hemingway, Steinbeck and Faulkner—and had the most impressive collection of African-American literature she had ever seen.

Angela stood in stunned silence. Nothing made sense. The pieces of the puzzle didn't fit, and the more she tried to figure Demetri out, the more confused she was. Bad boys didn't garden or cook or read classic books. And they never, ever professed their love. But Demetri had. His words played in her mind now, but she pushed them aside and continued perusing the shelves. Angela didn't want to offend him, but she couldn't resist asking Demetri the question on the tip of her tongue. "Do you actually read these books, or are they here just for show?"

"I'm more than just a baseball player, Angela. That's what I do, not who I am."

"Then who are you?"

"An honest, loyal guy who loves beautiful things, beautiful places and strong, beautiful women who aren't afraid to speak their mind." Demetri touched a hand to her face, stroking her cheek with the tip of his thumb. "There are a couple things we need to clear up."

His caress sent a quiver through her, and for a moment she couldn't speak.

"I didn't storm into your studio for kicks, Angela. Your *Athletes Behaving Badly* piece was poorly written and full of lies."

"Lies?" she repeated, nailing him with a cold, hard look. "Name one."

"I never threw a beer bottle at that college kid in New Jersey."

"He said you did. Even pressed charges."

"It was one of my security guards, and as soon as I found out, I fired him," he explained in a firm tone. "I would never condone that type of behavior."

"Anything else I got wrong?"

Demetri nodded. "I never messed around with my teammate's wife, and I'm not the father of her baby, either. She made a pass at me at a white party in the Hamptons, but I shot her down."

"That's hard to believe."

"I'd never hook up with Lexus Washington. She's an ex-stripper who's screwed half the guys on my team. If I ever brought her home to my family, they'd disown me!"

Angela bit the bottom of her lip, looked away.

"I'm attracted to women like you. Classy, professional types who care about giving back and making a difference in our community."

"Don't make me out to be a saint, Demetri. I'm far from it."

"You are to me and to a lot of other people in this city." Demetri leaned into her. His lips touched her mouth. "I could get used to this, baby. You being here with me every day."

Angela didn't trust herself to speak. Not when her heart was racing and her feelings were a jumbled mess. But that was no surprise. She always found herself flustered when Demetri was around.

"I love you, baby, and I'm ready to commit to you."

"Love!" The word burst out of Angela's mouth and ricocheted around the den like machine-gun fire. "That's outrageous. We only met a few weeks ago, and besides, we're just kicking it, just having fun."

"There's no time limit on love," he murmured, brushing his lips against the slope of her ear. "When you know, you know, and there's no doubt in my mind that you're the woman I'm supposed to be with. No doubt at all. I'm all in, Angela. Ready to..."

Closing her eyes, she soaked in the beauty of the moment. His words resonated with her, filled her with a deep sense of peace. As he spoke, her temperature rose and her body grew hot. That always happened when Demetri touched her. The way he was stroking her arms and hips incited her passion. Blood roared through her veins. Her breasts enlarged, her nipples hardened, and the lips between her legs grew moist. Last night, their lovemaking had been wild, but right now, her desire for Demetri was stronger than ever.

Angela pressed her lips against Demetri's, kissing him slowly as if she was savoring the feel and taste of his mouth. Sliding a hand under his T-shirt, she stroked and caressed his shoulders and abs. But touching him wasn't enough. It didn't quench her body's thirst. Feasting on his mouth, she nibbled on his bottom lip, eagerly sucking and teasing his tongue.

Demetri trailed his lips along her earlobe, down her neck and across her shoulders. He wasn't shy about sharing his feelings or afraid to say what was on his mind. "You have no idea how amazing it feels being inside you," he whispered, slipping his hands under her dress and cupping her butt. "I'll never get tired of loving you, Angela. You'll never have to worry about anyone or anything coming between us."

Overtaken by desire and moved by his sweet, earnest

words, Angela crushed her lips against his mouth. Sliding a hand inside his dark-wash blue jeans, she stroked the length of his erection. Her passion was through the roof. And when Demetri slid a finger inside her, she shivered. His stroke fueled her desire, infected her body with an undeniable hunger.

Angela couldn't take any more. She wanted to feel Demetri inside her, loving her only the way he could. Burning up from head to toe, she felt sweat trickle down her face and back. They were stuck together, but the warmth of Demetri's hard body only increased her desire.

Demetri took a condom out of his pocket, protected himself and plunged so deep inside her that she collapsed against him. Winded, she fought to catch her breath, to stay in the moment. He gave her what she wanted and more.

Bracing herself against the nearby window, she draped her hands around his neck and hiked a leg around his waist. They moved together as one, like dancers gliding across the stage.

Suddenly her orgasm slammed into her with the force of a category-five hurricane. And by the time Demetri scooped her up in his arms and carried her upstairs to the master bedroom, Angela was no longer thinking about leaving the estate. So desperate to make love again, she couldn't stop fantasizing about all the salacious things she was going to do to Demetri in his Jacuzzi.

Chapter 15

"I hate to toot my own horn, but toot, toot!" Remy shrieked, wearing a wide, toothy smile that made her eyes twinkle. "You look like a million bucks, girlfriend!"

Leaning forward in her leather swivel chair, Angela inspected her hair and makeup in the lit oval mirror. "Thanks, Remy. As usual you did a great job."

"I know!" Winking, Remy snatched her jean jacket off the silver coat hook and slipped it on over her orange Bob Marley tank top. "I'll catch you later. I have to be at Glamour Girlz by six, and it's already ten to. Have a great show, girlfriend. Knock 'em dead!"

Sitting in her chair, alone in WJN-TV's cool, bright makeup room, Angela wondered if it was too late to back out of co-hosting the live morning show. How could she go on the air when she was a nervous wreck? At times like this, when Angela was scared and stressed-out, she would usually call her dad. But he was en route to Nashville.

Fidgeting with her bracelet, she restlessly crossed and uncrossed her legs. Outside in the hallway, Angela heard loud footsteps, the security alarm beeping in earnest and high-pitched voices. The room smelled of freshly squeezed lemons, and her favorite Wynton Marsalis song was playing on the radio, but it did little to relax her. Her stomach was twisted in a knot so tight, Angela feared she was going to be sick.

I should have never agreed to fill in for Earl, she thought, wiping her clammy palms along the side of her black fitted pencil skirt. *What if I trip over my words or misread the teleprompter? Those bloggers from Gossip News will crucify me online!*

Angela pressed her eyes shut. In the darkness, she saw Demetri's face, heard his quiet, soothing voice in her ear. These days she thought of the gorgeous baseball star and nothing else. Last Saturday was supposed to be a onetime thing, a mere night of carnal pleasure. But since their first date, they'd made love on four other occasions. Five, if she counted the quickie they'd had on Wednesday night in the front seat of his tinted Mercedes-Benz SUV. Angela knew she had to stop sneaking around with Demetri, but every time he called and invited her over, she caved. It was hard not to. He was thoughtful and caring and gave her the freedom to be herself—her true, authentic self—not the person she pretended to be in front of the cameras. They were goofy together and had laughed so much while volunteering at the Cook County Food Bank that the other volunteers poked fun at them.

Being with Demetri had become addictive. She had to talk to him and see him every day. It didn't matter how late it was or how stressful her day had been; she was never too tired to make the hour-long drive out to his home. Seeing Demetri made everything better. And when they were in bed, making love, moving together in perfect sync, Angela was in heaven. Nothing else mattered or compared to the euphoria she felt when Demetri was buried deep inside her, whispering soft words in her ears.

A smile appeared across Angela's face when she thought about the unexpected surprise she'd received hours earlier. When she'd stumbled into her office that morning—after spending the night with Demetri—and seen dozens of vases filled with yellow tulips and bunches of helium balloons hanging from the ceiling, she'd let out a shriek. Her coworkers had come running. Everyone had squealed and cheered and told her how lucky she was to have found a sweet, romantic guy.

Angela agreed, admitted they were right. Everything in the gift basket was dainty and heart-shaped, but what touched Angela the most was the personalized, handwritten card from Demetri. He'd written her words of encouragement, and as Angela sat in her makeup chair, his words came back to her and slowly soothed her troubled mind.

Her cell phone rang, blaring her current favorite pop song through the room. Angela scooped her cell off the makeup table and immediately pressed it to her ear. The only person who would call this early was Simone. "Simone, what are you doing up this early? Raiding the fridge again?"

"I'm not Simone, but I *am* raiding the fridge!"

"Demetri?"

"Your one and only."

Angela checked the time on the wall clock above the oval mirror. "What are you doing up so early? It's only six-fifteen."

"You're cohosting the morning show, and I didn't want to miss it," he said, his tone full of excitement. "Ready for your big debut?"

"I thought I was, but now that it's almost showtime, I'm scared to death."

"Baby, you're going to do great."

"But what if I don't? What if my nerves get the best of me and I screw up on live TV?"

"It's not going to happen. You're smart and articulate, and you think fast on your feet. Don't worry. You've got this."

His words made her smile, but the butterflies in her stomach remained.

"Did you get the gift basket?"

"Yes, it was waiting in my office when I arrived. Thanks, Demetri. I shared the bottle of champagne and the edible roses with my colleagues, and now they all love me!"

"I'm not surprised. You're easy to love, not to mention gorgeous, intelligent and…"

Angela felt a tickle emerge in her throat. The times when

Demetri talked about his feelings and their relationship, Angela wanted to cry. She knew they would never be able to have a real future and share a life together.

An idea came to her, but she dismissed it when her doubts quickly flooded in. Telling Demetri about her past, about the wild and crazy things she'd done during her college days, was not an option. Not today, not ever. The risk of hurting him was too great.

"What time do you finish up today?"

"Three o'clock, maybe four. It depends on how long my afternoon meeting goes."

"When you wrap up, there'll be a town car waiting out front to bring you to my estate," he explained. "I have the whole day planned. We'll have a special celebratory lunch, play a round or two of golf, then watch the new James Bond movie in my home theater."

Angela frowned. "But that movie isn't out until November."

"I know, but since you're a huge Daniel Craig fan, I asked my manager to get it."

"Just like that?"

Demetri chuckled. "Yeah, baby, just like that."

"Wow, it must be nice having friends in high places."

"Only if it helps me get closer to you," he said, his voice soft and earnest. "I love having you here with me. If I had my way, you'd be living here permanently."

Growing up, her dad had never shared his thoughts or emotions, and over time Angela had adopted his passive approach in relationships. So instead of responding to what Demetri had just said, she changed the subject. "It's going to be gorgeous outside today. We should get out, maybe check out one of the music festivals?"

"I wish we could, but it's just not worth the hassle. We're better off staying in," he said. "I went to the grocery store late last night, and if not for my security guards, I'd still be in the produce section, fighting my way through the crowd."

"So, what are you going to do? Spend the rest of the summer holed up in your house?"

"Pretty much. I have everything I need at home, and since I schedule most of my meetings and appointments here at the estate, there's really no reason to go out."

"Oh, I know what this is about," she said, trying hard not to laugh. "You're strapped for cash and can't afford to take me out. Don't worry, baby. It's my treat!"

Demetri roared with laughter. "Where do you want to go?"

"I don't know. Let's jump on the L line and see where it takes us."

"Angela, we can't. I need to let my team know what we're doing beforehand so they can make the necessary arrangements."

"What arrangements, Demetri? It's not that serious. We don't have to go to a fancy restaurant or an upscale club. As long as we're together, I'm happy."

"Okay, then I'll have my assistant reserve Philander's for us. We can have a nice romantic dinner alone, then dance to the live jazz band."

"We don't need the entire restaurant, Demetri. Just one table." Angela slid off her chair and inspected her appearance in the mirror. The cropped, white blazer fit her curves just right, and her turquoise-hued accessories made the entire outfit pop. She sat back down in the chair and said, "The whole point of going out is to interact with other people, so let's just stroll around downtown and see where the night takes us."

"Maybe you're right. Maybe we should get out and do something different."

"Maybe?" she sassed. "Baby, I'm *always* right."

"Except when it comes to making breakfast. The entire house still smells like smoke!"

Angela giggled. "Hey, that's not my fault. *You're* the one

who wanted to have a quickie. I tried to stop you, but you just wouldn't listen—"

Salem stuck her head in the door and waved.

"I have to go," Angela said. "I'll see you later, okay?"

"For sure. Have a great show, beautiful. I'll be watching!"

Angela ended the call, slipped her cell phone back into her purse and turned to her boss.

"Are you all right?" Salem wore a concerned expression on her face. "You don't look too good, and we're live in fifteen minutes."

Angela swallowed. It was here. The moment she'd been waiting for her entire life. Her big break, the opportunity to show her producers she was more than just a pretty face. She replayed Demetri's words in her head. *You're smart and articulate, and you think fast on your feet. Don't worry. You've got this.*

Her breathing slowed, her hands stopped shaking, and the butterflies fluttering around in her stomach slowed. Angela smiled and hopped to her feet. "I'm great. Couldn't be better."

"Ready to head into the studio? Everyone's waiting."

"You bet your stiletto boots I am!"

Laughing, Salem led Angela down the bright, narrow hallway. On the walls were framed pictures of world leaders, prominent figures and the station's most celebrated reporters. Angela felt her confidence rise. One day, she'd be an acclaimed reporter, interviewing influential people and traveling all over the world. A question sneaked up on her, one that brought her thoughts back to Demetri. *Was he serious about us having a long-distance relationship? Would he really come visit me if I lived abroad?*

"I don't know how you did it, Angela, but convincing Demetri's brothers to join him on *Eye on Chicago* next month was a brilliant idea," Salem said, her tone one of awe.

Angela snapped out of her thoughts and gave her boss a grateful smile. "Thanks, but to be honest, it didn't take much convincing at all. Demetri called, and they agreed, just like that."

"The Morretti brothers are the hottest bachelors in the world, and since posting the details of the interview on Twitter and Facebook, I've received hundreds of messages."

"I'm not surprised. These days they're more popular than ever."

"Think they'll agree to do a fun *Love Connection*–type game?"

"I bet they'd love that, especially Nicco. He's a real ladies' man."

"That's what I heard." Salem winked. "That's not all I heard. I read online this morning in *Celebrity Scoop* that you and Demetri Morretti are lovers."

Angela gave a shaky laugh. "Those online publications will say anything to attract readers."

"I know. That's what I thought, until I saw the pictures."

"What pictures?"

"There you are. I've been looking all over for you!" The associate producer, a stout Polish man with fleshy cheeks, rushed over and grabbed Angela around the waist. "No time to waste! We're live in sixty seconds!"

Chapter 16

Madison's Steak Bar, a popular restaurant in the heart of downtown Chicago, was packed with chic, fashionable patrons every night of the week. Tables were close, only an arm's length away, but diners didn't seem to mind. Conversations were loud and spirited, and laughter flowed freely around the cathedral-shaped dining room. Crystal chandeliers, milk-white carpets and cozy booths gave the space an old-world feel, one that fit the mellow atmosphere perfectly.

"Want the last bite?" Demetri held out his spoon. His eyes were glued to Angela's lips, and he wore a devilish grin on his lean, handsome face. "This is the holy grail of gelato, baby. It doesn't get much better than this!"

Leaning forward, Angela parted her lips and slowly sucked the rich, creamy dessert off of his silver spoon. "You're right. That's good."

"I'm glad you suggested this place. It's nice, and everyone here is real chill."

"My dad and I used to come here all the time. We'd eat, watch the game and talk and laugh for hours," she said, a wistful expression on her face. "He's a long-distance truck driver, so I don't get to see him much, but when I do, it's just like old times."

"The next time your dad's in town, I'd like to meet him."

"Why?"

"Because I'm hot for his daughter, and I plan to be around for a *very* long time."

Angela giggled and shook her head incredulously. "Demetri, you're crazy."

"Not crazy, just grateful to have a second lease on life." His demeanor was calm but his gaze was intense. "I'm just a regular guy who fell in love with an extraordinary girl who completes me in every way."

"Stop playing around."

"I'm not playing, Angela. I mean every word." He touched a hand to her cheek. "I have everything a man could want. Wealth, fame, more money than I could spend in this lifetime. The only thing missing from my life was you."

His cell phone rang, but he didn't touch it. Instead, Demetri continued stroking and caressing her skin. Angela loved when he did that. He looked right at her when he spoke, no matter what he was doing or what was going on around him. He always gave her his undivided attention. Angela liked everything Demetri was saying, and she felt the same way, but she couldn't return the sentiment. Not because she didn't love him, but because the risk was too great. If Demetri ever found out about her past, he'd dump her like yesterday's trash. And she'd never be able to survive his rejection. It was better that they just hung out and had fun, rather than get serious. But when Angela told Demetri that, the smile slid off his face.

"What are you saying? That you don't see us together for the long term?"

Angela opened her mouth, but a booming male voice spoke over her.

"Sign this to Hakeem," the speaker barked. A scrawny, middle-aged black man with tattoo-covered arms tossed a receipt down on the table. "And I'll need a picture with you, too."

Demetri kept his eyes on Angela but spoke to the dark-haired stranger in the wrinkled Chicago Royals jersey. "Now's not a good time. I'm talking to my girl. Come back in an hour."

"Just hurry up and sign it. I don't have all day. I'm about to get up out of here."

"Then leave. No one's stopping you."

"I told my son I'd get your autograph, and I'm not leaving without it." The man pressed his palms down on the table, getting right up in Demetri's face. His fast, heavy breathing filled the air, and his booming voice attracted the attention of patrons dining nearby.

In seconds, there was a crowd gathered around the booth. Cell phones flashed in Demetri's face and the dining room was abuzz with excited chatter. "Signing this receipt is the least you could do," the stranger snarled, baring his teeth. "You played like crap last season. Hell, I've seen Little Leaguers play better!"

Demetri shot to his feet. The veins in his neck were throbbing, his hands were curled into fists, and his eyes were dark with rage. Angela stood and wrapped an arm around his waist. "Baby, let's go. He's not worth it."

"Chump, scram before I make you a knuckle sandwich to go."

Angela recognized the voice behind them, and when Rodney elbowed his way through the crowd and stepped forward, she felt a mixture of relief and apprehension. Her kid brother was a foot taller than the belligerent stranger and outweighed him by at least fifty pounds. The expression on Rodney's face could scare the Devil, and when he folded his broad arms across his muscled chest, the man gulped.

"Never mind," the stranger said, backing away from the booth. "You're not my son's favorite baseball player anyways. Jeter is."

The crowd dispersed, diners returned to their seats, and by the time the busty female manager hustled over, the dining area had returned to normal.

"Thanks, kid. What's your name?"

"Rodney Kelly."

Demetri glanced at Angela and then gave a slow nod. "It's good to meet you, Rodney. I've heard a lot about you."

"Only half of it's true. My sister exaggerates!"

"Rodney, what are you doing here?" Angela demanded, sitting back down in the booth.

"I came to see you."

"Now's not a good time."

Shaking his head, he threw his hands up in the air. "When is? I've been trying to get ahold of you for weeks, but you won't return my calls. We need to talk."

"I have nothing to say to you."

"Fine," Rodney said. "I'll talk and you listen."

"You guys need some privacy." Demetri squeezed her hand, then lowered his mouth to her ear and dropped a kiss on her cheek. "I'll be back. Don't rush. Spend as much time as you need with your brother."

Angela started to protest, but Demetri strode off. Her eyes followed him through the dining room and off into the TV-filled lounge. He took a seat at the L-shaped bar and made himself at home among the other patrons who were chatting, sipping wine and cheering on the Royals.

"Have you been getting my messages?"

Angela nodded and stared absently out the window. Golden lights sparkled in the night. The view of the Chicago skyline was nothing short of spectacular. Angela wished Demetri was beside her instead of her brother. Rodney was trouble, and she suspected he'd tracked her down to hit her up for money. Again.

"I'm sorry I took—"

"Don't you mean *stole?*" she said, cutting him off. "You betrayed my trust, Rodney, and I don't know if I'll ever be able to forgive you."

He drew up a chair, straddled it and sat down. "I didn't know what else to do, Angela. I was desperate and I needed the money fast."

"For what? To buy drugs?"

"Drugs?" A frown jammed between his thick, dark eyebrows. "I don't sell or use drugs. Never have, never will. That's not my speed."

"Then what did you steal the money for?"

Rodney stared up at the potted lights and then down at his big, beefy hands. "I—I—I took the money to pay off a bookie," he blurted out. "I bet on the Indy 500 and lost big. Icepick said if I didn't pay up he'd hurt Pops, and I got… scared."

"Why didn't you tell me?"

"I couldn't. I'm always screwing up, and I didn't want to let you or Pops down again. But I'm going to pay you back every penny of that money, sis. I swear."

"How, when you don't have a job and spend all day hanging out with your friends?"

"I don't kick it on the block anymore," he said. "Dad let me move back in if I promised to straighten up, and I've been searching for work all week."

Angela didn't speak, just nodded her head. She saw Demetri, sitting alone at the bar, and smiled when he glanced her way. He wore a concerned expression. She thought about the things he'd told her about his family, about all the messed-up things his relatives had done to him over the years. They'd sold him out to the tabloids, applied for credit cards in his name and pilfered items from his estate when they thought no one was looking. He'd forgiven each one, no questions asked. "You can't choose your relatives or decide who is worthy enough to share your last name," he'd said one afternoon while basking by his Olympic-size pool. "Your family is God's gift to you, *even* the crazy ones, and you're supposed to love them no matter what."

His words played in her mind now, but Angela still wasn't ready to forgive Rodney.

"I better let you get back to your date. Your man's been sitting at the bar a long time."

"Demetri's not my man. We're just...just hanging out."

Gesturing to the bar with a flick of his bald head, he broke into a grin that revealed his dimples. "Does he know that? Because he looks mighty sprung to me," he said, raising his eyebrows. "He's not watching the game. He's watching you!"

"Demetri and his brothers are doing my show next month. We just came down here to discuss the details of the interview." She could tell by the look on Rodney's face that he didn't believe her. Angela wasn't surprised. She didn't believe the words coming out of her mouth, either. Their relationship was different from anything she'd ever experienced before, but Angela wasn't going to tell her brother or anyone else that she was in love with Demetri. "We have a good time together, but it's nothing serious."

"That's too bad. I thought I was finally going to have a brother-in-law and some nieces and nephews to spoil and shoot hoops with!"

"Don't worry, Rodney. I'm working on it."

Angela's face held a serious expression, but inside she felt downright giddy.

"My man!" Her brother jumped to his feet and bumped fists with Demetri. "Now, that's what I'm talking about!"

Her cheeks burned red when Demetri slid back into the booth and draped an arm over her shoulders. He whispered in her ear in a sexy tone that caused desire to consume her body. Then he lowered his mouth to her lips. She tilted her chin and kissed him back.

"We should all hang out sometime." Demetri fixed his gaze on Angela but spoke to her brother. "Rodney, are you as crazy about the Royals as your sister is?"

"Naw, basketball's more my sport."

"Cool. Maybe we can check out a play-off game."

"Sounds good." Rodney took his cop-style sunglasses out

of the side pocket of his faded, blue jeans and slid them on. "I have to go. I have a job interview tomorrow, and I have a hell of a time waking up in the morning."

"I hear you, man. If it wasn't for your sister, I'd stay in bed until one o'clock!"

The men chuckled.

"'Bye," Rodney said, flashing two fingers, and then he turned and strode off.

Demetri took out his wallet, dropped several hundred-dollar bills on the leather billfold and grabbed his jacket. "Rodney, hold up. I think I'm going to need your help."

"To do what?" he asked, a quizzical expression on his face.

Demetri pointed at the front window. A group of twenty-somethings, holding their cell phones in the air, stood pressed against the glass, frantically snapping pictures. "Think you can clear a path from the front door to my Bentley?"

Rodney grinned and puffed out his chest. "You don't even have to ask."

Chapter 17

Demetri settled into his favorite leather chair and propped his size-twelve feet up on the chocolate-brown ottoman. He had a glass of Veneto in one hand and the remote control in the other. Demetri couldn't recall the last time he felt this relaxed, this happy.

The French doors, leading out onto the deck, were open, allowing the intoxicating scents and sounds of spring to fill his game room. Autographed baseball jerseys were displayed on the navy blue walls, barstools and low-hanging pub lights gave the space a cool, sophisticated feel, and the multicolored area rugs complemented the decor perfectly. Demetri owned every arcade machine known to man, dozens of table games and had over ten thousand video games in his collection.

Demetri turned on the ninety-inch wall-mounted TV, and when a commercial for *Eye on Chicago* came on, a grin exploded onto his mouth. These days, that was all he seemed to do. Eating breakfast with Angela in bed, watching the sunset on his balcony and luxuriating in his Jacuzzi was all it took to make him break out in an ear-to-ear smile.

Taking a sip of his wine, he cast a glance at his team. Todd was sitting at the bar, devouring his second bowl of penne, Lloyd was reviewing the terms of his new five-year Gatorade contract, and Nichola was typing on her beloved iPad. Demetri didn't want to kick them out, but it was time to bring their weekly meeting to a close. He wanted to be showered and changed by the time Angela arrived for their date. Though, if she wanted to join him in the shower he wouldn't mind. His grin doubled in length at the thought of making love to her in the middle of the afternoon.

For the past three weeks, he'd spent all of his free time with Angela, and when they were apart, she was all he could think of. It wasn't until meeting Angela that he realized how empty his life was. For years, he'd stumbled through life, searching for its meaning, its purpose. He loved playing baseball, had a great family and legions of loyal fans around the world, but he'd always longed for more. He had craved something deeper than just fame and fortune. Demetri wanted someone to share his life with, someone he could trust, and one warm, fateful day he'd found her.

Angela's love had changed him, restored his faith in people. Angela loved to socialize, found beauty in the smallest things in life and always had a smile. Nothing got her down—not her critics, not her hypercritical producers, not even the sexist male crew she worked with. Open-minded and always up for a good time, she thrived on trying new things and living in the moment. Demetri admired the way she carried herself and her zest for life. Being with Angela reminded him of the time—before fame and fortune came calling—when he was a fun, outgoing guy who didn't have a care in the world.

"That's the best damn penne I've ever had," Todd announced, leaning back into his chair and patting his stomach. "Thanks, Demetri. I owe you one."

Demetri snapped out of his thoughts and nodded at his agent.

"We've hit a roadblock in our plans for the Fourth of July extravaganza," Nichola announced, plopping down in the chair beside him. "I met with Claudia Jeffries-Medina and the director of the recreation center yesterday, and she shot down all of our ideas. We told her the Fourth of July extravaganza is for underprivileged kids, but she didn't seem to care."

"That's a bummer." Lloyd tossed his files into his briefcase, locked it and rested it on the floor. "You win some, you lose some, I guess."

"You can say that again. It's been one setback after another, and I'm starting to think we should postpone the event."

"How many families were you planning to invite?"

"This has been a major bone of contention," Nichola explained, combing a hand through her hair. "I wanted to make this a huge, over-the-top bash, but the hall can only accommodate two hundred people, and the director is dead set against having tents on the property."

Demetri raised an eyebrow. "Two hundred people? That's it? No offense, Nichola, but that doesn't sound like much of a party to me."

"Find somewhere else to have the fundraiser," Lloyd suggested, taking off his eyeglasses and cleaning them with his white silk handkerchief. "There are plenty of recreation centers in and around the Chicago area that can accommodate larger numbers."

Nichola sighed. "It's too late to find another venue. The fundraiser is only weeks away."

"Then we'll have it here."

His team exchanged quizzical looks.

"Here where?" Todd asked, his lean, tanned face screwed up into a frown.

"Here at the estate."

Eyes popped, jaws dropped, and foreheads wrinkled.

"No way." Lloyd gave an adamant shake of his head. "It's too risky."

"I agree. These kids come from bad, crime-ridden neighborhoods, and—"

Demetri drained his wineglass and put it on the side table. "Todd, relax. Everything will be fine. If something breaks, it can always be replaced."

"I'm not worried about something breaking," he mumbled. "I'm worried about those badass kids robbing you blind!"

"Having the Fourth of July extravaganza here is a wonderful idea. Imagine all the great press we'll get!" Clapping her hands together, Nichola whooped for joy. "And as long as the weather cooperates, we can set up everything outside."

A sly grin fell across Todd's mouth. "I like your way of thinking. Keep the runts and their thieving parents *far, far* away from the house."

Demetri glared at his agent but spoke warmly to his publicist. "Nichola, you're the best. I don't know what I'd do without you."

Her eyes lit up. "You don't have to thank me. You know I'll do anything for you."

"I know, but still. Just wanted you to know I appreciate all of your hard work." Resting the remote control on the ottoman, he swiped up his cell phone and stood. "I'm going upstairs. Feel free to eat and drink as much as you want."

"Where are you rushing off to?" Nichola asked, crossing her legs. "I thought we were staying in and watching old Al Pacino movies on TV."

"Can't. I'm taking Angela to Jazz Fest."

Lloyd scratched his head. "Jazz Fest? All the way up in Freeport? But you hate crowds."

"And road trips!" Nichola added.

"Yeah, but Angela is a huge Wynton Marsalis fan, and he's performing there tonight."

Todd pointed a finger at Demetri. "Have fun, but make sure your security guards take all the necessary precautions to keep you guys safe."

"I gave the guards the night off. I want to be alone with Angela."

"Are you sure that's a good idea?" Lloyd questioned, straightening in his chair. "I know you'll be wearing a disguise, but if someone recognizes you, all hell could break loose."

"No disguise tonight. I need to look fly as hell when I'm

out with Angela. She's gorgeous and I don't want to look like a scrub beside her!"

The guys chuckled, agreeing fervently.

"I almost forgot," Nichola said, her tone apologetic. "I told the Kids Awards you're not interested in being a presenter, but do you want—"

"I wish you would have spoken to me first before refusing the invitation."

"Why? Every year they invite you, and every year you turn them down."

"I know," Demetri said, "but this year I'd like to go. It might be fun."

Three sets of eyes stared incredulously at him.

Todd picked up his empty wineglass and sniffed it. "Someone must have drugged your Veneto, because you're talking crazy."

"One last thing before we wrap up," Lloyd said, sliding off his barstool. "My wife wants to know what time to expect you guys on Memorial Day. After last year's debacle, she decided to have invitations made and wants to have a general consensus before having them printed."

"Tell Trudy I'm sorry, but I won't be able to make it."

"Why not? You always spend Memorial Day with us."

"I'm taking Angela to Venice for the weekend," he explained, wearing a proud smile. "We're taking the Morretti family jet, and I've already booked the Ruzzini Palace, a driver and an English-speaking tour guide to show us all of the sights."

Nichola's face crumpled. "You're taking her to Italy for the weekend? That's insane! And ridiculously expensive!"

"Angela's worth it. She means a lot to me and…" Demetri broke off speaking, stopping himself from gushing like a lovestruck teenager. Morretti men didn't sweat females, and if his brothers ever found out he was head over heels for Angela— the woman who'd dissed him on national television—they'd tease him mercilessly. "These last few months with Angela have been incredible, and it's about time I wined her and dined her. Venice is one of the most romantic cities in the world, and I plan to make it a weekend she'll never forget."

"Wow, you're going all out." Todd whistled loudly.

"If you guys move any faster, you'll be married by Christmas!"

I'd like nothing more. The thought gave Demetri pause. Not because getting married after a three-month-long courtship was crazy, but because he'd never considered proposing to anyone before. But from the moment he first laid eyes on Angela, he knew deep down that she was as exquisite as a white diamond. And everything she'd said and done since their first date made him love and respect her even more. He liked having Angela right by his side, and the thought of spending the rest of his life with her didn't scare him; it filled him with pride.

"You know she's only using you to boost the ratings of her stupid show, right?" Nichola snorted. "I know her type. She'll do anything to stay on top."

"She isn't using me, Nichola—"

"Yes, she is! Open your eyes!" His publicist sounded worried, as if she was on the verge of tears. "Angela's dated dozens of pro athletes, and once you do her show, she'll dump you and move on to the next star. That's how she is. That's how she operates."

Demetri tried to remain calm, tried to act as though her words didn't faze him, but they did. They stung, burned like hell. His biggest fear was that Angela would leave him for someone else or that she'd choose fame and stardom over him. Nichola's comments just fueled his doubts.

"Women like Angela Kelly only look out for themselves," Nichola continued, her tone ice-cold. "She isn't going to stick around for the long haul, and she definitely isn't wife material."

"I disagree." Todd tore his gaze away from the TV screen

and addressed Demetri. "I like her. She's smart and talented and not afraid to speak her mind. She'll tell you the truth, not just what you want to hear, and that speaks volumes about her character. Angela's definitely the type of woman you need in your—"

"Todd, what do you know?" Nichola spat, cutting him off. "You're hardly an expert when it comes to love and relationships. You've been married three times, and your last girlfriend dumped you for a gardener!"

He coughed and then scratched at his crooked nose. "Whatever. I might be unlucky in love, but I know a good woman when I see one. And Angela Kelly is one of the great ones."

"Thanks, man. I feel the same way. That's why I want Angela to meet my parents."

"Your parents!" his team shouted.

"What do you even know about her?" Nichola asked, now pacing the length of the game room. "I mean, besides the fact that she's on TV and that she's a good lay?"

"Don't," Demetri warned, his teeth clenched and his eyes narrowed. "Angela's special to me, and I won't let you or anyone else disrespect her."

A crooked smile crossed Nichola's face, one that darkened the shade of her eyes. "I know your parents and your family really well, Demetri. They're not going to like her."

"I think they will. Angela makes me happy, and that's all that matters."

"I thought you wanted to settle down, get married and have a bunch of kids?"

"I do, Lloyd. That hasn't changed."

"And Angela's down for that?" Todd asked, a quizzical expression on his face. "I'm a pretty good judge of character, and I don't see her swapping red-carpet events for breastfeeding and changing diapers."

"Maybe not right now, but in time she'll come around."

Nichola touched his forearm lightly. "Demetri, she's going

to hurt you. I just know it. She reminds me a lot of Shai, and…"

Demetri felt his body stiffen and all the muscles in his neck tense. He didn't want to think about his ex. The woman who had chosen fame and stardom over him. Whenever he heard one of her chart-topping pop songs on the radio, he wondered what could have been. Or at least he used to. Ever since meeting Angela, he'd forgotten about every other girl. Finally, after years of being lied to, used and deceived, he'd met a woman who thrilled him and completed him in every way.

"Oh, I'm sorry. I had no idea you had company."

At the sound of Angela's voice, Demetri cranked his head to the right. There, standing beside the French doors, was the woman who made his heart sing. Her knee-length leopard-print dress, which clung to her curves, looked amazing on her. And her sky-high heels showed off her long, toned legs.

Three long, quick strides and Demetri had Angela in his arms. "Baby, you hit it out of the ballpark tonight," he praised, looking her up and down. "I might have to bring my security detail with us to Freeport after all."

"You need to come down to my set more often," she quipped. "You're great for my ego!"

"Well, you're great for me, period." Unable to resist, Demetri crushed his lips against her soft, luscious mouth. Caressing her cheek, he kissed her thoroughly as if he had all the time in the world. Her perfume filled his nostrils with its rich fragrance and aroused his hunger and desire for her.

"Baby, your team's staring at us," she whispered, breaking off the kiss and smiling sheepishly. "And your publicist looks pissed. If looks could kill, I'd be six feet under."

"Never mind her," Demetri said, stealing another quick kiss. "Her favorite contestant got voted off *The Song* last night and she's been in a funk ever since!"

Angela giggled.

They strolled across the room with their fingers intertwined.

"Hi, I'm Angela. It's great to meet you both."

Todd and Lloyd scrambled to their feet and almost tripped
over each other in their haste to reach her first. After shaking hands and enjoying a few minutes of conversation with
the guys, Angela waved at Nichola.

"It's good to see you," Angela said brightly. "How are
things going?"

Nichola didn't smile or wave back. Instead she stood staring at them intently. Her eyes were narrowed, her arms were
crossed, and she tapped her heeled foot impatiently on the
floor. Demetri didn't know what her problem was, but he intended to find out. But before he could speak, Nichola said,
"Angela, you're here, *again*—how nice."

Demetri shot Nichola a what-the-hell look, and she turned
away.

"I'm out of here. See you guys later."

Within seconds, she packed up her things, grabbed her
lightweight red coat and left. Demetri was relieved to see her
go, but when Lloyd and Todd made themselves at home on
the couch and started asking Angela dozens of questions, his
good mood fizzled. At this rate, they'd never leave! He tried
to catch Todd's attention, but his agent was too busy making
googly eyes at Angela. And Lloyd was no better. The happily
married father of three had flushed cheeks, and every time
he opened his mouth, he tripped over his words. Demetri had
never seen him smile so wide or heard him laugh so loud.

"I don't mean to be rude, guys, but it's time for you to
leave."

"Go shower and change. We'll keep Angela company while
you're gone."

"Yeah," Todd agreed, eagerly nodding his head. "I want
to hear all about her show."

"I got an idea." Demetri grabbed the leather briefcases beside the bar and shoved one into each of their hands and then gestured to the door. "Why don't you guys go home to your kids and significant others? Bet they're dying to see you."

Their faces fell and their shoulders slumped.

"Come on," Lloyd whined. "Angela was just about to tell us which Oscar-winning actor has a secret foot fetish!"

"You guys don't have to go home," Demetri said, trying hard not to laugh, "but you have to get the hell out of here… now!"

Chapter 18

Should I go for classy chic or sex kitten? Angela wondered as she cast a critical eye over the trendy designer dresses she was holding up under her chin. An hour after getting out of the shower, she was still standing in front of the mirror, stressing over what to wear. Dinner was simmering on the stove, scented candles had been lit and her favorite CD was playing on the living-room stereo. Soft, sensuous music filled the air, creating a romantic vibe that put Angela in a mood for slow dancing and passionate lovemaking. All she needed now was her man, and life would be perfect.

Her body warmed and flushed with heat at the thought of Demetri. Angela never imagined she'd ever claim a man as her own, let alone cook, clean and wax for him, but that was exactly what she'd done. Dating Demetri was an adventure, one filled with laughs, tender moments and toe-curling sex. And he was so ridiculously romantic. Angela went to bed every night with a smile on her face. But Demetri was more than just a great guy. He was everything she'd ever wanted in a man and more.

Angela's eyes drifted to the digital clock sitting on her dresser. She couldn't stop counting down the seconds until Demetri would arrive. Her behavior was juvenile, completely out of character, but these days Angela wasn't thinking like a mature woman; she was acting more like a love-struck teen. Since meeting Demetri, she'd become someone else. Someone her producers and crew seemed to like much bet-

ter. Maybe it was because she smiled more and wasn't so up-
tight about everything.

Or maybe, a little voice inside her head said, *you're happier because for the first time in your life you're being your
authentic self.*

Pondering the thought, Angela realized it was true. Every
day after taping *Eye on Chicago,* Angela jumped in her car,
anxious and excited to meet up with Demetri, not fretting
about her on-camera performance or what her critics would
say. And since attending Jazz Fest in Freeport two weeks earlier, Demetri had taken her from one public event to the other.
On Thursday they went to a movie premiere, the following
afternoon they dropped the top on his Rolls-Royce Phantom
and cruised down to the beach, and yesterday he'd surprised
her with front-row tickets to see the Jabbawockeez. At the
show, fans approached Demetri for pictures and autographs,
but he didn't trip. He held babies, shook hands and smiled
for the cameras. Angela loved seeing that side of him, loved
watching him talk and laugh with his adoring fans.

Eyes wide with alarm, Angela cast a glance over her shoulder. She waited, listened intently. A loud crackling sound
filled the air, and a thick, heavy mist drifted inside the bedroom. Chucking the dresses onto the bed, Angela tore down
the hall and burst into the kitchen as if it was on fire. And
it was. Smoke was rising out of the pots, and the stench of
charred meat was suffocating. The smoke alarm wailed so
loud, Angela's head throbbed.

Grabbing the frying pan with one hand and the stainless-
steel pot with the other, she dumped them into the sink and
turned the water on full blast. The pots fizzled as steam rose
from the rubble. The blackened meat looked like rubber.

Angela threw open the window and took deep gulps of air.
The sky was overcast, a dark, menacing shade of gray, and
the wind was blowing hot and fast. After cleaning the stove
and mopping the floor, Angela ambled over to the kitchen

table and plopped down on a chair. Her hair was damp, her short silk robe smelled like charcoal, and sweat drenched her arms and legs.

Fanning a hand to her face, she stared at the gold wine flutes, the gleaming utensils and flickering candles. The plates were empty and would stay that way unless she could find a restaurant that would deliver. It was Friday night, the last day of classes for university students, and no doubt her favorite spots were jam-packed with inebriated graduates.

Angela glanced at the pantry, stocked to the brim with food, and smiled despite her frustration. Last Sunday, Demetri had shown up at her house with bags of groceries and whipped up a to-die-for Italian brunch. Maybe all wasn't lost, she thought, straightening in her seat. Maybe she could still surprise Demetri with a home-cooked meal. But what? Angela thought for a moment and came up empty. But she knew just whom to call. Simone was a whiz in the kitchen, and she'd know just what to do.

Confident she could salvage her romantic evening, Angela surged to her feet and swiped the cordless phone off the cradle. It was the perfect time to call. Jayden and Jordan were already in bed, and Simone and Marcus were probably relaxing on the couch, watching their favorite TV show. And if Simone came through for her, Angela was going to treat her to lunch. They hadn't been to the Skyline Grill in weeks, and they were overdue for a relaxing gabfest at their favorite hotspot.

"Hello?"

"Hey, girl," Angela said when Simone answered the phone. "What's up?"

"Who's this?"

"Quit playing. It's me."

"Me, who?"

Angela heard the edge in her tone and knew her friend was upset. And Angela knew why. "Sorry for not returning your calls," she began, leaning against the kitchen counter. "Things have been crazy the last few weeks. Between taping, volunteering at the shelter, doing the live morning show and—"

"Doing Demetri," she tossed out.

"Don't be like that, Simone. You know I'd never choose a guy over you."

"I've seen the tabloids. I know what's up."

Angela felt her face harden. "What's that supposed to mean?"

"You have a man now, so you ditched your girls. Even me, your best friend, and I'm eight months pregnant and swollen like a beach whale!"

"You're right, Simone. I haven't been a very good friend lately. Do you forgive me?"

"I will if you babysit the boys next Friday," she quipped, giggling.

"Sure, no problem. They can spend the whole weekend with me," Angela said, sighing in relief. "Every time we talk, you're planning another trip. Where are you and Marcus going now?"

"To a couples spa in Las Vegas." Her tone brightened with excitement. "Girl, I need some R & R in the worst way. And some cute new maternity clothes, too, because nothing in my closet fits anymore!"

The friends laughed.

"Simone, I need your help."

"Sure, no problem. What's up?"

"I burned dinner."

"What else is new?" Simone joked. "You *always* burn dinner."

In the background, Angela heard someone chuckle and knew Simone's husband, Marcus, was listening in. "Today was Demetri's last day at the Sports Rehab Clinic," she explained, drumming her fingertips absently on the counter.

"I wanted to surprise him with a home-cooked meal, but the steaks just went up in flames."

"Do what you always do," Simone advised. "Order in from an expensive restaurant, put the food on your favorite set of china and pretend you slaved over a hot stove for hours."

"I can't do that again. Not tonight," she argued. Angela's gaze drifted to the sink, her shoulders slumped in defeat. "I want to do something special for Demetri, something he'd never expect."

"Answer the door buck naked!"

Angela cracked up, but when she heard the doorbell chime, she killed her laughter. "Gotta go. Demetri's here!"

"Have fun, girlfriend. Rock his world!"

Hustling out of the kitchen, spraying air freshener as she went, Angela rushed down the hall and reached the foyer in ten seconds flat. At the thought of seeing him, a girlish smile exploded across her face. The night wasn't ruined. She could still do something special for Demetri. She'd treat him to dinner at his favorite restaurant, then spring for the penthouse suite at Trump International Hotel and Tower. Demetri loved it there, and so did she. *We can play dirty card games again,* she thought. *And this time, I'll let him win!*

The doorbell chimed. Again and again.

Angela whipped off her robe, dropped it at her feet and slipped on her leopard-print sandals. Checking herself out in the mirror, Angela decided she'd never looked sexier. Her eyes were bright, her skin was glowing, and her thick hair was a wild, tousled mess.

A smirk pinched her crimson-red lips. That was just the look she was going for—bold, brazen, down for anything. But when Angela opened the front door and saw Nichola standing on her porch, her smile froze. "Hey," she said, shielding herself with the door. "Um, what's up?"

"We need to talk."

Whipping off her oversize sunglasses, she strode past Angela with the air of a runway model. Her perfume was strong, and her white business suit was so tight, it fit like a corset.

"I'm a very busy woman, with no time to waste, so I'm going to make this quick."

Angela snatched her silk robe off the floor and shrugged it back on. "What's going on?" she asked, closing the front door. "You're scaring me. Is Demetri okay?"

"Of course. Why wouldn't he be?" Her eyes roamed over Angela's body, moving slowly from top to bottom. "Demetri doesn't date fat girls, so I couldn't figure out how the hell you sunk your claws into him, but now that I know the truth about your past, it all makes sense. Sex-trade workers are the most manipulative people in the world."

Confused, Angela belted her robe. "I don't know what you're talking about."

"I bet you don't," she snapped, swiveling her neck. Her diamond, teardrop earrings tinkled like chimes. "You went to great lengths to hide your past, but I was smart enough to uncover the truth."

A cold chill snaked down Angela's back, and goose bumps seared her skin.

"I hired the best private investigator in the country, and he uncovered so much dirt on you, I could do my *own* three-part series." Nichola stared at her, her eyes blazing and her lips drawn tight. "And you know what I'd call my salacious exposé? *Newscaster for Hire.*"

The floor fell out from underneath Angela's feet. Fear infected her entire body. She remained calm, but inside she was dying a slow, painful death. It felt as if her heart had been pierced with a knife. She was so overtaken by guilt and shame, water filled her eyes.

"I must admit, I was shocked when the P.I. told me the truth. You seem so polished, so sophisticated. I never would have guessed you were once a paid whore."

Angela winced and swallowed the lump wedged inside her

throat. This was a nightmare, the moment she had been dreading for years. Her heart pounded violently. No one knew—not her friends, not her family, not even Simone—that she'd worked as an escort to pay for university, and she had no intention of ever telling them. That was why she didn't do relationships, why she shied away from love.

"Don't tell Demetri," she pleaded. "Not now, not yet. He won't understand."

"Few men would. I mean, really, what guy wants to date a former prostitute?"

Angela felt a strong attack of guilt, but she looked straight at Nichola and spoke the truth. "I was never a prostitute. I was an escort. There's a big difference."

"No, there isn't. *Escort* is just a sophisticated word for *ho.* You screwed men for money, and from what the P.I. told me, you had a lot of fun doing it, too. In fact, you worked for Elite Escorts an entire year. That's a lot of sex and a lot of men, Angela."

"I never slept with any of my clients. Ever. Not one."

"Right, and that's your natural hair color!"

"It wasn't like that," Angela argued, refusing to back down. "My scholarship fell through, and I needed to make fast money. But after I paid my tuition, I quit."

"Cry me a river," she spat, twirling a finger in the air. "I heard that became-a-ho-to-pay-my-university-tuition story before."

"It's the truth."

"No, it's a crock of bull." Nichola rolled her eyes to the ceiling and swept a hand through her hair. "You became an escort because you're a whore, plain and simple."

"Leave," Angela said, pointing at the front door. Her head was throbbing, her nose was running, and she couldn't control the tremble in her voice. But Angela didn't care how she looked. All she cared about was getting rid of the publicist from hell. "Get out of my house and don't come back."

Nichola batted her eyelashes, wore an innocent face. "But we're not finished talking."

The cold, menacing look on Nichola's face shook Angela to the bone, but for the life of her she couldn't figure out what she'd done to warrant her wrath. "What have I ever done to you?" she asked, her confusion turning to anger. "Why are you doing this? Why are you trying to ruin my relationship with Demetri?"

"Because you don't deserve him."

"But you do?"

"Damn right I do! I've been by Demetri's side for the last twelve years, and thanks to me, he's one of the most popular athletes in the world." Nichola lifted her chin and threw her shoulders back. She looked pleased with herself, proud, as if she'd developed a cure for a deadly disease. "Things were going great until you came along. Now I hardly get to see him, and when I do, all he wants to talk about is how intelligent you are, how generous you are, how fun you are to be around. I'm sick of it!"

Her gaze was lethal, as cold as a trained assassin, and when she spoke her tone was shrill and bitter. "I have plans for me and Demetri, *big plans,* and I'm not going to let a two-bit whore who grew up in the hood steal my place. Got it?"

Angela lowered her eyes to the floor, stared intently at her stiletto-clad feet. She wished she had the power to just vanish into thin air. Listening to Nichola made her feel worthless, insignificant, and the more she insulted her, the smaller she felt. "What do you want from me?"

"I thought you'd never ask." Nichola broke out into a twisted smile. "Break up with Demetri tonight, or I'll tell him about your whoring past."

"You can't," she croaked, choking back a sob. Her eyes burned, heavy with tears. Angela willed herself to be strong, to keep it together, but when she imagined her life without Demetri in it, tears broke free and coursed furiously down her cheeks. The truth about her past would tear him apart, and the last thing Angela wanted to do was hurt him. Not after all the sweet, thoughtful things he'd done for her over the past three months. "Demetri can never find out about it."

"Fine, then do what I say and I'll keep my mouth shut."

"Can't we work something else out? I'll give you anything you want—"

"Don't you get it? All I want is Demetri. That's it." Nichola took her car keys out of her Hermès bag and slid her sunglasses back on. "Ta-ta. Gotta run. I'm meeting a producer from the network for drinks, and I can't afford to be late."

"Wait! Please! Can't we discuss this?"

Throwing open the front door, Nichola sashayed down the paved brick walkway wearing the brightest smile.

Seconds later, Nichola sped down the street in her red two-door coupe, her music blaring so loud, the windows in Angela's house shook. Unable to move, she slumped against the wooden railing, a sick, aching feeling in her heart.

Angela blinked back tears, pressing her eyes shut tight. The thick, warm air blew across her skin, but her body trembled uncontrollably. Her palms were damp, slick with perspiration, and her erratic heartbeat pounded in fear.

Albany Park was filled with the sounds of summer. Children shrieked and laughed as they jumped through sprinklers, cyclists zoomed up the sidewalk, and the ice-cream truck crawled down the street carrying the scent of milk chocolate. Angela didn't know how long she stood on her front porch, replaying Nichola's words in her head, but with each passing second, her feelings of despair and isolation grew.

It took supreme effort for Angela to turn around and walk inside the house. And when she saw the glass vase—the one Demetri had surprised her with last night—filled with a dazzling array of colored tulips, she broke down and started to cry again.

Dropping her face in her hands, she slumped against the

door and slid down to the cold hardwood floor. Grief consumed her, a sense of loss so profound, her heart throbbed in pain. Angela didn't have psychic powers, but as deep, racking sobs shook her body, she was certain of one thing: life as she knew it was over.

Chapter 19

Baseball fans in Chicago Royals jerseys and T-shirts were everywhere—on the sidewalk, standing on the hoods of their cars, waving frantically across the busy, traffic-congested street. And when Demetri strode out of Skyline Field, a cheer went up.

Angela had never seen anything like it. The crowd outside of the stadium seemed to be growing by the second, and everywhere she looked people were smiling and cheering. Teenage girls in tank tops and Daisy Dukes were crying, grown men where hollering Demetri's name, and a group of inebriated college kids were singing a slurred, off-key rendition of "Take Me Out to the Ball Game."

"Are you okay?" Demetri squeezed Angela's hand and sent her a reassuring smile.

"Yeah, I'm fine. Just a little overwhelmed, that's all."

He hit a button on his car keys, and the lights on his gleaming, white Jaguar flashed. The windows slid down, the sunroof opened, and the car stereo blared.

"Baby, get inside," he said, opening the passenger-side door. "People are pushing against the barricades, and I don't want you to get hurt."

Angela slid inside the car and watched as Demetri entertained the crowd. He signed posters, magazine covers and posed for dozens of pictures with his adoring fans. Twenty minutes after exiting the stadium, Demetri hopped into the front seat, threw it into Drive and shot down the block like a rocket.

"What's wrong?" Casting a glance at her, his facial expression filled with concern. He reached out and gently stroked the back of her neck.

"What makes you think something's wrong?"

"You're usually upbeat and chatty, but you haven't said more than a few words all day."

"I'm fine. I just have a lot on my mind."

"Want to talk about it?" His eyes twinkled when he smiled. "Go on, baby. I'm all ears."

His words made her feel a powerful rush of emotion. Tears burned the backs of her eyes. Willing herself not to cry, Angela ordered herself to be strong, to keep it together. It was the first time she'd seen Demetri all week, but instead of being excited about spending the entire day with him, she felt anxious and afraid. *Will this be the day Nichola tells Demetri about my past? Will he ever forgive me once he learns the truth?*

Angela thought about last Tuesday night, the day her life took a turn for the worst. After Nichola sashayed out of her house, Angela called Demetri and canceled their date. When he pressed her for an explanation, Angela told him she was sick. And she was. She had a queasy stomach and an excruciating headache that pulsed behind her right eye. A week later her symptoms remained.

"It's nothing." Angela tried to smile, to put his fears to rest, but her lips wouldn't curve upward. She couldn't summon the effort it took. Probably because she'd spent the past few days crying and stressing about the vicious threats Nichola had made. "I'm just tired," she lied, forcing a yawn. "A good night's rest and I'll be as good as new."

A shadow of disappointment fell across Demetri's face. They drove on in silence for several miles, and when he finally spoke, there was a note of sadness in his voice. "Didn't you enjoy the tour of the stadium and our picnic lunch?"

"Yes, of course. It was amazing. I loved every minute of it."

Demetri raised an eyebrow. "Are you sure?"

"I said I had a great time. Why don't you believe me?"

"Because you've been quiet and distant all afternoon, and every time I touch you, you tense up." He lowered his hand from her neck to her thigh, giving it a soft, playful squeeze. "Don't worry, baby. When we get home, I'll make everything better. A deep tissue massage will—"

"I can't stay with you tonight," Angela said, cutting him off. "I have to be at the station at five a.m., and I don't want to make that long drive back to my place in the morning."

"I know. That's why we're staying in the city tonight."

"You got a hotel room?"

"Just wait and see. We're almost there."

Angela turned toward the passenger-side window and pretended to admire all the tall, attractive buildings they sped by. Her mind replayed the afternoon. Strolling around the old, historic stadium, chatting with Demetri's teammates and sharing a romantic picnic lunch out on the field. It had been a memorable day, but it was hard staying upbeat when Nichola was texting her threatening messages. Angela thought about the last text message Nichola had sent, the one that caused her blood to run cold.

I wonder what would happen if the president of WJN-TV found out his hotshot new broadcaster used to be a call girl.

"I almost forgot. I have something for you."

Angela blinked and shook free of her thoughts. "Sorry, I missed that. What did you say?"

At the intersection, Demetri opened the center console and took out a thin, black blindfold. "I'll take it off as soon as we get to our mystery destination," he said with a wide smile. "And no peeking, baby. I want it to be a surprise."

Angela hated the thought of being blindfolded, but she didn't argue. A power nap would do her some good, and when Demetri tied the soft piece of cloth at the back of her

We're players, lady-killers, men who live for the thrill of the chase. That's just who we are, Demetri. It's in our blood."

Rafael scratched his head and then gave it a hard shake. "Nicco, what are you talking about? It's not in our blood to mistreat women or dog them out. Mom and Dad have been happily married for almost forty years, and he still dotes on her!"

"Yeah, but Moms is old-school. They don't make 'em like her anymore. If they did, I would have burned my player card a long time ago!"

"Nicco's right. Modern women are out for themselves," Rafael conceded with a shrug. "I went out with that cute boutique buyer again last week, and after dessert, she gave me her bank-account number and told me to deposit her weekly allowance in a timely manner."

"At least she didn't steal your Benz and hightail it down to Tijuana!" A scowl wrinkled Nicco's tanned face. "All women do is take, take, take."

Demetri heard the edge in Nicco's tone and sympathized with him. Unfortunately, he knew exactly what his brother was talking about. From the day he'd turned pro, he'd seen how ugly and manipulative people could be. He didn't trust easily and had always believed that everyone outside of his inner circle was out to screw him over.

But then he'd met Angela.

Over time, she'd changed his views about the world. She didn't care about his wealth or his fame, or spending his money, either. Angela loved him—just him—and she wasn't afraid to check him when he was wrong. His girl told him what he needed to hear, not what he *wanted* to hear, and Demetri respected her for always telling him the truth. "Angela's never asked me for a dime," he said. "Hell, she wouldn't even let me take her shopping, and every time we went out for dinner, she insisted on leaving a tip *on top* of my tip!"

The brothers chuckled.

head, her eyes grew heavy, and her muscles relaxed. As she snuggled down into her seat and curled up against the window, Angela felt the car jolt forward and then roll to a stop.

Ten minutes later, Angela was clutching Demetri's forearm and moving along the sleek tiled floor with short, measured steps. She heard an elevator ping, boisterous conversation around her, and the glare of bright overhead lights seeped in through the corner of her blindfold. Angela didn't know why she'd agreed to let Demetri blindfold her, but when she heard soft, romantic music playing, her trepidation waned and her interest peaked.

"Surprise! Welcome home!"

Demetri untied the blindfold, and when Angela saw the lavish suite decked out in marble and luxurious furniture, she recognized it immediately. They were in the penthouse suite at Trump International Hotel and Tower, their secret getaway in the heart of the city. The wall-length windows overlooking downtown Chicago provided a spectacular panoramic view, but Angela's favorite spot in the suite was the enclosed wraparound balcony.

Angela glanced around the suite, confused. The living room looked a lot like the one in her house. There were fashion magazines on the glass coffee table, a red velvet armchair, and a statue—just like the one she'd bought in Cancun—was sitting on the bookshelf. The teal walls weren't covered in expensive abstract paintings. Instead they were filled with dozens of framed candid pictures that Demetri had snapped on his cell phone when they were goofing around at his estate. Angela smiled when she thought about all the great times they'd had the past few months.

"What do you think? Do you love it?"

"Yeah, it's great. But why did you have the hotel redecorate the suite for one night?"

Demetri came up behind her and wrapped his hands around

her waist. "Not for one night. This is permanent, unless you want to redecorate again."

"I don't understand."

"This is our new place."

Angela stared at him, puzzled and confused by his words. "*Our* place?"

"I hate you making the drive to Lake County after dark, and since you don't like my driver picking you up after work, I decided to buy this penthouse." A proud grin stretched across his face. "Now you don't have to steal the designer bathrobes or pilfer the candy in the mini bar. Everything in here is yours for the taking!"

"This suite is amazing, and I appreciate the gesture, but we can't live together."

"Why not? We're practically living together now!" Demetri held her tight. "Angela, I love spoiling you and doing things to make you smile. Because of you, I have a new lease on life. For the first time in years, I feel as rejuvenated and healthy as I did my rookie year."

Angela shook her head and held her hands out in front of her. "This is all too much. The expensive gifts, the penthouse, this insane notion of us living happily ever after."

"What's so crazy about that?" Demetri turned her around to face him and cupped her chin softly in his hands. He pressed a gentle kiss to her forehead and spoke in a tender voice. "Baby, I'm committed to you, one hundred percent, all the way in. If I wasn't, I wouldn't be making future plans or taking you with me to Italy to meet my parents."

"Italy!" Angela shrieked, widening her eyes. "Please tell me you're joking."

"We're going Memorial Day weekend. And that's not all. We're staying at the…"

"Demetri, I can't go with you to Italy."

"Of course you can. You already booked the time off work, remember?"

"Yeah, so I can work on my next series, not to fly halfway around the world."

"You can work on the jet. It has everything you need. An office, a computer…"

"Demetri, I don't want to meet your parents."

His eyes darkened. "Why not?"

"Because I don't want them to read too much into our relationship. We're lovers, nothing more, and that's not going to change." The lie seared her lips and filled her mouth with such a bitter taste she couldn't swallow. Her stomach lurched, pitched violently to the right. "I told you from day one I wasn't looking for anything serious. We're having fun, lots of laughs and great sex. Don't make this out to be more than it is."

He gave her a blank look and rubbed his fingertips over his eyes. "Angela, what are you talking about? Where is all this coming from?"

A war was waging in her heart as Nichola's words tormented her troubled mind. An unseen force urged her to tell Demetri the truth about her past, but she couldn't make her lips form the words. Her eyes were teary, her throat was dry, and when Demetri sank onto the leather couch and raked his hands over his head, her heart broke in two. Angela loved Demetri with all her heart, more than she'd ever loved anyone before, and the days they had spent together were the happiest of her life. His kisses were magical, his touch made her feel sexy, and being in his arms was the best feeling in the world. It killed her to know that he was hurting and that she'd been the one to cause him pain, but Angela couldn't tell Demetri—or anyone else—that she used to be an escort.

"I'm not cut out for relationships—you know that," she said, adopting a playful tone. "I hate being tied down, and after a while, dating the same person gets boring. That's why I like to play the field, you know, keep my options wide open."

Demetri's head snapped up. Lines of confusion creased

his forehead. He was breathing so heavily, Angela couldn't hear the music from the stereo.

"You're dating other guys?" His tone was sharp, filled with anger and accusation. He stared at her with contempt in his eyes. "Who? How many?"

"Why does it matter? We're both free to date and *do* whoever we want."

He slammed his fists on the armrest and rose to his feet. For a long moment he studied her with a lethal expression. The veins in his neck were stretched so tight, Angela was scared they'd snap. The next words he spoke were through clenched teeth, in a tone she'd never heard him use before, one that made her feel empty inside. "I won't share you, Angela. Not now, not ever."

"That's not your decision to make."

"Then we're through."

Angela didn't know what possessed her to touch him, to reach out and rest a hand on his cheek, but she did. To her surprise, he didn't pull away. This was the last time they'd ever be this close, the last time she'd ever have Demetri all to herself, and the thought made it hard to breathe. Angela saw pain etched on his face, a heartbreaking sadness that tore her up inside.

"Look me in the eye," he ordered, gripping her shoulders, "and tell me you don't love me. Tell me the last three months meant absolutely nothing to you."

Angela opened her mouth but quickly closed it. She couldn't do it, couldn't lie.

"I'm not the right girl for you, Demetri. You deserve someone better, someone you can be proud to take home to your parents."

"Baby, what are you talking about? You're the most remarkable woman I've ever met," he praised. "You work your ass off down at the station but still find time to volunteer, mentor teenage girls and burn dinner for me at least once a week."

Angela smothered a laugh, but inside she was smiling. She was being a royal first-class jerk to Demetri, but here he was, complimenting her. For as long as she lived, she'd never forget him or the love they shared.

"I want you, Angela. Only you, and no one else."

"I'm sorry, Demetri, but I can't do this anymore. I need my space and the freedom to do what I want, whenever I want. You're a great guy, but I'm tired of feeling smothered."

"Smothered?"

"Yeah, smothered," she said, opening her purse and rummaging around inside for nothing. Her eyes were stinging, and Angela knew if she didn't leave soon, the tears would surely fall. "I better get out of here. I have a full day ahead of me tomorrow."

"Angela, you sure this is what you want?"

His voice was muffled, and for a second Angela feared that he was going to cry. He wouldn't, of course. He was Demetri Morretti, a superstar athlete who had beautiful women like Nichola Caruso at his disposal. Men like Demetri, young, handsome, ridiculously wealthy, didn't stay single for long, and Angela knew he'd have another girl on his arm by the end of the week. At least that was what she told herself when guilt troubled her conscience.

She leaned in and gave Demetri a peck on the cheek and forced a smile. "Have fun in Italy. And good luck this season."

Then Angela turned and walked away. She'd played her role to the hilt, but when she stepped onto the private elevator and the heavy steel doors closed, her facade cracked. Her vision blurred, and for a long, dizzying moment she couldn't breathe. Angela slapped away the tears as they spilled down her cheeks, but nothing could assuage the aching void in her heart.

Chapter 20

Angela opened the refrigerator, took out the plastic container filled with barbecue chicken wings and strode out the back door. The sky was free of clouds, the air was thick and humid, and a hot breeze blew through her. Her colorful, long dress whipped around her ankles as she ambled through the backyard.

Angela fanned a hand in front of her face. It was scorching outside, at least ninety degrees, but her dad didn't seem to mind the sweltering heat. He was standing beside the grill, singing in perfect pitch to the Motown classic playing on his battered stereo. Like the CD player, the grill looked as though it was on its last legs. Every few minutes, it conked out, and when her dad turned it back on, smoke billowed out the hood. *Tomorrow, I'm buying him a new one,* Angela decided, resting the container on the wooden picnic table. *And a new stereo, too!*

Within the hour, the backyard would be filled with family and friends looking to celebrate Memorial Day by cutting loose, getting down and eating finger-lickin'-good barbecue. Angela was looking forward to catching up with her relatives and playing a game or two of dominoes with her uncles. But every time she heard an airplane in the distance, she couldn't help but think about Demetri. This was the weekend they should have been in Italy, visiting his family and taking in the sights, but because of the things she'd said and done, they were over. Angela told herself it was for the best, that it was better being alone than living a lie, but if that was true, why did she feel as if she were going to die of a broken heart?

It had been a week since their breakup, and each day was harder than the one before. At work, Angela was the consummate professional, but at night, when she was alone, thoughts of Demetri and the love they'd shared consumed her. For hours, she'd lie in bed, staring up at the ceiling, lamenting over what could have been. These days she was such a basket case she considered seeking professional help. When she wasn't crying, she was on her laptop watching old Chicago Royals games and interviews.

Eye on Chicago was still number one with viewers, but ever since her interview with Demetri and his brothers had gone up in smoke, Salem had been giving her the cold shoulder. *Who cares?* Angela thought, raking a hand through her windswept hair. *The man I love hates me.*

Loud music filled the air, and when she heard a car door slam in the distance, she knew her brother had arrived. Rodney strode into the backyard carrying a case of beer in one hand and plastic bags filled with junk food in the other.

"Hey, sis, what's up?" Rodney asked, flashing a smile at her.

Angela had nothing to smile about, so she nodded her head instead. It was the first time she'd seen him since running into him at Madison's Steak Bar a few weeks back with Demetri. But he leaned over and dropped a kiss on her cheek anyway, as if everything were cool between them. It wasn't, but Angela knew better than to argue with Rodney in front of her dad.

"Here, this is for you." He pushed a wad of money, secured with a plastic elastic band, into her hands and winked. "Don't spend it all in one place."

Frowning, Angela glanced from the cash to her brother. "Where did you get this?"

"From work, of course!" Rodney rolled his eyes. "I got my

first paycheck today, and after taking out a grand for you, I still have a little left over in my savings to buy—"

"You have a savings account?" Shaking her head, Angela dropped down in the checkered lawn chair behind her. "Someone pinch me. I must be dreaming!"

"I told you your brother would get his act together." Cornelius wagged his plastic spatula at his daughter. "He just needed some time."

"And a break," he added, sending Angela a smile. "Thanks again for the hookup, sis. Working for the Royals is a real sweet gig."

"You're working at Skyline Field? How did that happen?"

"A couple days after I ran into you and Demetri at that posh restaurant, he called and told me the stadium was looking for new ushers. I wasn't interested *until* he told me the pay was twenty bucks an hour. Then I told him, 'Hell yeah!'"

"I had no idea he called you."

"Really, but Demetri said he was hiring me as a favor to you."

Angela shook her head. "I had nothing to do with you getting the job."

"For real? So, my charm and good looks got me the gig?" Rodney smiled wide. "I guess I'm just fly like that!"

Cornelius stroked his beard reflectively. "Maybe I was wrong about Demetri Morretti. Maybe he isn't as bad as I thought."

"Pops, Demetri's mad cool," Rodney said, his tone full of admiration. "He's real laid-back, and everyone down at the field loves him."

"Is that right?"

"Demetri knows everyone by name—even the janitors—and he's the best tipper on the team. Yesterday, he gave me a hundred bucks just for vacuuming his Bentley!"

"That's hard to believe." Cornelius opened the cooler, took

out a can of Pepsi and broke the tab. "I read that he's a troublemaker, a real hothead."

"Now that I've gotten to know him, I don't believe the hype anymore."

Cornelius grinned. "Rodney, you don't know Demetri Morretti any more than I do. You've only been working there a couple weeks."

"Yeah, but I've seen firsthand all the crap Demetri and his teammates go through."

"Please." Cornelius dismissed his son's words with a flick of his hand. "They live in million-dollar homes, drive flashy sports cars and can afford to buy the very best of everything. What's so hard about that?"

"I used to envy pro athletes, but now that I know what goes on behind the scenes, I actually feel sorry for them," Rodney said. "People are always trying to provoke Demetri into fights so they can cash in on his money. Everyone wants fifteen minutes of fame, and they'll do just about anything to get it, including…"

Angela sat up, listening with rapt interest as Rodney spoke. What he said was true, every single word. She'd seen firsthand how cruel society could be to celebrities. Whenever she was out with Demetri, he was constantly looking over his shoulder. He craved privacy and didn't want to be surrounded by the paparazzi. But to make her happy he'd taken her to festivals, shows and anywhere else her heart desired.

"Demetri said if I work hard and have the right attitude, the team might even pay for me to go to trade school. Isn't that crazy?"

"You want to go to trade school? Since when?"

Rodney shrugged. "I'm just thinking about it. Demetri thinks I'm smart, and he said if I apply myself, I could make something of myself…"

Angela slid farther down her lawn chair. She tried to manage her emotions the best she could, but it was hard to keep her composure when all she wanted to do was cry. Being without Demetri was killing her, and hearing Rodney talk about what a great guy he was only intensified her guilt. Her brother was spot-on, though. Demetri was an amazing man, hands down the sweetest, most generous person she'd ever met.

"Demetri doesn't sound half-bad," Cornelius said, slowly nodding his head. "Now I see why you and Angela like him so much."

Not like, Dad, love. I love him with all my heart.

Her gaze fell on her cell phone, which was sitting on the pile of board games. Angela wanted to call Demetri to apologize for the way she'd acted last week and thank him for helping Rodney, but she was too afraid. What if Nichola had told him about her past?

The sun was still strong, making Angela unbearably hot, yet her entire body was shaking. Her past was hanging over her head, tormenting her day and night. The dirty little secret she'd been keeping for years had prevented her from falling in love and giving herself completely to any man, and Angela was tired. Tired of running from her past and the man she loved. She'd let fear stop her from telling Demetri the truth, but she knew if she didn't come clean to the people she loved, she'd never be able to move forward.

"Did you invite Demetri and his people to come over today?"

Angela glanced up at her dad and shook her head.

"Why not? I'd love to meet him."

"It's not going to happen, Dad. We're through."

Her father's jaw dropped, and Rodney groaned.

"Baby girl, what happened?" Cornelius put his soda can down on the wooden picnic table. He plopped down in the chair beside her and took her hand. "You've been talking my ear off for weeks about how great Demetri is. I thought you really liked him."

I love him, Dad, more than I've ever loved anyone before.

"It's a long, sad story. One you definitely don't want to hear."

"Of course I do. I'm your dad, and anything that affects you affects me."

"But I did something *really* stupid. Something I'm deeply ashamed of."

Cornelius hugged her to his chest and dropped a kiss on her forehead. "Everyone makes mistakes, Angela, and there's nothing you could ever say that would make me love you any less."

"Same here, sis. You're my shero!" Rodney's eyes were watery, but he wore a big, goofy grin. "Now, stop crying. We're having a party this afternoon, remember?"

Angela didn't realize she was crying until her dad grabbed a napkin off the picnic table and wiped her cheeks. His slim, narrow face was pinched with concern. The setting was all wrong, and so was the timing, but Angela knew if she didn't tell her dad the truth now, she'd never do it. So, she swallowed the knot in her throat and gave his hand a light squeeze. "Dad, can we go inside and talk?" she asked, ignoring the butterflies flittering around in her stomach. "There's something I have to tell you. Something I should have told you years ago."

Chapter 21

Demetri stepped up to the plate and tried a few practice swings. His right arm felt strong, better than it had in months. *How fitting,* he thought, shaking his head. *The same week I'm cleared to practice with the team my relationship with Angela goes up in smoke.*

Tired of lifting weights in his gym, he'd headed outside to his enclosed seven-foot batting cage, determined. The air was still and held the faint scent of rain. It was the first time Demetri had been outside all week, and the sun was so bright, it irritated his eyes.

Tucking his baseball bat under his arm, he took his shades out of his back pocket and slid them on. Now he could focus. Or at least pretend to. These days, he thought about Angela, and nothing else. He had been so bummed about their breakup, he didn't have the strength to leave the house. It was easier to stay home than deal with the world. For the past week, he'd done nothing but eat, sleep and relive every second of his last conversation with Angela. And, still, after all this time, he couldn't make sense of what went wrong.

The machine spit out a fast ball, and Demetri swung the wooden baseball bat with such force, he felt a slight twinge in his right shoulder. It was probably nothing, but he made a mental note to speak to his surgeon about it tomorrow at his checkup.

For the next hour, Demetri took his frustration and anger out on the pitches. And by the time he was finished practicing, his blue Nike T-shirt was drenched in sweat.

"Lookin' good, bro! You'll be back on the mound in no time!"

Demetri looked up and saw Nicco and Rafael leaning against the metal chain-link fence and gave them a nod. "What's up? I had no idea you guys were coming to town."

Rafael gave a shrug of his shoulder. "It was a last-minute decision."

"How was Argentina?"

"Sinful," Nicco said with a straight face. "But I loved every minute of it."

"I bet you did." Demetri narrowed his eyes and zeroed in on his brother's left forearm. The words *Dolce Vita* were tattooed in block letters down the length of his arm. "I see you got some new ink while you were in Buenos Aires."

"It hurt like a bitch, but the female tattoo artist gave me *exceptional* care afterwards."

"That's why you skipped my cricket match? Because you were too busy hooking up with some random chick?" Rafael looked relaxed in his striped polo shirt and khaki shorts, but when he glared at Nicco, his entire disposition changed. "Do you have to bed every woman you meet?"

"Of course not." Nicco wore a sly smile. "Only the sexy ones, bro. You know that."

Demetri and Rafael shook their heads.

"Speaking of chicks, are you still bangin' that smokin'-hot TV newscaster?"

Demetri's jaw tightened. "Her name is Angela."

"My bad." Nicco chuckled, held up a hand in a gesture of peace. "You still hittin' that?"

"Knock it off, Nicco. I'm not in the mood."

"You got too clingy, and she dumped you, huh?" Releasing a heavy sigh, he stepped inside the batting cage and clapped Demetri on the shoulder. "When are you going to learn that love doesn't last? Guys like us aren't cut out for relationships.

"I'm never settling down," Nicco announced, raking a hand through his short, curly black hair. "I'll be a player until I die!"

"Not if Mom can help it," Rafael said. "She wants daughters-in-law and grandbabies, and she's not beneath plotting and scheming to get them, either!"

"Forget about Angela Kelly and move on to the next chick."

"That's just it, Nicco. I can't," Demetri confessed, staring out into the bright blue sky. Being in a loving, committed relationship was who he was, who he'd always been. He wanted Angela—and no one else.

"The best way to get over a girl is by banging a new one." Nicco grinned. "That *always* works for me."

"If I can't have Angela, then I don't want anyone."

Two weeks had passed since Angela walked out on him. He thought of her day and night and would look at the pictures of her on his cell phone for hours. Demetri had racked his brain trying to piece together why she'd lashed out at him. But he'd come to only one conclusion and that was that Angela had lied to him. She wasn't dating other guys, wasn't seeing anyone else. When she wasn't at work, she was with him, and on the few occasions she went out with her girlfriends, she texted him throughout the night. So, why would she make up a story about sleeping with other guys? Why would she intentionally try to hurt him?

"If I were you, I'd..." Nicco broke off speaking and whipped out his cell phone. "Hold up, guys. I need to take this call."

"Something Angela said at the penthouse has been bothering me for weeks," Demetri said aloud. "She said I deserve someone better, someone I could be proud to take home to my family. At the time, I didn't think too much of it, but now it keeps playing in my mind."

"It sounds like your girl's running scared."

"Of what?"

Rafael gave a shrug. "You won't know unless you talk to her."

"I can't."

"Why not?"

"Because she doesn't want me. She wants to play the field." Inwardly, Demetri winced, but outwardly he wore a hard, stern face. He had to. He couldn't let anyone know— not even his brothers—how much he was hurting. The truth was, he missed Angela so much, his body ached with need. He yearned to hear her voice, to feel her touch, to have her unconditional love, and he wondered how he could ever live without her.

"Son of a bitch!" Nicco shouted, kicking the metal chain-link fence.

"What's the matter?"

"My assistant quit and is threatening to sue."

Rafael narrowed his eyes and wore a disgusted face. "You slept with her, didn't you?"

"It was an innocent mistake." Nicco dragged a hand down the length of his face and released a deep sigh. "I had too much to drink one night, and one thing led to another..."

"You're unbelievable," Rafael fumed, folding his arms rigidly across his chest. "It's time to grow up, Nicco. You're not a kid anymore, and I'm sick of fixing your mistakes."

Nicco started to speak but stopped when his cell phone rang again. He put it to his ear and turned away from his brothers. He spoke soft Italian to the caller on the line.

"I've only met Angela once, but it's obvious she makes you happy," Rafael said, his scowl gone and his smile sincere. "Since you guys started dating, you've become more outgoing, and now you're using your celebrity status for good. That's great, bro."

"The woman called me out on national television! I had to get my act together, *fast*."

"Demetri, don't let pride or your fear of rejection keep you from the woman you love." Rafael blew out a deep breath. "I did that once and to this day I regret not fighting for her. If Angela's the one, don't let anything get between you."

Demetri pondered his brother's words, truly considering what he'd said, and realized that Rafael was right. He had to fight for Angela, had to do whatever it took to get her back. She was his world and he wanted to spend the rest of his life with her. He was ready to go the distance, ready to make her his lawfully wedded wife. He wanted kids, family trips and the whole nine yards.

"Thanks, bro. You're the best!" Demetri chucked his baseball bat to the ground, kissed his brother on both cheeks and ran out of the batting cage. "Gotta jet. See you guys later!"

Chapter 22

Demetri jogged past the greenhouse and raced through the patio doors as if his life depended on it. And it did. He had to get to his girl, had to see her right away. He refused to live another day without her. Demetri was so consumed with thoughts of reconciling with Angela, he bumped into Nichola as she stepped out of the kitchen pantry.

"Where's the fire?" she joked, dumping the bags of potato chips on the granite breakfast bar. "Do you and your brothers want to eat lunch outside on the patio or in the game room?"

"I'm not staying. I'm going to see Angela."

"You two broke up."

"I'll explain later." Demetri glanced around the kitchen and saw all of the food trays and bottles of wine artfully arranged on the glass table. "It looks great in here."

"I made all your favorites and a whole pitcher of that sangria punch you love so much."

"Thanks, Nichola," he said, patting her shoulder. "Ask the housekeepers to clean the master suite and to fill all the vases in the living room with yellow tulips. I'm bringing my baby back home tonight, and I want everything to be perfect!"

"Hell no! That bitch isn't welcome here."

Demetri felt his nostrils flare and his hands curl into fists. "Excuse me?"

"If you bring Angela here, I'm leaving."

"Okay. See you tomorrow."

"I'm serious, Demetri. I'll walk out that door, and I won't

come back." Nichola puffed out her cheeks. "You don't need Angela or anyone else. All you need is me."

"Nichola, it's obvious you've had too much to drink," Demetri said, trying to lighten the mood with a joke. "Go home and sleep it off, and we'll talk in the morning."

"But I have good news. That's why I'm here. We're celebrating!" She rushed over to the glass table, picked up two cocktail glasses and pushed one into his hand. "Your new reality show, *Demetri's Bachelor Pad,* starts filming in September!"

Demetri scratched his head. He'd been out of sorts all week, and as grumpy as an old bear, but he didn't remember Nichola ever mentioning a TV deal. "I don't want my own show, Nichola. I'm a baseball player, not a reality star."

"But the network is rolling out the red carpet for you." Nichola was so excited, she was practically shouting her words. "Since I came up with the concept for the series *and* developed a kick-ass marketing campaign, they've agreed to let me be executive producer of the show!"

"Still not interested," he said. "And I don't care how much they're paying."

"Why not? This show could open a lot of doors for you."

"I'm a private person. I'd hate the idea of cameras following me and Angela around twenty-four seven. It's creepy. I won't do it."

Nichola held up an index finger. "Would you stop talking about her for one second and give some serious thought about this million-dollar deal?"

"There's nothing to think about. My priorities are baseball, my family, Angela and—"

"Forget about that skank. She's a whore and you deserve better."

Demetri narrowed his eyes. The more he stared at his publicist, the more convinced he was that she was drunk. Her skin was pale, and her face possessed a crazed expression. It took supreme effort to control his temper, but he spoke in a calm, rational voice. "Don't ever talk about Angela like that again," he warned. "I don't know what your problem is with her, but I'm not going to let you disrespect her."

"I called her a skank because that's what she is." A smile filled her lips, and her eyes lit up like diamonds. "Your precious Angela used to be an escort."

Demetri heard what Nichola had said, but he didn't understand. He stood paralyzed as her words turned over in his mind. He didn't believe it. His publicist was lying, just trying to poison his mind. *But why?*

"I hired a private investigator to check her out, and he uncovered a ton of dirt about her."

"You did what?" The question exploded out of Demetri's mouth. "For what reason? I never asked you to."

"Thank God I did, or you would have done something stupid like marry her!"

"Nichola, watch yourself," he warned. "You're out of line."

"You know what else the P.I. told me?"

Her nose wrinkled in disgust, but the expression on her face was one of pure joy. Nichola was enjoying every minute of this. For some sick reason she took great pleasure in smashing his hopes and dreams for the future.

"Angela's mother died five years ago from a drug overdose. Shoot, for all you know, she could be a druggie like her crackhead mom."

"Dammit, Nichola. Stop!"

Closing his eyes didn't block out the loud, shrill noises in his head. He heard Angela's tearful voice, then Nichola's harsh biting tone, playing in his mind over and over again. *You don't deserve someone like me. You deserve better.... Forget about her, Demetri.... She's a whore and you deserve better....* He was puzzled for a second, surprised that both women had virtually told him the exact same thing, but then something clicked. Everything made sense.

Demetri's eyes shot open. Stepping forward, he asked Nichola the question circling his mind. "You confronted Angela about what the private investigator told you, didn't you?"

"Of course I did. It's my job. That's what any good publicist would do."

"You told her she wasn't good enough for me, that I deserve better?"

"Why does it matter? She's gone, so forget her and move on." Her tone was firm, all business, as if she were chairing a board meeting. And she looked the part, too, standing there in a fitted black dress and wearing millions in diamonds. "It's time to move on to bigger and better things, like your *own* show."

Anger burned in Demetri's veins. He was so enraged that he wanted to grab Nichola and shake some sense into her. But instead of going after his publicist, he paced the length of the room. Three months ago, he would have punched a hole in the wall. But he wasn't the same man he used to be. He'd matured. He'd learned to see the world through Angela's eyes. And he wasn't going to embarrass his family or the woman he loved ever again. "I can't deal with this right now," he said, dragging a hand down the length of his face. "I need some time to think."

"What's there to think about? I know what's best for you, and it's this opportunity."

"I'm not talking about the reality show. I'm talking about Angela."

"God," she raged, throwing her hands up in the air. "I'm sick of hearing her stupid name! Enough already! I got rid of her, and she's not coming back, so…"

Her tone consumed Demetri with such rage he couldn't see straight. It broke his heart to think that Angela was hurting and that Nichola—someone he trusted—was the cause. He wanted to hate her, but his heart wouldn't let him. Nichola had been his publicist for twelve long years, and he loved her like a sister. But that didn't mean he was going to forgive and forget what she'd done. Her behavior was hard to justify and impossible to condone. Demetri pointed at the front door. "Nichola, you're fired. Please leave."

Her smile vanished. "Y-y-you can't fire me."

"I'll have my accountant put your final check and an official letter of termination in the mail first thing tomorrow."

Nichola stared at him in horror, as if she'd just seen a ghost.

His heart was heavy, filled with frustration and disappointment. He was so disgusted by Nichola's behavior, he couldn't stand to be in the same room with her a moment longer. "I want you gone by the time I finish getting dressed."

"Demetri, don't do this," she begged. "I love you. I've always loved you."

"You don't love me. You love the benefits of managing a celebrity."

"Of course I do. Who wouldn't?" Nichola's smile was back, shining in full force. "With my brains and beauty and your talent, we could be the next celebrity power couple."

Demetri didn't bother to answer. Shaking his head, he turned toward the staircase.

Nichola grabbed his forearm and threw herself against him. "Come back!"

Breaking free of her grasp, Demetri strode out of the room and down the hallway. He heard glass break, then an ear-splitting wail, but he continued upstairs to the second floor.

In the master bedroom, Demetri fell down on the bed and dropped his head into his hands. *Angela used to be an escort...an escort...* The word froze in his brain. Demetri didn't know what to think, didn't know what to believe. He wanted to make sense of what Nichola had said. What if it was true? What if Angela used to be an escort?

So what? his inner voice said. *Everyone has a past, even you.*

The truth slammed into him with the force of a battering ram. He'd made a lot of mistakes in the past and had done things he was ashamed of, but things had changed for the better when he'd met Angela Kelly—the strong, tenacious TV newscaster who lived to help others. It didn't matter what Angela had done in her past. All that mattered to him was the here and now.

He wasn't going to shut her out or lump her in with all the other lying, conniving women he'd had the misfortune of meeting in the past. He'd known from the first time they'd met that Angela was different. She challenged him, inspired him and wasn't afraid to speak her mind. They had great talks about life, their families and the stress of being famous in a celebrity-obsessed world. Angela cared about him, loved him despite his faults and shortcomings and put his needs above her own. Finally, Demetri understood why she'd lied to him that night in the penthouse suite. It wasn't because she didn't love him, but because she *did*.

Demetri rose to his feet and headed into his walk-in closet. Kicking off his sneakers, he searched through his dress shirts for something to wear. "Call Angela at home," he said aloud. The cordless phone dialed the number, and after three rings, her voice mail picked up. Her sweet, sultry voice filled the room, and thoughts of loving her consumed him. "Baby, it's me. Call me back. We need to talk," he said after hearing the phone beep.

Demetri tried her cell phone next, and when she picked up on the first ring, he charged over to the dresser and snatched the cordless phone off the base. "Angela?"

"Hey," she said, her tone somber.

His shoulders caved, and his heart fell. He heard the apprehension in her voice and wondered how things had gotten so bad, so fast between them. "I need to see you. We have to talk."

"I can't. Now's not a good time."

"It's important that I see you as soon as possible."

"Why? What else is there to say?"

Demetri heard a loud, piercing scream and stared down at the phone.

"What was that?"

"I'm at the hospital."

"Why? What happened? Are you okay?"

"I'm good, but I can't say the same for Simone. Her water broke while we were having lunch at the Skyline Grill."

"How's Marcus doing?"

"Great," she said with a laugh. "His daughters aren't even born yet, but he's already handing out Cuban cigars!"

He loved to hear Angela laugh. He didn't want to ruin her mood, but he had to know the truth. He opened his mouth, prepared to ask her about the accusations Nichola had made, but the question died on his lips. This was the wrong time. More than anything, he needed to hold her in his arms. "I miss you, baby. I miss us."

"I do, too, Demetri, but things are confusing right now. I just need some time."

"Come to the estate after you leave the hospital."

"I don't know if I can…"

"Please?" he begged, not caring how desperate he sounded. He *was* desperate—desperate to touch her, to kiss her, to stroke her soft, smooth cheeks and her flawless brown skin. "If you don't come to me, then I'll just have to come to you."

"No!" Her tone was sharp enough to cut glass. "We can't do this today, not here, not now. I promised Simone I'd be in the delivery room for the birth of her daughters, and I'm not going to let her down. We'll just have to get together another time."

Demetri thought hard, racking his brain for the right words to say. He had to say something, had to prove to Angela once and for all that he loved her—unconditionally. "Let's meet at the penthouse to talk. I'm headed there now."

"I don't know."

"Come on, baby. You can do better than that. Say yes."

Every second that ticked by worried Demetri more. "I just want to talk. That's it."

Dead silence settled over the line.

"Okay, I'll be there."

Demetri released the breath he was holding and smiled for the first time all day. "Hurry, baby. I'll be waiting."

Chapter 23

"Good morning," the robust security guard said from his perch in front of the reception area. "Welcome to WJN-TV, home of five Emmy Award–winning shows."

Demetri couldn't believe his good fortune. The security guard, who'd taken him to Angela's studio that fateful morning three months ago, was on duty. *Finally, something's going my way,* he thought, pausing in front of the bronze statue to check his cell phone. There had been no missed calls or text messages. No word from Angela whatsoever. She hadn't turned up at the penthouse suite on Monday night, and if not for Nicco threatening to disown him, he would have stormed Mercy Hospital looking for her. But that morning, after waking from a restless night of sleep, he'd decided enough was enough. He had to see Angela today. No matter what. And he'd driven to WJN-TV at the first light of day. He had to talk to her face-to-face.

As Demetri strode past the elevators, a hush fell over the lobby. He heard people whispering, saw cameras flash, felt the heat of a dozen wide-eyed stares. Hearing his cell phone buzz, he stared down at the screen.

His muscles tensed as he furiously clutched his phone. For the past three days, Nichola had been blowing up his phone, but he hadn't answered any of her calls. He didn't want to talk to her. At least not yet. Once he worked things out with Angela, he'd hash things out with his former publicist—but not a moment sooner. "What's up?" Demetri said, approaching his favorite security guard. "It's good to see you again, man."

The smile slid off the guard's wide, fleshy face. "What do you want?" Anger clouded his eyes and crimped his lips. "Because of the stunt you pulled the last time you were here, I got written up, and my hours were cut."

"My bad, man. I didn't mean to get you in trouble."

"You insulted a newscaster! What did you *think* was going to happen?"

Demetri noticed the security guard's name tag and then lowered his eyes to the floor, as if he were consumed with shame. "I feel terrible."

"You should. Everyone's not a millionaire like you." His voice was heavy with sarcasm. "I need this job to support my family."

Demetri reached into his back pocket, removed a small white envelope and offered it to the security guard. "Jorge, this is for you. I want you and three of your friends to be my guests at the celebrity baseball game next month."

His tongue lay limp in his open mouth. "Y-y-you do?"

"Of course. You're my number one fan, right?"

The security guard snatched the envelope out of Demetri's hand. "These are box seats! Box seats!" he chirped, waving the tickets in the air. "Those seats are worth five grand apiece."

Demetri clapped the security guard on the shoulder and motioned toward the corridor with his head. "I need you to take me to Angela's studio one last time."

The security guard shook his head. "I can't. Company rules. Unauthorized visitors aren't allowed in Studio A anymore. Not even celebrity ones."

"I'm not here to make trouble."

"But the last time you were here—"

Demetri cut him off. "The last time I was here I was trippin' big-time, but I'm not here to upset Angela."

"I don't know about this." Sweat broke out across his forehead and drenched the front of his navy blue shirt. "I can't afford to lose this job. My old lady will kill me."

"She'll be happy to see me, Jorge. I know it."

"You're sure?"

"Positive." Demetri forced a smug look. The truth was, he didn't know what to believe anymore, but if he wavered, even for a second, the security guard would toss him out. And nothing was more important to Demetri than seeing Angela. He had to trust his gut. Something told him they were going to make it, that they'd be okay. "We've been dating for months. Haven't you heard?"

"I heard this morning on the radio that she dumped you."

"It was one big misunderstanding. That's why I'm here. To apologize."

Jorge wore a small smile and nodded as if he understood. He spoke quietly to the receptionist, and after several minutes of heated conversation, the frizzy-haired blonde buzzed open the door to her left. As Jorge led Demetri down the corridor, he jawed about the celebrity baseball game and fretted over whom he should bring to the event.

Outside Studio A, Demetri put a hand on Jorge's shoulder and gave him a stern look. "Turn off your cell phone, Jorge."

"My phone? What phone? I, ah, left it in my truck."

"The last time I was here, you recorded my conversation with Angela and posted it online. Not cool at all," he said. "I don't like being the butt of people's jokes."

"It wasn't me. I swear."

"Don't play me." Demetri glared at Jorge to let him know he meant business. "I could tell by the angle the video was shot. You were standing right here, just inside the door, filming your little heart out."

Jorge shuffled his feet and fiddled with the walkie-talkie in his pocket. "I recorded the video just for kicks, but I wasn't the one who posted it online. I sent it to a couple friends, and the next thing I know it was on the six-o'clock news! Sorry, man. I didn't mean for it to get out."

"No screwups this time, okay? My entire future is riding on the next ten minutes."

"I won't let you down, Demetri. I promise." Jorge straightened his hunched shoulders and gave a salute. "What do you want me to do?"

"Just stand here and keep watch over this door," he said, gripping the shiny gold doorknob. "Make sure no one comes in. Think you can do that for me?"

"Of course. That's what they pay me for." Jorge chuckled. "Go get your girl, Demetri. Good luck!"

"Thanks, man. I have a feeling I'm going to need it."

"I want to do it all. Act, sing, dance, model," announced the bubbly tween star with the pink braces and glittery eye makeup. "I want to be the next big thing and nothing's going to stop me!"

Angela wanted to roll her eyes but smiled at the pop star instead. The twelve-year-old girl went on and on, jumping from one topic to the next. It was virtually impossible to stay focused, and when she broke out in song, Angela's mind wandered. Out of the corner of her eye, she studied the large wall clock at the back of the studio. *Ten more minutes and I'm out of here!*

"I'd love to come back on your show when my album drops this fall. It's called *Celebrity Love* and..."

Angela nodded, keeping her smile fixed in place. She needed to move the segment along, but she couldn't get a word in. Not one. Instead she sat there rehearsing what she wanted to say to Demetri when she arrived at his estate later that afternoon. Now that her family knew the truth, she could finally come clean to Demetri.

To ward off the tears stinging the backs of her eyes, Angela bit the inside of her cheek. Witnessing the birth of her twin goddaughters, Victoria and Aaliyah, had been a life-changing experience, and seeing how happy and close Simone and Marcus were made Angela hanker for a rock-solid marriage, too. She wanted babies—Demetri's babies—and the thought of spending the rest of her life with the man she loved, who completed her in every way, made Angela's heart swell with unspeakable joy.

A bright light suddenly flooded the studio, and a cold gush of air whipped through the room. Shivering, she crossed her legs and clasped her hands around her knees. Angela opened her mouth, a question poised on the tip of her tongue, but when she saw Demetri striding into the studio through one of the side doors, her mind went blank. Empty. Angela was so shocked, so stunned to see him, she convinced herself he was just a figment of her imagination.

Angela blinked, told herself to snap out of it. She had to be dreaming, fantasizing. No way Demetri was on her set, live and in the flesh—again. Only this time around he wasn't shooting evil daggers her way. He smelled dreamy, and if his smile was any bigger it could eclipse the sun. Angela expected security or her producer to stop him as he strode onto the set, but no one moved a muscle. She wanted to tell him that they were on live, but Angela couldn't get her mouth to work.

"I knew the first time I saw you, here on this very set, that you were the only woman for me." His voice was soft, as tender as a kiss along the curve of her spine. "I never dreamed that three months later I'd be madly in love with you, but I am. I love you with all my heart, with all that I am, and I want to spend the rest of my life with you."

Angela cupped a hand over her mouth to trap a scream inside. Her eyes filled with tears. Angela felt her heart pounding in her ears like a mighty rushing wind.

Demetri took her hands and helped her to her feet. Her palms, like her legs, were drenched in sweat and shaking uncontrollably. His gaze was intense, but the smile on his lips was comforting. His eyes glistened with amusement, making her feel light-headed and weak.

One of the station's interns marched onto the set carrying a silver tray. Wearing her brightest smile, she looked straight into the camera and whipped off the cover with a dramatic flourish. A velvet ring box sat on a bed of red rose petals. The fragrant scent filled the studio.

"I love everything about you. Your infectious smile, your upbeat attitude, the way you burn my breakfast just right." A grin crossed his lips when he winked. "I want to cook for you and laugh with you and watch *Family Feud* every morning with you in bed."

His words made her heart melt to a puddle at her feet. But Angela knew if they were going to have a future together, she had to tell Demetri the truth about her past. "There are things about me you don't know," she began, unable to hide the quiver in her voice. "Things that could affect our relationship and our future."

"Angela, there is absolutely nothing—" he reached out to her and cupped her chin "—you could say that will change how I feel about you. I believe in us, and I won't let anything or anyone come between us again."

The crew oohed and aahed.

"You're so beautiful, so perfect for me in every way," he praised, leaning forward and brushing his nose against her cheek. "You were made to be cherished, and I vow to love, honor and adore you for the rest of our lives."

A tear broke free and trickled down Angela's cheek.

"I want you to know and believe that." He rested a hand on her chest, and Angela covered it with her own. "You brought love and laughter back into my life, and for the first time in years, I'm genuinely happy. And it's all because of you."

Without looking, Demetri snatched the velvet ring box off of the tray and dropped to one knee. The cameraman wheeled the camera forward.

"I can't live without you, Angela. You mean everything to me, and I'm nothing without you." Demetri popped open the velvet ring box. "Baby, marry me. Make our love complete by becoming Mrs. Demetri Morretti."

Angela gasped. The radiant-cut canary-yellow diamond was the size of a marble. It flashed under the bright studio lights, easily the biggest diamond ring Angela had ever seen, and when Demetri slid it onto her fourth finger on her left hand, more tears spilled down her cheeks.

"I want to say yes, Demetri, but I can't. Not until I tell you everything."

"I know everything and I don't give a damn. I want you to be my wife."

"You know?" she asked, struggling to breathe.

Demetri placed a finger to her lips. "I know, but I don't care."

"You don't?"

He shook his head. "Nothing's changed, Angela. You're still the only woman I want by my side." He leaned forward and whispered softly in her ear. "Just so you know, I'm not leaving this set until you say yes. I'll camp out right here on the couch if I have to."

Laughter filled the studio, and Angela immediately knew Demetri's words had been picked up by the tiny microphone clipped to the front of her fitted suit.

"I'm not trying to pressure you, but you have to give me an answer before the commercial break. My friends and family are watching, and if my mom has to wait another ninety seconds, she will lose her mind!"

"Demetri, I'm so sorry I pushed you away." Angela dropped to her knees, and cupped his face in her hands. "I was scared and afraid, and I didn't know what else to do."

"I should have known something was up. You loved the penthouse suite!"

They laughed and shared a soft kiss on the lips.

"So do you accept my proposal?" he asked, clutching her hands in his own.

Throwing herself into Demetri's arms, she showered his face with hundreds of kisses. She wanted the whole world to know how much she loved Demetri Morretti. "Of course I'll marry you, baby! I'd love nothing more!"

Demetri kissed her forehead, the tip of her nose and her mouth over and over again. His lips ravished her, one succulent nibble at a time.

"Do you like your ring?" he asked between kisses. "Your dad helped me pick it out, so if you don't like it, take it up with him."

"Baby, I love it, but I love you even more."

Cheers, applause and whistles filled the studio. Her crew snapped pictures on their phones, and Salem hustled over with glasses of champagne. In the crowd Angela even spotted the president and vice president of WJN-TV. Angela was so overcome with joy and happiness, she felt as if she were floating on air.

Long after the studio cleared, her heart was still beating a thousand miles an hour. But there, on her set, Angela told Demetri everything—about how her scholarship to the University of Chicago had fallen through and how desperation had led her to answer an ad in the newspaper for a "paid companion."

Demetri listened patiently and only interrupted once to ask if she'd told her dad and brother the truth. When Angela finished telling Demetri about her past, he took her in his arms and pressed a kiss on her forehead before telling her they'd never have to discuss it again. They were together now, and that was all he said he cared about.

By the time they left the studio, night had fallen. Demetri hustled her into his truck, grinning from ear to ear, and

Angela knew he had another surprise up his sleeve. And she was right.

When Demetri pulled into the driveway of his estate an hour later, Angela saw all of their friends and family mingling on the lavishly decorated grounds. Her eyes instantly misted with tears. She was home, with all the people she loved, and nothing could mar the joy she was feeling inside. Finally, after years of running from her past, she was free. Free to laugh, live and love without the chains of guilt and shame.

One morning she'd met a loving, sensitive man who fulfilled her every desire, her every wish. And as soon as Angela became Demetri's lawfully wedded wife, she was going to make all of *his* dreams come true.

Demetri opened her door and offered his right hand. Angela took it and intertwined her fingers with his as she stepped out of the truck. As they joined the party and reveled in the excitement and well wishes of their friends and family, Angela decided there was no reason to wait. *Tonight's the perfect night to make a baby,* she thought, gazing longingly at her new fiancé. *As soon as our guests leave, of course.*

Epilogue

"Can I interest you in a cold beverage or a light snack from the kitchen?"

At the sound of the stewardess's voice, Angela snapped out of her thoughts and turned away from the airplane window. "I'm sorry," she said. "I missed that."

"I asked if you'd like something to eat or drink."

Angela smiled at the blue-eyed stewardess. The concierge staff offered exceptional service and pampering beyond her wildest dreams. Demetri had been in the office for only ten minutes, but in that short time, each staff member had stopped by and welcomed her to the family. "No, thank you. I'm still full from breakfast. That third course did me in!"

"The Morretti family loves their food and their wines, and unlike most people, they live life to the fullest."

"You can say that again! This jet looks like a hotel in the sky." Angela had never been inside a private jet before, and when she'd stepped into the Morretti family plane for the very first time and had seen the luxurious interior and impeccable designer furnishings, her eyes had widened in shock. The words *Dolce Vita* were emblazoned in gold on both sides of the gleaming, white aircraft, and everything inside the custom-made plane *did* typify the "sweet life." The Rolls-Royce jet was a marble-paneled space filled with oil paintings, crystal floor lamps and personal TV screens for every seat.

"If you need anything, Ms. Kelly, please, just give me a buzz."

A grin exploded across Angela's face. Every time she thought about her fiancé, she wanted to squeal. She had been engaged to Demetri for only three short weeks and was still in the beginning stages of planning her engagement party with celebrity planner Claudia Jeffries-Medina. But everywhere she went, people were calling her Mrs. Morretti-to-be. Probably because of her fiancé's very public proposal. The ten-minute clip had received a staggering number of hits on YouTube, and nearly a month later, bloggers were *still* raving about it.

They were the most talked about couple in the nation. Paparazzi camped out in front of Demetri's Lake County estate, followed Angela when she was leaving the television studio and snapped pictures of them every time they left the house. So when Demetri had suggested they get away, Angela had readily agreed.

After a week in Italy visiting Demetri's relatives and childhood friends, they were headed back to Chicago. Back to work, his legions of adoring fans and the celebrity-crazed paparazzi. The past seven days were a blur, filled with one sightseeing excursion and family dinner after another, but Angela had fond memories of Venice. They'd strolled through the quiet, moonlit streets hand in hand, laughing, kissing and admiring all of the breathtaking sights. But best of all was meeting her future in-laws. Demetri's parents, Vivica and Arturo, had welcomed her to the family with open arms.

Angela still couldn't believe that Demetri had proposed. And every time she thought about all of the heartfelt things he'd said to her on live TV—in front of her crew and one-point-three million viewers—she teared up.

Her gaze fell on her engagement ring. It was so big, Angela couldn't stop staring at it or running her fingers along the massive stone. Thanks to her nosy, Google-happy girlfriend Remy, she knew it was a twenty-carat Harry Winston original and valued at a million dollars.

Glancing around the main-floor cabin, Angela wondered how much longer Demetri would be on the phone with his conditioning coach. He'd been gone only a few minutes, but she missed him, hated being apart from him for even a second.

A scented breeze filled the room. The soft, soothing fragrance made Angela think about her adorable goddaughters, Victoria and Aaliyah. Opening her purse, she took out her iPhone and fired off a quick text to Simone. They hadn't spoken in days, and Angela wanted to know how her best friend was coping with her new one-month-old babies. Seconds later, Simone replied.

You know I hate you, right? I've got sore boobs and cramps from hell, and you're on a private jet, sipping cocktails and making out with your man. You should be here, suffering alongside me. Some friend you are! ☺

"I thought you were going to take a nap?"

Angela glanced up from her cell phone, seeing Demetri stride through the plane toward her, and hopped to her feet. He smiled at her, and lust shot straight to her core. Every time Demetri looked at her, Angela felt an uncontrollable desire to kiss him. And being fifty thousand feet in the air didn't change that. If anything, being at the dizzying altitude made her want him even more.

Licking her lips, she admired how in charge Demetri looked in his black V-neck shirt, dark jeans and casual leather shoes. His passion and energy always made for earth-shattering sex. Angela could only imagine all the wonderfully wicked things he'd do to her inside the vanilla-scented master bedroom at the rear of the jet. Angela flashed Demetri a flirty look, but instead of breaking out into his trademark grin, he wore a puzzled face.

"What's the matter?" Angela asked, touching a hand to his cheek.

Demetri raised an eyebrow. "What makes you think something's wrong?"

"Your eyes. They're a dead giveaway."

He lifted his cell phone. "Nichola called while I was on the phone with Coach. She said you told her it would be okay."

"I did."

"When did you guys talk?"

"We met up a few weeks ago," Angela said, keeping her voice even and her tone nonchalant. "We cleared the air, and now things are better."

Demetri's eyebrows knit together. "Why did you agree to meet her?"

"It seemed like the right thing to do. You guys have been friends for years, and I didn't want your friendship to end on account of me."

"She tried to break us up and destroy your career."

"As one wise, very intelligent and *very* sexy baseball star once told me, forgiveness is a gift I give to myself, and I didn't want to waste any time or energy holding a grudge."

"I love when you quote me. It makes me feel smart!" Demetri said with a chuckle as he put his arms around her waist.

"I used to struggle with forgiveness, because I couldn't forgive myself, but now I'm free of my past."

"I can't believe how cool you're being about everything."

"We'll never be BFFs, but at least we're not sworn enemies."

Nodding, he tightened his grip around her waist, held her close in his arms. "So, you think I should give Nichola her old job back?"

"Hell no!" Angela adamantly shook her head. "But maybe you could put in a good word for her at Dolce Vita. Nicco's still looking for an assistant, and ordering people around is right up Nichola's alley."

"Nichola would never work for Nicco."

"Why not?"

"Because he's a hard man to work for and fires people at the drop of a dime."

"Really? That's hard to believe. He seems so laid-back."

"Yeah, when he's around beautiful women," Demetri said, grinning at her. "But when it comes to Dolce Vita and expanding his brand, he's as tenacious as a pit bull!"

Hearing the theme music to her new show, *News at 6 with Angela Kelly,* drew Angela's gaze to the front of the cabin. There she was, on the gigantic flat-screen TV, smiling into the camera. Angela cringed and looked away as the commercial played. Much to her boss's delight, her exclusive sit-down interview with Demetri and his brothers, Nicco and Rafael, was back on. Single women all across the country had flooded the WJN-TV website, hoping to win a dream date with one of the brothers. And these days Angela couldn't go anywhere without females asking her about her future brothers-in-law.

"How does it feel having two hit shows?" Demetri asked, gesturing at the TV screen.

"Amazing, incredible, like a dream come true," she confessed. "But you know what I'm most thankful for?"

"The new mini fridge I put in your dressing room filled with Snickers bars?"

Giggling, Angela swatted him playfully on his forearm. "No, I'm most thankful for you. I've never, ever been this happy, and you're the reason why."

"Me? But I didn't do anything. Your shows are a hit because you work damn hard."

"You gave me the strength to face my fears." Angela touched a hand to his face and tenderly caressed his cheek. "Most men would have bolted when they learned about my past, but you stayed *and* encouraged me to share my story."

"Going on the air and coming clean about your past took a lot of courage, Angela, and I'm very proud of you. Your confession helped free a lot of people from the guilt and shame of their past, and that's a remarkable thing, baby."

"I wasn't expecting my *True Confessions* series to receive national attention, or for so many celebrities to Tweet about it, either, but I'm sure glad they did!"

Demetri nodded. "Me, too. Now the whole world knows my wife-to-be is a dime piece with a killer bod *and* a heart of gold."

They shared a soft, sweet kiss.

"Are you excited about playing your first game of the season on Sunday?"

"Baby, you have no idea!"

Angela shrieked in laughter when Demetri lifted her off the ground and swung her around the main-floor cabin. He looked more excited than a kid at SeaWorld, and his smile couldn't be any wider. Seeing him so excited filled Angela with joy.

"During my last practice, I smashed every pitch out of the stadium, and Coach said my form is better than ever. He thinks this could be a record-breaking year for me!"

"I'm not surprised," Angela said, stroking the back of his head. "You've been practicing around the clock and working out like a madman."

"I'm not that tired. I still have the energy to come home every night and make love to my beautiful fiancée." Demetri pressed his lips against her ear and tickled her earlobe with the tip of his tongue. "When we get home, we're making better use of the golf course."

"Oh, no, you're not. The Fourth of July extravaganza is tomorrow, and Claudia Jeffries-Medina is already at the estate setting up."

"Shoot, I forgot." He gave a dismissive shrug. "No biggie. It *is* a twenty-room mansion."

Tilting her head to the side, Angela broke into a cheeky smile. "Yeah, but you know how loud you get. People in the next county can probably hear you hollering my name!"

Demetri threw his head back and roared.

"I love you, Demetri. Always, no matter what, even when I'm sleep-deprived and acting like a diva."

Demetri chuckled.

His cell phone rang, and after checking the number, he smiled sheepishly. "Baby, do you mind if I take this call? It's my mom, and I haven't talked to her all day."

"But we're crossing over the Atlantic Ocean." Angela pointed at the window and flashed him a seductive smile. She rubbed her body against his chest and her hands along his broad, muscular shoulders. "It's the perfect backdrop for making love."

"Awww, hell. Moms can wait!" Demetri chucked his cell phone on the plush tan sofa and scooped Angela up in his arms. "You're so incredible, so damn beautiful, I could never, ever get tired of loving you."

Angela nuzzled her face against his cheek, basking in the warmth of his love.

"I love you with all that I am, Angela," Demetri said before lowering his mouth and kissing her passionately on the lips. He then set off for the master bedroom at breakneck speed. "*Now,* let's practice for the honeymoon!"

* * * * *

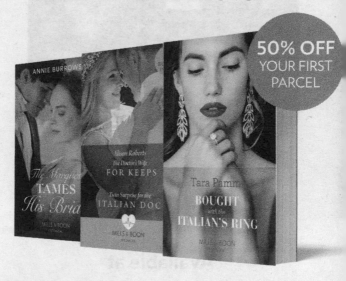

MILLS & BOON
Desire

Indulge in secrets and scandal, intense drama and plenty of sizzling hot action with powerful and passionate heroes who have it all: wealth, status, good looks… everything but the right woman.

MILLS & BOON

THE HEART OF ROMANCE

A ROMANCE FOR EVERY READER

MODERN

Prepare to be swept off your feet by sophisticated, sexy and seductive heroes, in some of the world's most glamourous and romantic locations, where power and passion collide.

HISTORICAL

Escape with historical heroes from time gone by. Whether your passion is for wicked Regency Rakes, muscled Vikings or rugged Highlanders, awaken the romance of the past.

MEDICAL

Set your pulse racing with dedicated, delectable doctors in the high-pressure world of medicine, where emotions run high and passion, comfort and love are the best medicine.

True Love

Celebrate true love with tender stories of heartfelt romance, from the rush of falling in love to the joy a new baby can bring, and a focus on the emotional heart of a relationship.

Desire

Indulge in secrets and scandal, intense drama and plenty of sizzling hot action with powerful and passionate heroes who have it all: wealth, status, good looks…everything but the right woman.

HEROES

Experience all the excitement of a gripping thriller, with an intense romance at its heart. Resourceful, true-to-life women and strong, fearless men face danger and desire - a killer combination!

To see which titles are coming soon, please visit

millsandboon.co.uk/nextmonth